FORGED IN PAIN AND SHADOW

Please Leave a Review on Amazon

J McCorMick

Copyright © [2025] by D McCormick

All rights reserved.

No part of this publication may be reproduced, distributed, or transmitted in any form or by any means, including photocopying, recording, or other electronic or mechanical methods, without the prior written permission of the publisher, except as permitted by U.S. copyright law. For permission requests, contact DMcCormick-author@mail.com.

The story, all names, characters, and incidents portrayed in this production are fictitious. No identification with actual persons (living or deceased), places, buildings, and products is intended or should be inferred.

Paperback ISBN: 978-1-0686799-2-6

E-Book ISBN: 978-1-0686799-6-4

"Cover designed by Getcovers."

CHAPTER 1

The Journey to Ireland

The scent of rain-soaked cobblestones filled my nostrils as I wove through the crowded streets of London. My eyes, a mix of vulnerability and steely resolve, darted between the bustling pedestrians and the looming grey buildings that seemed to close around me.

"Watch it!" A businessman in a crisp suit snapped as I accidentally bumped into him.

"Sorry," I mumbled embarrassedly; ducking my head, I quickened my pace. The weight of my backpack felt heavier with each step, like a physical reminder of the burden I carried in my heart.

Turning onto a quieter side street, My thoughts drifted to My mum. The ache that bloomed in my chest intensified, a familiar emptiness that threatened to consume me. I paused, leaning against a cool brick wall, and closed my eyes, picturing my mum with her infectious smile.

"Mum, I miss you so much," I whispered, my voice barely audible above the distant hum of traffic.

A gentle breeze caressed my face, carrying with it the faint chime of Big Ben. I opened my eyes, blinking back tears. Pushed myself off the wall and continued walking my solitary journey through the streets4 of London, the city's vibrant energy a stark contrast to the quiet despair that had become my constant companion. Each step reminded me of the life I once had and the uncertain future ahead.

Laying on my bed, I clutched my mum's old journal to my chest, my thumb stroking its soft, subtle leather cover. The leather-bound book contained more than words; it was a gateway to a world of Celtic myths and Irish landscapes that my mother had painted vividly with her stories.

Laying there, I wished I could hear her Tell me about the faerie rings, elves and gateways to other worlds and how she would weave tales of giants and monsters from the myths and legends she was raised on. My breath caught in my throat as I opened the journal to a dog-eared page. My eyes traced the delicate sketches of mushroom circles my mother had drawn, along with little stories and poems.

A sharp knock at my bedroom door startled me from my reverie. "Jess? There's a letter for you," my dad called out.

My curiosity piqued, I set the journal aside and padded it to the door. My dad stood there, an envelope in his outstretched hand, his eyes crinkling with a warmth that had been rare since my mum's passing.

"It's from me, actually," he said, a hint of nervousness in his voice.

My brow furrowed as I took the letter. "From you? But why—»

"Just read it, sweetheart," he urged gently.

With trembling fingers, I opened the envelope and unfolded the letter inside. My eyes widened as I read, and my heart began to race.

"Dad, is this... are we really going to Ireland?" I asked, voice barely above a whisper.

He nodded, a tentative smile forming. "I thought it was time. Your mum always wanted to take you there, to show you where she came from."

CHAPTER 1

Tears welled in my eyes. "I can't believe it. We'll see the Cliffs of Moher? The Ring of Kerry?"

"All of it," my dad confirmed. "And maybe we can spread some of your mum's ashes there. If you'd like."

Unable to contain my emotions, I threw my arms around him, burying my face in his chest. "Thank you, Dad. Thank you so much." I cry, unable to stop my tears.

As we embraced, I felt a flicker of something I hadn't experienced in a long time: hope. The chance to walk the lands my mum had loved, to breathe the air that had inspired her stories—it felt like a lifeline, a connection to the part of myself that had been adrift since my mum's death.

"When do we leave?" I asked, pulling back to look at him.

He chuckled; relief was evident in his features. "Next week. Think you can be ready by then?"

I nodded eagerly, cheeks damp from crying, and I began mentally cataloguing what I'd need to pack. "I'll start right now!"

As my dad left the room, I returned to bed and picked up my mum's journal again. As I ran my fingers over the pages this time, the stories within felt less like distant fantasies and more like a map to a part of my mum I was finally ready to explore.

***

My fingers danced over my laptop keyboard, eyes wide with excitement as I scrolled through images of lush green hills and ancient stone circles. "The Hill of Tara," I murmured, jotting down notes in a leather-bound journal—a gift from my mother years ago. "I can't believe I'll actually see it in person," I muttered.

I glanced at my half-packed suitcase, a mess of clothing and guidebooks across the bed. Picking up a worn copy of

Irish folklore, I hugged it to my chest, the scent of my mum's perfume still lingering on its pages.

"I wish you were here, Mum," I whispered, a bittersweet smile tugging at my lips. "But I'll bring you with me, in my heart."

Deciding the room felt stifling; I needed some fresh air to clear my head; I slipped on a jacket and headed out into the London twilight. The city's familiar din enveloped me as I navigated the familiar bustling streets, but something felt different tonight. The shadows seemed more profound, more alive somehow.

A flicker of movement caught my eye as I passed a narrow alley. Pausing, I peered into the gloom. "Hello?" I called, my voice trembling slightly with uncertainty.

No response came, but the hairs on my neck stood up. I quickened my pace, my thoughts racing. 'What was that? Just a cat, probably. Get it together, Jess.'

The street lamps flickered as I hurried past, casting eerie patterns on the pavement. I couldn't shake the feeling of being watched; my excitement about the trip was momentarily overshadowed by an inexplicable sense of unease.

"You alright, love?" a gruff voice startled me.

I spun around to face an elderly man walking his dog. Forcing a smile, "Yes, thank you. Just... lost in thought, I suppose." I said, trying to sound cheery

As I continued my walk, I couldn't help but wonder if the mysteries of my mother's homeland were already reaching out to me here in the familiar streets of London. The city I thought I knew so well suddenly seemed full of secrets, whispering promises of the adventure to come.

***

This trip to Ireland was meant to be another recovery for us. We had always dreamed of visiting the land of my mum's

CHAPTER 1

birth before she passed, and now, after her passing, we were making the pilgrimage in her honour. As we boarded the tour bus in Dublin, I felt excitement and apprehension. Could a place I had never seen really feel like home?

My dad took the window seat and began fiddling with the new camera. It was a recent birthday gift he had given himself to help celebrate his 40th. He was tall and robust but had a softness, a rounding of the edges. I liked to think of him as an oak tree in autumn, sturdy but beginning to show the first signs of change.

"Got it figured out yet?" I asked, peering over his shoulder.

He grinned and held up the camera, displaying a blurry self-portrait. "I think there's a learning curve."

I laughed a short, sharp bark that surprised even me. It had been a long time since I had found something genuinely funny. The last few years had been hard— seeing the cancer eat away at the vibrant woman that was my mum made it hard to see the bright side of things. But I had promised her before the end that I would always try to look forward and be positive.

The bus lurched forward, and I settled into my seat, letting my thoughts wander. The city gave way to suburbs, then to rolling green hills dotted with sheep. It was exactly as I had imagined, like something out of a postcard. I closed my eyes and tried to picture My mum here, walking these same hills, her red hair bright against the green. It was a comforting thought. And brought a genuine smile to my face.

"Jess," my dad said, and I opened my eyes. He was holding the camera out to me. "Take a look. I think I got a good one."

I took the camera and studied the screen. It was a shot of him looking out the window, the green hills reflected in the Glass. There was a melancholy to it, an unintentional artistry.

"It's beautiful," I said, and I meant it. "You're a natural."

He shrugged, but I could tell he was pleased. "So, what do you think?"

I nodded. "It's beautiful, but this feels more wild and mysterious than I'm used to. I can see why she wanted to come here."

Silence settled between us, not uncomfortable but heavy with unspoken things. I thought about the box of letters my mother had left for me, the last one still unopened. I wondered why I'd brought it with me; maybe I hoped that reading it here, in the place my mother had loved from afar, would make the words easier to bear.

The bus pulled into a small village with stone cottages and narrow streets. The tour guide, a cheerful woman in her fifties, announced that we would have an hour to explore and grab lunch. So my dad and I stood and stretched, then made our way to the front of the bus.

"Where do you want to go first?" My dad asked as we stepped onto the cobblestone street.

I looked around, taking in the quaint shops and bustling market square. "Let's just wander," I said.

We strolled through the village at a leisurely pace, poking our heads into shops and chatting with the locals. I felt a strange sense of déjà vu as if I were walking through a dream I'd had a hundred times. Everything was familiar yet just out of reach.

We found a small pub and ordered fish and chips. My dad took out the camera and started scrolling through the pictures he'd taken during the morning's drive.

Our food arrived, and we ate in companionable silence. I thought about how easy it was with my dad, how we didn't

CHAPTER 1

need to fill every moment with words. He was the only person in the world I could just be with.

After lunch, we made our way back to the bus. My dad stopped to take a picture of a flower stall that was filled to bursting with every variety of flower available, their scent intoxicating and then handed the camera to me.

"Here," he said. "You should have this."

I frowned. "I thought you were starting to like it."

"It's a little advanced for me. Besides, you're the one with a natural eye for beauty."

I took the camera reluctantly.

"Thanks," I said and tucked it into my bag.

We boarded the bus and found our seats. The village receded into the distance as the bus wound its way through the countryside. I felt a drowsiness settle over me, the kind that comes after a good meal and a long morning in the sun.

"Dad," I said, my voice already thick with sleep. "I'm happy we're doing this."

He patted my hand. "Me too, Jess. Me too."

I closed My eyes and let the motion of the bus rock me towards sleep. In a half-dream state, I saw my mother again, this time with my father, the two young and laughing. Then I was with them, a little girl with my mother's red hair, running through the green hills of home.

A scream shattered my dream like a rock through Glass. And I sat up, disoriented, and looked around the bus. A woman near the back was standing, her face a mask of terror.

"Oh my God," the woman screamed. "He's not breathing!"

My heart pounded in my chest. And I turned to my dad, who was already on his feet. He looked back at me, his eyes full of the fear mirroring the feelings I was trying to suppress.

"Stay here," he said and rushed to the back of the bus.

I craned my neck to see what was happening. An older man lay sprawled in the aisle, his face blue. My dad knelt beside him and checked his pulse, then started chest compressions. The tour guide was on her mobile, shouting for an ambulance.

My mind raced. My dad was a biology professor, not a doctor, but he knew enough first aid to be dangerous. I wanted to go back and help, to do something, but I was frozen in place, my hands gripping the seat in front of me so tightly that my knuckles were white.

The man's wife was sobbing now, a high, keening wail that set my teeth on edge. I watched as my dad counted out loud, his face grim and determined. This was supposed to be a healing trip, a time for us to recover and remember. It wasn't supposed to turn into this.

After what felt like an eternity, the bus pulled over and two paramedics rushed on board. They carried the man out on a stretcher and took over chest compressions from my dad. The passengers filed out to the roadside slowly, dazed and silent.

It took me a minute to push through the crowd. I found my dad standing in the road alone, just staring at the paramedics as they loaded the man into the ambulance with his crying wife. My dad's hands were shaking as I reached his side. I took his hand in mine and squeezed.

"You did everything you could," I said.

He nodded, but I could tell he wasn't convinced. "Let's hope he makes it." Was his only reply

The tour guide announced that the bus would wait until the ambulance left and that passengers were free to return to the village in the meantime, as it was only a ten-minute walk away. I looked at my dad, wondering if he had the energy to continue. He looked old to me now, older than I had ever seen him.

CHAPTER 1

"Let's get a coffee," he said, walking toward the village.

We found a café and took a seat outside. My dad ordered a cappuccino, and I got a mint tea, hoping to settle my stomach after witnessing what had just happened. As we sat there, I watched him stare into the distance, his mind clearly elsewhere. I didn't want to break the silence but knew I had to.

"Dad," I said softly. He turned to her, and she saw that his eyes were wet. "Do you remember when I had my first asthma attack?"

He closed his eyes and took a deep breath. "I was just thinking about that. How scared I was, not knowing what to do."

"I made it, though," I said. "Because someone called 999 and got me to the hospital in time. You did that for him today. You gave him a chance."

He opened his eyes and looked at me, the hurt and fear slowly receding. "You're right. It's just… seeing him like that, it brought a lot back."

"I know."

The ambulance drove past, heading toward the nearest city. My dad watched it until it was out of sight, then sipped his cappuccino.

"Do you think we'll ever return here?" he asked.

I considered the question. This trip had been years in the making, a once-in-a-lifetime thing. But now that we were here, I could see us returning and maybe one day bringing my own children.

"I hope so," I said.

We finished our drinks and made our way back to the bus. The passengers were subdued, speaking in hushed tones. Someone asked if the man would be okay, but no one had an answer.

As the bus started its journey again, I took the camera from my bag and turned it on. I began to flip through the pictures my dad had taken, each one a small, precious memory. When I got to the one of him reflected in the window, I paused and then raised the camera, framing a shot of the countryside rushing past. Then, I clicked the shutter, capturing the green blur, the essence of a place in motion.

I turned to my dad, who was gazing out the window with a faraway look. "Dad," I said, and he looked at me. I love you."

He smiled, and I saw the oak tree in him again, firm and unbending. "I love you too, Jess."

The bus rounded a corner, and the sun broke through the clouds, casting the hills in a golden light. I took another picture, then another, trying to capture how the light played on the grass and how the shadows stretched and yawned. I didn't know if a photograph could do it justice, but I liked the challenge and the attempt.

I thought about my mum's journal sitting in my suitcase. Maybe tonight, I would read it with my dad beside me, and we would cry, laugh, and remember. And perhaps the words would be exactly what we needed to hear, the kind that helped you recover and move forward.

For now, though, I let the camera rest in my lap and leaned My head on my dad's shoulder. The bus carried us through the green hills, a land starting to feel like home.

***

Our guide stood at the front of the bus, her voice lilting as she told stories of Irish folklore. I listened intently, my mind alight with the tale of Finn McCool and the Giant's Causeway. I imagined the great warrior biting into the salmon of knowledge, the landscape reshaping under his

CHAPTER 1

enormous hands. Each story kindled a spark in me, a longing for adventure that transformed ordinary lives into legend.

My gaze drifted to the window. The sky had grown sullen, and a light drizzle began to speckle the Glass. The landscape was a patchwork of ancient stone walls and verdant pastures dotted with the occasional ruin. I raised the camera and clicked, hoping to capture the brooding beauty of it all.

A sharp turn jolted the bus, and I gripped the seat before me. My heart quickened, not with fear, but with a strange excitement. The guide's voice crackled over the speakers, drowned momentarily by the engine's roar as the driver downshifted. Another sharp turn and the bus swayed precariously. Someone muttered a curse; another person laughed nervously. My pulse was a drumbeat in My ears. I looked out the window again, and in the distance, I thought I saw a figure standing on a hilltop, silhouetted against the stormy sky. It vanished as quickly as it had appeared, leaving me with an uneasy sense of foreboding.

The road narrowed, and the bus slowed to a crawl. I let out a breath I hadn't realised I was holding. The guide resumed her narration, but my thoughts drifted elsewhere—on the figure on the hill, Finn McCool, and my mother's Journal.

The bus's horn blared, and time seemed to stretch and bend. A blinding flash illuminated the bus, followed instantly by a deafening crack. My eyes flew open as the world tilted violently.

"Dad!" I screamed, reaching for him as the bus careened off the road.

Metal screeched against rock, and I felt myself thrown from my seat. My head slammed against something hard, and darkness engulfed me.

When I came to, the world was a haze of pain and confusion. Rain pelted my face, and the coopery tasted blood filled my mouth.

"Dad?" I called out weakly, struggling to my feet. "Dad, where are you?"

I stumbled through the wreckage, My vision blurring. Twisted metal and shattered Glass surrounded me, but there was no sign of my dad or the other passengers.

"This can't be happening," I muttered, my breath coming in short gasps. "It's just a nightmare. Wake up, Jess. Wake up!"

But the cold Rain and the throbbing pain in my head told me this was all too real. I limped away from the crash site, each step sending jolts of agony through my body.

"Help!" I cried out in vain, my voice swallowed by the howling wind. "Somebody, please help us!"

The landscape around me seemed to shift and blur, unfamiliar and threatening. My thoughts raced.

Where am I? Where's Dad? Oh God, what if he's... I stopped myself from thinking like that. Only despair would find me if I started to feel like that. Pushing the thought away, I focused on putting one foot in front of the other. The sky grew darker, and shadows danced at the edge of my vision.

"Stay calm," I told Myself aloud, trying to channel the strength my mum and dad always seemed to exude. "You can do this. Just find help, and everything will be okay."

But as I stumbled through the alien terrain, My mother's stories of Ireland took on a sinister new meaning. What if there was more to this land than I knew? What if something was out there, watching Me?

I shook My head, wincing at the pain. "Don't be ridiculous," I muttered. "Focus on finding help. That's all that matters now."

CHAPTER 1

Yet as night fell and the shadows lengthened, I couldn't shake the feeling that I was no longer alone in this desolate landscape.

A twig snapped behind me. And I whirled around, nearly losing my balance. I stumbled slightly, my heart pounding. Two figures emerged from the shadows, their outlines blurred by the misty darkness.

"Well, well," a grating male voice cut through the air. "What do we have here?"

I stumbled backwards. "S-stay away!" I warned, hating that my voice sounded so weak.

Another man's laughter, cold and mirthless, joined the first man's. "Oh, darling," he purred, "you're in no position to make demands."

As they stepped closer, I caught glimpses of their features. One was tall and gaunt, his lab coat stark white against the gloom. The other's eyes glinted with a predatory gleam.

"Who are you?" I demanded, trying to inject strength into my voice. "What do you want?"

The man adjusted his round spectacles, light glinting ominously off the lenses. "I am Jeremiah Blackwood, and this is my associate, Mallory. As for what we want..." He smiled, revealing teeth that seemed unnaturally sharp. "You'll find out soon enough."

Before I could react, Mallory was behind Me, pinning my arms to my side. "No!" I cried, thrashing against His iron grip. "Let me go!"

"Shh," Jeremiah cooed, producing a syringe filled with an ominous liquid. "This will only hurt for a moment."

As the needle plunged into my neck, My last conscious thought was of my dad.

"Dad, I'm sorry. I couldn't find help."

***

When I awoke, I found myself in a damp, cavernous space. My head throbbed, and my limbs felt like lead. Panic rose in my throat as I realised I was chained to a cold stone wall.

"Hello?" I called out, My voice echoing in the darkness, feeling hopeless and more alone than ever. "Is anyone there?"

A low rumble answered, accompanied by the clink of heavy chains. My eyes widened as they adjusted to the gloom, revealing a massive form nearby. My breath caught in my throat as I made out scales glimmering like moonlight on water.

"W-what the fuck are you?" I whispered to myself, fear and awe mingling in my voice.

The creature's eyes opened, revealing irises of deep purple that seemed to hold centuries of wisdom. "I am Lyn," an ancient and melodious voice projected into my mind. "And like you, young one, I am a captive here."

My mind reeled. I must be seeing things. "Are you a dragon? But that's... that's impossible." I ask aloud, trying to keep my voice calm

Lyn's laugh again sounded in my head. It was gentle and intensely comforting despite the circumstances. "Many things you once thought impossible are very real, Child, and yes, I am a dragon."

I sat there open mouth as I gazed at the hulking form beside me.

"There is much to explain," Lyn said softly. "But first, tell me, how did you come to be here?"

As I Began recounting my ordeal, I told Lyn everything from my dad's surprise that we were taking this trip to now sitting here chained to a wall, vocalising recent events to

CHAPTER 1

this strange creature; I began to feel a peculiar calm settling over me. Lyn listened patiently, her presence a balm to my frayed nerves.

"I'm so scared," I admitted when I finished my story. "What's going to happen to us?" I ask

Lyn's eyes glowed with compassion. "Fear is natural, young one. And I don't know for sure what he will do. But remember, we face this together."

I felt a flicker of hope for the first time since the crash. Whatever trials lay ahead, I was not Going to face them alone. As this realisation hit me, my eyes closed and I slipped into the dark embrace of sleep.

CHAPTER 2

Captured

My eyes fluttered open, and I squinted at the dim, flickering Light above me. My head throbbed, and my body felt heavy and weak as I tried to sit up. Panic surged through me as I slowly started to remember everything that had happened the night before. "It wasn't a nightmare; it all really happened," I gasped, not expecting anyone or anything to respond.

But then I heard the sound of heavy chains dragging across the rough ground. My breathing became erratic as I took short, sharp gasps, my heart pounding frantically in my chest. "Hello?" I called out softly, hoping for no response.

"Hello, young one. Are you feeling better now that you've rested?" A familiar voice filled my mind, bringing comfort and relief.

"Lyn!" I cried out in joy as the image of a vast, beautiful dragon slowly emerged from the shadows. It was heavily shackled with thick chains wrapped around its neck, legs, tail, and wings, preventing them from unfurling. As the dragon lowered its head and approached me cautiously, I noticed that it was severely injured - missing teeth, claws, and scales, with one cloudy eye that seemed recently damaged. "What happened to you? Oh my god," I exclaimed, not knowing why seeing this magnificent creature in such a state upset me so deeply. Until now, I never even knew dragons existed.

The sound of footsteps echoed around us from nowhere, growing louder and more deliberate. My body tensed, every muscle a coiled spring. Then, a steel door creaked open, and the men entered the room. Jeremiah and Malory wore white lab coats, and Jeremiah's was pristine white, with his hands casually thrust into the pockets. The Light caught his face, casting eerie hollows beneath his cheekbones. A slow, sinister smile spread across his dry, cracked lips. Malory was the polar opposite. His lab coat was stained and dirty, and he looked unkempt and scruffy, continually fiddling with something to keep his mind occupied.

"Good evening, Jessica, Lyn", he said, dipping his head in greeting each of us, his voice low and grating. "I trust you're comfortable?"

Lyn growled in response that only seemed to amuse the men before us. My mind raced. Who was this man? What did he want with me? "Let me go!" I demand "You have no right to—" I demanded, though my voice wavers slightly with fear.

Jeremiah removed a hand from his pocket and stroked his chin thoughtfully.

"Rights," Jeremiah interrupted, his smile widening. "Such a quaint concept. You must understand, Jessica, that what we're doing here is far beyond the realm of rights and wrongs. This is about knowledge. About pushing the boundaries of what is possible."

As Jeremiah spoke, Malory gazed at me hungrily. Giggling as he mutters to himself. "Now you are going to behave like a good girl as Malory leads you to the lab, but just remember he isn't very tolerant, and he enjoys hurting things", Jeremiah said. As he turns to leave, he glances back

CHAPTER 2

to Lyn, who is still straining against the chains that hold her, snarling and growling like a savage beast. "Don't worry, Lyn, I haven't forgotten about you. I will be back later for more samples. Your eye is healing nicely, so I might take the other one to have a matching set."

I realise then that all her injuries are from him, and I feel enraged. "You animal, how could you" I scream as Malory starts to drag me away.

"Oh, don't worry, Jess. I have much more exciting things planned for you". The glee in his voice is unmistakable.

The horrifying realisation of my situation finally sunk in, causing a surge of panic to course through my body. I doubled my efforts to resist Malory as he dragged me from the chamber into a dimly lit hall; I thrashed and struggled against his monstrous grip as he held onto my hair with an unyielding grasp. Each time I tried to pull away, he only tightened his hold, causing me to cry out and whimper in pain. The sharp tugs on my scalp felt like he was tearing chunks of my hair out, but I didn't care. All I could think about was escaping from this nightmare. As I continued to scream and fight with all my might, I could feel the tears streaming down my face. My mind raced for a plan as I desperately searched for any way out. And then, a glimmer of hope - I felt Malory's grip loosen ever so slightly. Without hesitation, I made a break for it in the direction we had just come from, but my legs were slow to respond. It felt like I was running through quicksand as fear and adrenaline coursed through my veins. But despite my efforts, Mallory's hand closed around my arm before I could get far, bringing me crashing to the ground with a painful thud. The frustration and terror inside me only grew stronger as I attempted to lash out at everything around me. Mallory's hand shot out, striking me with a force that sent me stumbling into a rough wall. Mallory pinned me to the wall, his iron grip twisting into the fabric of my shirt. "Are you going to behave now, or do I get to hurt you even more?" he snarled, his eyes glinting with twisted satisfaction.

I met his gaze head-on and spat the small amount of saliva in my mouth at him. "Go screw yourself, you scumbag!" It was a reckless move, but I couldn't help myself. Without hesitation, he raised his fist and drove it straight into my solar plexus, knocking the wind out of me. I gasped for air, struggling to breathe as tears welled up in my eyes.

Just as Mallory prepared to strike again, Jeremiah's voice cut through the tension. "Enough." We both turned to see Jeremiah standing behind us, his presence intimidating and commanding. "Mallory, you know better than to let your anger get the best of you. We need our 'lab rats' to be healthy if we want this experiment to succeed. I hope you haven't caused too much damage."

"I'm sorry, master," Mallory replied meekly, like a scolded child seeking approval from his parent. I might have chuckled at the sight if I wasn't so terrified for my life.

Still clutching me tightly, Mallory dragged me along as his master led the way. We soon arrived at a solid-looking door that seamlessly blended into the wall. Mallory stopped abruptly, still holding onto me like a rag doll. Jeremiah traced something in the air with a glowing finger before muttering an incantation. The door suddenly swung open, revealing a pitch-black room beyond.

Panic set in as we were plunged into complete darkness; I couldn't take it anymore – the fear, the uncertainty, the pain. Tears streamed down my face as I realised that I was at the mercy of two madmen who had something terrible planned for me. Desperately, I tried to wake up from this nightmare,

CHAPTER 2

but it was all too real. This was my reality now, and there was no escaping it.

As I was dragged in to the room I was suddenly engulfed in a blinding explosion of Light, causing temporary blindness. As my vision slowly returned, I found myself bathed in the warm glow of a brilliant blue light emanating from strategically placed spots around the room. Jeremiah stood before me imposingly, his figure silhouetted against the eerie blue Light.

From behind him, I could make out a metal surgical table that seemed to have been plucked straight out of a horror movie, resembling something out of a twisted torture chamber. Intravenous poles surrounded the table, each holding numerous bags filled with unknown fluids connected by tubes to various points on the contraption. Fear and dread filled me as I realised I was about to become a part of this twisted experiment. With rough hands, I was thrown onto the ominous table and held down by Mallory. At the same time, Jeremiah cuffed my arms and wrists in metal restraints, rendering me practically immobile. Desperately, I struggled against their grip, determined to resist them even if it meant causing harm to myself. But their hold was too strong, and my efforts were futile. I even attempted to kick out at my captors, hoping to inflict some damage, but it was no use. Within minutes, I was utterly restrained, with only my neck and head still able to move. But this small freedom didn't last long as leather restraints were quickly fastened over my forehead and neck, effectively silencing any further attempts at resistance. As I resigned myself to my fate, one last plea escaped me in a desperate attempt to appeal to their humanity: "Please, if you're going to kill me, just do it."

Jeremiah turned to look at me with genuine curiosity. He brushed stray hairs from my face as he spoke once again.

"I have no intention of killing you...yet," Despite my fear and anger towards this man for using people as his guinea pigs in this dank and dark cave, I knew arguing or pleading would be pointless.

Tears welled in my eyes. As I thought of my dad, unmoving in the wreckage of the bus. Of my mother, taken from us too soon. Of the life I still had to live.

"Why me?" I asked, my voice small and defeated.

Jeremiah set the scalpel down with a delicate, almost tender care. "Why not you? You were in the wrong place at the wrong time, my dear. Or perhaps the right place at the right time. Fate has a funny way of guiding us where we need to be."

"What do you hope to achieve by bringing me here?" I asked, a mix of resentment and resignation evident in my voice. Jeremiah turned and regarded me. "Very well," he said, brushing some stray hair from my eyes as he spoke again. "I don't want to kill you, well, at least not yet. You see, my experiment is very near completion. I Just need a few of my test subjects to survive, then I will show the lord that his faith in me wasn't misplaced." My heart raced with both fear and disgust at the thought of being used as a mere pawn in this madman's twisted game. But I knew there was no use in fighting against it now. The only thing left was to wait and see what horrors awaited me as a test subject in this dark and sinister place.

As I lay strapped to this torture device, the room seemed to close in on me as I listened to my captor's words. My body trembled with fear as they prepared to inject me with an unknown concoction. The smell of disinfectant and chemicals filled my nostrils, making me want to gag.

"I am going to start by giving you an IV," he stated calmly, their voice devoid of any emotion. "Or several. The

CHAPTER 2

different compounds will force a change in your body over the coming days and weeks."

I couldn't believe what I was hearing. This was all some twisted experiment, and I was just a mere subject.

"After every successful course of treatment, I will change the various drugs and compounds," he continued. "And monitor what these multiple things do to you. Most don't survive the first few days of the first treatment. But occasionally, I have subjects that live through several treatments."

My fate was sealed. There was nothing I could do but accept it.

"How long do you think you will last?" He asked a hint of sadistic amusement in his voice.

But then came the final blow - "I forgot to mention that you will be a plaything for Mallory between your treatment and tests". It was too much to bear. They had destroyed my life and now reduced me to nothing more than an object for their sick games.

But before I could process this new information, the pain started. Needles pierced my skin in various areas - arms, legs, neck, chest - and fluids were pumped into my body. The burning and freezing sensations sent shockwaves through my veins and muscles, causing me to cry out in agony.

I tried to stifle my screams, not wanting these monsters to revel in my pain, but I couldn't help it. The intensity was unlike anything I had ever experienced before. Tears streamed down my face as I thrashed against the restraints holding me down.

When I thought it couldn't get any worse, Mallory leaned in and whispered his final words. "I hope you survive. I really am looking forward to breaking you." And then they left, leaving me alone with the eerie blue Light and my own screams as my only company.

As my senses slowly faded, the pain overwhelmed me and dragged me into an abyss of darkness and oblivion.

I was grateful for the temporary oblivion. But I couldn't escape the agony that consumed my being for long, I seemed to have periods where the pain would lessen, bringing me back to wakefulness. In these periods, My mind was a chaotic storm of suffering, anger, and desperate longing for death. Sometimes, hours passed; other times, it felt like only minutes before the pain returned.

But gradually, the periods of unconsciousness became shorter and less frequent. Each time I woke up to searing pain, my throat raw from screaming, I couldn't help but wonder if this would be the time that I might finally die. But as each day passed and I remained alive, it became clear that he enjoyed prolonging my suffering.

I lost track of how many times I woke up in agony. Still, eventually, there were moments when I awoke to blessed relief, and I wept with gratitude. My sobs echoed in the empty room, my voice hoarse and strained from the countless hours of screaming. And in those moments of peace, I clung to the hope that perhaps death had finally claimed me

and that was the only reason I wasn't strapped into that torturous table anymore.

My body ached as I pushed myself up, struggling to stand on shaky legs. My surroundings were foreign and unfamiliar, the rough surface of the cave floor cutting into my exposed skin as I fell back down. Disregarding the pain, I desperately looked over my sensitive skin for any sign of injury. "I can't be dead," I muttered to myself. "I shouldn't still bleed if I was dead, and I wouldn't still be here...would I?" My eyes scanned the cave walls until they landed on a faint glimmer in the distance - a door. Without hesitation,

CHAPTER 2

I rushed towards it, driven by a need to escape this place. I needed to get out and find my father if I was alive. And if there was even a chance that he was still alive, I had to save him at all costs. The adrenaline coursing through my veins drowned out the pain and fear as I focused on reaching that door, desperate for a way out of this nightmare.

My mind flashed back to the harrowing image of my father's arm hanging limply from the shattered window of our tour bus. The memory fuelled me, pushing me to charge faster towards the door in front of me. I needed to escape this nightmare as quickly as possible. As I neared the door, a faint distortion in the air caught my attention, but I ignored it and continued my sprint. With all my might, I slammed my shoulder into the door, only to be thrown back by a blinding flash resembling the flares used by SWAT teams on TV. I flew through the air, landing roughly 30 feet away on the hard cave floor. The impact knocked the wind out of me, leaving me gasping for breath as I struggled onto my hands and knees. But even as I tried to recover, I couldn't help but scream in frustration, "WHAT THE FUCK? JUST LET ME OUT, YOU PRICKS! YOU'VE HAD YOUR FUN!" My words echoed off the walls, met only with eerie silence. Defeated for the moment, I collapsed onto the floor. I curled into a ball, allowing self-pity to consume me in that dark, desolate cave.

I lost track of time as I lay on the cold, hard floor, my tears drying against my cheeks. My gaze was fixed on the intricate patterns of cracks on the ceiling, but my mind was trapped in a cycle of self-pity and fear. Why did I have to be the one to survive? Why was I stuck in this horrifying place with no hope of escape?

As I lay there, consumed by my thoughts, I heard the faint sound of claws scraping against the rough rock floor. A chill ran down my spine as I remembered that I was not alone in this dark, dank cave. And then I heard it - a voice whispering into my mind.

"Hello again, little one. Do you remember me?"

Things started to click back into place. I remember Lyn comforting me when I first woke up before Jeremiah's experiment. She now stood before me, a massive, fierce dragon with a certain regal beauty. Her scales were mesmerising shades of purples and silver greys, reminiscent of storm clouds, with a pearlescent shimmer that caught the Light. However, upon closer inspection, I noticed that large patches of scales were missing all over its body, revealing raw and wounded flesh beneath. The creature held itself with pride and dignity but was clearly in poor shape; its claws and horns were chipped and broken, and streaks of dried blood marred its beautiful hide. One of its eyes had a milky white film over it, giving it a haunting appearance. It was heartbreaking to see such a magnificent creature suffering so greatly. Who could have inflicted this kind of damage on something so beautiful?

Tears immediately sprang to my eyes as I gasped, taking in the sight of the chained dragon before me. Its once proud and majestic form was now marred by cruel mangles on its legs and a heavy chain around its neck. "What happened to you?" I cried out, unable to contain my sadness and shock.

"Little one, do not cry for me. I am but a captive Like yourself," Lyn replied with a gentle voice that belied her massive size. It continued, "I have been held captive here for many years, my power suppressed by these chains. A hatchling could easily defeat me right now."

Feeling helpless and defeated, I turned away from the dragon's sorrowful gaze. I couldn't bear for this magnificent creature to see me cry.

CHAPTER 2

But the dragon spoke again, reassuring me, "Do not cry, little one. All hope is not lost. You have survived longer than any other human brought here. Your will to survive must be incredible and unfortunately necessary in this place."

Through sniffles and tears, I managed to ask for more information about our situation. "Can you tell me how long I've been here and what he has planned for us?"

After a pause, Lyn answered gravely, "You have been here for several weeks. Most humans brought here last only a few days before succumbing to their fate. In all his years of doing this, you are the first to survive being brought back to this chamber."

Her words hung heavily in the air, emphasising our dire situation.

"I think I know what he is attempting to achieve, but I can't be a curtain. Please allow me to explain". I listened to her words, and images of a distant past flooded my mind. "In a time long ago, when war raged among all the realms - humans, elves, vampires, shapeshifters, harpies, and all manner of creatures battled for dominance. Even the older species, like the watchers, the dragons, and the elementals, were not immune to the conflict. While some chose to stay neutral, others were forced to defend their borders against those who dared to challenge them.

A solution was devised to combat this constant threat a force of soldiers where created who could be controlled. The process involved a powerful ritual that combined human soldiers with the blood of dragons and a significant amount of magic. The result was extraordinary - enhanced strength, speed, intelligence, dexterity, longer lifespans, and increased magical abilities. They even gained innate gifts from the Donner of the Blood. At first, this solution brought peace and satisfaction to all parties involved. But then something went wrong. The details are hazy, but it is believed that a group known as the "blood born" rose and attempted to seize control of all the realms. This led to an unprecedented war that left devastation in its wake.in response to this chaos, the council was formed - representatives from each species came together to govern and maintain order. However, even they were answerable to a higher power - the watcher council. In their first act as a united front, they issued an order for the extermination of all the blood born and any who were created by it's ritual. They then banned any further creation of blood born or the use of the ritual.

The memory of this dark period still lingers in the minds of all creatures, serving as a reminder of what can happen when power falls into the wrong hands."

My brow furrowed, my thoughts fixed on the man who had kidnapped me. The man who may have given me abilities beyond human comprehension. "You think he made me into one of those things?" I asked, my voice laced with fear and uncertainty.

"I honestly don't know," Lyn replied, eyes scanning the room for any sign of danger. "From what I've observed, he can't be doing that, but I can't think of what else it could be. I know he's trying to develop a weapon, but that's all I know." I felt relief at Lyn's words, but it was quickly replaced by a surge of uncertainty. "Wait, you said these blood worriers are stronger than most other things, so if that's what he's trying to turn me into, surely I will get stronger too, right?" I asked, my mind racing with possibilities.

The corner of Lyn's mouth twitched into a small smile. "Not that straightforward, little one. Look at your ankle!"

Confused, I glanced down at my ankle and saw for the first time a thin silver band encircling it. The intricate markings etched onto its surface glinted in the dim Light of

CHAPTER 2

the chamber. Panic rose in my chest as I turned to Lyn with wide eyes. "What's this?"

Lyn's expression darkened. "If I had to guess, it's something similar to what he has on me to stop me from escaping."

I took a step back as it dawned on me. I was trapped here, just like Lyn. But I refused to let fear take over. "Okay, that just means we need to be more creative with our escape attempt," I declared with determination.

A low, menacing growl rumbled from within Lyn as I watched her eyes flash with fury. She warned me of Jeremiah's approach in a voice that only I could hear. The chains that bound her were pulling her back, preventing her from attacking. But she refused to be silenced, letting out a deafening roar that echoed off the stone walls.

As I turned towards the door, it creaked open slowly and in strode Jeremiah, followed closely by his sleazy lackey Mallory. Their presence made my skin crawl and fear spike through me.

"Oh, look, master sleeping. Beauty is awake," Mallory's voice was sickeningly sweet and full of malicious delight.

Jeremiah sneered at me, his cold eyes gleaming with arrogance. "So it would seem, Mallory."

Mallory giggled to himself, the sound sending shivers down my spine.

"So Jessica, are you ready to be a well-behaved little girl, or are you going to make me punish you?" Jeremiah asked with a sly grin.

I tried to hold onto my confident defiance. "Why don't you just let us go and leave us alone?" I blurted out, surprising even myself with my boldness. But Jeremiah only recoiled at my words for a moment before quickly he regained his composure. He took a step towards me, his hand raised threateningly. "You'll learn to watch your tongue," he spat before striking me with the back of his hand across the face.

I stumbled backwards and fell to the ground, pain radiating through my cheek where he had hit me. My vision blurred for a moment as tears welled up in response to both physical and emotional pain.

Meanwhile, Jeremiah formed a glowing ball of purple mist in his hand. With a silent command, he sent it flying towards Lyn, who was still struggling against her chains. The mist washed over her body, causing her to let out an agonising roar that shook me to my core.

As the events played out before me, I could see Mallory's twisted joy and amusement in his sickening giggles and claps. My heart broke at the thought of what they were doing to Lyn, a mighty dragon reduced to this helpless state.

"Now Jessica, come with me quietly, or I will be forced to continue hurting your friend," Jeremiah threatened, forming another ball of mist in his hand.

My resolve shattered at the thought of Lyn suffering more, so I sobbed and tried to look obedient as I followed Jeremiah out of the room with Mallory close behind. But inside, I was seething with rage and determination. I would find a way to free Lyn and make them pay for their cruelty.

Just then, I heard Lyn's voice in my mind, urging me to be brave. "Please be strong, my little dragon," she whispered.

"The things I plan to learn from you will change the world," Jeremiah's excited voice brought me back to the present. "You're the first step to realising my dream. If I can unlock how you survived, my research will finally be near completion. Nothing in history has ever been as special as you will be."

He led me out of the room and into a different part of the facility, with Mallory following closely behind. With my

CHAPTER 2

head down and shoulders hunched in a show of submission, I tried to take in my surroundings and create a mental map. One day, when we escaped from this place, it would help us get far away from these sadistic men and their experiments on creatures like Lyn and me.

CHAPTER 3

The Experiments

Fear and adrenaline coursed through my veins as I continued to follow, too afraid to speak up. My eyes darted around, taking note of the downward incline and the twists and turns we were
making. As our path seemed to lead further and further into darkness, I desperately tried to commit the route to memory so I could make my escape later. But for now, I had no choice but to keep following; trying to appear weak and timid, I kept my posture hunched and meek, hoping they would underestimate me. After what felt like an eternity, we finally reached a massive steel door. Its surface was etched with intricate symbols that seemed to glow in the faint light. My heart raced as I wondered what kind of horrors awaited me on the other side. Jeremiah typed in a code on the keypad, his fingers moving with practised precision. With an unsettling grind, the door slid open,
revealing a cloud of dust that momentarily obscured my vision.

I braced myself as we stepped inside, my mind racing with fear and anticipation. What did these psychos have in store for me? The unknown was terrifying, but I knew I couldn't give up without a fight. Steeling myself, I followed them into the unknown depths beyond the steel door. Jeremiah strode into the Chamber confidently, showing he was at ease in his surroundings. This was where he held all the power and control, and it made my skin crawl just being near him. Seeing him so comfortable here only made me uneasy, and I hesitated to follow. But Mallory, always eager to please his master, pushed me forward none too gently. "Hurry up, the master is waiting," he sneered. My feet dragged along the cold stone floor as I resisted his prompt to move forward. He grew impatient and shoved harder, causing me to stumble towards the centre of the room, my eyes widening as I took in my surroundings. My blood turned to ice as I realised that the operating table placed prominently in the middle of the room was not for traditional medical procedures. Instead, it was surrounded by a trolley filled with sharp scalpels, saws, and other ominous-looking tools I had only ever seen in horror movies.

The walls of the Chamber were lined with shelves upon shelves of specimen jars, each holding a different body part or organ preserved in formaldehyde. Some were recognisable, while others were distorted beyond recognition. My stomach churned as I spotted jars containing claws, teeth, and even scales from unknown creatures.

But what horrified me most was the eye displayed front and centre on a pedestal. It could have belonged to someone, but I felt it was Lyns. I don't know if a dragon could regenerate an eye. But his earlier statement now made sense. My mind raced with gruesome possibilities as I fought back a wave of nausea and terror. This was no ordinary laboratory it was a house of horrors controlled by a madman.

With a frustrated grunt, Mallory shoved me harder, his hands digging into my shoulders as he tried to force me onto the table. The cold stone of the Chamber sent shivers down my spine as I resisted his push. "I said move," he growled, his face twisted in anger. "We don't keep the master waiting." I

CHAPTER 3

stumbled to the side as he pushed me further into the room, my heart racing with fear and adrenaline.

But then, in a moment of blind courage, I took my chance. Ignoring Mallory's threats, I bolted back towards the Chamber where my fellow captive was being held. My feet pounded against the smooth stone floor as I desperately searched for a way out. I followed a narrow path that led upwards, praying it would lead me to freedom. As I ran, I could feel Mallory's heavy footsteps behind me, but for some reason, he didn't seem to be giving chase. My mind raced as I wondered why they weren't pursuing me more aggressively. Was it some kind of trap? Or were they simply overconfident in their ability to catch me? But there was no time to dwell on these thoughts; all that mattered was finding a way out. Suddenly, the path split into two directions, and without hesitation, I veered left. My instincts told me it was the right choice, and I prayed silently that it would lead me closer to escape. And then, just like a beacon of hope, a bright light appeared at the end of the tunnel. A surge of relief washed over me as I realised this could be my way out.

With renewed energy and determination, I picked up my pace and sprinted towards the light. But just when I thought I had made it, something struck me from behind with an intense burst of pain. The shackles around my leg glowed with an eerie light, and I could feel searing heat spreading through my body. Before I knew it, I was on the ground, my body convulsing in uncontrollable spasms.

The pain was unbearable, and all I could do was scream as tears streamed down my face. I had no idea how long this went on, but when it finally stopped, I gasped for air, and my whole body was exhausted. My throat felt raw from screaming, and my cheeks were wet with tears, but at least I had survived for now.

Jeremiah knelt in front of me, gripping my face tightly between his hands. His eyes burned with a maniacal glint as he spoke to me. "I have allowed you to roam free in my facility, to indulge your desires and run wild. But do not be fooled, little one. You can never escape me. You are mine to control, a mere plaything for my pleasure. And when I am finished playing with you, I will dispose of you like trash." He stood up and dusted off his clothes, looking at me with disdain. "Now, enough wasting time on your foolish attempts at escape. It is time for me to begin my work," he sneered.

I remained still, knowing that resistance was futile. What was the point of struggling against this madman if death was inevitable? But Jeremiah wasn't satisfied with my silence. "So you refuse to walk?

Very well then," he snapped his fingers and suddenly my limbs became stiff and frozen, locked in place by some unknown power.

Jeremiah began to chant with a wicked grin in a language I couldn't understand, but it sounded almost musical. Despite my anger and fear, I couldn't help but find it absurdly comical. After a few moments of chanting, he stopped and walked away, leaving me levitating in his wake. This was undoubtedly an interesting way to force someone to follow.

As we returned to the cave where I had tried to escape from earlier, I saw Mallory sulking in the corner, his rage barely contained. Jeremiah gestured towards the operating setup, and my body floated into place without any resistance from me. I couldn't move or fight back, which only infuriated me more. Jeremiah seemed to sense my thoughts and sneered at me. "Even if you could move, do you really think you stand a chance against me?"

CHAPTER 3

As he secured restraints on my arms, legs, hands, feet, and even my neck, I noticed that holding whatever magic he used in place seemed to exhaust him. At least his power was not infinite, giving me a glimmer of hope. I tried to wriggle free from the restraints, but they were tight and unyielding, just like his hold over me. My captor's deep, rumbling voice filled the dimly lit Chamber, his words echoing off the cold stone walls. His eyes flickered with curiosity and malice as he pondered aloud, "Now we know the dragon can regenerate, but with the first treatment done, do you think you will be able to" With a grim smile, he lifted a glinting scalpel. He sliced through my filthy clothes, the sharp blade leaving trails of blood in its wake. Each cut sent waves of pain coursing through my body. Methodically, he peeled away the layers of fabric, revealing my wounds in all their rawness. His hands ran over them like a macabre artist examining their latest masterpiece, pressing into the torn skin and urging the wounds to bleed even more freely. I could feel my blood mingling with the grime and filth on the table, creating a sickening pool underneath me. The metallic scent of iron filled my nostrils and made me lightheaded. Every beat of my heart seemed to throb in time with each cut and gash on my body. But despite the agony pulsing through me, I refused to show any weakness in front of this man who seemed determined to push me to my limits.

Mallory bounced eagerly on the balls of his feet, causing his entire body to shake with excitement. He couldn't contain his giggles as his master leaned closer to inspect his handy work, a mischievous twinkle in his eye. The air was tense with anticipation, as if the ground they stood on held its breath. Mallory's hands twitched eagerly, waiting to see what his master would do next.

Jeremiah's face was lit up with a frenzied joy as he gazed into my eyes. "Yes, they are already healing faster than anything I have seen before," he exclaimed. His voice trembled excitedly as he continued, "Oh, do you know what this means?" But he didn't wait for a reply, too consumed by his thoughts. "I've done it," he declared triumphantly. "My superiors will be ecstatic. But now, it's time to collect more data." A predatory grin spread across his face as he stepped closer, wielding a scalpel.

As soon as the cold metal touched my skin, I let out a blood-curdling scream. Ignoring my cries of pain, Jeremiah began cutting deeper and deeper, carving chunks of flesh and muscle from my arms and legs. It felt like an eternity as he worked methodically and relentlessly, focusing solely on obtaining more data.

My screams turned into whimpers long before he was finished. My voice had abandoned me, leaving only the searing pain that engulfed every inch of my exposed injuries. Each passing gust of air felt like hot coals being pressed against my raw flesh. At that moment, all I could do was suffer in silence as Jeremiah completed his brutal experiment.

Excruciating pain wracked my body, reducing me to nothing but a quivering mess. I could do nothing but whimper and writhe in agony, my muscles contracting and spasming uncontrollably. In the dimly lit room, Jeremiah leaned close to my ear and whispered, his voice dripping with sadistic glee. "I hope you've enjoyed this as much as I have. Next time, we'll push the boundaries of your healing abilities even further. We'll see if it's just the flesh that can regenerate or if you possess the power to heal organs," he chuckled darkly, relishing in my suffering. He turned to Mallory, who was waiting eagerly in the corner. "I'm

CHAPTER 3

finished for now. Take her back to the holding area And make sure she receives the new solution," he said with a hint of excitement in his voice. "I've mixed in traits from multiple more paranormal specimens, more than what we used in the original batches. Let's see how her body responds to a higher concentration and dosage." With a final order, he strode out of the room, leaving me alone with Malory. My body was on the verge of giving up, unable to handle the brutal treatment any longer. As darkness enveloped my mind, I heard Malory's sinister laughter echoing through the room, serving as a cruel lullaby before I succumbed to unconsciousness.

*

As my consciousness returned, I found myself on a hard cot in the main cavern. Lyn's face hovered above me, her eyes locked onto mine with concern. I tried to sit up, but my body was heavy and sluggish. It was then that I noticed I was completely naked, covered in a thick layer of blood and filth. An IV filled with a strange liquid dripped into my arm, next to the cot lay a pile of empty fluids bag. Panic set in as I wondered what else they had decided to injecte into my system. Every inch of my body throbbed and ached as if I had been beaten with a metal bat.

"Hey Lyn," I croaked, struggling to form words. "How long have I been out?"

"He brought you back two days ago. And hanging a new bag to your iv every few hours, Honestly, I didn't think you would survive. But I'm glad I was wrong. What he did to you... it's horrific, and I hate that you had to endure it."

"I tried to escape. I think I made it to the entrance but couldn't go any further. The cuffs on my legs triggered something. The pain was so intense it dropped me to the floor when he came to retrieve me; he just laughed, like it was all just a game." The memory of my failed attempt at freedom filled me with anger and frustration. How could someone be so cruel and heartless?

Lyn's expression turned grim as she snarled. Her anger about what had happened was evident. "He enjoys playing with his prisoners. It's sickening." She replied

We sat silently, pondering our next move, when Lyn spoke in my mind again. The words fell from her like a heavy and resigned boulder rolling down a mountainside. "Thank you for trying," her voice laced with exhaustion. "We will bide our time. Maybe they will slip up, and we will escape soon." I could hear the desperation in her voice, and the hope that was slowly fading away.

"When he took me, he hit you with a spell," I said softly, trying to keep my voice steady. "He didn't hurt you too badly, did he?"

"No, I was fine within a few hours," she replied, but I could see the pain etched on her face.

"I'm assuming it was more of your blood in those bags," I pointed to the empty IV bag. Her blood had been drained and used to heal me. The thought made my stomach churn.

"It was, but I don't think it was only mine". she said, her voice barely above a whisper. "But if it helped you recover, I'm happy to give it."

A shudder ran through me at the memory of the place he had taken me to. It was a nightmare come to life. "When you said he was harvesting tissue from you, I did not know how bad it had been," I said quietly. "Lyn, I think I saw your eye preserved in a jar; he had body parts and organ specimens. Is that what will end up happening to us? Are we just going to end up dissected and put on display for this psycho's pleasure?" My words hung heavy in the air as the gravity of our situation sank in. We were nothing but pawns

CHAPTER 3

in his twisted game, mere objects to be studied and used for his sick pleasures. And there seemed to be no escape from it all. At this realisation, My tears began to flow freely, like a waterfall cascading down a rocky cliff. Gradually, they slowed and then stopped altogether, leaving behind a sense of relief and release. I took a deep breath, my chest rising and falling with each inhale and exhale. I felt like I could finally move forward at that moment, no longer weighed down by unshed tears and bottled-up feelings.

"Jessica," Lyn began, her voice deep and resonant, carrying hints of wisdom and experience. "I am a dragon and have lived for centuries, enduring countless traumas and unspeakable horrors, many of which have been forgotten by history. It has been a long time since I was last among my people; until I met you, I was unsure if I would ever get to walk the world again or if I would choose to take my last sleep just so I could escape this hell.

Pausing, she glared at me with her one good eye and continued, "But meeting you in this place has given me hope and has swayed my decision. I will venture out into the world once more and see the realms with fresh eyes."

Lyn's words brought me great comfort and strength. Together, we shall fight, and we shall persevere. For now, let us focus on staying alive and finding a way to defeat our enemies." She growled.

The hours since I woke had been a blur, but I could feel my strength slowly returning. Only one visitor had come to see me, aside from Lyn. It was Mallory, the snivelling creep who strode into the Chamber and threw a crusty loaf of bread and bottle of water at me before snatching the IV equipment away. "The master will continue his tests shortly," he grumbled before Leaving with an air of authority. As he dragged the equipment out the door, I took a tentative bite of the bread to find it was stale, and I had to force every down mouthful down with a gulp of water.

As I swallowed the last chunk. Jeremiah Appeared in the doorway, his voice taunting as he spoke, "Are you looking forward to today's session, pet?" I refused to give him the satisfaction of a response and just lay on the cold hard floor, my body already tensing the thought of being strapped down. "Oh, are you not feeling talkative today? That's okay; I'm sure you'll find your voice soon enough." His words dripped with malice as Mallory appeared beside him. "Come along nicely so Mallory isn't required to use much force, he said."

Mallory rushed over to me and dragged me all the way to the same Chamber that used for the previous treatment. I got on the table, and Mallory quickly began securing my limbs. I could feel his hot breath on my skin as he muttered about how excited his master was to harvest organs from me today. The thought sent shivers down my spine. I had known Jeremiah wanted to cut me open again, but surely Mallory was lying. I couldn't survive something as brutal as having my organs removed. "Now, Jessica," Jeremiah's voice whispered as he slowly entered the Chamber, "since you're so brave, I'll let you in on what I have planned for you."

He was fidgeting from side to side, unable to contain his excitement. But before he could begin, he wanted to instil fear in me first. "Your cells have undergone incredible changes while you were recovering. We've closely monitored your healing process as your muscles and flesh knit themselves back together remarkably. However, some beings possess similar abilities, so I need to push your body to its limits and see just how much it can take before it stops recovering." He clapped his hands together eagerly.

CHAPTER 3

"First, I'll make a Y-shaped incision," he explained as he pointed to where he would cut on my body, tracing his finger along the imaginary path his blade would take. "Then, I'll have to go through your ribs to access all the fascinating organs inside of you. And for that, I have this." He gestured towards a metal contraption that appeared straight out of a medieval torture chamber. After carefully placing it back on the table, he picked up a scalpel.

My sense of horror deepened as I realised what was about to happen. But the man seemed oblivious to my distress. "Don't worry, Jessica," he said with a twisted smile. "I want you to survive this experiment so we can repeat it over and over again. I must replicate my results, after all."

But that was only the beginning of his twisted plan. "You see, a normal human body cannot survive without lungs, kidneys, spleen, appendix or gall bladder," he continued nonchalantly. "And we already know that your body can withstand more than a regular human's. So now, I want to see how strong your healing factor is. One by one, I'm going to remove these vital organs and time your recovery while you lay helplessly on this table with your insides exposed for me to observe." He paused, his eyes gleaming with excitement. "Isn't that going to be fun?"

The man was clearly insane. But I refused to give him the satisfaction of seeing me scared.

With a sickening squelch, the blade sliced into my skin, and I felt the warm rush of blood soaking my chest. The metallic tang filled my nose and made me want to retch. But I resisted the urge to scream, I didn't want to give him the satisfaction of hearing me in pain. Instead, I focused on the sound of my own harsh breathing, trying to drown out the wet scrape of the knife against my flesh. When he was done with the first round of cuts, I thought it was over, but then came the excruciating moment when he pulled back the flap of skin to expose my ribs. My sobs turned into desperate wails as I felt like every nerve ending in my body was on fire. How could anyone endure this? How much more could I take? "Such a beautiful reaction," he sneered, his eyes gleaming as he gazed at my exposed chest. A shiver ran down my spine as he reached for the rib shears, his excitement palpable as he brought them

closer to my torn body. At that moment, I didn't care about anything except escaping this nightmare. And I started to blacked out, thankfully I wouldn't have to feel anymore. Perhaps I wouldn't wake up and have to suffer through his twisted pleasure. But even as I drifted into unconsciousness, part of me knew that there would be no escape from this hellish torture for long.

***

After enduring countless experiments at the hands of Jeremiah, it turned out that my healing factor was strong enough to regrow organs no matter how many times or how roughly they were removed. Every time I lay on the cold metal table, waiting for the next round of torture to begin, I couldn't help but feel a sense of dread wash over me. But to my shock and surprise, each time Jeremiah attempted to use his rib shears to break through my rib cage or remove any organs, my mind would shut down and spare me from the excruciating pain. After each session, I would wake up a couple of days later, bruised and battered hooked up to a fresh iv bag filling my veins with whatever Jeremiah decided to test this time but with no lasting damage.

With every experiment in which I passed out, it seemed to infuriate Jeremiah more and more. His once calm demeanour was replaced by one of madness and obsession. And then, one day, maybe six or seven months after his first

CHAPTER 3

attempt at organ harvesting, he strolled into the cave with Malory at his heels. As he made his way over to me, I could see the crazed gleam in his eye and knew that whatever he had in store for me would be brutal.

"You haven't been proving to be the sort of test subject I was hoping for recently," he snarled, circling around me like a predator stalking its prey. "And I must confess, this has put me in a foul mood." He let out a chilling cackle and continued, "You see, part of the fun in doing these tests is seeing your reactions and emotions. It's all important data that must be collected. But every time we start, you decide to blackout."

I tried not to shiver under his gaze as he towered over me, revealing my fear. But I refused to give him the satisfaction. I knew that was what he got off on- my anxiety and pain. He leaned in closer, his hot breath fanning against my face as he whispered, "Don't worry, pet. You won't escape me today. I have lots of delicious treats in store for you." My heart raced with terror as I braced myself for what was to come.

I was dragged, trembling and terrified, to the room that haunted My nightmares. The walls were lined with specimen jars, I was sure a few of which now held some of my organs. As soon as we entered, I was thrown onto a stiff metal table, my body shivering in the cool air. In this place of fear and pain, I had become accustomed to being stripped of my dignity no longer seen as a human only as thing to be used and discarded. But today I couldn't help but shiver as Mallory approached me. Without a single word, he began strapping me down, making sure I was completely immobile. His words slithered into my ear like snakes, sending goosebumps down my spine. "No escape for sleeping beauty today," he chuckled darkly. My heart raced as I realised what he meant - there would be no mercy this time. Dread filled my mind as I anticipated what horrors Jeremiah had planned for me. "I hope he will let me have a turn," Mallory sneered, his eyes glittering with sadistic pleasure. My worst fears were about to come true, and I could do nothing to stop it.

Mallory instinctively backed away as Jeremiah advanced, his eyes studying the shackles that bound me to the table. I could see the wheels turning in his mind, his usually calm demeanour replaced with a frenzied determination. He pulled a syringe from his pocket, filled with an eerie green liquid that glowed under the harsh lights of the laboratory.

The colour and consistency of the liquid reminded me of dish soap, but I knew it was something much more sinister. "No more passing out for you," Jeremiah said in a singsong voice before violently jabbing the needle into my upper arm. I cried out in pain and shock, unable to believe what was happening. "Ouch, that hurt asshole!" I screamed, immediately regretting my outburst when I saw the look of pure rage on Jeremiah's face.

The colour drained from my face as I realised the gravity of my mistake. "Well, aren't you a mouthy little lab rat today?" Jeremiah sneered, his voice dripping with malice. "I was going to wait till later, but I think I'll do it now. Yes, now will be good. Maybe it will teach you who's really in charge around here," he muttered, almost as if he needed to convince himself that what he was about to do was justified. I shuddered as I watched him discard the now-empty needle, knowing that I was entirely at his mercy.

Terror coursed through my veins, paralysing me as I braced for the inevitable. Every time he had inflicted his cruel ministrations upon me before, I had been fortunate enough to pass out and escape the pain. But not this time. This time, I would have to endure it all. "Now I'm going to

CHAPTER 3

show you just what a little slut does," he taunted, his words dripping with sadistic glee as he stripped off his clothes. My heart pounded as I realised what he had in store for me. Panic consumed me, and I thrashed against my restraints, desperate to break free from the nightmare unfolding before me.

To make matters worse, Mallory stood by watching with sick fascination, applauding and cheering like it was some kind of twisted game. I endured his ministrations, trying to switch off my emotions as best I could. As he had his way with my body, the feel of his clammy skin on mine was revolting, but I refused to let it show; when he was done and satisfied, he went on with his experiments, and I lay there Like a dead lump of flesh. I tried to stay quiet and not to shed a tear. He wasn't worth it.

***

As I lay there hours later, broken and butchered, I couldn't remember how I had made it back to the cave where Lyn and I were imprisoned. Lost in my own misery I slowly regained my sense of reality, I felt Lyn projecting a calmness to me, assuring me that we would be alright. It wasn't until I tried to move that I realised the true extent of my injuries - I was in worse shape than I could ever imagine. Another IV line was pumping another unknown fluid into my veins. A bowl of stew and bread sat by my side, providing me with much-needed sustenance. Still, I could barely stomach anything through the excruciating pain coursing through my body.

"Stay still," Lyn cautioned as she saw me attempt to move. "Your bones need to set properly."

Bones...the word echoed in my mind as memories flooded back. Memories of him - the man who had raped me and then systematically broke my bones with careful precision. He started with my legs, shattering them into multiple pieces before carving away at the flesh to better observe their healing process. The sound of my own screams filled the room as he took pleasure in watching my bones fuse back together.

I thought I was going insane - the constant breaking and slicing was enough to drive anyone mad. But even when he grew bored with my legs, he moved on to my arm and fingers, dislocating each one before breaking them in different ways just for his own twisted curiosity. And all the while, I was forced to witness this torture, unable to do anything to save myself.

"How often do they change the IV bag?" I managed to ask through gritted teeth, determination filling every fibre of my being. I had a plan - escape or die trying.

Lyn's head was tilted to one side, her eyes fixed on me as if trying to decipher my thoughts. "I think the bag needs to be refilled every few hours," she said, nodding towards the IV bag above me. I furrowed my brow in thought, realising that they must have given it to me to speed up my recovery for their experiments. "But how does that help us now?" Lyn asked, confusion evident in her voice. I turned to face her and asked, "Can your teeth or claws cut through a bone?" Her response was hesitant but confident, "Yes, but it will hurt. What are you planning? How do you expect us to get out of here?" My mind raced as I formulated a plan. "When Mallory comes to change the IV bag, I'll kill him," I stated coldly. The realisation hit me that these people were no longer humans in my eyes; they were ruthless and cruel individuals who deserved to be taken out of this world. My determination grew more potent at the thought of ridding the world of their presence.

It was finally time. Lyn had successfully removed the silver band from my ankle without removing my entire foot,

CHAPTER 3

although it wasn't as easy as I had hoped. Luckily, the drug Jeremiah gave me to stay awake was still working. I gritted my teeth and endured the excruciating pain as the metal tore through my skin and muscle, knowing it would all be worth it soon. Once the process was complete, I approached the cave entrance and waited for my prey to arrive, allowing my leg to heal. As Mallory sauntered through the doorway hours later, I could feel my injured leg throbbing beneath me. Despite this, I stood tall, bracing myself against the cold wall for support. My eyes never left his form as he entered the room, too consumed with his mutterings to notice my presence. "Maybe next time," he muttered under his breath, a sickening grin spreading Across his face. "Master will let me have a turn; I want to make her cry too." The thought of him causing any more harm made my skin crawl, and I knew then that I had to put an end to this monster.

Summoning all the strength in my body, I swung the IV pole with all my might into the side of his head. The sound of impact rang out through the room, followed by a sickening thud as his body hit the floor. But even as I approached him, seeing the damage I had caused, I could still see he was breathing. With a primal rage burning inside me, I crawled towards him, dragging the pole along with me as I delivered blow after blow to his head until it was nothing but a pulpy mess.

Catching my breath, I looked down at his unrecognisable form and couldn't help but think how fitting it was for such an evil creature. Doubtful that he would survive such injuries, I turned towards the door and shouted to Lyn, "I will be back for you." My promise hung heavy in the air as I slowly made my way out of that nightmare and into the safety of the outside world.

My heart raced with fear as the warning echoed, "Go before it's too late." I scrambled to my feet and navigated the maze-like corridors of the dungeon, my memory guiding me towards the quickest route to freedom. My injured leg burned with each step, but I refused to let it slow me down. I repeated, "I can endure this", like a mantra, pushing myself beyond what I thought possible. And then, finally, I was out. The bright blue sky stretched above me, the salty smell of the ocean filling my lungs. In that moment of relief and triumph, I heard a slow applause, like a mocking soundtrack to my escape. "Well done, Jessica," came Jeremiah's voice behind me. "I never would have imagined you capable of such an act of brutality." He leaned casually against the rocky wall beside the exit as if we were simply having a friendly chat instead of being mortal enemies. But then I noticed the ball of crackling energy hovering in his palm. "But don't worry," he continued nonchalantly. "I won't make that mistake again." With a flick of his wrist, he sent the energy hurtling towards me. The impact knocked me unconscious immediately.

***

After my failed escape Lyn and I then developed a daily routine that we clung to with all our might. Every morning, Jeremiah would stride into our makeshift prison, his eyes gleaming with malice as he decided which of us he would experiment on first. His cruel intentions were evident in the way he handled us - rough and forceful, trying to break our spirits and leave us broken. Once he was satisfied, he would go, leaving us trembling and bruised.

But through it all, we held onto each other and our routine. Each day, We were given meagre rations - a bowl of thin stew and stale bread for me, and once a week, Lyn received two slaughtered cows for food.

In those moments, we would forget about our captivity and revel in the taste of our food.

CHAPTER 3

But amidst the darkness and despair, there was a glimmer of hope in the form of Lyn's stories. She would tell me stories of the paranormal world - of other realms filled with creatures beyond my wildest imagination. Her words transported me from this hellish place and gave me hope for something more. I hung onto her every word, hungry for any escape from the darkness that consumed my days with Jeremiah.

With each passing day, Jeremiah's behaviour became more erratic and cruel. As time went on, he delved deeper into his twisted experiments, even going so far as to remove my limbs in a sick attempt to see if they would grow back. In the days that I would need to recover, I was forced to bear witness to the atrocities he inflicted on Lyn. At the same time, I was restrained in my cot within the dark, damp Chamber we called home. The days dragged on slowly, blending together until I no longer kew how many months it had been since my captivity began.

But during this time, I could feel changes happening within myself. Was it because of the constant IV drip of unknown substances that Jeremiah forced into me? Or was it simply because I was growing older? My body was taller now, my figure changing and developing in ways I couldn't fully understand. But it wasn't just my appearance that was transforming; my once timid and submissive nature was fading away, replaced by a newfound sense of defiance and strength.

Jeremiah's punishments were always cruel and merciless, but they became even more extreme whenever I dared to talk back. Which I often did.

He tried to expand his pool of test subjects and would chain me to the unforgiving cave walls and floor, just as he had done with Lyn, to ensure we could not interfere when he brought in his next test subject. As we watched, their bodies writhed in agony under the influence of his experimental drug. None were unable to endure for even 24 hours before succumbing to its effects; with every dead test subject, Jeremiah's rage grew. He would unleash his fury upon me, beating and violating my broken body until I was nothing but a shattered and battered mess, unable to even stand on my own two feet.

After one such ruthless experience in the lab, I found myself seeking solace in Lyn's comforting presence. I leaned against her strong front legs, finding peace in her calming energy. She projected stunning images of soaring over snow-capped mountains, the beauty of nature momentarily distracting me from my ordeal. Suddenly, she spoke up.

"So what did you do to make him remove your fingers and break your toes?" Her voice was gentle but curious.

Despite the pain still fresh in my mind, I couldn't help but laugh at the absurdity of it all. "Well," I began, "after he was finished raping me, I noticed one of my restraints had come loose. So, being the feisty person that I am, I may have thrown something at his crotch and given him the finger." A smirk tugged at my lips as I remembered his enraged expression. "Needless to say, he was not amused by my actions. And as punishment for damaging his precious manhood, he broke each of my fingers and toes with a hammer." My words were laced with bitterness and humour.

I chuckled again, remembering how I had goaded him even further by sarcastically asking if he was done with my manicure and pedicure he could wax my eyebrows next. The image of his bewildered stare was too much for me to handle, and I burst into uncontrollable laughter once more. "Maybe it wasn't the wisest decision," I gasped between

CHAPTER 3

giggles, clutching my ribs with my stumpy hands. "Because then he decided I didn't need my fingers for a while."

As I recounted the ridiculousness of the situation to Lyn, her chest rumbled with laughter alongside mine. Despite the pain and trauma, we found humour in my misfortune together.

I couldn't help but think that at least Lyn enjoyed my sense of Humour, as she looked at me quizzically and asked, "What warranted such an outburst? You rarely lash out without reason." Taking a deep breath, I tried to compose myself. "While he was doing his business," I explained, my voice trembling, "he said just think how proud my mother would be that she raised a freak slut." The memory of those cruel words sent a wave of anger and self loathing coursing through me. "After that, I just wanted to hurt him even though I knew he was going to punish me after." Before Lyn could say anything more, we felt a massive tremor reverberate through the cave. The walls shook, and debris fell from the ceiling as we braced ourselves for whatever was causing the disturbance.

CHAPTER 4

Rescue and Revelation

We felt a massive tremor reverberating through the cave. The walls shook, and debris fell from the ceiling as we braced ourselves for whatever was causing the disturbance.

With lightning reflexes, Lyn threw her body in front of mine, shielding me from any potential debris that may have fallen from the crumbling ceiling. Chaos and destruction echoed outside, causing our hearts to fearfully race. I could hear screams and explosions, a cacophony of danger and uncertainty. My heart raced as I dared to hope that someone had finally found us. But deep down, I knew better than to get my hopes up too high. In this cruel world, anything was possible, and nothing was certain.

With a resounding creak, the heavy door leading out of the damp cave swung open, revealing Jeremiah as he came charging in. Behind him, a group of people dressed in sleek, black tactical gear followed closely, each wielding their own unique weapon or power. The air crackled with sparks of energy as they made their way forward, determined and focused. Unlike most invading forces, there were no guns among them. Some carried swords and daggers, while others held orbs of shimmering energy, much like Jeremiah.

As they entered the dimly lit cave, one figure stood out. His posture exuded confidence, and his sharp gaze scanned the room with authority. In his hand, he held a pulsating orb of vibrant red energy that seemed to pulse with a life of its own. Without hesitation, he spoke in a commanding tone that left no room for question or disobedience.

The commanding officer made a swift gesture to his team, signalling them to keep their distance from the impending confrontation.

Fear and caution were evident on their faces as they took several steps back, creating ample space for the two men to face off.

With a confident tone, the officer called out to Jeremiah," Tell you what, if you can defeat me in battle, my team will release you as free as a bird." Without hesitation, Jeremiah charged forward with an explosive burst of energy, hurling balls of power towards his opponent. But the officer remained unfazed, gracefully dodging each blast with fluid movements that seemed almost otherworldly.

As Jeremiah attempted a physical attack aimed at the officer's solar plexus, the skilled fighter effortlessly evaded it with a mesmerising display of agility and grace. With one swift movement, he pivoted on one foot while whipping the other around, delivering a crushing blow to Jeremiah's rib cage. The sound of breaking bones filled the air, followed by a piercing scream of agony from Jeremiah.

"Restrain him!" the officer commanded as he calmly watched Jeremiah crumple to the ground in pain. "He won't be down for long." The rest of his team immediately sprang into action, swiftly restraining Jeremiah and efficiently neutralising his abilities.

As the red orb of energy dissipated from his hand, the officer removed his helmet and face coverings to reveal a strikingly handsome face. A five o'clock shadow adorned his strong jawline, highlighting his piercing blue eyes. His nose showed signs of being broken multiple times, adding to his

CHAPTER 4

rugged appearance. But what caught my attention were the faint laughter lines etched in the corners of his eyes, hinting at a kind and humorous soul behind his tough exterior. He walked towards Lyn with slow and steady strides, exuding confidence and control in every step.

The officer appeared suddenly, his footsteps muffled by the damp rock of the cave. He greeted Lyn first, bowing slightly before addressing her as "Lady Saar." His voice was firm and confident, tinged with an air of authority that seemed to command respect.

"We will have you out of these shackles as soon as possible," he assured her. "We also have healers waiting on standby for you."

"Thank you, Commander," Lyn replied, "But I am more worried about my comrade. This is Jessica, and she requires urgent medical aid. She shouldn't be forced to walk as he broke all her toes earlier today, and she will not be questioned until I am with her. Do I make myself clear?"

The commander nodded quickly, already turning to leave the cave in search of healers. "Yes, ma'am. I will retrieve a healer immediately. And I will also get a team working on your restraints."

He rushed out of the cave, barking orders at everyone he passed. Lyn turned to me as I sat up and watched the scene wide-eyed.

"Lyn, that wasn't very nice," I scolded playfully.

"I didn't notice," Lyn shrugged nonchalantly. "That being said, he should have had better priorities. You are a human girl who has been held captive by a lunatic. Still, instead of focusing on you, he comes over, trying to fawn over me like I'm some injured kitten. The nerve of some people." Her tone was laced with sarcasm and a hint of bitterness towards the commander's misplaced attention.

The commander's sharp tone and condescension had rubbed Lyn the wrong way, igniting a fierce sense of defiance within her. She stood tall and straight, asserting dominance with every word and movement. She was determined to show that being a captive hadn't broken her spirit. "Anyway, I wanted to talk to you before they ask questions about what has happened." Her words held a sense of urgency that caught me off guard. "I need you to trust me and let me handle everything. And do not leave my side unless I give you explicit permission."

I couldn't help but feel worried as I looked into Lyn's intense gaze. "Lyn, why are you acting like this? Aren't these people supposed to be the good guys?"

She gave me a small, reassuring smile. "You need not be concerned. We must just tread carefully until we know what's happening and who pulls the strings. Once we have all the information, we can decide how much to disclose."

I nodded, trusting in Lyn's judgment and leadership. But there was still one nagging thought on my mind. "Can you try to find out what happened to my father?"

Her expression softened as she placed a comforting hand on my shoulder. "Child, I will do everything in my power to find out the truth about your father and reunite you with him if that's at all possible. But for now, we need to put our game faces on. He is coming back, and remember, let me do the talking."

I took a deep breath and braced myself for whatever was about to happen. I was grateful to have Lyn by my side in this uncertain situation.

The Commander sprinted towards us, his face flushed with urgency as he led a team of equally harried individuals.

"Well, commander," Lyn called out, "are your people going to tend to my injured comrade? And while you're at

CHAPTER 4

it, perhaps this team can finally free us from these wretched chains."

She paced back and forth, her vast bulk causing the chains around her foreleg to clang together in a menacing rhythm. The metallic sound only added to her fierce determination to be freed from captivity.

Time flew by in a blur, the hours melting into what felt like minutes as I was tended to and healed. Their magic was astonishing, easily regrowing my missing fingers and fixing my broken bones. As the healer's hands moved over my body, I felt a sense of calm and rejuvenation. My restraint bracelet had been removed, freeing me from the heavy weight that had held me back for so long. With each step, I felt lighter and more alive, my toes no longer throbbing in pain but dancing across the ground. Adhering to Lyn's instructions, I kept my interactions minimal and brief, not wanting to cause any trouble or draw attention to myself. Once my healing was complete and I was released from the healer's care, I eagerly returned to Lyn's side. They were still struggling to remove the chains that bound her, but as I approached, I saw the final cuff clatter to the ground with a satisfying thud.

The relief was palpable as she let out a deep sigh, finally able to release the tension that had been building in her muscles. She shook out her limbs and stretched her wings with fluid motions, arching her back like a graceful cat basking in the sun's warmth. She extended her talons, leaving deep gouges in the solid rock beneath her, a testament to their strength and sharpness. I couldn't help but marvel at this magnificent creature's raw power and flexibility.

With Jeremiah detained and the magical bindings removed, Lyn felt her power rush back to her like a long-lost lover. It embraced her in an all-consuming, exhilarating embrace. The air in the chamber crackled with raw energy, the stillness was shattered as lightning bolts and gusts of wind whipped around Lyn like a hurricane. She stood at the centre, shrouded in an otherworldly aura that obscured our view. But we caught glimpses of iridescent scales shimmering in the light and arcs of electricity dancing across her body.

As she transformed from dragon to human, time seemed to slow down, and each second stretched out into an eternity. We watched in awe as her features shifted, and her form grew petite and beautiful. And then suddenly, there she stood before us - a powerful and regal young woman radiating strength and authority.

Despite her physical appearance as a young woman in her late twenties or early thirties, it was clear that Lyn was ancient and wise beyond measure. In that moment, she commanded respect and held herself with a poised grace that demanded attention and reverence.

The woman's voice was like a gentle caress, soothing and comforting. "It's nice to be in my human form again now, child," she said, her eyes sparkling with joy. "Come here so I can hold you. I have dreamt of comforting you from the day I met you and will no longer be denied." Her voice was like honey, sweet and alluring, drawing me closer with each word. As she enveloped me in her arms, a sense of safety and warmth washed over me as if I had finally found my true home. And in that moment, I knew that she was right - I would no longer be denied the comfort and love I had longed for all this time.

As Lyn's strong arms wrapped around me, I felt a sense of safety and comfort wash over me. My worries and fears seemed to melt away as she held me tightly against her chest. At that moment, nothing else in the world mattered. All I could focus on was the warmth of her embrace and the sound of her steady heartbeat.

CHAPTER 4

During this intimate moment, I heard Lyn speaking to the commander. Her tone was firm but respectful as she addressed him.

"Yes, commander, I understand your need for answers, but as I have told you, we are leaving. We will accept an escort, but our destination is a hotel. We must bathe, eat, and perhaps find some new clothing suitable for this location," she stated confidently. It was then that I realised we were both completely naked.

Feeling my cheeks flush with embarrassment, I shifted slightly in Lyn's arms. She noticed my discomfort and casually added, "Also, do you have any spare clothing we could borrow for our Journey to a hotel? It would be much appreciated. As I would prefer not to check into the hotel unclothed." The commander's shocked expression only made her request all the more amusing to me. It was clear that we were a pretty strange sight. As the dust settled and all preparations were completed, we were given a change of clothes - essential combat gear that would protect us on our Journey. We were then escorted to the Aurora lodges, a hidden oasis where the extraction team had established their command centre. The scent of freshly cut grass greeted us as we entered the lodge, its walls made of sturdy logs and its roof adorned with shingles. Maps and charts covered every surface while agents in tactical gear worked busily on computers and radios. It was clear that this was a serious operation.

We arrived at the lodge and were escorted to a breathtaking cabin we insisted on sharing. The commander grumbled, clearly disappointed that his plans to interrogate me would be hindered by Lyn's presence. She was immediately on the phone, trying to reach anyone who could help us in our current situation. As she handled the logistics,

I went to the bathroom, eager to wash away the memories of Jeremiah's touch. I was stunned by the luxuriousness of the bathing area - a shiny silver freestanding bathtub and a pile of fluffy white towels awaited me. The sight nearly brought me to tears as it starkly contrasted the fear and danger we had been facing. Taking a deep breath, I ran one of the hottest bubble baths I could remember and spent hours scrubbing every inch of my body to rid myself of any lingering contamination. Even after my skin turned pink from the scrubbing, I couldn't shake off the memories.

Desperate for some semblance of peace, I drained the tub and filled it again with fresh water, hoping it would soothe my troubled mind and allow me to contemplate my uncertain future.

As I lay submerged in the warm water, a dreamy aroma of lavender wafted through the air from the bubble bath concoction I had used. The soft bubbles tickled my skin and eased my tension as I contemplated what lay ahead. It was hard to fathom just how long I had been held captive, and the thought made my head spin with uncertainty. Had my Dad perished in the accident? If so, where would I go? Where would I call home now? These unanswerable questions swirled around me, taunting me with their weight. And so, I let out a soft cry, tears mingling with the fragrant water as I wallowed in my grief. Eventually, I noticed the once warm water had turned cold, and my body began to shiver. Slowly, I dragged myself out of the tub and wrapped myself in the softest towels imaginable. Taking a deep breath, trying to steel myself for what was to come, I reminded myself that I had already allowed myself this moment for my emotional breakdown but now it was time to put on a brave face and confront whatever challenges awaited me. But I think I deserve a nap first. Lyn had given me permission for some

CHAPTER 4

much-needed rest, and nothing would take that away from me. With determination fuelling my steps, I made my way to the bed and crawled under the comforting folds of the duvet. I had missed duvets - how they cocooned you in warmth and protection. As exhaustion overtook me, I relished in the comfort of this momentary reprieve from reality.

My exhaustion caught up with me when my head hit the soft, downy pillows. Thankfully, it was a dreamless sleep, free from any worries or fears. When I woke, I saw the sun peeking through the window and could hear a heated conversation coming from the next room. As well as the delicious aroma of food wafting into my room, causing my stomach to let out a demanding growl for sustenance. I chuckled to myself and my rumbling belly and took in my surroundings. A pile of clothes and boots sat neatly on a chair beside the bed, with a note on top that read, "I hope these are to your liking." I eagerly dressed in the offered attire - stone-washed jeans, a long-sleeved black shirt, a pair of sleek timberland boots in black, and a flowing cardigan in matching black. As I glanced at myself in the mirror, I couldn't help but feel transformed - my new outfit fitting perfectly and gave me a look of sophistication. The only thing that didn't quite fit was my hair length, which was now reaching past my waist. It made me look older, not old per se, just more mature. My features seemed more pronounced, and my eyes somehow seemed brighter than I remembered. For a moment, I almost didn't recognise myself in the mirror. But before I could dwell on it too much, my grumbling stomach reminded me of my mission - to find some food. Without hesitation, I headed out of my room and towards the source of the commotion and, hopefully, a warm meal.

As I stepped into the dimly lit cabin, my gaze was immediately drawn to Lyn. Dressed in a similar style to mine, she exuded an aura of confidence and power that demanded attention. Her posture was straight, and her shoulders were squared as she sat at the head of the long wooden table, her presence filling the room with energy.

Across from her sat the Commander who had rescued us, his stern expression giving away nothing of his thoughts. Beside him was an official who looking man who appeared out of place and less than thrilled to be there. Next to Lyn sat a man with a friendly smile, his face radiating genuine interest and excitement.

But it was Lyn who commanded the room. Her voice was vibrant and commanding as she addressed the other official with a steely determination. "I am not saying you cannot speak to Jessica," she asserted, her gaze never wavering from them. "But I will not allow you to hold her accountable for something that was done against her will." The tension in the room thickened as she spoke, drawing everyone's focus towards her.

"I can personally testify that she shows no signs of madness," Lyn continued, her voice unwavering and confident. "And as I have already informed you, she is protected by both the dragon and elf council's.»

Silence hung in the air as Lyn glared at the official beside the Commander. Before anyone could say something that could worsen the situation, the gentleman beside Lyn cleared his throat to shift the room's attention to him. Then, rather boldly, he said, "I, for one, would rather you not question Jessica. I feel she has been through enough trauma. Do you think we should force her to relive it just to satisfy our curiosity? There is enough evidence for all of us to be busy investigating for months. But if you insist, then get on with it." His words hung in the air, a transparent order for the official to follow.

CHAPTER 4

The official sat nervously, obviously out of his element, before reluctantly relenting. "Fine, have it your way. But I want to be kept in the loop on all relevant investigation details moving forward," he huffed with obvious resentment.

The gentleman beside Lyn clapped his hands together, the sound echoing in the room like a resounding symbol of his delight. His beaming smile lit up his face, revealing rows of perfectly white teeth. "That's wonderful!" he exclaimed, his voice filled with genuine enthusiasm. "Now, before we go any further, I'm famished." His eyes sparkled with anticipation. He asked. "Will you both be joining us for breakfast, or do you have somewhere else to be?" The official who sat with the Commander stood abruptly and excused himself. At the same time, the Commander remained seated, his expression still serious and focused. After a tense few minutes, the commander spoke. "Well, that went better than expected," he said, a hint of relief in his tone. "So what's For breakfast," he added with a slight chuckle, "the three of them broke down laughing." The tension in the room dissipated as they all shared a moment of lightheartedness amidst the grave situation. Their laughter filled the air and echoed off the walls, bringing a brief sense of warmth and camaraderie to the otherwise austere atmosphere.

My throat felt tight as I cleared it, trying to announce my presence in the room. The group turned to look at me, their eyes curious and assessing. Lyn, the woman who had been there for me through this ordeal, spoke up with a warm smile. "Ah, there's my Little Dragon. I should explain everything over breakfast."

We all made our way to the dining table, but before we could sit down, a woman who appeared slightly older than me informed us that the food would take a bit longer. As she ushered us to make ourselves comfortable, I couldn't help feeling out of place and vulnerable. I sat close to Lyn, seeking her protection and guidance. The commander and another man, who seemed like a mystery

The gentleman was kind enough not to comment on my behaviour as Lyn made introductions.

"These gentlemen," she began, gesturing to them, "are Commander Killian Robinson and Alexander Elric." Her voice held respect and admiration for both men. "Commander Robinson leads a joint task force between the paranormal military and the paranormal investigation agency. And Alexander here is the head of the paranormal investigation agency." She paused, then added with pride, "He is also an ancient friend of mine and a member of the elf's council." Lyn turned to me with a reassuring smile. "He has vouched for you."

I couldn't hold back my confusion any longer. "I'm sorry, but I don't understand why I need to be vouched for or what that other man was so angry about. Can someone please explain what's going on?"

"This is a complicated subject, but I will explain," said Alex

"Our joint councils made a treaty long ago when my grandparents were still young. This treaty decreed that anyone who dabbled in ancient blood magic or created a blood-born would be sentenced to life in Tartarus." The mere mention of this place sent shivers down my spine.

And then came the final blow - "a clause in the treaty that stated all products of these experiments would also be destroyed." Fear and confusion raced through my mind as I looked at the three wide-eyed.

"So... does that mean you're going to kill me?" My voice trembled with terror as I finally managed to choke out the

CHAPTER 4

question, unable to hide the fear and vulnerability that consumed me.

Alexander's head shook slowly, the firelight from the cabin fireplace casting shadows across his face.

"Jess, we are not going to kill you. But we are concerned about the risk you represent," he said, his tone serious. "The paranormal world has changed and evolved significantly since then, but we elves have always guarded the secret of how to create blood-born warriors." He paused. "I examined Jeremiah's workspace in those caves while you slept and spoke with him. I even took a look at your genetic makeup." My heart skipped a beat as he continued, "Don't worry; I did not touch you or cause any harm. But what he did to you is something that cannot be easily explained, his eyes scanning my face for any hint of understanding. "You see, what I found in those caves revealed that he has manipulated your DNA, giving you not just dragon blood but also genetic markers for multiple supernatural beings – feline shifters, mages, vampires and dragons, to name just a few."

My mind reeled at this revelation. "So...what does that mean? What will happen to me?" I couldn't help but feel a twinge of fear creeping into my voice. "Are you going to lock me up and experiment on me like he did?"

In a flurry of movement, Alexander and Lyn rushed to my side, their concern palpable. Lyn's grip on my hand was firm yet comforting, while Alexander's calming touch on my shoulder helped ground me. A peculiar sensation washed over me as I struggled to regain control of my breathing. It was as if sparks of electricity were buzzing under my skin, disrupting any sense of calm I had left. My mind raced with thoughts and emotions, making it difficult to focus on anything else.

Lyn's voice sounded like a gentle breeze, cutting through the thick haze of fear and uncertainty. "Don't worry, Jess," she said, her voice soft and reassuring. "We won't let anyone harm you or use you for their own twisted experiments." Her words were like a shield, protecting me from the dangers that lurked in the shadows.

My gaze fell to my outstretched hand, and I was shocked to see tiny sparks of electricity dancing between my fingertips. In a panic, I attempted to wrench away from Lyn's grip on my other hand, but she held on with fierce determination. The energy surged through me like a wild current, coursing up my arm and filling me with a buzzing, crackling sensation that was frightening and strangely alluring. The air around us seemed to hum with the power of it all, as if the atmosphere had been charged with electric energy.

My eyes were glued to the magnificent display of power before me as I pleaded with them. "How do I make it stop?" My voice was desperate, my heart racing with fear and confusion. "What is happening to me?" Every inch of my body felt like it was on fire, and each cell was pulsing with unknown energy. I could feel the weight of their gazes on me, their expressions of awe and apprehension. The air around us crackled with electricity, and I couldn't help but wonder if this was all just a dream or some kind of nightmare.

Alexander and Lyn exchanged a glance, their eyes filled with understanding. I could sense the tension building in their bodies as they faced me. "We can't say for certain, but it appears that removing the power nullifying cuff and your heightened emotional state has triggered your body to adapt to the changes by Jeremiah," Alexander's voice was calm, but his words held a hint of uncertainty. His brow furrowed in deep concentration as he explained the situation.

CHAPTER 4

The light in Lyn's eyes became radiant and proud as she spoke, her voice soft yet full of conviction. "You are on the brink of a powerful transformation and are evolving into something entirely new, Jess. And though the Journey ahead may be dangerous and uncertain, we will be by your side to help you navigate it."

Lyn squeezed my hand gently as she continued, her voice barely above a whisper. "Just close your eyes and focus on your breathing. Imagine each breath is filling you with energy, becoming one with your being." I followed her instructions, inhaling deeply

and feeling the warmth of energy coursing through my body like a river. The air around us seemed to vibrate with an otherworldly power, crackling with untapped potential. With each exhale, I let go of doubts or fears, letting the vibrant energy from the world around me. pulse through my veins, filling me with renewed strength and clarity

I slowly opened my eyes, taking in the curious gazes of those around me. Their expressions ranged from awe to admiration, and a sense of accomplishment washed over me.

The woman cooking breakfast stood at the stove with a wide grin as she stirred a bubbling pot of scrambled eggs with one hand and flipped golden pancakes with the other. The sizzle and aroma of bacon wafted through the air, making our stomachs growl in anticipation. "That is impressive for your first time," she exclaimed, giving a hearty clap before announcing, "Breakfast is served." The table was filled with steaming dishes overflowing with fluffy eggs, crispy bacon, and perfectly browned pancakes. Each dish looked more tantalisingly scrumptious than the last, and we couldn't wait to dive in.

At that moment, all thoughts of anything else disappeared as we focused solely on the feast before us. I ate heartily, unable to remember when I had enjoyed a meal so much. Despite my apparent gluttony, no one seemed to care as conversation flowed easily between us.

As soon as every last bite had been savoured and every dish cleaned, the woman I had not yet met clapped her hands together and the table was magically cleared. Steaming pots of tea and coffee appeared in its place, inviting us to sit back and relax after our hearty meal. Unable to contain my amazement any longer, I turned to her and exclaimed with a grin, "That was incredible! How did you do it?"

She laughed lightly, brushing off my praise. "Oh, it was nothing. Maybe I'll show you how it's done one day. I'm Mini, by the way. It's nice to meet you."

"Hi, Mini, I'm Jessica," I replied with a smile, still in awe of the incredible display.

Just as things began settling down again, Alexander cleared his throat to get everyone's attention. "Jessica, I have a proposal for you," he said earnestly. "I want to invite you to join The Agency's training program. It will not only help you adjust to your new worldview but also provide a safe place for you to call home. And with our protection, you'll never have to worry about being attacked by anything again." He motioned towards Mini beside him. "I brought Mini along because she's currently in the training program herself, and I thought you might like to discuss the possibility with someone of a similar age." His offer filled me with relief and security, and I couldn't wait to learn more about this mysterious organisation.

As I considered the offer, my mind raced with possibilities. The idea of having a mentor, someone to confide in and guide me, was like a shining beacon of hope in this uncertain situation. His words were like a tantalising lifeline, promising a way out of the dark cave I had been

CHAPTER 4

trapped in for so long. But could he truly be trusted? Lyn clearly trusted him, but I couldn't help the nagging doubts that crept into my mind as I weighed my options.

It was a tough decision, but ultimately, what choice did I have?

"What do you get out of this?" I finally asked, unable to contain my curiosity any longer. "Why help me?" The room fell silent as though my question had caused a great insult, and even Alexander seemed taken aback by my boldness.

After a moment to regain his composure, he replied calmly, "There are a few reasons why I'm offering this. Firstly, my friend asked me to help you and I am more than happy to oblige. Secondly, I strongly feel that you will be an invaluable asset to our team. And lastly, I hate seeing potential go to waste, and I can see that you have great potential." He paused before adding, "Does that answer your question?"

Feeling sheepish for questioning his motives, I nodded and said, "Yes, it does. But I have two more questions - has anyone been able to find out what happened to my Dad? And how long was I held captive by Jeremiah?" My voice trembled slightly as memories of my time in captivity flooded back. But determined to move forward, I waited anxiously for Alexander's response.

The mood in the room shifted as all eyes turned to Alexander. His face became grim as he replied, "We have received reports that there were no survivors at the crash site. Your father's body was found in the wreckage, along with the bodies of the other Passengers. As for how long you were held captive, it was almost five years." He paused before adding, "I have spoken to Lyn, and we understand if you find that hard to believe. But due to Jeremiah's experiments on you, there were periods when you would slip into a coma for days or weeks at a time. This may have skewed your perception of time." A heavy silence fell over the table as I processed this new information. Despite the uncertainty of my future, I felt grateful that they didn't sugarcoat the truth but delivered it bluntly.

As I sat there, surrounded by these newfound allies who had already become a support system, I couldn't help but feel a sense of loss and displacement. Even if I tried to rejoin the world and pick up where I had left off, nothing would be the same. I wasn't just a girl anymore; my experiences had forced me to grow up too quickly, and now I was a woman faced with unimaginable challenges.

A stray tear fell down my cheek; before I knew it, Lyn had enveloped me in her arms. She held onto me tightly as if afraid that one more shock would break me completely. Maybe she was right, but despite everything, I had made my decision - it was time to move on.

CHAPTER 5

Beginning Anew

I fidget nervously, shifting my weight from foot to foot as I looked up at Alexander. His tall stature and commanding presence made me falter, unsure how to address him. "Excuse me, sir...I mean, Alex," I stuttered, stumbling over my words. He simply grinned, his eyes twinkling with amusement at my obvious discomfort. "No need for formalities," he said casually. "Just call me Alex. Although some of the other recruits have given me...less respectful and more colourful nicknames," he chuckled, causing Minnie's cheeks to flush a bright pink before she quickly looked away.

This interaction reminded me of my past life as a student, with teachers and authority figures who were approachable and friendly. It brought a sense of normality and comfort to my daunting situation.

My nerves got the best of me as I blurted out my next question: "So when do we leave?" I tried to sound eager, but my voice came out shaky. I turned to Lyn, seeking reassurance from her steady presence, but she seemed lost in her own thoughts.

"You will be leaving shortly," she replied with a hint of sadness. Knowing what was coming next, my heart sank at her words. "Unfortunately, I won't be joining you."

The news hit me like a physical blow to the stomach. I stared up at Lyn with wide eyes, desperately searching for any sign that she was joking. But there was only sorrow in her gaze.

"I have been away from dragon society for too long," she explained softly. "I need to make my presence known before others get the wrong idea." An underlying growl in her tone sent a shiver down my spine.

As if sensing my distress, she leaned down and gently kissed my forehead. Her cool lips left a lingering warmth on my skin as she whispered, "My little dragon." It was a term of endearment that only she used for me. "I won't be gone for long, and if you ever need me, just let Alex know, and I will be there. But now I must leave. I'm sure you will Make me proud."

A lump formed in my throat as she spoke, and I couldn't help but feel a sense of loss at the thought of her leaving. With determination in every step, Lyn strode confidently out of the cabin, her boots crunching against the gravel path. A surge of energy radiated from her, making my heart race in anticipation. As the door closed behind her with a resounding thud, I felt a pang of loneliness wash over me. She had been my only companion for the last five years and was leaving me behind. I longed to chase after her and plead for her to stay, but I knew deep down that this was my chosen path.

Lost in my thoughts, I suddenly noticed Mini's presence beside me. Her knowing look conveyed understanding and support. And then it happened - with a swift whisper of power rippling through the air, Lyn transformed into her majestic dragon form. Through the window, I caught a glimpse of the magnificent creature I had come to know so well. But seeing her scales glisten in the sunlight for the first time left me breathless.

I couldn't help but be taken aback by the sight before me. Her dragon form's sheer size and beauty will stay etched

CHAPTER 5

in my memory forever. No words could fully capture or do justice to this view.

As I turned away from the window, watching the majestic Dragon take flight and disappear into the distant horizon broke my heart. But I couldn't let that hold me back. Determined, I faced the room and asked aloud, "So what happens now?" I asked, my voice not feeling as confident as I would like

Alex's voice answered, "I have arranged for a car to pick us up outside. It will take us to the nearby airport, where a private jet will transport us to the agency's exclusive training facility." I felt excitement and unease tingled at the thought of what lay ahead. "Make sure you rest on the flight," he continued, "Because once we land, we will hit the ground running with your training." My mind raced with anticipation as I followed him out of the cabin, ready to embark on this new chapter of my life.

***

I had taken Alex's advice, and as soon as I sat in my seat, I was out like a light. I was shaken awake as we landed by Mini, who seemed to be hovering around me, never straying far. She somehow made me feel calm and like everything would work out.

Despite Alex warning me that I would hit the ground running, I hadn't taken him totally seriously. Still, as soon as we landed, I was thrust into the clutches of Hargreaves, who tossed a set of pristine gym clothes at me. "Don't just stand there gawking; the changing room is over there!" he barked, his harsh tone sending shivers down my spine. In stunned silence, I stood there with my mouth wide open, feeling like a deer caught in the headlights of an oncoming car. Shaking his head in frustration, Hargreaves pointed to a door with a sign that read 'changing room' and let out a deep breath before bellowing, "MOVE YOUR ASS! I WANT YOU CHANGED AND BACK HERE IN FIVE MINUTES. DON'T KEEP ME WAITING!" Without pausing for a response, he began counting down in his aggressive drill sergeant voice. Panic raced through my veins as I sprinted to the changing room, not wanting to anger the strict instructor further. The adrenaline pumping through my body matched the urgency in Hargreaves' voice, making me realise that this was just a glimpse into the gruelling training ahead.

As I emerged from the changing room, my heart raced with nervousness as I approached him. I was relieved that he was still counting, his strong jaw set in determination. "Well, at least you can follow basic instructions," he said with a sneer, his piercing gaze scanning over me. Without hesitation, I replied loudly and confidently, "Yes. Sir," I could feel my nerves causing my volume control to skyrocket.

A small glimmer of a smile crossed his lips before he turned and motioned for me to follow him. "We will assess your physical fitness so I know where to focus your training. Do you understand?" he asked in a commanding tone.

I nodded, eager to prove myself and show that I was ready for whatever challenges lay ahead. As we went to the gym, he started conversationally, "I'm assuming you have no combat training?"

I replied in a more normal volume this time, voice still shaking, "No, if I'm being honest, I used to be a complete pacifist." Even as the words left my mouth, I surprised myself with how open and honest I was being.

He stopped walking for a moment and looked at me seriously. "I hope all that is in the past because if you think pretty words will be enough to survive in this world, you are sorely mistaken."

CHAPTER 5

My heart sank at his harsh words, but deep down, I knew he was right. "I am well aware of that", I admitted quietly. "And I am determined to move forward and learn how to survive."

With a curt nod, he continued leading the way to the gym. My mind raced with fear and anticipation as I prepared for the gruelling physical assessment. But despite my nerves, I felt a spark of determination ignite within me - I was ready to face whatever challenges were thrown my way in this new world.

With a confident push, he swung open the heavy, frosted glass door, which let out a soft whoosh as if inviting us into another world. We stepped inside and were immediately greeted by a sleek, modern design that emanated luxury and sophistication. As I followed behind him, I couldn't help but feel like I was entering the sort of place I had only seen on TV shows. For someone like me, who had never prioritised physical fitness before my abduction, this was a completely new experience.

The gym was unlike anything I had seen before - it was like stepping into the future; there was an M.M.A. cage in one corner, rows of shining treadmills lined up against the wall, various weight machines scattered around, and an array of free weights in another area. I looked around, impressed and slightly intimidated by the high-tech equipment surrounding me, with what I assumed were other cadets using them. Hargreaves approached a treadmill and started punching buttons on its control panel. Carefully, I approached his side, hoping to avoid another outburst. "What is your first command?" I asked anxiously.

"Step up onto the treadmill and begin running," he directed. "I will handle the controls. Simply attach this monitor to your wrist. It will track all of your vital signs. And do not fret - if you collapse, the machine will automatically stop."

Feeling a mixture of anticipation and unease, I climbed onto the sleek, high-tech treadmill and started running as instructed. The floor thrummed beneath my feet as Hargreaves expertly adjusted the speed and incline. With each stride, I could feel my heart pounding faster and my muscles working harder. Despite my initial hesitation towards physical exertion, there was an undeniable thrill in being in this futuristic gym and pushing myself beyond my limits.

"Don't worry, you'll get the hang of it," said a tall, muscular woman with short-cropped blonde hair. She extended a hand. "I'm Morgan. Been with The Agency for ten years now."

Jessica took the hand, noting the calluses and the firm grip. "Jessica, it's nice to meet you."

"So, what's your story?" Morgan asked, leaning casually against a weight rack. "Most of us have some kind of background in this stuff. You seem... new."

Jessica hesitated. How much could she reveal? How much did she even understand herself? "I'm still figuring things out," she said finally. "But I'm a quick learner."

Morgan shrugged. "Everyone starts somewhere. Just remember, it's not all about the physical. The mental game is just as important."

With that, Morgan walked off, leaving me to contemplate the mountain I had to climb. As I settled into a steady rhythm, my heart rate and breathing gradually increased before levelling off. Hargreaves diligently monitored my vitals, his sharp eyes scanning the monitors and machines around us. "Keep going for as long as you can," he urged, "just focus on running. This will give me a better

CHAPTER 5

understanding of your endurance." My legs burned with fatigue, and my chest heaved with each breath, but I was determined to meet Hargreaves' expectations. Between gasps for air, I asked, "What would be considered a good starting score?" But Hargreaves only responded sternly, "Do not worry about that now. Just keep running." And so I did, my feet pounding against the treadmill belt as my body strained to maintain the pace. The room began to blur around me as sweat dripped down my forehead, and my muscles screamed in protest, but I refused to give up. This was just a small step towards achieving ultimate physical fitness. I was determined to see it through until the end. I lost track of my surroundings as I determinedly put one foot in front of the other. The air was thick and humid, making it hard to breathe. My legs felt heavy, and my body ached, but I refused to give up. Suddenly, a wave of dizziness hit me like a ton of bricks.

I stumbled forward, trying to steady myself, but it was useless. My vision blurred, and my head spun as if I were on a carnival ride gone wrong. As I struggled to push through the dizziness, my knees buckled beneath me, and I fell to the floor with a thud.

I vaguely remember someone placing a cold cloth on my forehead and saying comforting words. But all I could focus on was the intense nausea building in my stomach. With a very violent heave, my body emptied itself, and I couldn't stop it.

Thankfully, Hargreaves appeared by my side, holding a bucket that easily caught everything. It seemed like this was common for him as he calmly helped me through the ordeal. Even in my weakened state, I couldn't help but feel grateful for his presence and care at that moment. My chest felt tight, constricted by the rapid thumping of my heart. My stomach churned and threatened to bring up the rest of my breakfast. I reached for a towel and dabbed at my face, only to find Hargreaves handing me a water bottle. "You can glare at me all you want," he sneered, "but it's my responsibility to push you until you break and then push some more." His smug expression made my blood boil. "If you don't like it, then quit." He paused momentarily before adding, "But don't forget, you managed an hour and a half, that's comparable to most professional human athletes." As much as I detested him at this moment, I refused to let him win. Jeremiah never broke me, so this asshole wouldn't either. With fierce determination, I dragged myself onto my feet and took a swig of water to settle my roiling stomach.

I waited for Hargreaves to continue with the next part of my assessment. My muscles were already burning from the intense physical training, but I refused to show any sign of weakness. "Alright, if you're ready," Hargreaves said, his voice betraying no emotion. "Next, we will do a flexibility assessment. For this, I need you to copy the poses I perform as accurately as possible. Once in position, you must hold still while I inspect how close you come to achieving the pose."

He paused before adding, "If you have ever tried yoga, it is very. similar to that." A small burst of relief coursed through me at his words. I remember doing yoga back in school, and it wasn't that difficult.

With a nod of understanding, I kept my mouth shut tightly, not wanting to risk vomiting again.

Hargreaves led me to a softly padded floored area; being a tall and muscular man who could easily pass for Arnold Schwarzenegger's twin, he seemed out of place in an area designed for gentle movement.

CHAPTER 5

I quickly realised that this was not your typical yoga. The poses were unfamiliar and complex, and no matter how hard I tried, I couldn't seem to contort my body in the same way Hargreaves effortlessly demonstrated. The contortions seemed impossible for someone of his build. Let alone someone with little to no expense in this discipline.

After an hour of trying to mimic his movements, I found myself repeatedly falling on my face in defeat. Hargreaves didn't seem fazed though, and finally called an end to the torture. "Well, that was a disaster," he chuckled. "We'll definitely need to work on your balance and flexibility. Luckily, some martial arts you'll be learning will help with that."

When I thought this fitness assessment couldn't get any stranger, Hargreaves asked me about my experience with dance. "What does dancing have to do with anything?" I snapped in frustration. Is this some kind of messed-up hazing ritual?"

Hargreaves' expression turned serious as he explained, "Dance training can actually help build muscle, increase stamina, improve mobility and flexibility...the list goes on." his words carried a subtle edge of menace, making me realise that I may have crossed a line." I apologise," I quickly interjected. "This is all new to me."

He softened his tone as he explained, "Everything I'm teaching you has a purpose to prepare you for anything that could happen to you." It was clear that Hargreaves was not just a fitness instructor but a trainer in every sense of the word.

Hargreaves barked out his instructions with an air of stern authority, his voice cutting through the tense silence of the gym. My heart sank as I realised this test would not be a walk in the park like I had hoped. "Do you know how to do a push-up?" he asked, his eyes boring into mine. "Yeah," I replied curtly, trying to brush off my sense of disappointment and frustration. He gestured for me to get into position on the mat beside him.

"Good. You will lower yourself slowly and with controlled movements when I say down. And when I say up, you will push yourself back up to the starting position," he explained, his tone leaving no room for questioning. "Just like with the treadmill, we will continue until I say stop or your body gives out." With a deep breath, I got into position, my body already tensing in anticipation of the upcoming challenge.

As I began the first push-up, my muscles strained and trembled under the weight of my own body. The room was filled with heavy breathing and the unmistakable scent of sweat. Every fibre in my being screamed at me to give up, but I was determined to push through until the end. This was not going to be easy, but I was ready to give it everything I had

After another gruelling hour of intense push-ups, Hargreaves finally took pity on me and allowed me to stop. My trembling arms gave out as I collapsed onto the gym floor, sweat pouring down my face and my muscles screaming with exhaustion. "You can rest now," Hargreaves said, a hint of amusement in his voice. "I have all the information I need. Go sit on one of the weight benches while I review everything, and we can discuss a basic training plan." As I stumbled towards the bench, my body felt made of lead, and my breaths came in ragged gasps. The clang and thud of heavy weights being lifted filled the air, accompanied by the unmistakable scent of sweat and determination. But despite the physical toll, I couldn't help but feel a surge of excitement, knowing that soon I would embark on a journey to better myself both physically and mentally.

CHAPTER 5

However, that excitement was short-lived, as I succumbed to exhaustion. I decided to lie on the weight bench, resting while Hargreaves reviewed his notes. It wasn't long before my eyes grew heavy and slowly began to close. I didn't know how long I had actually managed to nap - it felt like mere seconds - but suddenly, I was jolted awake by an angry presence towering over me. Hargreaves' face was red with fury, veins pulsing in his forehead and neck as he bellowed at me. If the situation weren't so intimidating,

I might have been slightly impressed by his intensity. "I told you to sit, not get comfortable and have a nap!" he thundered, his face turning an alarming shade of purple.

"Join me," he beckoned, leading the way with quick, purposeful strides towards the glass door we had entered through. I hastened to keep up with him, feeling a sense of urgency in his movements. He stopped just a few doors down from the main gym, forcefully pushing the door open and holding it for me to enter.

"Take a seat," he gruffly commanded, pointing to one of the few chairs in the small room. Without hesitation, I sat down and remained silent as he settled into a chair behind a plain wooden table.

As his intense gaze locked onto mine, I could feel the weight of his determination and authority bearing down on me. Every word he spoke carried a heavy presence, settling deep in the pit of my stomach. He began to delve into the details of my training plan, laying out expectations for me going forward. "Firstly," he said, his voice firm and direct, "I want you to know that you impressed me in the stamina and muscle assessment." His words stirred a sense of pride within me, but I could tell there was more to come. "Considering that you have never done this, your performance was remarkable. However, it should be noted that your comparison is only impressive when compared to humans." He paused, studying me carefully as he continued. "From the information I've been given, you should be able to grow quickly in these areas." His tone shifted then, becoming more serious and stern. "But my biggest concern lies in your flexibility and movement style. Even when compared to humans, your level is severely lacking." I could feel my cheeks flush with embarrassment as I remembered my clumsiness, even in life before all of this. Letting out a soft moan, I hoped he wouldn't probe further into this weakness.

But despite his stern words, I could sense a genuine care behind them. And as he spoke, I couldn't help but feel a wave of determination wash over me. This was where I belonged, and I was ready for whatever challenges lay ahead. "So starting tomorrow," he declared with a commanding tone, "you will be meeting me here at 05:00 for our first run of the day." The thought of such an early start made me groan inwardly. "This will be one hour outside on the base grounds - you are to keep pace with me for the entire run and do not eat breakfast before coming." His instructions were clear.

"At 06:00," he continued, "we will go to a secure gym - just the two of us. And I will be pushing your muscles way past breaking point." A sadistic gleam flashed in his eyes as he let this sink in. "This will continue for six hours, followed by a lunch break. But you must return to the gym by 13:00, where we will spend the next ten hours working on your flexibility." The thought of such rigorous training was daunting, but I knew it was necessary to succeed in this new life.

Now, for the remainder of today, we will return to the gym and practice basic hand-to-hand combat techniques. Although you are safe on this base, I feel more comfortable knowing

CHAPTER 5

that all recruits have the basic skills to defend themselves. Let's head to the cage and see how you fare against me.

The fighting cage was like nothing I had ever seen before. It was a massive circular structure constructed entirely of sturdy metal bars. The floor was covered in a thick mat that showed signs of countless battles and struggles. The air inside was thick with the scent of sweat and adrenaline, sending goosebumps rippling across my skin as I tentatively stepped into the ring.

My stomach churned nervously as Hargreaves led me into the centre of the cage. He began to speak, his tone serious and determined. "These skills are crucial for survival," he explained, sweeping his arm around to indicate our surroundings. "You never know when you may be caught off guard or outnumbered."

He motioned for me to take a fighting stance as we prepared to spar. Hargreaves would be my opponent, training me to defend myself and others from harm. "For the foreseeable future, this will ensure your safety and prevent any unnecessary injuries," he stated firmly.

Despite my nerves, I nodded in understanding and breathed to steady myself. Before we began sparring, Hargreaves taught me basic fighting techniques and stances. His movements were lightning-fast and precise, easily deflecting my clumsy attacks. But with each round, I could feel myself improving.

Not only did Hargreaves teach me how to fight effectively, but he also helped me use my newfound strength and agility to my advantage in combat. He showed me how to dodge attacks quickly and deliver powerful blows with enhanced stability.

As we trained, I couldn't help but feel grateful for this opportunity to learn from someone as skilled as Hargreaves.

Though he could be stern and intimidating at times, it was clear that he genuinely wanted me to succeed and become a formidable fighter.

After hours of intense training, Hargreaves called for a break. We stepped out of the cage and sat on nearby benches, panting and wiping sweat from our brows. "You're a quick learner," he remarked with a small smile, and I couldn't help but feel a sense of pride in my progress. With a nod and a gesture towards the exit, he led me to my dorm for the night. As we walked, my mind was buzzing, anticipating our training the following day. A sense of release and calm settled over me as we made our way through the quiet halls, our footsteps echoing off the polished floors. The building's perfect lighting and warm temperature created a peaceful atmosphere, like a sanctuary from the chaos outside. I couldn't wait to continue my training tomorrow, eager to learn more from the drill sergeant from hell.

CHAPTER 6

The Training Intensifies

For 18 gruelling hours each day, my body was pushed to its limits. My feet pounded against the rough terrain of the nature trails, leaving a trail of sweat as I ran tirelessly toward my goal. The weights felt heavier each time I lifted them, my muscles screaming in protest as I pushed through one more rep. Even practising yoga, dance drills and martial arts forms became a battle against my trembling, exhausted body. But beyond the physical challenges, there were also mental ones: yoga and dance classes tested my physical endurance, focus, and discipline. Every night after training, I dragged myself back to my room. I collapsed into bed, too tired to even think about anything other than sleep.

The only person I saw besides my intense instructors was Mini – she never failed to offer words of encouragement and support. Her calm presence and soothing voice provided a much-needed respite from my demanding routine. One particularly tough night, when I was on the brink of giving up and calling it quits, she spoke sternly to me. As an empathic water witch, she could sense my emotions and knew I could do so much more than I believed. Her gentle yet firm guidance reminded me of Lyn's belief in my strength and encouraged me to push through. From then on, I gave 100% every day, determined to become the strong, fierce woman Lyn believed I could be. Each day presented a new challenge, but with Mini's unwavering support and Lyn's belief in me, I was ready to face them head-on.

Over the next few weeks, I threw myself into the training with a fervour that bordered on obsession. I ran drills without complaint, sparred with Hargreaves, and practised more complex dance exercises and yoga poses. Hargreaves even started to include gymnastic training, saying my coordination and flexibility were no longer disappointing. I also discovered that I needed less sleep than I used to, with a bit of downtime after my physical training. I would head to the facilities library and study the extensive archives detailing The Agency's history and the supernatural world they policed. Every night, she collapsed into bed, her body exhausted but her mind racing with new knowledge and possibilities.

When training, I discovered that my speed was not just a burst of adrenaline like I thought but something that I could sustain. My wounds, even the deep gashes from training and heavy bruises, closed and healed within hours, much quicker than when I was being tested by Jeremiah. The most startling was my endurance; I could go days with only 2 or 3 hours of sleep and still function at peak performance.

Yet, it was not these abilities that excited me the most. It was the skills and knowledge I was gaining, like how to track a rogue vampire, the signs of a werewolf den, and the intricate politics of the fae courts. I was building an arsenal, not just of physical prowess but of understanding.

One evening, after a particularly gruelling session, I sat alone in the locker room. My mind wandered to thoughts of my mum and dad, to happier days.

"I'm doing this for you," I whispered, unsure if I meant my mother or my father. Perhaps both.

CHAPTER 6

The door to the locker room swung open, and Alex stepped in. "How are you holding up?"

I wiped the unshed tears from my eyes and stood. "I'm managing."

"You're doing more than that. Hargreaves is impressed. Hell, I'm impressed."

I shrugged, trying to downplay the swell of pride his words brought. "I have good teachers."

Alex studied me for a moment, his expression unreadable. "You know, you don't have to do this alone. The Agency is a family. We take care of our own."

A family. The word struck me with a bittersweet force. "Thanks, Alex. That means a lot."

He nodded and turned to leave, then paused. "Remember, we're here for you. But I just wanted to check on you. And also say that whether you decide to join the Agency fully after your training or not, we will always be a family for you."

When he was gone, I stood in silence, the weight of his last words settling over me. Whatever you decide. I knew that Fully joining The Agency was not a commitment to be taken lightly. It was a pledge to a cause, a surrender of my old life for a new one.

I walked to a mirror and looked at myself. The woman who stared back was not the same Jessica Dyer who had set out for Ireland years ago. That Jessica had been fragile, a little broken by loss but still hopeful. This new Jessica was harder, tempered by pain and forged in the crucible of experiences.

Could I still be the daughter My parents loved? The friend others relied on? Or would this new identity consume me, leaving nothing of the old me behind?

I thought of the people I had met through my training: humans turned vampires, people bitten and changed to werewolves, cursed witches. All of them were trying to navigate lives that had been irrevocably altered, just as mine had been. They were not monsters but individuals struggling to maintain their humanity in the face of overwhelming change.

In the mirror, My own eyes stared back, unblinking and fierce. I saw not a Monster but a woman with a choice.

I took a deep breath and exhaled slowly, letting the tension drain from my shoulders. I was stronger than I had ever been physically and in spirit. My future was too terrifying to contemplate, but it was a future I was ready to face. I was no longer just a victim of circumstance. I would be an agent of change with the power to shape my destiny.

I would use that power to protect others, to ensure that no one else had to suffer as I had. This was my new reality, my new purpose.

***

"Again," Hargreaves commanded, echoing through the training hall. I was breathing hard but nodded and reset my stance. In a blur, I launched myself at the target, My movements a symphony of speed and precision. The dummy shattered, pieces skittering across the floor like autumn leaves.

"Better," Hargreaves conceded, tossing me a towel. "But you're still holding back."

I wiped the sweat from My brow. "I don't want to hurt anyone."

He raised an eyebrow. "You think the vampires, shifters or anything else will show you the same courtesy?"

I sighed, knowing he was right. "It's just... this strength. It's not natural."

"None of this is natural, Jess," Hargreaves said, his tone softening. "But you need to own it. These abilities could save your life."

CHAPTER 6

I looked at My hands, flexing my fingers. "Could save, or will save?"

Hargreaves shrugged. "Depends on how seriously you take your training. And speaking of abilities you will be starting to train with one of the mages as of tomorrow for one hour per day to see how you get on «

We walked together toward the locker rooms, the hum of machinery filling the air. I was the first to break the silence. "Why did The Agency take me in? I mean, I'm just a human with some... enhancements."

"You're more than that, and you know it," Hargreaves said. "And The Agency sees potential. We don't just protect humans, Jess. We protect the balance. Sometimes that means recruiting people who can walk in both worlds."

"Walk in both worlds," I repeated, testing the phrase on my tongue. "Is that what you do?"

He stopped, turning to face me. "I believe in what The Agency stands for. That's all you need to know."

I held his gaze, searching for the man behind the mission. "I just want to understand, Hargreaves. Why are you helping me so much, or the Agency? Why do any of you care? Jeremiah made it clear that he believed the paranormal worlds don't exactly hold humans in great regard." I said shocking myself with what I said

Hargreaves looked away, the briefest flicker of something—regret, perhaps—crossing his features. "We take care of our own," he said, walking again.

CHAPTER 7

Mastering Power

With each punishing rep, my muscles screamed, my body a taut wire ready to snap. Sweat poured from my brow, stinging my eyes as I forced myself through another set of pull-ups. The gym's fluorescent lights cast harsh shadows, making me look like a gaunt spectre of my former self. Every inch of my lanky frame, now carved into sinew and bone, is a testament to the sheer brutality of my training regimen.

"That's ten. One more set," barked Hargreaves, his voice a gravelly command that brooked no disobedience. He stood with arms crossed, a mountain of a man whose sheer presence could cow a lesser being. His salt-and-pepper hair and the deep lines etched into his face spoke of hard-earned experience, the kind that came from decades of conflict and survival.

I dropped from the bar, my hands raw and blistered, arms shaking uncontrollably. I bent over, hands on my knees, gulping air like a drowning woman who'd just broken the surface of the water. My mind screamed for rest, for mercy, but I knew better than to hope for either in Hargreaves' presence.

"You're not done yet, Dyer," he growled, stepping closer. "You think the enemy will give you a breather? That your enemies will wait while you catch your breath?" His eyes were flint, his gaze cutting through me like a whetted blade.

I straightened, every movement an act of willpower, and met his stare. "I can take it," I said, my voice steadier than my body.

"Prove it," he said, tossing me a weighted vest. "Wear this. Now run."

I strapped the vest on; its heavy bulk crushed my little strength. I staggered toward the treadmill, each step a small victory over my rebelling limbs. Hargreaves set the machine to a brutal pace that would challenge even an Olympic sprinter.

As I ran, my mind drifted to the past—to my mother, father, and life I once knew. The pain in my body was now a familiar companion, but it was the ache in my heart that indeed drove me. The thought of the people I'd hurt, the promises I'd broken, the future that now lay in ruins. Every memory was coal in the fire of my determination, fuelling me beyond the limits of my physical endurance.

The treadmill's timer beeped, and I collapsed to the side, my body like a wet rag doll. I lay on the cold, hard floor, chest heaving, vision swimming in and out of focus. Hargreaves loomed over me, his expression unreadable.

"You're getting stronger," he said, and for a moment, I thought I detected a note of approval in his voice. "But strength isn't enough. You need to be unbreakable."

I wanted to tell him that I already was, that nothing could break me after what I'd been through. But I held my tongue, saving what little energy I had left. Hargreaves wasn't the type to be convinced by words; only actions would sway him.

"Same time tomorrow," he said, turning to leave. "And Dyer—rest. You'll need it."

I lay still, letting the cool floor leech the heat from my overworked muscles. I closed my eyes and breathed deeply,

CHAPTER 7

willing my heart to slow and forcing my mind to calm. In the darkness behind my eyelids, I saw the face of jeramiah, the cold, clinical detachment in his eyes as he subjected me to one experiment after another.

Unbreakable, I thought. That's what I have to be.

With a groan, I pulled myself to sit and unstrapped the weighted vest. My body was a wreck, but I took a grim satisfaction in the fact that I'd survived another session. Hargreaves was right—I was getting stronger. Whether it would be enough, I didn't know. But for now, it was all I had.

I stood slowly, every joint protesting, and made my way to the locker room. As I opened the door, I glanced back at the empty gym. The shadows seemed to stretch and yawn like the maw of some great beast waiting to consume me.

Tomorrow, I thought, and the day after until I'm ready.

With that, I stepped into the locker room and shut the door behind me, leaving the shadows to their hunger.

***

A few days later, I was squared off against a sparring partner, a towering shifter named Gregor. Gregor cracked his neck and rolled his shoulders, a predatory grin spreading across his face. I tightened my fists, my knuckles whitening with the pressure.

"Begin," Hargreaves barked from the sidelines.

Gregor moved first, a blur of muscle and sinew as he launched a haymaker at my head. I ducked and pivoted on my heel, my enhanced reflexes turning what should have been a bone-crushing blow into a harmless rush of air. Without pausing, I drove an elbow toward Gregor's ribs, but he twisted away, his movements fluid and serpentine. A man of his size should not be this nimble.

We circled each other, testing and probing each other for weaknesses. My mind raced, calculating angles and trajectories. My body was a finely tuned machine responding to my opponent's actions. Gregor feinted with a left jab, then came in low with a sweeping kick. I leapt, my body arcing gracefully over his leg, landing in a crouch, ready to spring.

Gregor rushed me again, and this time, I met him head-on. Sidestepping his initial charge, I caught his wrist, using his own momentum to fling him toward the mat. He landed with a thud but was on his feet instantly, a dangerous gleam in his eye. I didn't wait for his next move; I closed the distance with rapid strikes, my fists and feet a blur. Gregor blocked and parried, each contact producing a sharp, percussive crack.

"Good, Dyer," Hargreaves called. "Keep that pressure up."

My lungs burned, and my muscles screamed, but I pushed through the fatigue, driven by a need to be better and ready. I launched a roundhouse kick at Gregor's head; he caught My ankle and yanked, sending me sprawling to the mat. Pain shot through my shoulder, but I rolled with it, coming to my feet in a defensive stance.

"Again," I demand with a growl.

Gregor hesitated, glancing toward Hargreaves, who gave a curt nod. With a shrug, Gregor lunged, and the dance began anew. We moved with a lethal grace, a choreographed violence that spoke of countless hours of training. My strikes grew more precise, blocks more effective. I was learning and adapting.

After what felt like an eternity, Hargreaves blew a whistle. "That's enough."

Gregor and I stepped back from each other, both breathing heavily. Sweat dripped from my hair, stinging my eyes. Gregor extended a hand, and I took it, his grip firm but not crushing.

CHAPTER 7

"You're getting there," he said, not unkindly.

I nodded, too exhausted to speak. I knew I still had a long way to go, but hearing it from someone like Gregor gave me a tiny spark of hope.

"Take five," Hargreaves said. "Then we'll go over technique."

I sank to the edge of the mat and wiped my face with a towel. My body was a mass of bruises and sore spots, but I took grim satisfaction in the fact that I'd held my own. I closed my eyes and let my mind drift, thinking of the battles yet to come and the enemies I would face.

"Dyer," Hargreaves said, and I opened my eyes to see him standing over me. "You're doing well. But remember, strength and speed are nothing without skill. You need to be precise. You need to be perfect."

"I know," I said, trying to keep the frustration out of my voice. I stood slowly. Every joint protested, but I ignored the pain. "I'm ready."

Hargreaves handed me a set of training pads. "Let's see how ready."

For the next hour, I practised under Hargreaves' watchful eye. I worked through a series of drills, alternating between striking and blocking, and my movements grew more economical and practical. Hargreaves offered occasional corrections, his tone more mentor than taskmaster.

"Elbow in. Rotate the hips. Breathe."

Each adjustment sank into my muscle memory, my body absorbing the lessons with a sponge-like eagerness. I visualised real opponents with every strike and imagined life-or-death scenarios with every block. This wasn't just training for me; it was preparation for a future I could not afford to face unprepared.

"That's enough for today," Hargreaves finally said. As he lowered the training pads, my arms trembled with fatigue. "You're making progress."

"Thank you," I said, knowing progress was insufficient. I needed to be more than just better; she needed to be unbreakable.

***

I stood in the dimly lit chamber, starkly contrasting to the bright, sterile gym where I spent most of my waking hours. Here, the air hummed with latent energy, and the stone walls were etched with runes that glowed faintly, like embers in a dying fire. This was the heart of the Agency's arcane division, where ancient magic met modern technique.

My spell-casting instructor was a wiry man named Eamon with piercing blue eyes. He circled me slowly. "Focus, Jessica. Spell casting is not about force but precision and control."

A small orb of light flickered unsteadily in my hands, casting erratic shadows that danced across Eamon's gaunt features. My brow was knit in concentration, my eyes unblinking as I willed the light to hold its form.

"Good," Eamon said, though his tone was more analytical than encouraging. "Now, disperse it gently."

I exhaled and imagined the orb dissolving like mist in the morning sun. It burst with a soft pop, and tiny motes of light drifted down like snowflakes. I allowed myself a small, tired smile.

"You're getting there," Eamon conceded. "Remember, these are just the basics of energy manipulation. Without a foundation, you'll crumble when you try something more advanced."

I knew he was right. The abilities Jeremiah had awakened within me were raw and untamed. Here, I was learning to

CHAPTER 7

shape and give them form and purpose. It was like learning to walk after being forced to run.

"That's it for today," Eamon said, turning away. "We'll continue tomorrow."

I wiped a bead of sweat from my temple. "What about elemental manipulation? You said we'd start that this week." I asked unable to hide my eagerness

Eamon paused at the doorway, his fingers tracing one of the glowing runes. "i want you to continue with me for another week. I have spoken with Zara and they will begin with you then ," he said.

***

The following week, I found myself in a different chamber, this one larger and more cavernous, with a high ceiling that dripped with stalactites. Pools of water dotted the floor, and the air was humid. I liked this room; it felt alive.

My new instructor, a tall woman with olive skin and dark, curly hair, went by the name Zara. Where Eamon was reserved and clinical, Zara was passionate, almost fiery.

"Elemental magic is the purest form of spell casting," Zara said, her hands moving in fluid arcs as if conducting an invisible orchestra. "It requires not just control, but a deep connection with the element itself."

In front of me, a small flame danced atop a stone pedestal. I held out my hand, feeling the warmth on my palm. It wavered, then shrank.

"Don't be afraid of it," Zara said. "Respect it, but do not fear it. The flame knows your heart."

I took a deep breath and closed my eyes, shutting out the world. I pictured the fire growing, stretching like a cat after a nap, its orange tendrils licking the air. When I opened my eyes, I held a flame double the size of what Zara had demonstrated, but It felt wild and unrestrained.

"That's good," Zara said, a hint of approval in her voice. "Now, make it move."

This was the part I dreaded. It was one thing to grow the flame, to feed it my energy and let it flourish. Moving was like trying to command a wild animal. I extended my hand and motioned as if trying to guide a pet forward. The flame flickered, then shot away from me in a streak of light.

"Excellent," Zara said. "You see? The element responds to your will when you meet it with confidence."

For a moment, I felt a surge of pride. I was beginning to understand, to truly grasp the nature of what I was doing. These were not just tricks or tools; they were extensions of myself, manifestations of my own inner power.

"You're progressing faster than I expected," Zara said. "

I didn't respond, but the words gave me hope. I needed to believe that I could do this, that I could potentially master these abilities and use them for something greater.

"Come back tomorrow," Zara said. "We'll see how you handle water."

***

The next day, Zara stood by one of the pools, her reflection wavering on the water's surface. I approached cautiously, remembering the warmth of the flame. I began wondering what the cool touch of water would feel like in comparison.

"Fire is passionate and immediate," Zara said, not looking up. "Water is patient and enduring. It's an element that can wear down mountains given time."

I joined Zara by the pool, peering into the depths. "So it's harder to control?" I asked

"It's different," Zara said. "Each element has its own nature. To master them, you must understand that nature and find a balance within yourself."

CHAPTER 7

Zara held out her hand, and a sphere of water rose from the pool, defying gravity. It swirled and eddied, a miniature ocean in her palm. "Watch."

With a flick of her wrist, Zara sent the water flying. It arced through the air and landed in another pool with a soft splash, not a single droplet escaping its target. "Your turn."

I extended my hand over the pool, feeling the coolness radiate up my arm. I imagined the water rising to meet me, forming a ball like the one Zara had created. For a long moment, nothing happened. Then, the pool's surface began to ripple, and a small water column wobbled upwards.

"Good," Zara said. "Now catch it."

I cupped my hands, and the water fell into them, sloshing over my fingers. It was colder than I expected, almost biting. I tried to will it into a sphere, but it dribbled through my hands.

"Feel its fluidity," Zara instructed. "Let it take shape naturally. Don't force it."

I closed her eyes and focused on the sensation of the water moving in my hands. My body gently swayed, rocking, mimicking the motion of water, and it began to coalesce, a fragile orb forming in my grasp.

"That's it," Zara said softly. "Now, make it fly."

I slowly opened my eyes and lifted my hands. the small orb of water wasn't as impressive as Zara's, and it was still dripping, but I imagined the water soaring like a bird. It wavered and rippled, then shot upwards, its trajectory unsteady. It burst in mid-air, and the droplets fell like rain, catching the light in a brief, sparkling shower.

I let out a laugh. I hadn't managed to do what I was supposed to, but the sight of what I had achieved brought me more joy than I could imagine. It had been a long time since I had heard myself laugh.

"You're a natural," Zara said, and I thought I saw the instructor smile.

For the rest of the session, Zara had me alternate between fire and water, growing flames and summoning spheres of water, then extinguishing one with the other. Each exercise was a dance of opposites, a lesson in balance and harmony.

By the end, My hands were shaking, and my body was exhausted, but I felt a deep sense of accomplishment. These were more than just small victories; they were steps towards a future I could begin to see taking shape.

"Remember," Zara said as I prepared to leave, "the elements reflect your inner state. Control them, and you control yourself."

I nodded, taking the words to heart. I knew that true mastery was still a long way off.

But as I walked through the corridors of the arcane division, my mind drifted to the life I once had, to the person I once was. I was changing, evolving, becoming something new. Something stronger.

Unbreakable, I reminded myself, and I almost believed it this time.

With that thought, I headed towards the gym. The shadows in the hallways seemed less oppressive, the air less heavy. I was progressing, not just in my training, but in reclaiming a sense of self and the person I needed to become.

***

Mini and I often retreated to the small lounge area, after training. It was a sanctuary of worn couches, throw pillows, and blankets. It was here that I first learned the depth of Mini's compassion. When I spoke of my abduction and the painful experiments, Mini listened with an intensity that went beyond mere hearing. She felt my pain, fear, and the enduring hope that I clung to.

CHAPTER 7

"You're stronger than you know, Jess," Mini said one afternoon, her blue eyes shimmering with unspoken emotions. "To survive all that and still be standing... It's incredible."

I shrugged it off. Although I was uncomfortable with the praise, I was touched by Mini's sincerity. "I didn't have much of a choice. It was either keep going or give up, and giving up never really seemed like an option."

We laughed together, something I had almost forgotten how to do. Mini told stories about her eccentric grandmother and the chaotic life of a young mage. It always provided a welcome relief from the intensity of my training.

"She once tried to summon a rainstorm for the garden and ended up flooding the entire village," Mini recounted, giggling. "We had to evacuate the sheep to higher ground."

Through these moments, I saw Mini as more than just a teammate. She was the first real friend I had made since my life was turned upside down.

The camaraderie we built gave me a renewed sense of purpose and strength, something I would need for the challenges ahead.

One morning, I arrived at the training hall to find an elaborate obstacle course set up. It snaked through the cavernous room, a series of daunting physical and magical challenges designed to test every skill an agent might need.

"You've come a long way," Zara said, appearing at my side. "Let's see if you're ready."

I surveyed the course. There were walls to scale, elemental traps to disarm, and target dummies to neutralise. It looked like something out of a nightmare, but I felt a thrill of anticipation.

Taking my place at the starting line, I closed my eyes and took a deep breath to centre myself. The first obstacle was a towering wall, slick with conjured rain. I sprinted towards it, leaping and grabbing for handholds. My fingers slipped, but I willed the water to freeze and create a protrusion, giving me a ledge to grip. The climb was hard. I manipulated the water to avoid the handholds, which made the climb harder. As I reached the top, I hauled myself over.

I landed in a roll, coming up quickly as fireballs shot from the walls. With a flick of my wrist, I summoned a water shield from the moister in my soundings , its surface rippling as the flames hissed and died. I moved with fluid grace, My body and mind in sync as I navigated through a gauntlet of swinging blades and arcane sigils.

Halfway through, My muscles began to protest, but I pushed the pain aside. I thought of My time in captivity, of the endless tests and the torture. Jeremiah had tried to break me and failed. Instead, he had forged me into something unyielding.

The final stretch involved a series of platforms suspended over a chasm, each rigged with elemental traps. I leapt from platform to platform, disarming the traps with quick bursts of energy, my movements precise and economical. The last platform gave way as I landed on it, and without thinking, I hurled myself towards the finish line, a bolt of lightning arcing behind me.

I hit the ground hard, skidding to a stop. For a moment, I just lay there, chest heaving, every part of me screaming in agony. Then I heard the slow clap of hands and turned her head to see Zara, a smile on her face.

"Well done," Zara said. "You completed it in record time."

I struggled to my feet, a wave of pride washing over me. Looking back at the course, I could hardly believe I had conquered it.

CHAPTER 7

"Remember this feeling," Zara continued. "The real challenges are yet to come."

***

I strolled through the dimly lit corridors of the Agency's headquarters, my body a symphony of bruises and sore muscles.

I paused before a large, reflective pane of glass and studied my face. The eyes that stared back at me were the same as always, but there was a new depth to them, a hardness tempered with understanding. My cheekbones looked sharper, jawline more defined. Even my posture had changed; I stood taller, more assured. The physical changes were the easiest to accept. It was the other changes—the ones that went deeper—that I struggled with.

A powerful paranormal being. That's what Zara had called me, and I knew it was true. The abilities that had been forced upon me were growing stronger every day, and with them, my understanding of the world I'd been thrust into. The supernatural community, the hidden society, the delicate balance the Agency sought to maintain—and I was a part of it all now.

Yet there were moments, alone in my Spartan quarters, when the weight of it all threatened to crush me—the loss of my old life, the fear of what I was becoming. Closing my eyes, I took a deep breath, centring myself. This was the path I had chosen. To survive, I had to move forward. To move forward, I had to accept what I was.

Acceptance. That was the hardest part. I had to accept that I was no longer just Jessica Dyer, the girl from a small town with big dreams. I was something more now, something different—a paranormal being with responsibilities and allegiances I was still coming to terms with.

I made my way to the living quarters and stopped outside My room. The door was adorned with a small plaque, which you'd find in a college dormitory. It read "Dyer, J." in neat, laser-etched letters. I ran a finger over the plaque, thinking about the name and its meaning. My identity was changing, but the core of who I was had to remain. That was the balance I needed.

With a sigh, I opened the door and stepped inside. The room was as spartan as ever, with a single bed, a desk, and a small wardrobe. On the desk sat a framed photograph of me and my father, taken on the day we left for Ireland—the only tangible piece of my old life.

I put the photo back on the desk and lay on my bed, staring at the ceiling. My mind raced with thoughts of the future, the missions I would undertake, the people I would have to protect, and the enemies I would face.

Sleep took me slowly, like a rising tide, and in my dreams, I was running through the gauntlet once more, each obstacle a memory, each trap a choice. I woke with a start, my body tensed as if ready to spring into action. The soreness from the day before had dulled, and I felt a strange sense of calm.

Today would be another test, another step in my transformation. I was ready for it. Or as prepared as I could be.

***

I stood at attention, my heart pounding with a mix of anticipation and disbelief. The training hall was silent, the kind of silence that holds its breath, waiting for something momentous to break its stillness. Around me, the other recruits watched with a mixture of respect and envy. I had been one of them not long ago, struggling to keep up, wondering if I would ever find my footing in this new, perilous world.

CHAPTER 7

"Exceptional work, Dyer," said Instructor Hargreaves, handing me a dossier with the Agency's sigil on its cover. Your dedication and resilience are noted. Few make it this far, this fast."

I took the dossier with a steady hand, though I felt like a child on Christmas morning. Hargreaves words were more than just praise; they were validation. The long nights, the physical pain, the constant fear of failure—they had all been worth it.

"We're proud of you, Jessica," added Instructor Zara. "You've shown a remarkable capacity to adapt. Keep this up, and you'll be one of our finest."

I allowed myself a small, controlled smile. Coming from Zara, whose standards were notoriously high, the compliment felt like a medal pinned to my chest. I remembered the first week when even the simplest tasks had left me exhausted and despondent. Now, I could see the transformation in myself—physically and mentally. I believed I could do this.

"Thank you," I said, my voice steady and sincere. "I couldn't have gotten this far without everyone's guidance."

Hargreaves and Zara exchanged a glance, something unspoken passing between them. "Guidance is only as good as the one receiving it. You've earned this, Jessica. Remember that." Hargreaves finally said

With that, the two instructors left me to the congratulations of my fellow recruits. Some offered handshakes, others a pat on the back. I accepted each gesture with humility. My mind was already racing ahead to what the dossier contained: the next phase of training, real missions. The future I had dared to imagine now seemed within my grasp.

Back in my quarters, I opened the dossier with the reverence of a scholar unsealing an ancient manuscript.

The first page listed my accomplishments: top marks in combat simulations, high scores in tactical assessments, and glowing evaluations from my instructors. I lingered on each line, letting the words sink in, feeling a swell of pride that threatened to overtake me.

The following pages outlined what was to come: advanced training modules, field exercises, and the all-important apprenticeship with a seasoned agent. It was daunting but also exhilarating. I closed the dossier and leaned back in my chair, staring at the ceiling. The cool, blue tones of the night had given way to the first light of morning, casting soft shadows that danced like spectres on the walls.

I stood and walked to the small bathroom to splash cold water on my face. I looked at myself in the mirror, at the woman I was becoming—stronger, more confident, yet still recognisable, still Jessica.

I knew the next phase would be harder—the challenges would be more severe, the stakes higher—but I was ready to face them—I had to be.

I dressed in My training gear, tying my hair back in a tight ponytail. Each movement was precise, practised, the routine of someone who had found their purpose. I grabbed the dossier and headed for the door, pausing momentarily as if to take a mental snapshot of this point in her life.

Unbreakable, I reminded myself once more. And this time, I believed it.

With a deep breath, I stepped into the hallway, ready to meet whatever the day—and the future—would throw at me.

CHAPTER 8

New Horizons

The door creaked open as I timidly entered the room. I could feel my heart racing; it was like being called to the principal's office in school. "Hi Alex, the information in the dossier informed me to come see you today. Is now okay?" I ask, trying to keep the nerves out of my voice.

"Yes, Jessica, thank you for coming," Alex replied, gesturing for me to sit. As I sat down, my palms started sweating, and I tried to steady my breathing.

"I have some things I would like to discuss with you." My mind started racing. Had I done something wrong? Am I not performing well enough?

"Of course, have I done something wrong?" I blurted out before he could continue.

"No, you have done brilliantly, and that is why I need to speak to you."

As I looked at Alex with confusion and disbelief, he reached out to reassure me. His expression was one of concern as he continued speaking.

"Your progress has been remarkable, far surpassing our expectations. In the few months you have been here, you have completed the basic training requirement for recruits to be sent on general assignment." His words were a blur to me as my mind struggled to process this new information. Faster than expected? It all seemed too surreal.

I was struggling to get to this point. A sense of pride and accomplishment swelled within me as I realised how much I had accomplished.

"The training is challenging, but that's what I expected. I spoke honestly.

As I sat across from Alex, his expectations weighed heavily on my shoulders.

So now, I'd like to discuss the plan with you. Going forward," I couldn't help but feel apprehensive about what would come. and I could sense that it would be no easy feat." We will still focus on physical training first," he continues. "The intensity and duration decrease. This means your mornings will be dedicated to building strength and endurance. After lunch, we will switch gears in the afternoons and give you some time to rest and recover. This part of your day will involve learning about our weapons and tactics. Once you have a good grasp on that, I will begin sending you on missions with instructors so you can get some hands-on experience. In your downtime, I want to start giving you some books to read on subjects like demonology, folklore, and paranormal history to help you understand more about the types of things you might encounter. Be warned, the workload will be extreme." I paused for a moment to let everything sink in before continuing

"Do you find this proposal acceptable?" The words hung between us like a delicate spiderweb waiting to be shattered. The weight of his question pressed down on me, making my heart race and my palms sweat. His eyes bore into mine, full of intensity and expectation. I took a deep breath and replied, "Yes, that sounds acceptable." My voice sounded small and hesitant, but I knew this decision was momentous. His face relaxed into a smile, and he leaned back in his chair, relieved by my answer. But there was still a lingering tension

CHAPTER 8

in the air as he asked, "When do we start the new program?" I asked feeling the gravity of this conversation - it would shape my future with the agency. My mind raced with excitement and nerves as I thought about what lay ahead for me.

"You will start your new training plan tomorrow, Jess. Take the rest of the day off and enjoy some leisure time. Perhaps you could visit the rec area and unwind, or Mini is available if you desire some company." Alex's warm smile radiated understanding and compassion. "Thank you for all your help and support, Alex. I am grateful for everything you are doing for me." I said, my voice filled with appreciation and gratitude as I slowly exited the room, feeling a sense of relief washed over me like a gentle wave.

***

Despite the intense physical demands, my time in the gym had become a welcome respite from the chaos of my other daily Classes. The workouts pushed me to my limits, each exercise more challenging than the last. We abandoned traditional cardio and focused more on weight training for the first part of our morning. Then, we incorporated sparing and dance practice into our midmorning, which helped give my movements an element of grace and fluidity. . As I settled into this new routine, we waited a few weeks before we started my physical weapons training focusing more on lessons regarding strategy and tactics, wanting to ensure that the change in the physical aspect of the training wasn't too much. After a few weeks of this new regimen, Hargreaves announced he had a surprise for me during our morning warm-ups. My curiosity mixed with trepidation as I wondered what twisted form of torture he had planned for me now. He loved to tease and torture me like this, so after our warm-up, which consisted of a five-mile jog on the treadmill and a 30-minute yoga session, he led me past the regular gym where we usually worked out. We passed several unmarked doors, building up my curiosity and anticipation. Hargreaves always loved surprises; I knew he wouldn't give anything away. Finally, we exited the gym through a door I had never noticed before and entered another building on the other side of the yard. There were guards posted at the entrance, heightening my excitement even more.

The building loomed before me, a place I had yet to explore. It held little interest for me in the past; always too exhausted or occupied to spare a thought for it. The guards performed practised motions as we approached and waved us through the gates. I felt Hargreaves' excitement radiating off him with each step. "Are you ready, kid?" he asked with a grin plastered on his face. The nickname irked me, but I let it slide for now. I had no idea what awaited me inside, but my heart was racing with anticipation. I nodded eagerly, and Hargreaves let out a booming laugh.

"Laugh it up, big guy. I'll have my revenge when we spar later." My words made him laugh even louder, and I couldn't help but chuckle a little to.

My heart fluttered with anticipation as the led me through a corridor towards a pair of intimidating steel doors. "The surprise is just through that door, and it's also today's lesson," he said with a sly grin. I couldn't help but wonder what was waiting for me on the other side. The doors were colossal, towering over me at nearly twice my height. In the paranormal world, I had begun to grow accustomed to such imposing structures. Yet, these doors seemed almost exaggerated in their size. I could feel their weight bearing down on me as we approached. Hargreaves gestured for me to open them, I hesitated, feeling a sense of trepidation. But I

CHAPTER 8

pushed aside my fears and placed my hands on the smooth metal surface, pushing with all my strength. To my surprise, they did not give easily - they were much heavier than expected. With a grunt of effort, I gritted my teeth and put more power into my thrust. Finally, with a loud groan, the doors creaked open. Once fully opened, they stayed in place, revealing a short, dark and mysterious passage beyond. "Impressive," the Hargreaves said with admiration. "Those are testing gates. If you can't get through them, it's usually straight back to training. Only a select few can do it on their first try, but I knew you had it in you, kid." He playfully ruffled my hair like an uncle would to their favourite niece or nephew. Blushing at this unexpected show of affection, I stepped through the gates into the unknown realm that awaited me.

"Now come on, let me show you around," Hargreaves said, beaming excitedly as he led me through a doorway into the weapons testing and training facility. As we stepped through, the darkness lifted, and my eyes adjusted to the bright lights that illuminated the room.

I couldn't help but gasp in amazement as I took in the different target setups: a traditional shooting range, what looked like an archery setup, and other weapons target setups. Hargreaves chuckled at my reaction, clearly pleased with himself.

"Wow, what the actual fuck? Why did the room change when we walked in?" I asked in shock.

Hargreaves' smug grin grew wider as he explained, "There is an illusion spell on the entrance, so you can't see anything until you step in. Adds a bit of mystery to the place."

I couldn't help but marvel at the level of magic involved in creating such an illusion. The air was buzzing with energy and anticipation, making it clear that this was a serious training facility for skilled warriors. It was both exhilarating and intimidating.

My excitement was palpable as I eagerly asked, "This is awesome, so where do we start?" I couldn't wait to get some weapons and start training.

"Well, let's just go through a few things first," he said with a smile, clearly enjoying my enthusiasm.

"You can use this facility during your downtime to get in some extra practice outside your normal training" His words were like music to my ears. "Second, you will still be required to do physical training. The sort of work we do isn't just about using weapons. We must become weapons if the situation requires it."

He explained the facility's layout as we walked through the sleek halls and past various rooms. "This place goes six levels up and six down," he gestured to the elevator doors nearby. "The lower levels are for research and development, so you probably won't need to go there anytime soon. They get a little protective over their projects." He winked playfully before continuing.

"The upper six floors are pure weapons training grounds," he paused dramatically. "The first two floors are dedicated for ranged weapons, the next two are for mid-ranged weapons, and the final two are for close-ranged combat." A thrill ran through me at the thought of testing various weapons and finding my strengths.

My mentor grinned mischievously. "Today, I have you all to myself." He reached out to squeeze my shoulder encouragingly.

I couldn't believe my luck. A whole day to experiment with different weapons? It was a dream come true. And I knew I would learn so much with my Hargreaves by my

CHAPTER 8

side. "Also, as we explore and try different things, I want you to keep an open mind and give everything a try; I have a feeling I know where your talents are going to lie", he added, his voice filled with excitement. I nodded eagerly, ready to dive into this new world of weapons and training.

As Hargreaves spoke, I nodded in agreement. But beneath the surface, my excitement quickly morphed into apprehension. The thought of handling a weapon, any weapon, filled me with terror. "Come on," Hargreaves said, beckoning me to follow him. Let's go see the quartermaster."

We approached a large weapons cage where a towering man stood guard. He seemed to be expecting us. As we drew closer, the quartermaster warmly greeted Hargreaves with an embrace. From their interaction, it was clear they were old friends.

"I assume you're Jess," the quartermaster said, turning to me with a friendly smile. "Hargreaves has told me about your progress, and I've arranged some toys for you to try out." His eyes twinkled mischievously as he gestured towards the weapons lining the walls. "Now, am I correct in assuming you had no prior experience with weapons before coming here?" His question hung in the air, causing my nerves to jump even more at the realisation that I was about to handle deadly instruments for the first time.

I nodded my agreement, too nervous to articulate a response. The words hung in the air like a heavy and suffocating fog. "That's good," he said with a slight smile and a calm and reassuring tone. "It means we don't need to train out any bad habits, and we can teach you the most efficient ways to handle your weapons."

My heart raced at the mention of weapons, but I tried to push aside my fear and focus on what he was saying. "I've been told you are fairly strong," he continued, eyes assessing me. "So we don't need to worry about recoil on firearms."

His words did little to ease my apprehension as he mentioned firearms. However, I knew I needed to face my fears to learn how to use them properly. "That's what I would like you to start with today," he said, gesturing towards a table covered in various guns. "I have a few sidearms and shotguns. How do you feel about trying them?"

My hands trembled slightly as I approached the table, eyeing the array of deadly weapons before me. "I can give them a go," I managed to say, though my voice betrayed my apprehension. "But I am apprehensive about them," I admitted

"It's good to be apprehensive of them," he replied in a serious tone, his warm demeanour vanishing for a moment. It will ensure you treat them with the required care and respect." His words carried a weight of importance, and they made me realise that these were not just mere objects. They were weapons designed for one purpose: to kill. And that fact sent chills down my spine.

He then led Hargreaves and me to a section of a shooting range with a multitude of targets already set up. Throughout the entire exchange between the quartermasters and me, Hargreaves stayed silent, and it didn't look as though he had any plans of speaking soon, meaning I was purely in the quartermaster's hands.

We stopped at a bench that was set up in front of the target area and arranged in front of me where 3 shotguns and 3 handguns . Seeing them gave my stomach a nervous lurch. This is getting intense fast. I thought

The quartermaster gestured for me to sit on the bench, and I did so, my heart pounding. He picked up one of the shotguns and handed it to me, showing me how to hold it properly and explaining the different parts of the gun.

CHAPTER 8

. The quartermaster's deep, authoritative voice echoed through the shooting range as he introduced each firearm with precision and expertise. "We are going to see how you get on with the shotgun's first lass," he said, his thick accent adding a touch of charm to his words. His weathered hand gestured towards a row of guns on a long table.

"From right to left, we have the Tabor TS-12 gauge rotating tube-fed semi-auto shotgun, which holds 4 shells per tube and has 3 tubes with one shot in the pipe. It requires manual left or right rotation," he explained, my eyes scanning over the details of the weapon before moving on. And passing me the next one in the lineup.

"Next, we have the DP-12 pump action double barrel rear-loading shotgun with an impressive 16-shell capacity." again, we studied every detail before he handed me the next one.

And last but not least, the KSG pump action with a maximum capacity of 14 shells."

"Now, before we start shooting, I want to stress the importance of safety," he said sternly. "These are not toys; they are dangerous weapons and must be treated with caution and respect at all times."

I nodded, feeling a sudden wave of anxiety wash over me. I had never held a gun before, let alone fired one.

"First things first, we need to ensure the gun is unloaded," he continued. "Always check the chamber and barrel before handling any firearm."

I followed his lead as he showed me how to check for ammunition and safely unload the gun. Once it was cleared, he demonstrated how to load and hold it properly for aiming.

"Now, aim at that target over there," he said, pointing towards a large paper target about 20 feet away.

My hands shook as I raised the shotgun and tried to steady my aim. My heart was racing so fast I could barely concentrate on what he was saying next.

"When you're ready to shoot, take a deep breath in and slowly let it out as you squeeze the trigger," he instructed.

I followed his directions as best as I could manage, feeling adrenaline rush through my body when I pulled the trigger. The loud boom of the gunshot echoed through the shooting range, and I felt a jolt through my shoulder from recoil.

"Hmm, not bad for your first shot," the quartermaster commented with a small smile. "Let's try again."

He helped me adjust my stance and grip until, eventually, I could hit closer and closer to the centre of the target. By my third shot, I was feeling more confident and less anxious.

After practising with each of the shotguns for a while, the quartermaster me and instructed me to unload the weapon I was using. Once the shotgun was safe he continued. "right then, lass, next is the handguns," he said as he pulled out a sleek, black handgun from the case

and placed it in my hands. "This is the HK45 tactical," he said, his voice tinged with admiration. "It holds ten rounds per magazine and one in the chamber. Notice the 3 dot sight system for improved accuracy." I held the gun carefully, taking note of its weight - 27.68 ounces when empty. The powerful .45 calibre rounds it fired promised lethal force.

Next, he handed me a smaller gun, the Sig M11-A1 9mm. "This one is designed for concealed carry," he explained. It has a 3-dot adjustable sight system and can hold up to 15 rounds in the magazine, plus one in the chamber." I took aim at an imaginary target as he continued to describe its features. This gun was slightly heavier, at 32 ounces, when empty.

CHAPTER 8

Finally, he revealed the Beretta M9, a classic firearm used by many soldiers. "This one also has a 3-dot sight system, but it fires 9mm rounds instead," he stated confidently. Its weight was comparable to the sig—33.3 ounces when unladen.

After thoroughly familiarising myself with each weapon, the quartermaster led me to a shooting range where I could practice my newly acquired knowledge. He showed me how to hold each gun properly, adjust my stance for stability, and fire with precision. Despite his expert guidance, it quickly became apparent that guns were not my forte. I struggled to hit even a stationary target with any accuracy.

With a final nod of approval, the quartermaster and I decided that the sig M11-A1 9mm was my best option. As he handed me the weapon, his weathered face took on a serious expression. "Jess," he said in a low voice, "everyone around this facility is armed. Our work is dangerous, and you must always be prepared to defend yourself. I can tell from your brief training that guns are not your forte, but I insist you carry this with you." His words hung in the air, heavy with the weight of responsibility. Reluctantly, I agreed to take on the burden of this new tool.

The quartermaster then equipped me with a sturdy waist harness containing three fully loaded ammo clips for my chosen weapon. Though I had never been fond of guns, especially after growing up in a society where violence was rare, I felt a sense of empowerment knowing I had a reliable means of protection at my disposal. With a deep breath, I braced myself for the challenges ahead as he sent me off to explore the upper levels of the facility. The gun suddenly felt heavier against my side, and I couldn't shake off the feeling that I was about to enter into a world much darker and more dangerous than anything I had ever known before.

As Hargreaves and I made our way through the facility's sterile, metallic corridors, I couldn't shake off the unease that clung to me. Each sharp turn and security checkpoint reminded me of the danger lurking around every corner.

I couldn't help but notice that we bypassed the mid-range weapons section, jumping straight to the higher levels. When I questioned Hargreaves about it, he replied with a confident smirk, "No need to waste your time. We can always come back if my intuition is wrong." But his words were tinged with a hint of hesitation, making me wonder what was happening in his mind.

Pushing aside my doubts, I followed him up the winding staircase that seemed to go on forever. With each step, my nerves grew more frayed. What is waiting for us on these upper levels? I had a sinking feeling that I was about to find out.

Finally, we reached our destination: the close combat floors. My eyes widened at the sight before me—a traditional dojo setting complete with tatami mats and training equipment. In the centre of it sat a stunning woman in athletic wear that could have been mistaken for high fashion. Her dark hair was pulled back into a sleek ponytail, and her posture exuded confidence and grace.

She addressed us by name: "You are here earlier than expected, Hargreaves. And you must be Jess," she said with a hint of amusement in her smooth and melodic voice, giving no indication of aggression or hostility despite our sudden appearance. The corners of her mouth turned up in a delicate curve, revealing dimples that added to her charming demeanour. "I'm Hiyori," she said, her voice gentle yet confident. " I've been expecting you, Jess. I'm one of the close-quarters combat trainers here at the facility. My job is to train recruits like yourself in weapons-based combat and other close-range techniques."

CHAPTER 8

A surge of excitement mixed with nervousness flooded through me at the thought of learning how to fight using my weapons instead of relying on my own body. But I couldn't help but wonder why Hargreaves hadn't brought me here sooner.

"Why didn't Hargreaves bring me here sooner?" I asked, trying to keep my voice steady despite my heart racing. "He's been showing me basic self-defence, but if that's your speciality, shouldn't you have been teaching me?"

Hiyori's expression turned serious as she answered, "There have been reports of increased threats and attacks against our agency and its agents. We believe it is necessary for all agents to be well-rounded in their training and prepared for any situation that may arise. However, this is advanced training; not all agents require this level of combat training. That's why we had Hargreaves get you up to speed before I steep in to help.»

My determination to prove myself grew at the mention of danger and being prepared for anything. "So, what do you need from me?" I asked, determined to show that I was willing to learn and do whatever it takes to protect myself and others.

«I will assess your current skills and tailor a training regimen specifically for you," Hiyori replied as she motioned for me to step onto the mat.

As we went through various exercises and drills, I could feel myself improving under Hiyori's expert guidance. Her style was fluid yet precise, and each movement had a specific purpose.

After hours of intense training, Hiyori finally called for a break. As I sipped some water and caught my breath.

"Well done, Jess," she said with a proud smile. "You have more talent in this area than I was told." There was admiration and surprise in her eyes as she looked at me.

"Thank you, but Hargreaves deserves all the credit," I replied with a grin, feeling accomplished. Despite my initial doubts about my abilities, I was starting to believe that I did have what it takes to be an agent for this agency.

"Before we continue, there is something of great importance that we must discuss," Hiyori's words were weighted with meaning as she glanced in Hargreaves' direction. Taking a seat, she motioned for me.

To join her as she spoke again. "Aside from teaching hand-to-hand combat, I am also responsible for the agency's enchanted armoury."

My confusion must have been evident because Hiyori continued to explain. "Throughout history, there have been countless tales of enchanted weapons - some called magical, cursed, or blessed. But the truth is, that it's the user who wields these weapons that usually causes such phenomena and attributes it to the weapon so that they can hide that they have powers. However, there are exceptions, and it is those rare weapons that I am tasked with handling."

Her tone grew more serious as she spoke, and her eyes gleamed with knowledge and experience. My mind raced with questions as I struggled to process this new information. "So these weapons are real? And they possess powers?" I asked.

Hiyori nodded solemnly. "Yes, but it's not so simple. These weapons can be unpredictable and even dangerous at times. Some are truly what the legends say - cursed, blessed, imbued with magic, or containing sealed souls. These magical weapons are well-documented and usually only require a basic understanding of magic to wield. The ones I am responsible for are rare and powerful; they are hardly handled by anyone, not even agency personnel. You see, some weapons are created using magic, and anything

CHAPTER 8

touched by magic in its creation has something akin to a soul - something that seeks its match. Think of it like a destined weapon. But sometimes, even ordinary weapons used in the paranormal community for extended periods can gain sentience due to their exposure to powerful beings."

Anticipating my next question, Hiyori added, "Not everyone can wield one of these weapons. They can be too powerful and can easily overwhelm an individual. However, since Hargreaves has brought you directly to me and is rarely wrong about these things, let us take you to the vault and see what happens."

Her words lingered in the air, leaving me awestruck and filled with wonder at the thought of such powerful and sentient weapons. The once unremarkable armoury now held a mysterious and awe-inspiring presence, as if it were a sacred temple to these ancient combat tools.

With a graceful movement, Hiyori turned and beckoned us towards a narrow staircase tucked away at the back of the dojo. The wooden steps creaked under our weight as we made our way up, anticipation building with each step.

CHAPTER 9

Finding Her Weapon

The top floor of the dojo was reminiscent of a sacred temple, with its traditional setting and soft floor mats that seemed to hug my feet as I walked. The air smelled of old wood and polished steel, with hints of incense and sweat. As I took in the sight, Hiyori called to grab my attention.

"Jess," she said, her voice grave and tinged with respect. "This area is reserved for those chosen by a weapon. If you are not deemed worthy, you will never be allowed past this point again." With her warning ringing in my ears, she motioned for me to follow her to a nearby bench.

As we sat down, Hiyori explained the significance of the weapons in front of us. She spoke of their ancient history, immense power, and the great responsibility of wielding them. I listened intently, trying to absorb every word as though they were precious gems.

After her brief lesson, Hiyori stood up and placed a hand on my shoulder. "Close your eyes," she instructed in a serious yet gentle tone. "Take a few deep breaths and tell me how you feel." As I followed her instructions, I couldn't help but feel a heavy weight pressing down on me. This room had an overwhelming aura as if thousands of unseen eyes were watching and judging me. My every flaw and insecurity was being exposed under their scrutiny, but I refused to cower to this feeling. I was not the little girl I used to be; nothing would make me feel weak or unworthy.

A feeling of unease washed over me as I stood in the centre of the weapon room. It was as if thousands of eyes were watching my every move, each pair bearing its unique voice or emotion. Hiyori's expression softened as she listened to my explanation.

"You have a strong connection with the weapons," she said, her voice calm and soothing. "It is not uncommon for those chosen by a weapon to feel drawn towards it. It is a sign of your potential and compatibility."

I let out a breath I didn't realise I was holding. The weight on my shoulders lifted slightly, and I knew there was some reason behind my unexplainable attraction to these powerful objects.

"But how do I choose?" I asked, looking around at the vast array of weapons before me.

"You must listen to your heart," Hiyori replied, gesturing towards my chest. "Close your eyes again and concentrate on which weapon calls out to you the strongest."

With a nod, I closed my eyes and tried to block out the noise and distractions around me. As if on cue, two distinct melodies began to play in my mind - one soft and gentle like a lullaby, the other strong and determined like a battle cry. They were vying for my attention, neither overpowering the other.

"Which one is it?" Hiyori's voice broke through my thoughts.

"I-I don't know," I admitted, overwhelmed by the conflicting melodies.

"That's okay," Hiyori reassured me. "It takes time to fully connect with a weapon. Just trust your instincts."

Holding onto Hiyori's words, I took a deep breath and opened my eyes again. My gaze scanned the room, searching

CHAPTER 9

for any sign or indication of which weapon was calling out to me. And then suddenly, something caught my eye in the distance -

"There," I said, pointing to a display on the far wall. "It feels like I'm being called in that direction. It's hard to explain, but it's like Lyn would speak in my mind, but it's a silent melody."

"Ah, I see," Hiyori nodded, understanding my explanation. She signalled for Hargreaves, standing nearby, to approach us.

"Jessica, tell us what is calling you, and we will bring you to it," she said.

With determination, I pointed to the display

on the far wall. Hargreaves gently picked me up and ran towards the display. My heart raced as we got closer and closer until finally, we reached the display - full of different types of daggers and oriental looking swords.

Hiyori followed us with eager steps and opened the case I had been pointing to. Her eyes widened in approval as she nodded at me, giving me the go-ahead. I reached into the case, my fingers trembling with excitement, as I slowly caressed the hilt of two swordsmen slightly shorter than the other but they where definitely a matching pair as my fingers danced delicacy over the hilt I pulled the blade from their scabbards. The curved Blades glided smoothly through the air as I examined them, the sharp single-edged Blades glinting in the light. As soon as the Blades sat in my hands, a sense of calm washed over me, like everything in the world was suddenly right . I sat infant of the display case where the scabbards lay abandoned placing the blades delicately on my lap I ran my fingertips along the razor-sharp edge, feeling a rush of adrenaline and contentment coursing through me. It was almost like the blades where purring in happiness.

Glancing up at the two instructors, I could see shock and awe written all over their faces. We sat there in silence, allowing me to fully bask in this feeling of completeness that only these Blades seemed able to bring me.

"Jess, we should probably head to one of the training rooms to discuss what's happened and to talk about what happens now," Hargreaves said in a calm and reassuring voice that cut through the fog that filled my mind. I stood up as if in a trance, my body moving on autopilot as I followed him and Hiyori towards one of the training rooms me with my blades still out of their scabbards which Hargreaves's kindly carried for me . My heart was racing with anticipation, fear, and a sense of pure bliss. With each step, the ground felt unsteady beneath my feet, like I was walking through a dream. We entered one of the training rooms, its walls bore with weapons and equipment, and Hargreaves quickly contacted Alex. Hiyori remained by my side, her presence a comforting weight against my shoulder. Her dark eyes watched me intently, like a predator stalking its prey. As we waited for Alex to arrive, Hargreaves joined us and spoke seriously. "Alex is on his way. We must discuss the ramifications of this and how it might affect the planned training. He's also bringing Killian." His words hung heavy in the air, adding to the already tense atmosphere of the room. "Jess, are you okay? You have been very quiet." Hargreaves' concern was evident in his gentle voice, but I couldn't find the words to respond. My mind was still trying to process everything that had happened.

My voice wavered, uncertain and filled with emotion. "Yeah, I'm... I don't know. It's hard to describe." I paused, trying to describe the feelings that swirled within my head. "I feel calm and whole; it's like I didn't even realise a piece of myself was missing until it had been filled. And now I

CHAPTER 9

feel more aware like everything has a sharper definition." As I spoke, I noticed the intricate details of the room around him - the fine lines on the furniture and the subtle variations in colour on the walls. "Sounds are clearer, and smells are more pronounced," I continued, my eyes taking in the vibrant colours and rich scents that filled the space. "Why is everyone so shocked?" I turned to look at my Trainers, seeing their expressions of disbelief and amazement. "I thought you took me there to see if a weapon would choose me...but it feels like something more profound has happened."

"We will wait for Alex to arrive before giving a full explanation, but I must say, it is quite uncommon for someone to have such an intense reaction. Most individuals do not have any unaided response at all. This only adds to our surprise, as finding candidates with any connection to the weapons is challenging for us," Hiyori replied, her voice laced with concern and fascination. She paused, "It's almost as if these blades has been waiting for you specifically." The weight of her words hung in the air, thick with mystery and wonder.

The door to the training room slid open, and Alex entered the room with Commander Killian Robinson trailing behind him. The Head Trainer's face was curious and concerned as he looked at me. "Hargreaves contacted me about Jess's reaction," he said, his gaze flickering between Hiyori and me. "I want to see for myself what is going on."

Without hesitation, I held my hands towards Hiyori, offering her the Blades that had Claimed me moments earlier. She leaned in to take them from my hands, but before her fingerers touched them. The Blades discharged a spark of energy, shocking Hiyori, so her hand withdrew like she had just been burned.

Alex nodded, his eyes scanning over the Blades and then Hiyori's hand before meeting my gaze again. "We will discuss this further later, but first, we must assess if these weapons have impacted your combat ability," he said firmly. "Killian will be your opponent."

My heart skipped a beat at the mention of sparing. The thought of sparing was something had begun to enjoy since coming to the agency, but fighting while wielding a weapon was completely new territory.

As if sensing my unease, Killian gave me an encouraging smile before taking a blocky-looking sword from the closet weapons rack and assuming a defensive stance across from me. I mirrored his movements before bracing myself for his first attack.

The fight was intense and fast-paced, each of us dodging and parrying as we tried to gain the upper hand. Killian was clearly skilled in using his weapon. Still, I moved almost instinctively - anticipating his next move and countering it effortlessly.

It wasn't long before our sparring session ended, with me pinning Killian down on the ground with my own weapon pressed against his throat. As soon as I released him, he stood up with amazement. "You pick up things remarkably fast.

My mind reeled as I stumbled backwards, shock and confusion coursing through every fibre of my being. "Alex, what's going on?" I asked, my voice trembling with nerves. "And how did I do that?" My hands shook as I gestured to the weapons in My hands, still trying to process what had just transpired.

"Did I do something wrong? Was I not supposed to touch this?" The weight of my actions hung heavy in the air, the uncertainty and fear creeping into my words.

"No, Jessica, you did nothing wrong," Alex reassured me, his tone filled with awe and amazement. "According to

CHAPTER 9

our records, these blades have only ever been used by the original warrior who owned them. And now, it's responded to your touch." His eyes widened as he spoke, a sense of wonder and reverence colouring his words. "This is truly remarkable."

The sound of gasps and murmurs filled the room as all the instructors looked at each other with wide eyes, their faces stricken with shock. I could feel the weight of their gazes on me, but I didn't quite understand the full ramifications of the situation. "What's going on? Are you all alarmed because of who the blades belonged to? Was it someone evil or dark?" Hiyori's expression was one of surprise and concern. "No, nothing like that," she reassured me quickly. "We would never allow something tainted in this facility. But if it will ease your mind, I will investigate and gather all information about the Blade's origins for you." Her words gave me a slight sense of comfort, and I felt slightly relaxed. Then, I became aware of a faint humming coming from the Blade, almost like a gentle lullaby. But it was a sound only I could hear or feel, like a secret shared between just me and the Blade. The soothing hum reminded me of a group of kittens purring contentedly on my lap, a feeling of peacefulness washing over me.

As the months passed, I noticed my training becoming easier. Hiyori had spent countless hours researching my weapons and discovered that they where a katana and wakizashi. The use of a katana and wakizashi together, known as a daishō, these particular blade where used in the 1300 wielded by a mighty dragon during the various wars and conflicts throughout this realm and many others world. This Blade was not just an ordinary weapon but a tool to protect the innocent and refugees. They have never been recorded as being used another user since their creation.

Under the guidance of both Hiyori and Hargreaves, my training was a mixture of workouts in the gym and hand-to-hand combat and weapons training. At first, I had to use blunt practice swords to learn proper form and technique without causing any permanent harm to myself or others. But even with these restrictions, I quickly realised that a blunt weapon could still be deadly in skilled hands. My mentors showed me how to attack pressure points and control my opponents' movements with minimal force. Even showing me how to take down opponents while my blades remained in their scabbards, I was instructed to always keep myself armed with my swords and SIG Sauer. As Hiyori delved further into the history of my Blade, she discovered that they were

"Once known as the blades of shadow and flame," the name resonated with me, and I decided to adopt it for myself.

Every day brought new challenges and lessons, but I revealed the opportunity to hone my skills with such unique and powerful weapons at my side. As I continued on this path of training and self-discovery, I couldn't help but wonder what other secrets these elusive Blades held.

My time with the agency was a continuous journey of learning and understanding. The instructors were incredibly patient with me, always willing to spend as much time on a subject as needed. Through their teachings, I discovered the intricate rules and systems that governed supernatural society. Each species and subspecies had a council overseeing their affairs and decisions. And above them, all sat the elder's council, made up of leaders from multiple groups, united as equals. But even above this influential body was the agency - the enforcers of the rules and protectors of our world. Working with all groups, including humans, they ensured the safety and secrecy of our existence.

CHAPTER 9

But above everyone else stood the watcher council - the highest authority. Though Alex tried to explain their role to me, I couldn't fully grasp it. He had me poring over materials and information about them. Still, their purpose contradicted everything I thought I knew about our world. Ultimately, we agreed that it wasn't necessary for my education and would revisit it later. Despite my lack of knowledge about them, I couldn't help but feel a sense of intrigue and curiosity surrounding this mysterious group.

Under my instructor's tutelage, I have come to learn about the vastness and complexity of our world. They have opened my eyes to the truth behind the legends and fairy tales passed down for generations. Every creature and story holds a glimmer of reality, from pixies and trolls to mermaids and unicorns. At first, believing such fantastical beings existed in our world was complicated. Still, as I delved deeper into my studies, everything made sense. My mind expanded and absorbed all the knowledge imparted to me as if by magic.

But there were moments when I questioned my own sanity. Was it possible that I had lost touch with reality and all of this was just a figment of my imagination? Perhaps I was a deranged patient locked away in some asylum, kept away from society for the safety of others. But then, a gruelling combat training session would bring me back to my senses. Or Mini, my loyal mentor and friend, would sense my troubled state and talk me through it with her words of wisdom. She was a remarkable companion - always there to support and guide me through the darkest times.

As my studies progressed, I encountered a new problem - Commander Killian Robinson. He had shown a reluctance to taking on an active role in the practical aspect of my magic training, he was a battle mage and From what he had demonstrated during my and Lynn's rescue, he was an extremely powerful one. His presence alone commanded respect, and his skills were unparalleled. But despite his expertise, there seemed to be an underlying tension between us.

He was always professional and efficient during our training sessions. Still, something about him made it hard for me to warm up to him. And then it hit me -he had seen me at my most venerable, and every time he looked at me, I was reminded of the person I was then. A dirty, broken experiment that needed to be saved. The realisation turn my stomach sour. But I had to get past it. During one of our earlier training sessions, he confided in me that he had spoken with the dragon breed about what abilities they expect me to manifest after what Jeremiah had done. Although they couldn't give any conclusive answers due to the ongoing investigation they were doing into what Jeremiah was actually trying to do, they gave him a run down on what they believed I might be capable of. The list they had given them was long and daunting, and it seemed like a lot of pressure for someone like me who was still trying to grasp the new realities of what had been done to me.

Every lesson with Killian seemed to get progressively more difficult. And I soon discovered that being a mage wasn't about learning frilly words or spells or incantations; it was about force of will and mental fortitude. I learned that I had to visualise the outcome I wanted and guide the energy to accomplish my desire. When Zara initially introduced me to magic, it was with gentle coaching that I had to hold the energy and mould it carefully. but Killian's method for teaching me this was to toss lighting, fireballs, ice spears and a host of other magical constructs at me with

CHAPTER 9

the intent to kill and see if I survived the barrage. When I confronted him about his barbaric training methods,. His response surprised me - he believed in pushing people beyond their limits for them to reach their full potential. To him, my potential as a mage far exceeded what I thought it was, and it was his duty as my instructor to help me realise it.

His words struck a chord, and I couldn't help but feel grateful for his belief in me. But at the same time, I also felt overwhelmed by the weight of his expectations. Everyone around me seemed to see something in me that I didn't even know existed.

Killian's training sessions were tough. He pushed me harder than anyone else, but my showed little improvement. My control over my abilities hardly improved under his guidance. Still, I developed a deeper understanding of battle tactics and strategy. For dealing with magic users and mages, But more than just this, Killian taught me valuable lessons about humility and determination. He showed me that possessing great power and natural ability was not enough. It was about being able to bounce back when you encounter failure. As my training progressed, Killian quickly established that my strength, speed, and endurance had increased much more than I could have imagined. He said I was about as strong as a young dragon breed in human form, After enduring a gruelling day, where every aspect of my training seemed to go awry, frustration consumed me, I reached my breaking point. No longer willing to dodge my opponent's attacks or play by the rules, I stormed to the training field and plopped down on the ground. The sun beat my face, adding to my already simmering irritation. "What in all hell do you think you're doing, Jess?" My Killian's voice boomed above me.

"Simply sitting," I replied, my tone dripping with sarcasm. The look of outrage on his face was almost comical, but my mood was too sour to appreciate it. I might have found it amusing enough to laugh at if circumstances had been different.

"And how do you think you are going to dodge my assault if you are sitting, or is this you telling me you can now harness your power and Don't need to dodge?"

What a jackass" Nope, I suck at this, I suck at shooting, and most of what Alex tries to teach me is now just confusing the fuck out of me, so if you're going to attack, get on with it." I crossed my arms and glared at him. I knew I was acting like a spoilt child, but I didn't care at that point.

"oh, so you want a pity party, is that it?"

I sat there silently. I wouldn't give him the satisfaction of a reply.

But he didn't stop there. "What is it too hard? Your Just like I thought, in the end you are worthless. Can't hit a target at ten paces, can't protect against magic. I bet you're even failing basic combat trying. No one wants to tell you because they don't want to upset the poor little experiment." "What the fuck did you just call me" I snapped Before I knew what I was doing,

I was up and moving towards him, getting ready to attack. He raised his hand, and I was flung into the air. It was like I had been hit by a gale-force wind. "What? Are you scared a girl might hit you?" I screamed as I hit the dirt

"Oh, does the experiment think I'm scared of her. That must be a joke. I've seen toddlers with more skill than you have. The only reason you are here is that people feel sorry for you. You are useless. What would your parents think to see what a joke you've become. You must be happy they can't see you like this. I might ask Alex to forget about

CHAPTER 9

training you and let the doctors run their tests on you. At least we might learn something then." He goaded me. Every word that came out of his mouth directly hit my emotional insecurities.

Without thinking, I snapped. I don't know how, but electricity burst from my body and shot straight toward Killian. Power was coursing through me; it was like a dam had broken, and the power wouldn't stop poring out of me, but I didn't care. I would show that prick, Killian, that I wasn't weak or helpless. The wind whipped around me, kicking up dirt and

flinging my hair wildly. I felt my feet leave the ground. It was like I was in the storm's eye for a moment. I forgot everything around me and just felt the. Power, it was. Beautiful. Nothing else mattered. Then it stopped, and I plummeted to the ground. I landed in a heap tangled up in my clothes,

"Jess, are you okay talk to me" Great, it was Killian the jackass.

"Why do you care? I'm just a useless experiment," I said. I could feel tears build this. I knew that's what they all secretly thought of me. I just wasn't prepared for anyone to say it. I got to my feet and made a quick retreat to my room. I couldn't stand anyone else looking at me with pity today.

CHAPTER 10

First Assignment

For the next few days, I locked myself away in my small room, surviving on the meagre supplies from my mini-fridge. The thought of facing the people I once trusted and considered friends

was unbearable. Would they see me as a lost puppy, pathetic and useless? Or worse, a failed experiment that needed to be disposed of? My heart raced at the idea, and with each passing moment, I could feel sparks of electric energy coursing through my body, visible arcs dancing between my trembling fingers. It was a constant reminder of what had happened, how it had left me broken and afraid. The fear grew each day, gripping me tight and suffocating any hope of escape. They would surely lock me up for being too dangerous, unable to control this new power that had emerged within me. The walls of my room seemed to close in on me, trapping me in this nightmare.

A rhythmic knocking on the door echoed through the empty room. Mini's voice, muffled and concerned, called out from the other side. "Jess, it's me. We all know what happened, so we've been trying to give you space, but I'm getting worried about you." I can feel your emotions, and they're not good. Remember, being alone is never a good idea when you feel like this." Silence followed her words before she continued, "Come on, let me in. I've brought some food for you. You must be sick of surviving on mini fridge snacks." Slowly, I rose from my bed and went to the door. Feeling like every step was a burden. With a twist of the doorknob, I let her in. Mini stood there with a concerned expression on her face. And a tray of warm food in her hands. "I brought some real food," she said with a small smile before stepping inside and closing the door behind her as I retreated back to my bed, curling up under my blanket as if seeking comfort and protection within its soft folds, she made her way forward slowly making her way towards me, the aroma of a home-cooked meal filled the air. It was comforting and overwhelming at the same time.

Mini sat on the edge of my bed, placing a food tray on my nightstand. I couldn't bring myself to look at her, afraid of what emotions she might sense from me. But as she started talking, her voice was gentle and understanding, and I slowly relaxed.

"We're all worried about you, Jess," Mini said softly. "We know it's been tough for you since the incident with Killian. But we're here for you, no matter what."

I didn't respond, still overwhelmed by everything that had happened.

"And I know you must be tired of eating mini fridge snacks," Mini continued, trying to lighten the mood. "So I brought some real food from the cafeteria. Your favourite, pasta Alfredo."

I managed a small smile at her attempt to cheer me up. Mini was always so thoughtful and caring. "Thank you," I whispered.

Mini reached out and squeezed my hand. But I pulled away at her sudden movement. Terrified that the energy that had been pulsing through me would hurt her.

CHAPTER 10

Suddenly realising why I was so scared, she pulled her hand away slowly. "You don't have to go through this alone, Jess. We're a team." Tears welled up in my eyes as I finally looked at her. She smiled warmly at me, keeping her distance for both of our protection. "I'm sorry," I sobbed. "I've just been so scared." "It's okay," Mini whispered soothingly. "Let it out." And for the first time since the incident, I let myself cry, allowing someone else to see my fear and pain. I was consumed with raw emotion as tears streamed down my face.

When I finally calmed down, Mini handed me a tissue, and I wiped away my tears.

"I'm here for you," she said firmly.

I nodded gratefully before digging into the delicious pasta Alfredo she had brought for me.

"would you be able to tell me what Killian told everyone," I said with dread

"Okay, but only if you think it will help. "He spent some time reviewing how your day had gone and then said that you seemed to have been hitting a wall recently and were getting frustrated." I couldn't help but snort a laugh at the mention of me getting frustrated. Frustrated was definitely an understatement. Ignoring my outburst, she continued.

"he then went into detail about everything that happened when you were training with him. I was there when he explained himself, so I assure you he wasn't lying in anything he said to us."

Before she said anything else, I whispered, "I'm sorry I should have known the only reason Alex wanted me here was because of the things Jeremiah did to me. He wants to make sure I'm not a threat. I see that now" as I spoke electricity crackled over my body, shit I need to calm down I need to breathe. Once I calmed down, Mini smiled at me.

Her hand flew up as she spoke, and she lifted a finger, emphasising the importance of what she was about to say. "First thing's first," she declared. "I want you to know that I and the others don't feel that way about you. In fact, we are all extremely pissed at Killian for what he did. He has been incurring the wrath of the entire base for his actions." As she finished her sentence, she held up another finger. "And what he said about you isn't true. No one, including him, feels like that about you," I objected, trying to defend myself. But she spoke over me, determined to get her point across. "Jess, he saw that you had a rough day and thought he would play on your insecurities to see if he could get you to unleash some of your power. And yes, you did show an impressive display of power. But the way he went about it was wrong. I can assure you that he regrets doing it, and I will ensure he suffers the consequences for his actions." Her words were filled with determination and justice as she stood up for me against Killian's cruel actions.

I nodded, my throat tight and tears threatening to spill over. "I'm sorry I worried you," I said, my voice breaking. "You don't hate me, do you?"

Mini reached out and brushed a tear from my cheek. "No, none of us could ever hate you," she reassured me gently. She then left my room, telling me to finish eating before resting for tomorrow's training. I did as told, but my mind couldn't rest as I worried about the potential fallout from my mistakes. As I lay in bed, my mind raced about what had happened. I couldn't believe that Killian would do something like that to me. But as Mini had said, he was probably just trying to push me to see how much power I had. But still, the thought of him hating me for my powers was unsettling. I didn't want anyone on the base to hate or fear me because of what I could do. I just wanted to be accepted and belong somewhere.

CHAPTER 10

Feeling exhausted from all the emotions and training, I drifted into a restless sleep.

***

The following day, I felt refreshed and ready to restart my training. As I went to the mess hall for breakfast, I noticed that Killian was already there with Mini and the rest of my trainers.

Seeing me, Mini immediately waved, indicating I should join them. I hesitated for a moment before walking over to them. As soon as I sat down at the table, everyone fell silent. It was obvious that they were all waiting for me to speak first.

"I want to apologise," Killian finally spoke up, breaking the tension. "I shouldn't have done what I did the other day. It wasn't right, and you didn't deserve it."

I looked at him with surprise in my eyes. This wasn't the reaction I was expecting from him at all.

"I forgive you," I said softly, relieved he wasn't angry with me.

"Thank you," he replied sincerely.

From beside me, Mini gave him a stern look before turning back to her breakfast.

The rest of breakfast was tense, with strained smiles and awkward silences between us. After the plates were cleared and we finished our morning meal, we all scattered about our activities.

I was headed for a training session with Hiyori and Hargreaves and the rest for whatever tasks they had when they were not training me. Later in the day, as I attended my training session with Killian, I couldn't help but notice his slight limp. When I asked if he was alright, he brushed it off and said he had just fallen earlier in the day. But his nonchalant attitude raised my suspicions, and I began to ask around discreetly. No one would tell me what really happened, only that he had slipped and hurt himself. The knowing looks exchanged between Mini and some of the other members only added to my growing suspicion that she was somehow involved in his accident. Everyone looked the other way, protecting her despite her potential involvement in harming one of the trainers.

After months of strenuous training, I stood tall and confident, my body finally reflecting the hard work and dedication I had put into mastering my abilities. The paranormal world still held many mysteries, but I knew that proper understanding could only be gained by fully immersing myself in this otherworldly realm. Though Alex's teachings often perplexed me, I continued pushing myself further, eager to unravel the secrets of this supernatural world.

Not only had my mental and physical strength grown, but my skills with a firearm had also undergone a remarkable transformation. While I would never consider myself a sharpshooter, my aim and accuracy had greatly improved from my initial attempts. With determination and perseverance, I could hit my target eight times out of ten—an impressive feat considering where I began. Holding the gun's weight in my hand felt familiar and comforting, a symbol of the progress and growth I had achieved on this journey into the unknown.

My hand-to-hand combat skills surpassed all expectations. My swords had become an extension of my very being, lethal instruments that moved with deadly precision and fluidity in the heat of battle. With each strike, I felt the rush of adrenaline coursing through my veins as I sparred fiercely with Hiyori and Hargreaves.

Though they still bested me when they unleashed their full strength, I held my own for several minutes before

CHAPTER 10

inevitably being thrown to the mat. And even then, I left them with their own injuries from our intense battles, bruises and cuts marking our bodies as badges of honour.

I honed my physical skills and focused on strengthening my mental fortitude. Killian's teachings on self-control and meditation were invaluable in sharpening my mind into a powerful tool. With each breath, I could feel a heightened awareness and clarity wash over me, allowing me to anticipate and react quickly in any situation.

But progress was not always linear. There were moments of frustration where I felt like I was lagging behind the other agents or would never reach their level of expertise. But Killian always reminded me that mastery takes time and dedication.

"You are already becoming a formidable agent," he would say reassuringly. "But true greatness comes from patience and perseverance."

And so I pushed on, determined to become the best Agent possible.

Each training session with Killian felt like a test of endurance and willpower. He seemed to enjoy watching me struggle, his smug grin never faltering. But I refused to back down, fuelled by the hope that one day I could wipe that smirk off his lips. And after countless gruelling sessions, I finally reached a point where I could hold my own against him. I was no longer just evading his attacks - I had learned to redirect them and launch counterattacks. But even with all my progress, those damn wind blasts always managed to catch me off guard. Still, I persisted and focused my energy, occasionally catching glimpses of iridescent scales on my skin during intense concentration. But they would disappear like a mirage when I tried to examine them closer. Perhaps it was just the sweat glistening on my body or my mind playing tricks on me in the heat of our training.

As my training progressed, I was allowed to shadow some of the senior Agents. Each experience was a mix of exhilaration and dread - so far, these had only been routine assignments like patrolling, guard duties, and escort missions. But each mission taught me valuable strategy, teamwork, and quick-thinking lessons. It was one thing to fight against Hiyori and Hargreaves in controlled training sessions; it was an entirely different matter facing real supernatural threats in the field.

As I drifted off into a peaceful slumber, the soft hum of my ceiling fan lulled me into a deep sleep. Suddenly, the loud banging of my door jolted me awake. Groaning in annoyance, I ignored it and rolled over in bed, pulling the covers up my chin. But the insistent pounding continued, growing more urgent by the second. Finally, Mini's high-pitched scream pierced through the quiet and shattered any hope of falling back asleep. With my pillow shoved tightly over my head, I prayed fervently to any higher power that might exist. My desperation and frustration were palpable as I begged for just a few more minutes of rest before facing the day.

But Mini's voice echoed through the walls like an alarm, taunting me with the promise of an exciting adventure. "Jess, I know you're in there. Wake up and open the door, or I'm not taking you with me..." My heart skipped a beat as her words registered. Could it be? Was she really saying what I hoped she was? The possibility of an adventure with my best friend made all the sleepless nights and early mornings worth it. In one swift movement, I threw off my covers and rushed to open the door, ready for whatever awaited us outside.

Standing before me was a very serious-looking Mini, her expression hinting at a thrilling and dangerous mission ahead. "Well, get dressed and meet me at Alexis's office,"

CHAPTER 10

she commanded sternly. "Do me a favour - try not to look so excited."

My heart raced with eager anticipation as I hastily changed into my mission attire, my fingers trembling with excitement. I meticulously smoothed out any wrinkles in my fitted jacket, adjusting it to ensure a polished appearance. With careful precision, I checked that my trusty gun and sword rig were securely concealed, taking comfort in the weight and familiarity of my weapons. My instructor's words echoed in my mind - never go anywhere without your wepons - and I knew I was prepared for whatever challenges lay ahead.

Taking a deep breath to steady myself, I made my way to our boss's office, the endless possibilities of this mission racing through my mind like wildfire. This could be the moment I had been waiting for, my chance to prove myself and join the esteemed ranks of active agents. As I knocked on the door, my mind whirled with excitement and nerves, unable to believe I would embark on this mission alongside Mini, my best friend and mentor at the agency. A wide grin spread across my face as I envisioned all the thrilling action and danger awaited us.

I felt a surge of confidence and readiness course through me as I stood outside the door, eagerly anticipating the mission. Whatever may come our way, I was determined to face it head-on and emerge victorious.

As I stepped into the office, a sense of tension and seriousness hung in the air. My trainers all wore sombre expressions as Alex motioned for me to come closer to his desk. "Jessica," he said gravely, his voice echoing in the quiet room. "Please take a seat, and I will explain your assignment." I sat in the chair opposite him, my heart racing with anticipation.

Without any preamble, Alex got straight to the point. "I would like you to join Mini on a case in London." My mind raced with excitement and nerves at the thought of being given such a responsibility. I had always dreamed of becoming an agent but never expected it to happen so soon.

"I know you have shadowed some instructors before," Alex continued, "but this will be different. You will be working this case like any other agent would." He handed me a leather wallet, and inside was a shiny badge and a plastic identification card. I couldn't believe it - they gave me active agent status for this mission.

"Thank you," I stammered, still trying to process everything. "But are you sure I'm ready?"

"Your instructors think you are ready," Alex reassured me. "And I agree. However, even though you will be actively working on this case, I still expect you to continue training." He then mentioned Commander Killian's comments about my powers and how I needed more practice to fully master them.

For a moment, I was speechless. I knew I had been putting in long hours and hard work, but I never realised that my instructors saw such potential in me. "Thank you," I finally said, a mixture of gratitude and determination filling my voice. "I will make all of you proud for taking a chance on me."

I stood nervously before Alex, as he delivered the news. "I'm sure you will do your best. I have partnered you with Mini," he said, his voice steady and reassuring. I gave my friend a quick glance, worried that she might see me as a burden, but her beaming smile put me at ease.

"As I was saying, this case isn't ideal for someone's first assignment, but it's also best to get it out of the way. You will be heading to London," Alex continued. My heart raced at the thought of such a high-profile case in a big city.

CHAPTER 10

"We have received a report of a series of unsolved murders concerning us. And just moments ago, we received word of another victim found. You will head straight to the crime scene and take over the investigation."

My mind whirled with questions and apprehension. "Where in London?" I finally managed to ask.

"Chelsea Park Gardens. One of the London offices top crime technicians will meet you at the site. The area has already been cordoned off for your arrival. You and Mini will be stationed at the London field office for the duration of the investigation." Alex handed us each a thick briefing pack and looked at us expectantly.

"I've assembled all our information so far, and I expect you. both to read it thoroughly before arriving at the scene. There is a direct flight to London Stansted waiting for you, along with a driver who will take you directly to Chelsea Park Gardens."

"I have faith that you will both make us proud," Alex concluded, dismissing us with a nod. "And remember, if you encounter any difficulties, don't hesitate to ask for assistance." With that, Mini and I left his office and began preparing for the daunting task ahead in the bustling streets of London.

My heart raced as Mini and I hurried to our rooms, frantically packing a bag of essentials while clutching the briefing file. The urgency in my movements was mirrored by the

tense set of Mini's jaw as she stood beside me, her eyes darting around the room. We both knew we had to move quickly if we were going to make it to the plane on time.

As we made our way out to the car that would take us to the airport, I sat next to Mini and immediately sensed her tension. It radiated off of her in waves, almost tangible in its intensity. "Do you want to talk about what's on your mind?" I asked softly, trying to respect her boundaries.

Mini's fingers tightened on the handle of her suitcase as we climbed into the car. She took a deep breath before turning to me, her eyes searching for the right words. "I'm just worried about this mission," she admitted, her voice laced with nervousness. "It feels like there are so many unknown variables, and I can't shake this feeling that something is going to go wrong."

I nodded in understanding, feeling a knot form in my stomach at her words. "I know what you mean," I said quietly. "But we have to trust in our training and our abilities. I'm sure we will come out on top."

Mini gave me a small smile, but she was still struggling with her worries. I reached over and touched hers, offering what little comfort I could.

We arrived at the airport and focused on getting through security quickly and making it to our gate on time. My nerves spiked when I was frisked, remembering too late that I was carrying a firearm and sword. The guard waved me through before I could panic and cause a scene. "Have a good flight agent, waved me through. Once onboard the plane, Mini and I settled into our seats and began reviewing the file, making sure we had all of the details memorised

I knew from experience that Mini's empathic abilities could sometimes overwhelm her. She would shut herself off from using them unless absolutely necessary, which meant she often carried a heavy emotional burden with her at all times. If emotions around her ran too high or someone touched her without warning, she would absorb their raw feelings like a sponge, causing her both physical and psychological pain.

But despite these challenges, Mini never complained or let them hinder her. She simply found ways to cope and

CHAPTER 10

manage, constantly adapting and evolving to help others. As we sat on the plane, I couldn't help but feel grateful for having such a strong and resilient partner by my side.

Her voice wavered slightly as she spoke, betraying a hint of worry and exhaustion. "Yeah, I'm okay, Hun," she reassured me. "I just glanced at the file, and it looks like you may have to do much of the heavy lifting in this case." Panic began to rise within me at her words. "What do you mean?" I asked, my heart beating faster. "I need help understanding Mini. You have more experience with working cases than I do. I thought I would only be assisting." The weight of fear and self-doubt settled heavily on my shoulders as I realised I would need to take the lead. But Mini's calm voice broke through my inner turmoil before I could go further into my own thoughts. "Jess, I have faith in you," she said firmly, her unwavering belief in me shining through her words. "And so does everyone else; otherwise, they wouldn't have chosen you for this case. But I need to warn you about something - as someone with an empathic gift, I can pick up on emotional echoes in any location that has experienced significant emotions. Although those echoes diminish over time, with this being such a fresh and intense case, it might be too much for me to handle without getting emotionally overwhelmed. I don't want that to affect our work or compromise your safety." Her vulnerability and honesty struck a chord within me, reminding me again why Mini was my partner and my closest friend in this dangerous line of work.

I took a deep breath and put on my best professional demeanour. "I understand completely, and I'll give it my all," I said, hoping to project a sense of confidence I didn't feel. Mini nodded appreciatively and motioned for us to move on to the briefings. As she smiled at me, I saw the tension behind her eyes. She tried to remain brave as we delved into the work ahead.

The flight felt like an eternity as thoughts raced about everything that could go wrong on this mission. But as Mini and I landed on the outskirts of London and made our way to meet our driver determination set in.

CHAPTER 11

Fog of fear

We arrived at the crime scene just as the morning fog began to lift, revealing the grim tableau that awaited us. After poring over the detailed file Alex had handed us, I could easily discern why Mini appeared so utterly terrified. The information contained within those pages painted a picture so gruesome that it seemed almost understandable for her to be so shaken. Her face was as pale as a ghost as if merely stepping any closer to the scene would induce a wave of nausea or worse. I turned to her with a reassuring smile and offered, "If you'd prefer to stay outside, I'm confident I can manage everything that needs to be done inside on my own." Despite her apprehensive demeanour, she took a deep breath and replied, "Thanks for the offer, but I think I should be okay."

Our driver, silently observing from the front seat, stepped out of the vehicle calmly. He addressed us with an air of quiet assurance, stating, "I will stay here with your bags and ensure they're safe while I await your return." His tone was so straightforward and matter-of-fact that it almost caught me off guard. I turned to look at him, my expression surely one of disbelief, as if he had unexpectedly slapped me across the face with a wet fish. It wasn't what I had anticipated from a driver, and his nonchalance took me by surprise. My reaction must have been quite evident because Mini suddenly burst into laughter, her amusement echoing in the stillness of the morning.

"Oh, I'm sorry," she managed to say between bursts of giggles, her voice trembling with unexpected lightness amid the gravity of our situation. "But the look on your face right now is so surreal," she continued, her words interspersed with chuckles that, although unexpected, offered a fleeting respite from the tightening tension that lay heavily over what we were about to face.

After briefly pausing to gather herself, we began our steady journey toward the police cordon. With every step we took, the closer we came to the sealed-off area, the more Mini's expression darkened—a silent portrait of dread and resignation. I silently vowed to respect her decision, withholding further mentions of what deeply troubled her. Yet, as we moved forward, I couldn't ignore the oppressive tension in the air, infusing my senses with a bitter taste that clung stubbornly to the back of my throat.

Just then, a uniformed officer stepped forward with apparent authority, his arms placating as he attempted to halt our progress behind the yellow police tape. "I'm sorry, ladies, but this is a secure crime scene—I can't allow you to pass," he announced before I could form a word in my defence. Without missing a beat, Mini slid in front of him with confident determination. "I'm sorry, officer, but could you please direct us to the person in charge? Our presence was specifically requested, and we should be expected." The officer hesitated for a moment. "Oh, I'm sorry, ma'am. I wasn't informed. If you could follow me," he offered, his voice betraying uncertainty and reluctant compliance.

Mini glanced at me with that knowing look, a silent acknowledgement that her subtle manoeuvring had hastened our advancement—a somewhat sly nudge of power

CHAPTER 11

that, at least, expedited our entry. He then led us toward the house, and as we approached, an odious stench assaulted my senses. It was a rancid concoction of fear, blood, despair, and pain. This aromatic miasma transformed the setting into something resembling an abandoned slaughterhouse. I tried desperately to shield my nose and switched to breathing through my mouth, only to find that this alternative was equally offensive. Even the uniformed officer couldn't help but wrinkle his nose as we stepped over the threshold.

Inside, the silence was palpable. Every instinct I had learned during my training and while shadowing in the field had taught me that crime scenes typically hummed with activity—chatter, heated theories tossed around in hushed whispers. Yet, in this place, an eerie stillness reigned; it was as if time had paused, and the only sound one could imagine was the faint drop of a pin. Every onlooker seemed absorbed in the moment's gravity; they were silently tracing over the contours of the unfolding tragedy, processing a scene far more horrifying than I had ever envisioned.

I stole a furtive glance at Mini, and it was immediately apparent that the nightmare unfolding before us was far more macabre and brutal than she had ever expected. As an empath, she seemed uniquely attuned to the lingering echoes of agony, terror, and the final, desperate despair that clung to the victim's spirit. Every subtle nuance of pain resonated deeply within her, as though she were drawing in the very essence of the suffering that had just taken place.

In a voice nearly devoured by the oppressive silence, I murmured, "Mini, do you need to wait outside? I know that this isn't easy for you." Soft yet imbued with unwavering resolve, her response reached me as she said, "Jess, I'll be fine. I'm shielding myself now. I just wasn't prepared for that overwhelming surge of emotions—it was intense and decidedly not in a good way." With a nod that echoed my resigned determination, I answered, "Alright, let's get this over with."

As Mini trailed after the uniformed officer, I turned my attention to the crime scene itself. We had entered through a narrow hall that served as a prelude to the chaos. While others ascended the staircase to the right towards the first floor, I chose a leftward path that led into what appeared to be a reception room. On this very spot, the assault had likely begun. Crime technicians bustled efficiently around me, frantically capturing photographs of the intricate patterns of blood spatter and meticulously cataloguing every minute detail, ensuring that nothing would escape our later reconstruction of events.

I drew a long, stabilising breath, following the techniques I had been taught, and let my mind project into an empty duplicate of the room. In that quiet visualisation, I allowed my other senses to awaken, combing through the lingering smells and subtle traces left behind, deliberately setting aside the fresher, more immediate anomalies in favour of those older and fainter signs. Focusing intently on the layout and atmospheric residue, I began to piece together the sequence of events: apparently, a woman had approached the door and invited two strangers. Then, something unsettling had occurred—the atmosphere shifting perceptibly as she returned to the reception area, a palpable nervous tension clinging to the space.

From the adjacent dining room, I discerned the scents of a man's cologne mingled with the understated aroma of children—one boy and one girl—who appeared to have been summoned, their arrival interrupting what once had been a peaceful dinner. Then, an overwhelming surge of fear, so potent it might have driven even the sturdiest mind to

CHAPTER 11

the brink of madness, struck me. The man and the children seemed frozen, as if time had halted their movement. Meanwhile, the two visitors lingered ominously close to the bewildered woman. At the spot where they had stood, a gruesome puddle of blood marked the carpet, with grotesque splatters adorning the walls and ceiling. This stark, violent tableau seemed deliberately designed to enforce a certain compliance or to make a grim statement.

Tracing further, I noticed from the viscous blood pool droplets leading steadily towards the staircase—the winding trails of evidence from all five individuals appearing to converge in the same direction.

Faced with a critical juncture, I found myself standing at a crossroads where my path split into two distinct directions: one descending into the realm of blood and brutality, the other promising an ascent toward Mini, whose presence was a comfort. In that fateful moment, a potent mix of curiosity and responsibility surged within me—my investigative instinct, fuelled by a hunger for truth, overpowered any lingering hesitation. I chose to follow the grim trail of blood, driven by the persistent, haunting scent it left in its wake.

The deeper I ventured, the stronger and more oppressive the odour became—not merely the smell of blood but also of a palpable terror that invaded every breath. When I finally reached the bottom of the staircase, I stepped into a room that, by its design, seemed meant for leisure—a sort of entertainment area—but the scene that unfolded was one of complete and utter disorder. Furniture had been carelessly thrown about, and everywhere I looked, from the walls to the ceiling and the floor below, grotesque splatters of blood painted a picture of indiscriminate violence. To my left, a pair of double doors hung uselessly on their hinges, beyond which lay a home office that had clearly been subjected to a frenzied ransack, as if desperate hands had been searching for something, anything, with no regard for order or preservation.

I tried desperately to refocus my scattered thoughts, piecing together the confusing barrage of sensory details surrounding me. The mingling trails of scent, the overwhelming presence of blood, and the chaotic dispersion of evidence blurred any attempt at logical deduction. Although the main bodies had been removed, remnants of flesh and dismembered parts lay stubbornly scattered throughout, each telltale sign of an event too horrifying to fathom. The prospect of an encounter with the medical examiner loomed over me like a dark cloud, its inevitability pressing on my already heavy heart.

I cautiously approached one of the forensic technicians to gather more information. My question, posed in a low, measured tone, inquired about the extent of the devastation—how bad the bodies indeed were and whether he might indicate roughly where they had been found in the room. His reaction was instantaneous; shock rippled across his face, and his voice quavered as he began to speak. With a noticeable stutter, he described the adult female victim's body as nearly unrecognisable—so mutilated that the only evidence of human identity was the skeletal structure itself. The grisly details churned my stomach, almost overwhelming me, yet I managed to keep myself together enough to listen.

He continued in a hushed, trembling voice: the boy was almost as horrifically transformed, discovered near the home office, and the male victim had suffered unspeakable torment. His account detailed how the fingers and toenails had been viciously torn away, the bones in his hands shattered, his joints forcibly dislocated, and even several teeth cruelly extracted in the process. With every word,

CHAPTER 11

the colour drained from the technician's face further until, once he'd finished his bleak narrative, he abruptly fled the room—presumably in search of a secluded place to vomit or perhaps simply overwhelmed by the mounting horror of the scene. I could only assume that his reaction was a mixture of revulsion and the instinct to escape; truth be told, had I not recently come to a critical realisation of my own, I might have found myself joining him in retreat.

In all, only three bodies had been discovered. Amid this chaotic tableau of violence and despair, there remained a single witness—an isolated sentinel to the unspeakable events that had unfolded in that disarrayed room.

I shot up the stairs, my heart pounding so fiercely it felt as if it might burst from my chest. Every step was propelled by the desperate need to find Mini and kick off the search without delay. As I reached the next landing, I heard her unmistakable voice drifting down from the reception room we'd left only moments ago.

I wasted no time and hurried back to that room. When I pushed the door open, I found Mini deep in a tense standoff with a plainclothes officer whose whole demeanour exuded unearned arrogance. His grim expression and superior tone left no doubt in anyone's mind: he believed himself above everyone present.

"Look, little girl, I didn't ask for your help—and I certainly don't need you meddling in my crime scene," he snapped, his voice dripping with condescension as he brushed Mini aside. In response, Mini puffed up defiantly, like an overgrown blowfish ready to burst. Her temper flared as she shot back, "Check your over-inflated ego at the door! They specifically requested us to be here, and it's painfully obvious you can't crack these homicides!" Her voice echoed with indignation and fierce determination.

At that very moment, I caught a low snigger from beside me. A nearby voice murmured loud enough for those nearby to hear, "Dame, she's on fire! Look at him—he's utterly struck dumb." Intrigued, I turned toward the source and asked, "And who might you be?" The man gave an apologetic smile as he introduced himself, "Sorry, I should have said hello earlier—I'm Keith. The London office sent me to help you all get settled in. Normally, I work behind the scenes in the lab. Still, with the situation escalating so dangerously fast and the threat of unwanted publicity looming large, it's clear that we're on an all-hands-on-deck mission right now."

"Alright, Keith, I'm Jess," I declared with unwavering resolve as I stepped in firmly. "We need to break this up right now—I have crucial and urgent information." Exchanging a quick nod with Keith, we returned to the duo at the centre of the bickering storm. It was all too apparent that the verbal jousting between Mini and that pompous officer was edging dangerously close to a full-blown confrontation. Keith and I grumbled in unison as we pressed into the heated fray.

Drawing a deep, steadying breath, I summoned every ounce of authority and bellowed, "ENOUGH!" My voice thundered throughout the room, reverberating power rattling the windows. In that suspended moment, everyone in the vicinity fell silent; all eyes fixed on me in startled stupor—I even suspected I had startled a few onlookers. Honestly, even I was taken aback by the sheer force of my own tone.

Glancing quickly at Mini and Keith, I noted that both struggled to conceal beaming smiles and stifled laughter, clearly savouring the fleeting moment of triumph. Seizing that precious pause, I took charge of the situation. "Now that you two have finally quieted down," I said crisply, "I have a question: How many bodies have been found so far?"

CHAPTER 11

The room stared back at me as if I had suddenly sprouted an extra head amid the chaos.

The previously defiant officer turned his glare upon me, a mixture of confusion and irritation in his eyes, his tone now laced with hostility. "And who the hell might you be, little Miss Loudmouth?" he demanded.

Meeting his challenge head-on, I replied evenly, "You can call me Jessica. I'm Mini's partner on this assignment." A hint of amusement crept into my tone as I continued, "I assume you have a name—unless you'd prefer I call you 'ass clown'?" The shock on his face was priceless, though it quickly gave way to a dark, seething scowl. "I'm DCI Duncan Lancaster," he snapped, desperate to reassert his authority. "As I explained to your associate, we don't need your help."

Not skipping a beat, I cut him off sharply, "Look, I'm not in the mood for a pissing contest. Just tell me—have you found the witness?" My question hit him like a bolt; he looked like he couldn't believe what he heard. "What are you talking about? There wasn't any witness. Just as before, we received nothing more than another anonymous call warning us of the massacre."

Amidst a rising tide of tension and a charged atmosphere that seemed to pulse with each breath, I carefully steered the conversation with unwavering authority. I was determined that this investigation would march forward regardless of any misplaced arrogance or bluster anyone dared to display.

"Tell me, how many bodies did you find?" I demanded, my voice cutting through the murmur of discontent.

"Three," came the curt reply. The man added, before I could press further, "They were all found downstairs. If you want to know the cause of death, ask your friend over there—he's already sent them for an autopsy at your facility."

I drew a deep, shaky breath, trying desperately to keep my anger in check. But something inside me snapped, releasing a torrent of raw fury. "Look around you, you fucking cock-womble! How many people live in this house? How many dinner plates have been left abandoned on the table, and how many bedrooms are there? It doesn't take a genius to see that two children—a boy and a girl—lived here, along with two fucking adults, who I'm assuming are their parents. So tell me, where the fuck is the girl when you haven't even found a body?" My words hung heavy in the air, each syllable charged as every eye in the room fixed intently upon me.

Taking another steadying breath to reassert my control, I added, "Why are you looking at me? Find the girl. she's still somewhere in this house." No sooner had the words left my mouth than the building exploded into a chaotic hive of activity. People scattered, meticulously combing every nook and cranny as if desperate to find even the slightest clue—each search driven by the belief that the missing child might be hiding in plain sight.

Realising that time was critical, I escorted Mini and Keith swiftly downstairs to the entertainment area. "I don't know why, but I'm positive she's down here," I stated as we descended into the murkier depths of the estate. With a heavy heart and a tone that betrayed my worry, I turned to Mini. I said, "Mini, I know this might be overwhelming, but I need you to tune into her emotions. Look for the slightest shift, any sign of fear or pain. I understand you're already struggling with the events upstairs and down here; it might get a lot worse."

Her voice was calm and resolute as she replied, "I will manage." The concern in her tone was palpable. "We need to find this kid. I can't even imagine what she's already been through."

CHAPTER 11

It didn't take long to stumble upon the hiding place—an unexpectedly secure and secluded wine cellar. I still had no inkling of how she managed to evade our earlier searches or how, in the chaos, she found her way into this fortified refuge. I suspected that even the two attackers might have found the cellar too daunting to penetrate, perhaps because it had been reinforced somehow.

Mini crouched carefully near the entrance, her voice soft and coaxing as she addressed the trembling child. "Hey there, my name is Mini. I'm here to help you. Can you open the door just a little for me, sweetheart?" Her tone was soothing, imbued with quiet magic—a gentle assurance meant to lower the child's guard and build trust.

Suddenly, the tense atmosphere was further disrupted by the abrupt intrusion of DCI Lancaster, who demanded, "Where is she?" as he stepped into the room. His tone was brusque, almost harsh. I interjected quickly, "Keep your voice down. My partner is trying to coax her out, and the safer she feels, the easier it will be." I stepped directly into his path, my stance firm and defiant.

"Get out of my way," he barked. Despite my protest, he managed to force his way past me just as Mini's gentle persistence finally convinced our frightened witness to open the door just a fraction. This small opening symbolically confirmed we would not hurt her.

Then, my heart sank as I saw the little girl cowering in the shadows, her fragile form trembling like an injured animal. Silent tears streamed down her cheeks, and her body shook uncontrollably. Yet, in her tiny hand, she clutched a knife with a resolve that belied her desperate state. In that split second, chaos erupted: Lancaster, undeterred, forced his way forward, shoving Mini aside and startling the child further. In a panic-driven reaction, she lashed out—her tiny hand slashing and thrusting with all the pent-up terror she held inside. Remarkably, she scored a shot, a brilliant and devastating hit upon Lancaster's arm.

I couldn't help but let out a brief, incredulous giggle at the absurdity of the moment. This sound might have been inappropriate under the circumstances. And was immediately met with a death glare from Lancaster, "Well, what did you expect? The kid is scared. Get out of the way and let us handle this." I said

And so, in that heated and unpredictable moment, emotions and tensions soared to an entirely new high. The air was charged with a complicated blend of panic, command, sorrow, and a surprising streak of stubborn defiance—a concoction of feelings that etched itself indelibly into every one of our memories.

I watched as Mini gradually edged nearer while Kieth and I diligently coordinated to keep the rest of the group safely at a distance. I couldn't help but notice a subtle but unmistakable surge of authority emanating from my partner. With a calmness that belied the chaos of the situation, she addressed the trembling girl, saying, "I'm sorry about that rude individual—he was completely in the wrong; he should never have tried to barge in uninvited." As these words washed over her, the girl's eyes, momentarily ensnared in a trance-like daze, lost their sharp focus. Gradually, as my Mini continued, her voice laced with an ever-strengthening sense of empowerment, the girl nodded in subdued agreement. Everything about her demeanour exuded relaxation, and though I anticipated that her grip on the weapon might falter under the influence of this newfound calm, it remained as tightly secured as it had been in our initial encounter.

I stepped closer to Mini and spoke in an almost whispered tone meant only for her ears, "Whatever you do,

CHAPTER 11

promise me you won't take the knife away." With a single, understanding nod, she silently affirmed her resolve.

Making my way over to Lancaster, I sought to gauge the extent of his injuries. His voice, edged with a biting mixture of cynicism and underlying discomfort, greeted me with a sneer as he quipped, "Well, that was something, wasn't it? Do you think I need stitches, or will some antiseptic and a dressing suffice?" Sensing his irritation, I said, "Clearly, civility is the last thing on your mind right now, so let's dispense with the pleasantries and get straight to business." The bluntness of my words appeared to catch him off-guard.

"I'm here because I have a job to do," I continued, treading carefully between professionalism and urgency. "We never intended to make a mess of things, but sometimes these situations spiral out of control. Your boss reached out for our assistance, and I need your cooperation to help. Specifically, I need the information that only you can provide." I paused, allowing my words to hang in the charged atmosphere as he processed the gravity of the situation.

With a resigned sigh, Lancaster replied, "I'm sorry, but this case is under immense pressure. Having you all interrupt—taking over—is more than a little exasperating."

I leaned in closer, lowering my voice to emphasise sincerity, "I completely understand your frustration, but let me assure you: we're not here to sideline you. Yes, we will pursue our own leads, yet that doesn't preclude you from continuing the investigation. All I'm asking for is an honest exchange of information so that we can put an end to these Killings. So, tell me, what can you reveal about the case? And I don't mean just the information scribbled in the file—I'm talking about the real, raw details, even those you think might sound far-fetched or even crazy."

The look on his face suggested that he was seeing me in a new light—as if realising for the first time that I genuinely sought his input. "You... you really want my input?" he stammered, surprised by my request.

"Yes, exactly," I affirmed firmly. "Now, can you please tell me: are there any similarities between this case and the previous ones? You were at the helm from the start of the earlier cases, so I need your impressions. Don't spare any details; leave nothing out—even if some seem impossible or far-fetched. We need every piece of information to stop these situations from spiralling further out of control."

"What good will that do you have my file? I included all my notes, but I don't think I left anything out." I began passing back and forth,

trying to use some of my nervous energy.

"I've read your notes, but it's human nature to skim over things that don't make scenes. I'm asking you, so tell me what you're thinking and your theories."

"I can't cover everything here. I need to review my notes and organise my thoughts, but I would happily share my notes, findings, and theories with your team."

"Do you think this is connected to the other cases? Could it be a copycat?"

"I think they are all connected. We have kept most of these out of the media, but we've had homeless people going missing for months and then showing up dead; child abduction cases have skyrocketed in the last 18 months, with a lot of the missing showing up dead with the COD (cause of death) being put down to substance abuse, drug dealers are turning up in the same state as this family like I said most of this has been unreported and I've only been able to connect it all after a lot of digging," he stopped to take a breath,

CHAPTER 11

This guy has connected the same dots as Alexander: "Okay, we must finish here. The kid will come with my team, and I'm assuming all evidence from all related cases is being sent to our facility" At my question, he just nodded in affirmative. I would also like you to bring your case notes to the office tomorrow. It will give us time to develop a working theory of what is going on. Is noon enough time for you to get everything together?" He gave me another nod "okay then I need to assemble my team and the witness then head to our office if you discover anything else brief us tomorrow but if it's urgent and you feel it's can't wait, call me immediately" I handed him my card hoping he would call us if he get's any leads, the last thing we need is a detective going missing, I made my way back to Kieth and Mini, and was shocked to find that they had managed to get the girl out of hiding altho she was still shielding herself behind them both and I could still see the knife clutched tightly in her tiny hands, "okay I've left things in the detectives hands and arranged a debrief with him for noon tomorrow at the office" they both nodded and mini interrupted me before I could say anything else" Jess this is Alisha I've explained that we are her friends and we are going to take her somewhere safe" as she was talking to me Alisha poked her head out and gave me a tentative look up and down she whispered something to her human shields and I could tell it had tickled Mini,

"oh, Alisha, I promise you wholeheartedly that she is very nice and not nearly as mean as she looks; I'll tell you a secret: she has a weakness for cupcakes and cookies. All you need to do is give her a cake, and she becomes as cute and adorable as a newborn kitten" My jaw hit the floor; first of all, I am not that bad; I just enjoy a good pastry, cake or cookie. Tell me, anyone who doesn't, and second, am I that scary-looking. Thinking back to how I used to be described before,

I lost everything. People always said I was cute, but all the training and exercise had changed me more than I realised. Alisha peeked at me again, this time with a Hughe grin. I knelt, bringing myself to eye level with her, "Well, since Mini seems to have a problem with sweet treats, it means there will be more for you and me, Alisha let out a slight giggle, and we led her back to the car, walking through the house we told her to keep her eyes on the floor and we did our best to block her view of the carnage around us, we could!t block everything but we did our best to block the worst, my heart broke as she started to cry silently; if I could hold her and cry, I would, but my tears would do nothing for her, and I couldn't indulge in my

sorrow not now, not when she and others like her depended on my strength, I need to be strong for this child, as we got Alisha settled in the back of the car so Kieth and Mini could be on either side of her like two imposing sentinels, I confirmed arrangements with DCI Lancaster and we made our way towards the field office within minutes of the drive starting I heard a quiet series of snores coming from behind me I looked around to find Alisha passed out with her head propped on Mini's shoulder, at my questioning look she shrugged "the

poor thing was exhausted, so I just gave her a gentle emotional nudge to get her to sleep, but she still wouldn't let go of that bloody knife," I wasn't surprised, the rest of the journey was completed in relative silence; I think, we where all just trying to process the horror that we had seen.

CHAPTER 12

The plot thickens

Upon arriving at the London field office, I was taken aback. I had anticipated it would be situated in a designated area of a police station or something of that nature. However, to my astonishment, it was housed within a sleek, modern office building. If I hadn't known better, I would have mistaken it for a high-end corporate headquarters rather than a field office for the paranormal defence agency. As I absorbed the unexpected surroundings, our driver declared, "I will take care of your luggage. The medical team is on standby, ready to examine the child and ensure she is healthy. Additionally, I have been informed that a conference room has been prepared for your use. All these details have been communicated via email to Keith, and I have been instructed to inform you that he will serve as your liaison for the duration of your visit."

Before I could comment or express my gratitude, our driver exited the car, swiftly moving to hold the door open for Mini. Instead of waking Alisha, we decided to carry her gently. Our initial destination was the medical wing, where we would ensure her well-being. Following Keith, we proceeded through the security checkpoint to the third floor. There, we discovered state-of-the-art medical facilities, complete with every modern convenience. Carefully, we placed Alisha on one of the available beds. We then conversed with one of the nurses, ensuring that Alisha would be well cared for.

Mini was adamant about remaining with Alisha so that when she awoke, she would be greeted by a familiar face. Moreover, Mini could utilise her empathic abilities to soothe and calm Alisha if the need arose. With everything in place, we felt assured that Alisha was in capable hands, allowing us to focus on the tasks ahead.

"Jess, I understand that our original assignment was to handle this as a team effort, but I simply cannot in good conscience leave her in such a vulnerable state—it just isn't right," Mini explained with passion lacing every word. She leaned in considerably closer, her urgency mingling with an unwavering resolve that resonated deeply. "I really need you to take the lead on this one, handling the situation as best as you can. And as you do, keep me updated at every single juncture. I plan to extract every piece of relevant information from Alisha. At the same time, I remain stationed here— and I'll ensure that every incoming detail is coordinated seamlessly." I couldn't help but observe how Mini interacted with Alisha; her decision to position herself so near was hardly surprising.

"Alright," I replied slowly, my voice dropping to a more serious, reflective tone as the weight of the responsibility began to settle in. "But promise me one thing—if things take a turn for the worse if the situation escalates beyond our control, you will immediately come out into the field with me to help set things right."

A soft smile played on her lips as she offered reassurance, "Of course, I will, hun," she replied gently, her calm confidence interwoven with an unspoken acknowledgement of my underlying concerns. "Though frankly, I don't anticipate you'll even have to call on my help—I trust in you

CHAPTER 12

and your ability." Her comforting words gave me a sense of cautious support. As I took them as an unspoken dismissal, I began to leave the room. Naturally, I expected Keith to follow right behind me. However, his raised hand halted my steps; he signalled that there was one more critical detail to address.

"If you plan to remain here with Alisha, I'll ensure that a fully equipped workstation is set up right in this area," Keith explained, his tone methodical as he outlined his plan. "This way, you can work directly on the case and video conference into the briefing room, sparing us the constant back and forth of relaying messages. I'm also going to see if we can rig you up with a dedicated communications link so that you and Jess can maintain seamless contact even when she's out in the field."

I paused momentarily, genuinely impressed by the foresight in his plans. "Wow, that would be fantastic, Mini. Do you think that setup will Help us?" I asked, my voice reflecting a blend of optimism and apprehension as the layers of our task unfolded before us.

"It sounds perfect to me," she replied, her voice carrying reassurance and finality as Keith pulled out his phone and began arranging the necessary equipment with practised efficiency.

"Now, go get organised and grab some rest," Mini said dismissively but with an undercurrent of urgency. "I have this gut feeling that we won't enjoy much more downtime anytime soon." With Mini's words marking the final dismissal from the ward, I turned to Keith, who was already deep in his work making the necessary technical arrangements.

"Keith, will you take me to the briefing room we're slated to use?" I asked calmly but assertively, despite the internal storm of emotions churning within me.

"Yeah, come with me," he replied, his tone imbued with quiet reassurance as we set off together down the corridor. "You'll be heading to the fifth floor—it's not only home to the briefing room but also houses the armoury. The briefing room is beside the facility chief's office, so I'm sure we'll be crossing paths with him throughout the coming days." As he led me toward the elevator, he confidently pressed the button for the fifth floor. He added with unmistakable certainty during our ascent, "So, you're going to be the lead investigator on this one."

Every word he spoke seemed to vibrate within that confined space, the palpable weight of responsibility intermingling with bursts of hope for what we might accomplish together, even under such challenging and unpredictable circumstances. I took a nervous gulp, allowing the full measure of his declaration to sink in before replying, "Yep, it looks like everything now depends on me to ensure it stays on track."

"I have complete faith in you, Jessica and the entire agency has your back, so if you need anything, you just need to ask," he said.

"Thank you, it means a lot."

"And I'm going to stick with you guys on the case so you won't be alone."

I gave him a grateful smile as he showed me into the briefing room. They had already set up the existing case files and whiteboards for us to work on. They had also developed a timeline for the cases we knew about. As I looked this over. I realised everything I assumed I would need to do tonight had already been done.

I looked at Keith, giving him an inquisitive look. "We were told that you had a long journey, and with everything you've experienced

CHAPTER 12

today, I thought I would get everything set up so now you can get a few hours rest before DCI Lancaster arrives with his notes and case files, I have also instructed the nurse to ensure Mini gets some rest! Would you like me to take you to your dorm room?"

"That would be great, but I thought we would stay at a hotel."

"The top few floors have been turned into living quarters for people that have a tendency to work too much or if we have visitors from

other facilities," he took me to my quarters in relative silence. Once we arrived, he handed me a key card and said he would wake me at 7 a.m. so we would have five hours to sort things out before the detective arrived with his insights. I was also informed that the room had a fully stocked kitchen."

"Thank you, but I will try to get some sleep; it's been a long day."

He left me to my thoughts as I closed the door.

***

It was a new day—a blank canvas—and I wasted no time checking on Mini and Alisha. Alisha still lay cocooned in sleep, her gentle, rhythmic breathing filling the silence of the medical ward with a calming presence. In stark contrast, Mini was fully alert and absorbed in her elaborate tech setup, where screens and gadgets hummed with life. Ever the proactive one, she wasted no time letting me know she was ready for the day ahead. "I'm prepped and waiting," she called out briskly, urging me to hurry to the briefing room to dive into the latest discoveries.

With anticipation pulsing through my veins, I strolled into the briefing room, and the sheer vibrancy of the space immediately struck me. The room itself seemed to pulse with energy. This tangible buzz came from the astonishing work of the tech crew that Keith had spoken of just the previous night. Every display screen in the room was alive with images: crisp photographs taken from multiple angles of crime scenes, meticulous lists cataloguing various pieces of evidence, and timelines that mapped out details with unsettling precision. As I marvelled at the rapid-fire influx of information, Mini's voice suddenly boomed over one of the screens. "Stop being impressed, and let's get on with some work," she declared with decisive efficiency. My startled reaction even brought a brief squeal from me, an involuntary response to her commanding tone, quickly met with her playful giggle. "That was so not funny, Mini—you nearly gave me a heart attack!" I managed to exclaim, a mix of irritation and amusement colouring my tone.

"Please," she teased lightly, "it would take a bit more than a little fright to get rid of you." That humorous exchange momentarily eased the tension, so I composed myself and shifted my focus back to the matter at hand. "Okay, so what have you discovered so far?" I inquired, keen to understand more about our challenging situation.

Instantly, Mini's tone turned serious as she started to carefully unpack the gravity of what we were facing. "We have a huge problem," she began, my eyes never leaving the images flashing before me. "Based on the evidence here and a swift database search matching missing person reports with various unsolved homicides, there's an ominous trend emerging. I believe this nightmare has unfolded for at least 18 months, perhaps even stretching to 24 months." At that moment, the main screen shifted, presenting a detailed timeline replete with case references and succinct descriptions of each discovery. "What's particularly disturbing," Mini continued, her voice dipping

CHAPTER 12

into a tone of grave concern, "is that the condition of the victims' bodies is deteriorating with each successive case. The earliest victims that I believe are connected were Killed with merciless violence like someone might use if they where in an uncontrollable rage. But they are nothing when compared to the more recent cases while the level of violence is the same if not worse its more controlled for example the bodies that were discovered just last night. Where tortured in order there was a purpose behind the violence that wasn't there before»

Before I could let the weight of her words fully sink in, Keith entered the conference room. His presence was gentle and comforting; he interjected himself smoothly into our conversation. "Good morning," he said, his tone Pleasant and welcoming. "I've got our lab technicians working tirelessly around the clock on the physical evidence. They're performing every conceivable test on every possible fragment to extract evidence that might finally give us a lead on the kind of monster we're dealing with." His comments added another layer of urgency to our gathering.

As we continued our discussion, I surveyed the multitude of display screens, absorbing every detail etched into the visual records. I noted the overturned furniture scattered throughout, the blood spatter and scorch marks that marred the walls, and the shattered remnants of glass from broken picture frames strewn across the floor—each element collectively narrating a story of unspeakable brutality. Yet, amid all this chaos, what truly seized my attention were the strange symbols etched into the doorframe. Their angular lines and cryptic script were entirely foreign, hinting at meanings and forces I had never encountered before.

A shiver ran down my spine, and my instincts warned me that this was no ordinary murder, even by the standards of the paranormal. There was an undeniable darkness at play, a sinister force that held the potential to consume everything in its path. My thoughts drifted to Alisha, whose delicate, small form had been clinging desperately to Mini when we led her through the carnage where she had been discovered. In that harrowing moment, I realised with brutal clarity that I would stop at nothing to shield this innocent child from the nightmares that lurked in the shadows.

Carefully, I continued my methodical sweep across the detailed scene images and whispered to myself in a tone heavy with dread, "I think there's more to this than meets the eye. The level of violence and those bizarre symbols... it's almost as if everything is part of a larger, ritualistic design that exudes something dark and twisted."

Mini's voice crackled through the speakers, laden with excitement and apprehension. "I think you might be onto something. I need to do a bit more digging, but I believe I've seen something similar before—in one of the Agency's archaic case files. That particular file was linked to a series of illegal experiments carried out on both humans and paranormals." Her voice faltered momentarily, trembling with the weight of her realisation before she pressed on. "If this connection holds true, we could be dealing with a conspiracy that stretches far beyond the isolated cases we initially suspected."

Keith's eyes widened in disbelief as the gravity of Mini's revelations settled over him. "Are you saying this is like some underground network using ordinary humans and paranormals as pawns in their twisted experiments?" he asked, struggling to grasp the magnitude of the implications.

"Exactly," Mini responded crisply. "And if that's the case, we need to unearth who's orchestrating all of this—and fast—before more lives are irreparably shattered."

CHAPTER 12

Searching his face for any further clues, I turned to Keith with a mixture of curiosity and apprehension. "Do you have any insights you'd like to share?" I inquired, eager to watch how he would articulate his reaction to our emerging theory.

Leaning forward with a serious Look, Keith lowered his voice, his measured tone underscoring the gravity of our predicament. "One thing's absolutely clear: this case is far larger than I initially thought," he explained, a trace of urgency threading through his words. "I can guarantee that we aren't even aware of all the potential victims. Many supernatural communities are fiercely private, determined not to let outsiders meddle in their affairs."

Staring at him in a blend of shock and confusion, I couldn't help but exclaim, "Are you seriously telling me that this disaster is being kept secret? How can that possibly be?" My words trembled with incredulity as I tried to wrap my mind around the notion of such a widespread cover-up.

Mini's voice resonated again over the speakers in that tense silence, offering a brief but poignant interjection. "Jess, remember what Alex mentioned to you before? The Agency we work for can only take action on matters that are formally reported. On the other hand, individual leaders within the paranormal community prefer to handle their own affairs through their trusted enforcers. Even though they acknowledge our authority, they loathe the idea of appearing weak by having to rely on us."

As her words echoed through the room, I couldn't help but recall many lessons Alex had tried to impart to me over my training. I still struggled to fully understand the chaotic world of paranormal politics. At that moment, I felt an enormous weight of frustration mingled with resignation. Sighing deeply,

I raised my hands in surrender, acknowledging that many aspects of my new, inexplicable reality remained cloaked in mystery and enigma. The morning's investigations had propelled us into a convoluted labyrinth of conspiracy and dark rituals. This complex puzzle promised to unravel even more layers of the unknown as we progressed. As I took one last extensive look at the array of flickering monitors and cryptic symbols that persistently haunted our screens, I understood that the path ahead would challenge every ounce of our resolve, every spark of our determination, and every shred of our humanity.

"Alright, I understand where you're coming from, but how do we determine if this problem is as significant as we suspect?" I asked, seeking clarity in the tangled web we found ourselves in. Keith raised his hand to capture our attention, a gesture reminiscent of days in a school classroom. "Keith, we're not in school anymore. If you have a suggestion, just go ahead and share it," I encouraged him, eager for any potential solutions.

He offered me a nervous smile, the kind that spoke of both apprehension and a hint of excitement. "Thinking that this might become a significant issue, I may have taken the liberty of arranging a few meetings with various representatives from the paranormal factions in the area right after you meet with D.C.I Lancaster," he revealed, his voice carrying a mixture of hope and caution.

"Okay, that sounds promising. Hopefully, we will be able to secure some assistance or, at the very least, gather some valuable information from them," I replied optimistically. Mini and Keith exchanged a look that suggested they weren't entirely convinced, but they kept their doubts to themselves. "So, who have you scheduled appointments with, and are

CHAPTER 12

they coming here?" I asked, my voice brimming with hope and anticipation.

"I have a meeting booked with the mages," Keith began, his tone measured and deliberate. "You have two meetings booked, one with the vampire council and the other with the dragon's court. However, they have insisted that they will only meet with you, you must go to them and no one else from the Agency can accompany you."

"Did they provide any explanation as to why it's so crucial that I attend alone?" I inquired, a hint of concern creeping into my voice.

"No, they didn't, but please exercise caution. Those two factions wield considerable power, and their influence surpasses what is healthy for any group. My gut tells me this could be some sort of test, so just please, do your best not to offend them," Keith advised, his voice tinged with a warning.

Dealing with two of the most powerful factions in London's vast and bustling city was certainly not something I had planned. Nonetheless, the fact that they were going out of their way to establish contact with me could signify one of two things: they were either frightened by some looming threat or perhaps profoundly entrenched in this complex web of conspiracy that had come to light. There was only one viable approach to uncovering the truth I desperately sought, and that was to agree to meet them. Yet, I had to do so with utmost caution, a steadfast determination, and an unwavering readiness to confront whatever challenges or revelations might lie in wait.

"Who's going to have a conversation with the sifters? Surely, there must be a ruling alpha within their ranks willing to engage in dialogue with us?" I inquired, my curiosity tinged with urgency.

"Regrettably," came the response, "they steadfastly refuse to cooperate at this juncture. They haven't provided any justification for their reticence, but it seems increasingly apparent that they are concealing something. I just can't discern what it is at this moment. Rest assured, if I receive any new information, you will be the first to hear about it."

***

The meeting with Detective Chief Inspector Lancaster unfolded as I had anticipated. He had diligently compiled an extensive list containing the names and descriptions of numerous missing persons. These individuals, however, had never been officially reported missing because they were vagrants and those living a transient lifestyle, often slipping through the cracks of societal attention. In addition to this, he had meticulously gathered an impressive list of suspicious deaths. These deaths had been casually attributed to drug overdoses, heart attacks, and other nebulous causes. Still, Lancaster's quick rundown suggested a deeper, more sinister pattern. He was defiantly on to something significant, though it seemed that no one else had taken the time or effort to connect the dots as he had.

After assuring him that I would keep the lines of communication open and available to him, I emphasised that if he had any leads or critical information, he could reach out to me at any time, whether night or day. Once our discussion concluded, I escorted him out of the building, ensuring that he felt supported in his investigation. With that matter settled, I focused on preparing for my upcoming meeting with the vampire council. This gathering promised to be as intricate and challenging as the one I had just concluded.

CHAPTER 13

Vampire Politics

Driving up to the vampire council's compound left me feeling thoroughly unnerved. The complex was enormous, an impressive fortress of Gothic architecture that loomed ominously against the sky. As I navigated the winding path leading up to the estate, I couldn't spot a soul on the grounds. Yet, an unshakeable sensation of being watched prickled my senses. The wrought iron gates swung open silently as if by magic, allowing me passage without braking. I continued up the serpentine driveway, my car's tyres crunching softly on the gravel, until I came to a halt before two imposing oak doors.

Pausing for a moment, I inhaled deeply, gathering my courage. The weight of the situation pressed on me as I stepped out of my vehicle. The air was thick with anticipation as I ascended the stone steps, each one echoing with the distant whispers of the compound's secretive past. Just as I reached the formidable doors, they slowly creaked open. A rush of heated air enveloped me, saturated with the rich aromas of aged whiskey, sweet pipe tobacco, and an indescribable essence that spoke of something far more ancient and mysterious.

Standing on the threshold was a vampire with a disarmingly artificial smile. His youthful appearance betrayed his recent transformation; he couldn't have been turned more than a few months ago. The crimson hue of his eyes was a dead giveaway, a sign of the insatiable bloodlust that newer vampires struggled to control. In contrast, the older vampires had mastered the art of concealing such traits, presenting a more benign visage to the human world. "You must be Jessica from the agency," he spoke, his voice carrying the faintest hint of Disdain. "My masters are waiting for you in the council chambers. Please, follow me."

He turned and led me down a dimly lit corridor without waiting for my response. The corridor was a realm of shadows, the flickering torchlight casting dancing silhouettes along the stone walls. My footsteps echoed softly, a hesitant rhythm in the council's inner sanctum. As we approached an ornate set of double doors, the intricate carvings depicting ancient vampire lore seemed to shift and come alive, their eyes trailing my every movement with an unsettling awareness.

Upon reaching the grand entrance, my escort halted and turned back the way we had come, leaving me alone with my mounting apprehension. The weight of the moment pressed upon me as I extended my hand toward the heavy iron handle. A palpable thrum of power emanated from beyond the doors, a testament to the presence of numerous elder vampires gathered for our forthcoming dialogue. This was no ordinary meeting; the stakes were high, and the room beyond promised a conversation that would be anything but mundane. I braced myself, my nerves tingling with fear and self-doubt, but I pushed myself forward, stepping into the unknown. This was going to be interesting, to say the least.

I prepare myself for the daunting task ahead with a deep, steeling breath. Firmly grasping the ancient, weathered handles, I yank the doors open with all my strength, the hinges protesting loudly as they screech

CHAPTER 13

and groan under the oppressive weight of centuries gone by. The chamber's grandeur is overwhelming, hitting me like a punch to the gut — vaulted ceilings stretch impossibly high above, their surfaces adorned with intricate frescos that depict, in vivid detail, the bloody and tumultuous history of vampire kind. Entering a room full of vampires is never a prospect one relishes, let alone the mere thought of stepping into a den belonging to the most formidable vampires in the region, those who occupy seats on the dreaded vampire council. Now that's the stuff of nightmares. It's time to gather all my courage, metaphorically don my big girl Panties, and face this storm head-on with unwavering resolve.

In the centre of this daunting room, the vampire elders are seated in a commanding semicircle, their ancient eyes fixed upon me with an intensity so fierce it could crush stone. Their regal presence and ageless elegance exude a raw, overwhelming power that demands nothing less than complete submission from any who dare to breach their hallowed domain. I step forward, each footfall echoing like thunder in the vast, cavernous void. As I position myself at the heart of the chamber, the suffocating weight of the council's scrutiny bears down on me with the ferocity of a tidal wave crashing against the shore. Their razor-sharp gazes pierce through to my very core, relentlessly hunting for any trace of frailty or deceit that might lurk within.

I stand tall, my shoulders a fortress against the relentless pressure, defying the crushing force of their eternal might. My mind remains laser-focused on my purpose, unwavering in their daunting presence. The memory of guiding Alisha through the remnants of her ravaged home serves as my anchor, a steadfast beacon amid the tempest of immortal eyes surrounding me. I hold onto this memory with every fibre of my being, allowing it to fortify my resolve as I prepare to confront the vampire council and ask for there aid.

I was acutely aware that each word, each carefully considered syllable, and every subtle inflexion in my voice held the potential to sway the outcome dramatically—either securing their much-needed favour or casting my hopes into a chasm of despair from which recovery might be impossible. The stakes felt as heavy as the silence that settled over the chamber, a silence that demanded both courage and precision.

"Esteemed members of the Vampire council," I began, my voice unwavering despite the swirling storm of nerves threatening to consume me from within. The grand chamber, dimly lit by flickering candlelight, cast long shadows that danced across the ancient stone walls. The air was thick with an air of solemnity and anticipation. "I come before you today with a matter of grave importance," I continued, my words echoing softly against the vaulted ceiling above.

The elders leaned forward slightly, their eyes narrowing with keen interest, piqued by my bold opening statement. Their robes rustled softly like leaves in a gentle breeze, and the air seemed to crackle with anticipation. I felt a flicker of hope ignite within my chest, a warm ember in the cold, solemn atmosphere of the chamber. Perhaps they would listen after all. I took a deep breath, gathering my thoughts, and prepared to lay bare the truth that had driven me to seek an audience in this hallowed chamber, its walls steeped in history and authority.

The fate of both human and paranormal worlds teetered on the edge of a knife, and I understood with crystal clarity that failure was simply not an option. Drawing a steadying breath, I resumed my address, my words ringing out through the vast chamber like a clarion call for justice and unity against an invisible foe lurking in the shadows.

CHAPTER 13

My voice resonated powerfully through the space as I laid out the grim details of the horrific murders that had cast a pall over the city. "In the past several months, a series of brutal killings has unfolded, claiming the lives of both humans and paranormals without discrimination. The victims have been discovered utterly drained of blood, their bodies mutilated in grotesque ways that suggest a level of savagery far surpassing mere feeding."

I paused, allowing the weight of my words to settle heavily in the room. The council members exchanged glances, their faces painted with concern and scepticism, brows furrowed and eyes darting from one to another. Yet, I pressed on, my resolve strengthened by the urgency to make them grasp the gravity of the situation.

"These murders," I began again, my voice firm and unwavering, "are not mere random acts of violence. They are a calculated assault on the very foundation of our society." I paused to let the words resonate, watching their expressions shift from doubt to unease. "The killer, or killers," I continued, "appear to be conducting macabre experiments with the victims' bodies, blurring the lines between human and paranormal in a way that threatens to expose our hidden world to the masses." The room was silent, the air heavy with the implications of such a revelation, as if the walls were straining to contain the tension within.

My eyes locked with those of the council leaders, my gaze steady and unflinching, piercing through the dimly lit chamber. the air thick with worry. "If we do not act now if we do not put aside our differences and work together to stop this looming threat, the consequences could be catastrophic. The delicate balance that has been meticulously maintained for centuries could be shattered, leading to chaos and destruction on an unimaginable scale. The very foundations of our society could crumble into ruins."

My words lingered in the hushed silence, the atmosphere heavy. The only sound was the soft rustling of robes—an almost imperceptible whisper—as the council members shifted uneasily in their ornate seats. My heart pounded like a war drum in my chest. Yet, I maintained my composure, my face a mask of determination, knowing that any flicker of weakness could undermine my urgent call for assistance.

The elders exchanged furtive glances, their aged eyes conveying a silent conversation, as a gentle murmur rippled among them like a soft wind stirring autumn leaves.

One council member, distinct with his silver hair that shimmered like moonlight and piercing blue eyes that seemed to see into one's soul, leaned forward. His brow was furrowed, etching deep lines of worry across his forehead. "While we understand the gravity of the situation, Miss Dyer," he began, his voice a smooth yet authoritative timbre, "we cannot simply ignore the potential consequences of involving ourselves in Agency affairs. Our community must remain our top priority."

His words carried an undercurrent of fear, a palpable anxiety that seemed to echo a deep-seated concern for the safety of his kin. I sensed this flicker of fear, a shadow of dread beneath his composed exterior. "I assure you," I responded, my voice steady and earnest, "we have no intention of jeopardising the well-being of your community. My goal is to protect all those who may be targeted, human and paranormal alike."

The council leader lifted a hand, a simple gesture that immediately silenced the low hum of murmurs filling the chamber. "And what of the balance of power?" he inquired, his voice a blend of caution and strategic deliberation. "The

CHAPTER 13

Agency has long been a persistent thorn in our side, an ever-present reminder of the fragile peace we strive to uphold, always eager to impose its regulations upon us. By aligning ourselves with you, we risk disturbing that delicate balance and inviting even more intense scrutiny."

My eyes narrowed, a sharp glint of resolve cutting through them as my posture straightened with unwavering determination. "With all due respect, the balance of power is already precariously perched on the edge. These murders, these grotesque experiments, they loom over us, threatening to rip apart the very fabric that holds our societies together. If we do not act decisively now, the repercussions will be far more devastating than any temporary disturbance. We are not asking you to place your trust in the Agency but rather in our mutual yearning for justice and safeguarding the innocent. We cannot shoulder this burden alone, but we stand a chance to stop this together."

The council spokesman leaned back in his seat, fingers steepled before him, a posture of contemplation as he carefully weighed his words. The room, dimly lit and filled with the scent of polished wood and old leather, fell silent. The air was tense, the gravity of the impending decision pressing heavily upon each person present.

Time seemed to stretch, every second an eternity in the tension-filled chamber. Finally, the spokesman broke the silence, his voice laden with resignation and solemnity. "Before I give you our decision, I have some questions for you."

"Okay, I will be happy to answer some questions," I said, unable to keep my voice steady and clear.

The spokesman's eyes narrowed, scrutinising, as he asked, "Am I correct in my information that you are the girl who was recovered in Ireland during that dragon rescue the agency took part in?" His gaze was intense, and there was a calculating glint in his eyes.

"Yes, you are right. I was rescued along with Lyn, but that is not why I am here," I answered, my voice calm and unwavering, though a hint of past trauma lingered in my voice.

"Interesting," he said, his voice a smooth, dark melody as he licked his lips, eyeing me like a predator sizing up its prey. It was as if I were a delectable morsel, tantalising and irresistible, waiting to be consumed. "I have only heard snippets of the things that happened to you while you were held there. I would love to get a firsthand account of your experiences," he continued, his eyes sparkling with a hunger that unsettled me.

I ground my teeth, struggling to suppress the biting retort clawing its way up my throat.

"Should I take your silence as a no?" he asked, his smirk barely concealed, a mocking curve of his lips that told me he was enjoying this little game.

"Very well," he conceded after a moment, his tone turning clipped and formal. "We have been appraised of the situation, but as it stands, we can't see why it concerns anyone from the vampire community. This council will not offer its support. We will not be beholden to the Agency any more than we already are, nor will we risk our own resources for the sake of this investigation." His words left me stunned, rendered speechless by their audacity. Could they truly be that blind, that foolish?

Before I could regain my composure, the council members rose as one, their movements synchronised like a well-rehearsed dance. They dissolved into the surrounding shadows, leaving me alone under the dim light. I struggled to reign in my fury, my breath coming in sharp bursts. The

CHAPTER 13

door through which I had entered creaked open on its own, and a chilling voice whispered in my ear, "I think it's time for you to leave."

As I exited the chamber with what little dignity I had left, I couldn't shake the feeling that they knew something more than they were letting on. Their actions were designed to provoke and distract me from the fact that they were terrified. I seethed inwardly, rushing toward the grand entrance, eager to slip into the car and escape before causing the Agency, a public relations debacle with the vampires.

Upon reaching the heavy oak doors, their dark wood polished to a gleaming finish, I was surprised to find a young woman, who appeared not much older than myself, lounging casually against the open doorway. Her posture was relaxed, and an air of nonchalance was surrounding her. In no mood to tolerate any more nonsense, I brushed past her, my focus solely on my escape. Unperturbed by my rudeness, she pushed herself away from the doorframe and began to walk alongside me as I hurried to the car, her presence almost ghostly in its quiet persistence.

"I'm Abigail," she announced, her movements a seamless blend of grace and authority, that would draw the gaze of everyone around her like moths to a flame. Her presence was akin to an exquisite dance, mesmerising and commanding attention. "Well, I'm sure that didn't unfold quite as you envisioned, your inaugural meeting with the Vampire Council of London." Her voice was laced with a playful amusement, a subtle hint of mischief devoid of malice. "Your speech was beautiful, delivered with such eloquence, if I might add. It elicited an emotional response, but they would never offer aid. Their true intent was simply to meet you and perhaps gather some leverage to use against you in the future. That was the purpose of the speaker's final comments; he wanted a negative reaction to hold against you." As we neared the car, its sleek body reflecting the shimmering light like a jewel, she paused, her insightful words hanging like an unfinished melody.

"But I must disagree with the council's stance on this matter."

Her words carried a weight that seemed to hang in the air, like a dense fog refusing to dissipate, demanding to be heard. "These murders and the suspected experiments pose a dire threat not only to the human world but to all of us in the supernatural community. I could not forgive myself if I stood idly by and allowed this to continue unchecked."

Abigail's voice grew more passionate, her conviction burning as she continued. Each word dripped with the intensity of her resolve. "We cannot afford to hide in the shadows any longer, content with maintaining the status quo. The time has come for us to emerge from the darkness and take decisive action, to unite against this common enemy and protect those who cannot protect themselves. To that end, I offer my assistance to you, not as a mere council member but as a determined ally in this fight. I hope we can uncover the truth behind these atrocities and bring those responsible to justice."

Her eyes shone with determination as if fuelled by an inner fire, and the air seemed to pulse with her fervour.

I felt an overwhelming surge of gratitude toward Abigail, sensing the deep sincerity in her words and the unwavering strength of her resolve. Her presence was like a steadfast beacon in a storm.

"Thank you for your support," I said, my voice tinged with a sudden fear. Are you sure you can offer to assist me if the council has already refused to help?" I asked, suddenly worried that this mischievous young woman might face

CHAPTER 13

punishment if she followed through on her bold declaration of assistance.

"Oh, it's fine. I usually do what I want anyway," she replied nonchalantly, her voice carrying a hint of defiance. "So, should we be heading off? I believe you have an appointment with the dragons next, and they tend to get grumpy if they are kept waiting." She declared boldly, flashing me a toothy grin that revealed the sharp tips of her fangs as she eagerly jumped into the passenger seat.

Without further argument, I gave in, my thoughts racing as I slid behind the wheel. I drove as fast as I could, the tires crunching over the gravel as we sped out of the vampire compound. The world outside blurred into a tapestry of shadow and light.

CHAPTER 14

Dragon's Keep

As I ponder the lessons on the various factions imparted to me by Alex, I recall his words vividly. "Dragons, like many other beings within the supernatural community, possess the unique ability to blend in with humans seamlessly," he had explained. "Lyn is among the most formidable dragons I've encountered in recent times. You might remember that in her true dragon form, she can easily dwarf a house. However, she is far from the oldest or largest of her kind. Legends speak of ancient dragons as colossal as mountains themselves. Generally, though, the dragons you might come across would be approximately the size of one or two double-decker buses. We rarely interact with them, and when we do, they usually take on a human guise."

These memories replay as I follow the satellite navigation directions to my next appointment. My new vampire companion sits beside me, humming softly to herself, while I focus intensely on the road ahead.

"You have now reached your destination," announced the sat nav, jolting me from my wandering thoughts as I eased the car to a halt at the curb. It took a moment for the scene before me to sink in, and I couldn't help but chuckle at the absurdity. This had to be a joke. We were supposed to meet at a quaint, old-style pub named the Dragon's Keep. The very name tickled my sense of humour—who would have guessed that dragons possessed such a whimsical side? Abigail exited the car with a casual grace, and I joined her at the pub's entrance.

The door was made of sturdy, dark wood, and its upper portion was adorned with an intricate inlay of stained glass. The design depicted a fierce dragon's head surrounded in vivid flames. The light spilling from within the pub gave the illusion of the flames flickering magically, as though they were alive and ready to leap from the glass.

As I pushed the door open, a wave of warm air enveloped me, carrying rich scents of roasting meat, aromatic spices, and an elusive, tantalising aroma that whispered mysteries yet to be uncovered. For a brief moment, conversations quieted as the patrons turned their eyes to the newcomer, assessing the strangers in their midst. Yet, I paid them no mind, my attention sweeping the shadowy recesses of the Dragon's Keep, seeking any potential threat. To my relief, nothing alarming presented itself, and the pub appeared to be an ordinary, everyday bar.

Abigail brushed past me with a nonchalance that suggested nothing out of the ordinary, and we proceeded inside. We were quickly approached by a waitress who seemed somewhat dishevelled, asking if it was just the two of us at our party. However, before I could respond, a tall, ruggedly handsome man interjected smoothly, "It's okay, Mona. These lovely ladies will be joining me in the corner booth."

"Gudmundur! I didn't see you there," she exclaimed with a surprised squeal. "I'll escort your guests to your usual table, sir. This way, please, ladies." With that, the waitress,

Mona set off briskly, her movements purposeful as she gestured for us to follow her through the throng of patrons. We wove through the lively pub, finally at a secluded

CHAPTER 14

corner booth. This spot was tucked away from the main bustle, offering a sense of privacy and an air of nostalgia, as if countless stories and secrets had been shared over the years. The booth featured a cosy wrap-around couch seating arrangement that provided a commanding view of the entire venue. From this vantage point, I could easily see all the exits and potential escape routes, a subtle indication that this dragon was revealing the vulnerabilities of his domain. This knowledge could be crucial if our conversation took a turn for the worse, much like my previous encounter with the vampires, which had not ended how I would've liked. Dealing with dragons would likely present similar challenges.

Gudmundur settled in next to Abigail, and their familiarity was palpable. It was as if they shared a history, a bond that was somewhat unsettling given the longstanding enmity I had heard existed between vampires and dragons. Their unexpected camaraderie made me uneasy, adding a layer of tension to the already charged atmosphere.

"Ms. Dyer," Gudmundur's voice resonated deeply, cutting through the ambient noise like a knife through butter. His tone was authoritative, commanding attention as he gestured to the seat across from him with a strong, calloused hand, inviting me to join them.

I slid into the booth, the aged leather groaning softly under my weight. With the dragon so close, I could feel the intensity of his golden eyes as they bore into me, examining and evaluating every aspect of my being. Gudmundur, with his centuries of knowledge and experience, likely saw my existence as nothing more than a fleeting moment, a mere blink of an eye in his long life. Here, in his place of power, surrounded by his element, the disparity in our positions was impossible to ignore.

As I leaned back, I consciously tried to maintain a neutral expression, even though my heart was racing, pounding a staccato rhythm in my chest. Showing any sign of weakness to someone like Gudmundur was not an option. While the Agency had its own formidable reputation, manoeuvring through these treacherous political waters demanded different strength.

I met Gudmundur's ancient gaze with unwavering eyes, determined not to let the weight of his scrutiny break my resolve. His eyes held the wisdom of centuries, and I felt the challenge of matching their intensity. "Thank you for agreeing to meet on such short notice," I began, carefully modulating my tone to convey a sense of polite professionalism. "I understand your time must be exceedingly valuable, and I appreciate you making room for this discussion."

Gudmundur's lip curled ever so slightly, revealing a hint of fang that glinted ominously in the room's dim light. "The Agency does not make social calls," he growled, his voice gravelly and ancient, like stones grinding together. "Should I presume this meeting pertains to the recent, unexplained murders that have been occurring around London, causing quite a stir among both the human and supernatural communities?"

I folded my hands on the rough-hewn surface of the table, the wood worn and scarred from countless past meetings. It was clear that Gudmundur was not one for small talk, which suited me perfectly, as I wasn't either. "Yes," I confirmed, my voice steady and deliberate. "We have reason to suspect that there may be supernatural involvement in these incidents. The Agency has offered resources and expertise to assist the human authorities in their investigation, hoping to shed light on these troubling events..."

CHAPTER 14

As I delved into the details, outlining the patterns and peculiarities of the recent crimes, I couldn't shake the persistent feeling that this was merely the opening gambit in a much larger, more dangerous game—one whose players had yet to reveal themselves fully and whose stakes were far higher than any of us could comprehend.

Gudmundur's gaze flickered momentarily to Abigail, who sat quietly, a brief flash of amusement crossing his chiselled, ancient features. I leaned forward, my elbows resting firmly on the table as I gauged the reactions of both Abigail and Gudmundur. "Your insights would be invaluable," I continued, scrutinising how he responded to my words. "As the dragons' representative, your unique perspective could illuminate aspects of this situation that we may have overlooked or misunderstood in our preliminary assessments."

Abigail's lips gracefully curve into a smile, a gesture that somehow manages to be inviting and unsettling. She maintains her silence, observing the unfolding scene with a palpable sense of enjoyment, her eyes dancing with curiosity and intrigue.

"Of course," he says with a measured tone, "the Dragon Council is concerned about the ramifications of these crimes. If a supernatural element is at play, we must resolve it swiftly and efficiently." His words carry an air of authority, underscoring the gravity of the situation.

As the conversation progresses, I find myself captivated by the intricate dance of linguistic sparring unfolding before me. Each word spoken, each subtle gesture exchanged, holds a significance that stretches far beyond the present dialogue. I am acutely aware that the assistance the dragons offer may come at a price higher than I am willing to pay, and the decisions made today could have far-reaching repercussions for both the human and supernatural realms.

Yet, even as I navigate this discussion's complex and treacherous currents, my mind races with a myriad of questions. What secrets are concealed within Gudmundur's stoic demeanour? What hidden agendas might Abigail be discreetly pursuing beneath her enigmatic smile? And most pressingly, how can I untangle the intricate web of this mystery before more innocent lives are lost to its dark depths?

I understand that the answers I seek will not come quickly or without significant effort. But as I sit at this table, facing two formidable powerhouses from the supernatural world, I feel a flicker of determination ignite. Regardless of the cost, I am resolute in my mission to see this through. For the sake of the victims, for the sake of the innocent lives hanging in the balance, I will not rest until the truth is brought to light and justice is served.

Abigail leaned forward with a poised grace, her elegant fingers forming a steeple beneath her chin as she gathered her thoughts. "If I may," she began, her melodic voice effortlessly slicing through the thick, smoky air that filled the room. "The patterns of these gruesome murders suggest a level of savagery that transcends mere human brutality. The nature of the wounds inflicted, the sheer ferocity of the attacks... these are not the acts of a human being. Rather, they bear the unmistakable hallmarks of a creature driven by an insatiable hunger that knows no bounds."

As I listened to Abigail, my eyes narrowed slightly, reflecting on the implications of her words. As a vampire with centuries of experience, her insights aligned disturbingly well with my growing suspicions. Despite myself, I couldn't help but harbour a grudging respect for her analytical prowess and her ability to piece together the macabre puzzle with such clarity. "You think it's a

CHAPTER 14

Wendigo," Gudmundur stated, his voice carrying more of an affirmation than a question, as if he, too, had reached the same chilling conclusion.

Abigail nodded thoughtfully, her gaze shifting between me and Gudmundur, her expression grave. "It's a possibility we cannot afford to ignore," she replied, her voice steady yet filled with an underlying urgency. "The escalating nature of the attacks, the horrific manner in which the bodies were... consumed. All these factors point decisively to a creature that feeds on human flesh and grows stronger with each life it takes."

Gudmundur's face darkened, his brow furrowing deeply as he pondered the grave implications of Abigail's analysis. "If a Wendigo is indeed responsible for these murders," he said, his voice heavy with concern, "then we are not merely dealing with a simple murder investigation. We are confronting a threat of a far more sinister nature. The creature's hunger is insatiable, and with every new victim, it will only grow in power, becoming more formidable and more difficult to stop. We must act swiftly and decisively before it becomes unstoppable."

As I absorb the information, my mind races with the potential ramifications of what I've just learned. I had never heard of Wendigo's before, and now the weight of this knowledge is beginning to press down on me.

"I have seen the results of Wendigo attacks before," Abigail says, her voice tinged with the gravity of past encounters. "Although the victims all exhibit injuries that confirm their presence, the behaviour is disturbingly wrong. The devastation these creatures can wreak if left unchecked is truly staggering. Just one of them could devastate an entire town within a matter of weeks, yet all your evidence points to this happening over the span of several months." Abigail and Gudmundur thoroughly briefed me on what to expect from a Wendigo. Despite my reluctance to acknowledge it, they were right. The mere thought of such a creature prowling the city streets, hunting unsuspecting victims, sends an icy shiver down my spine.

"We need to act quickly," I declare, my voice brimming with urgency and determination. "If we don't stop this creature, the body count will continue to rise. And with each kill, the risk of exposure increases exponentially. We cannot afford to let this situation spiral out of control." I then shift all my attention to Gudmundur, hoping to convey the seriousness of my request. "I came here today to ask for your assistance, whether in manpower or information. I am willing to accept whatever help you can provide," I say, striving to project confidence with each carefully chosen word.

He nods in agreement, his eyes glinting with a predatory intensity that suggests he's already several steps ahead in his calculations. "I have contacts in the city," he begins, his voice smooth yet carrying an undercurrent of authority. "Informants who can help us track the creature's movements. But what do I get in return if I choose to help you?" His voice takes on a demanding tone, leaving no room for negotiation.

I can feel the immense weight of responsibility settling heavily upon my shoulders, like an invisible mantle I never asked for. Every decision I make in this dimly lit room could very well mean the difference between life and death for countless innocent people out there, unaware of the looming threat.

Yet, even as the task's enormity looms like a dark cloud, I feel a flicker of determination igniting within my chest, a small flame that refuses to be extinguished. I've faced impossible odds before, stared down horrors that would

CHAPTER 14

shatter the resolve of lesser souls. seen things that would make others cower in fear, and I'll be damned if I let this creature—a twisted manifestation of hunger and violence—claim even one more victim without a fight. "Name what it is that you want," I say, my voice steady despite the tumult of emotions swirling inside me.

"You will owe me a favour of my choice when this is dealt with," he declares, his words like a binding contract as if already savouring the control he would wield over me in the future.

I imagine what he might ask of me, but at that moment, it doesn't matter; the situation's urgency outweighs any future consequences. We desperately need his help. "Okay, I will owe you a favour, as long as it is within my power, doesn't require me to harm myself or anyone I care about, and isn't illegal," I say with an air of finality, laying down the terms of our agreement.

"I agree with your terms," he says, his voice rumbling with a deep growl of satisfaction as though he has just secured a prize.

With a resolute nod to Gudmundur and Abigail, I steel myself for the battles to come, feeling the adrenaline course through my veins like a river of fire. "Let's get to work," I say, my voice ringing with newfound resolve. "We have a monster to hunt, and it's time we end its reign of terror."

Gudmundur clears his throat with a deliberate cough, drawing my attention back to him. "There's something else you should know," he begins, his voice low and imbued with a sense of gravity that makes the air feel heavier. "I am not certain if this is directly connected, but we've received numerous reports about multiple facilities where humans are allegedly being held captive. The rumour is that these individuals are subjected to horrific and unethical experiments."

My heart lurches violently in my chest, a wave of cold dread seeping through my veins like ice water. "What kind of experiments are we talking about?" I ask, almost whispering, afraid that saying it too loudly will make it more real. I brace myself for an answer I'm unsure I'm ready to hear.

Gudmundur's jaw clenches tightly, his eyes darkening with a barely contained fury that seems to make the room grow dimmer. "The specifics are still unclear," he admits with frustration edging his voice, "but from what we've managed to gather so far, it appears they are attempting to harness supernatural abilities within humans—an endeavour both dangerous and morally reprehensible."

My mind reels as it processes this information, the implications swirling around chaotically until the puzzle pieces click into place with a sickening clarity. The missing people, the savage attacks by the Wendigo... could it all be pointing to a far more sinister plot than I had initially suspected? Or am I merely drawing connections where there are none?

"I think we need to locate these facilities," I say, my voice trembling with a potent mix of horror and determination. "If they truly exist and are indeed connected to everything that has been happening, we have to shut them down and rescue the victims before we find any more bodies or before anything worse happens." My resolve hardens as I speak, feeling the weight of the responsibility pressing down on me, knowing that action is our only option.

Abigail gently extends her hand, placing it reassuringly on Jessica's arm. "We absolutely will," she affirms with a voice brimming with steadfast determination. "By harnessing the

CHAPTER 14

combined might of the Agency and the dragon's formidable power, we'll put an end to this insanity and ensure those responsible are brought to justice."

As the gravity of this revelation sinks in, we find ourselves enveloped in a profound silence, each of us immersed in our own thoughts. My mind whirls with various strategies and backup plans, the drive to take immediate action clashing with the necessity for meticulous planning. The duality of urgency and caution is a constant struggle.

Yet there is one undeniable truth: I am resolute in my mission, even if these facilities are not directly linked to the current case. I will not find peace until every single victim is liberated and those who have orchestrated these heinous acts are held accountable. Regardless of the cost, no matter the peril, I am committed to seeing this mission through to its conclusion.

In a world where the distinction between human and supernatural becomes increasingly blurred, where the essence of reality is at risk, I am responsible for confronting the darkness and championing the cause of light. The weight of our conversation lingers heavily as I rise from my seat, my gaze shifting between Gudmundur and Abigail in contemplation. "Thank you both for your time and cooperation," I say, my voice maintaining steadiness despite the turbulent thoughts in my mind. "I deeply appreciate your willingness to collaborate on this matter."

Gudmundur nods slightly, his eyes reflecting a blend of respect and wariness. "We all have a significant stake in this, Agent Dyer. It is in the best interest of everyone involved to ensure that this threat is effectively neutralised.»

I nod slowly, a faint smile briefly touching my lips, conveying a sense of determination. "Rest assured, I'll contact you soon with any information I uncover. In the meantime, do be careful and watch your back out there. It's a dangerous world."

As I turn away to leave, my mind is already racing ahead at full speed, meticulously strategising the upcoming steps in the investigation. The abandoned facilities, the mysterious disappearances, the ongoing murder investigation, and the possibility of a Wendigo—all these elements of the puzzle seem intricately connected, pointing towards an even more sinister truth lurking just beneath the visible surface.

I carefully weave through the eclectic mix of patrons gathered in the Dragon's Keep, my senses heightened and alert. The air is dense with smoke, exotic spices, and a distinctly otherworldly scent, serving as a constant reminder of the hidden world that exists parallel to mundane, everyday life.

Reaching the door, I pause momentarily, glancing back over my shoulder. Gudmundur and Abigail remain seated at the table, their heads bowed together in a quiet, intense conversation. For a fleeting moment, I allow myself to feel a flicker of hope. With their combined knowledge and resources, we could unravel this complex mystery before it's too late. Yet, even as this thought crosses my mind, a shiver runs down my spine. In this unpredictable life, hope is a perilous thing. It's all too easy to lower your guard, to believe that with enough determination and grit, the monsters can be beaten back.

No, I can't afford to become complacent. Not now, not ever. The only way to survive in this unpredictable world is to stay one step ahead and place trust in nothing and no one but your instincts.

With a final, resolute nod to myself, I step out into the crisp, fresh air, the weight of the investigation settling over me like a heavy shroud. The game is truly on now, and I swear I'll be damned if I let the bad guys win.

CHAPTER 14

The cool, invigorating air washes over me as I step onto the old cobblestone street, offering a welcome escape from the suffocating atmosphere of the Dragon's Keep. I pause for a moment, drawing a deep breath as the crisp, clean scent of the city fills my lungs and clears the fog from my mind.

The streets are unnervingly quiet everywhere around me—London's usual chaos and familiar bustle replaced by a silence that hangs as though the entire city is holding its breath, anxiously awaiting the next move in this perilous game of chess.

As I continue to walk, my thoughts race. Every new revelation from the meeting spins through my mind like the twists of a Rubik's cube, desperately seeking the pattern that will finally make sense of it all. The hidden facilities, the disturbing involvement of a Wendigo, and the volatile balance of power among supernatural factions blend into an overwhelming, dizzying storm of questions and possibilities.

I reach into my pocket and retrieve my car key. After unlocking the car and preparing to climb in, I'm suddenly startled by a bright voice cutting through the silence.

"Jess, wait for us! We've decided to stick with you," calls out Abigail in her cheerfully insistent tone.

Startled, I turn to see both Abigail and Gudmundur rapidly catching up to me. "What?" I exclaim, as their presence makes itself immediately known.

Abigail lets out a sigh tinged with frustration before explaining, "We promised to help you, so we're sticking together. It'll save us from the constant back-and-forth of relaying messages, which means you'll have backup when needed."

Gudmundur responds with a deep, approving grunt, his silent affirmation leaving no room for doubt.

Clearing my throat, I ask, "Alright, what's the first step?" I plan to send them off on one task while managing another independently.

"We all agreed it would be a good idea to visit the most recent crime scene," Abigail replies hesitantly.

I nod slowly. "I agree—seeing the site up close should provide us with the insight we need. But we can't head there just yet. I have to return to the Agency to get updates from the team and check in on Alisha first. And before either of you even considers going ahead of me, remember that you don't have clearance, and I can't risk the complications of any unauthorised personal entering an active crime scene. You have a choice: stay here until I contact you when I've wrapped things up, or accompany me as I handle these basic tasks."

Exchanging a look of resolute understanding, Abigail and Gudmundur nodded and said in unison, "We'll stay with you."

CHAPTER 15

Chaos at the Agency

Driving back to the agency was quite the fascinating experience. The atmosphere in the car was lively, with the vampire and dragon in my back seat behaving like a couple of teenage girls, caught up in a whirlwind of gossiping and giggling. Well, to be precise, Gudmundur didn't exactly giggle. He was more of a belly-laugh kind of guy, with a laugh so infectious it could fill the whole car, which was extremely annoying because it kept ruining my hard-ass image every time it coaxed a smile from me. As we approached the agency, I noticed police car parked at the front of the building, their lights flashing ominously. It was an unusual sight that instantly heightened my curiosity and concern. I manoeuvred my car into a spot right next to the police vehicles and quickly rushed up the front steps, my heart pounding with anticipation. As I got closer, the sound of raised voices grew louder, echoing through the hallway. "What the fuck is happening now?" I muttered under my breath, my mind racing with possibilities as I hurried inside to uncover the source of the commotion. What I found was Detective Duncan Lancaster, his face flushed a deep ruddy hue, standing mere inches from Mini's face. His meaty finger jabbed the air aggressively as he shouted, his voice booming through the space. Flanking him were representatives from child services, their expressions steeped in disapproval, brows furrowed and lips pursed in a clear display of discontent.

My eyes were instantly drawn to the sight of Alisha, the small, frightened girl huddled alone in the corner, clutching a worn-out teddy bear with her tiny arms. Her hazel eyes were wide open, brimming with fear, and tears cascaded down her pale cheeks like a sorrowful river. The sight gripped my heart with a fierce pang of emotion, threatening to crush it under the weight of helplessness and anger.

Propelled by an unwavering instinct to protect, I moved decisively towards her, positioning myself firmly between Alisha and the menacing trio that loomed threateningly. I straightened to my full height, squaring my shoulders with determination, my eyes blazing with a fierce wrath. My gaze locked onto Lancaster with an intensity that could cut through steel.

"Someone better tell me what the hell is going on here. Now," I demanded, my voice low and charged with danger, each word articulated with a chilling precision that left no room for defiance or delay.

Mini, standing nearby, turned her attention towards me, her face a canvas of relief as the tension eased from her delicate features. "Jess, thank the gods you're here," she exclaimed, her voice a mixture of gratitude and urgency. "They're trying to take Alisha away!"

Lancaster groaned audibly, clearly not wanting the situation to escalate any further. "This is official police business," he insisted, his voice carrying a note of authority meant to quell any objections. "The girl is a key witness in an ongoing investigation, and since she has no guardian on record, she needs to go with child services."

My hands clenched tightly into fists at my sides, rage simmering hotly in my veins. Like hell they were taking

CHAPTER 15

Alisha anywhere. Not as long as I was here to stand in their way.

I took a deliberate, menacing step toward the detective, making full use of every inch of my athletic frame to overshadow him with my presence. "I wasn't asking, Lancaster. I'm telling you," I declared firmly, leaving no room for argument. "Alisha stays with us. End of story."

The representatives from child services shifted uneasily where they stood, clearly sensing the threat in my posture and the unwavering determination in my eyes. "Now see here, miss," one of them began, his voice wavering slightly. "This is highly irregular..."

"You know what else is irregular?" I interrupted him sharply, my voice rising with passion and urgency. "A little girl, scared out of her mind, with no one looking out for her best interests. That ends now."

I turned to face them fully, locking eyes with each of them in turn, fire blazing in my gaze, daring any one of them to challenge my resolve. I stood there, unyielding, a protective force that would not be swayed or intimidated by titles or procedures. My stance was clear: Alisha was not going anywhere without a fight.

Mini gently placed a soothing hand on my arm, her voice calm and steady. "Let's all take a deep breath," she suggested, hoping to diffuse the tension in the room. "I'm confident we can reach a solution that ensures Alisha's safety while allowing us all to fulfil our responsibilities."

However, my patience had worn thin. These people had no comprehension of the perils Alisha faced. They couldn't possibly grasp the trauma she had endured. I was determined to protect her, even if it meant confronting the flames of hell itself. No one would harm Alisha as long as I stood by her side.

"This isn't up for negotiation," I declared firmly, turning my attention back to Lancaster. It took all my strength to maintain control over the fury simmering within me. "Now get them out," I ordered, my voice unwavering. "Before I take matters into my own hands and throw them out myself."

Lancaster's face flushed with anger, his jaw tightening as he took a step towards me. "I will address the concerns with child services, Dyer," he said, his voice firm. "But I have every right to be here, and I refuse to be cowed by your threats." With that, he led the child services personnel out of the building.

Once they were out of sight, I stepped back from Alisha, allowing Mini to approach her and try to calm her nerves. everything felt quieter now, though the tension lingered in the air like a thick fog.

It was at that very moment that I became aware of the sound of heavy footsteps resonating ominously through the corridor, immediately capturing my attention. The imposing figure of Aldrich the head London branch soon appeared, his demeanour a complex amalgamation of frustration and concern as he made his way toward me with purposeful strides. I instinctively braced myself for the confrontation that seemed inevitable, every muscle in my body tensing in anticipation as I prepared to defend the actions I had taken.

"Dyer, what the hell is going on here?" Aldrich demanded in a voice that was both low and terse, yet carried a weight of authority. "I've got Detective Lancaster outside trying to calm down child services personnel who are, as I understand it, threatening to unleash the full power of their department upon us, and you appear to be right at the centre of this entire mess."

I did not waver as I met his gaze directly, my voice steady and composed, yet imbued with a firmness that conveyed

CHAPTER 15

my conviction. "Sir, I had no choice but to intervene. They were planning to take Alisha away, to place her into a system that is utterly incapable of comprehending or protecting her unique needs. She's already endured more than enough hardship and pain."

Aldrich let out a weary sigh, running a hand over his face as if trying to wipe away the stress of the situation. "I understand where you're coming from, Dyer. Believe me, I do. But we can't just go around making threats against government personnel. There are protocols in place, procedures that we are obligated to follow, no matter how flawed they may seem."

"With all due respect, sir, there are times when those established protocols simply don't account for the harsh realities we encounter on the ground." I shifted my gaze towards Alisha, who had quietly retreated to a nearby chair, clutching Mini, her small form hunched protectively over a stuffed animal she had managed to obtain. Alisha was not just another case; she was unique and vulnerable. "Alisha is a special case," I reiterated. "She requires our protection, our guidance, and our understanding. To send her away now would be a grave mistake, one that could have significant repercussions."

Aldrich followed my gaze, his stern expression softening slightly as he observed the frightened child in the corner. His eyes lingered on Alisha, and I could see the subtle shift in his demeanour. "And you believe you're the person who can offer her what she needs? Especially after everything that's just transpired?"

"Absolutely not," I replied with a firm shake of my head. "But Mini, is an excellent empath. In this moment, I truly believe Mini will be better equipped to look after Alisha than any governmental institution that would dismiss her experiences as mere hallucinations." I spoke with unwavering conviction, knowing the gravity of my words. "We, here at the agency, understand what she's enduring, the challenges she will inevitably face. We possess the capability to help her navigate this daunting new reality, to shield her from those who might seek to exploit the trauma she has endured."

I paused deliberately, drawing a deep, steadying breath before continuing my plea. "However, we cannot fulfil this duty if she is taken away from us. We must keep her here, within the safe confines of the agency's care. It's the only viable way to guarantee her safety and well-being, to ensure that she receives the support she desperately needs."

Aldrich pondered my words, allowing the seconds to stretch into an almost unbearable silence. I felt the heavy weight of his gaze upon me, sensing the judgment and evaluation swirling in his eyes. I was acutely aware that my future with the agency was precariously hanging in the balance, yet I stood resolute, unwilling to back down. Not when Alisha's future and her well-being were at stake.

Finally, Aldrich began to speak, his voice calm and carefully controlled, each word meticulously chosen. "Alright, Dyer. I'll place my trust in your judgment on this matter. However, let me make one thing crystal clear: your team will bear the full responsibility for ensuring the girl's safety. Any mistakes, any additional incidents that might occur, and the blame will fall squarely on your shoulders."

I nodded solemnly, feeling a profound sense of relief wash over me, like a wave crashing onto the shore. "Understood, sir. I promise, I won't let you down. I won't let Alisha down."

As Aldrich turned his attention to managing the consequences of my actions, I allowed myself a brief moment

CHAPTER 15

to exhale deeply, to fully grasp the enormity of the task that lay before me. I was acutely aware that it wouldn't be easy, that the path ahead would be riddled with challenges and potential dangers lurking at every turn.

Yet, when I glanced at Alisha, at the spark of hope shimmering in her eyes like a beacon, I felt reassured that I was making the right decision. We would become her protectors, her guides through this uncharted territory, the steadfast anchor Alisha so desperately needed in this chaotic and unpredictable new world. Together, we would confront whatever obstacles lay in our path, advancing one determined step at a time.

***

The door slams shut with a resounding thud, echoing through the secure meeting room as I usher my team inside, urgency crackling in the air like static electricity. Gudmundur's massive frame dominates the space, his imposing presence casting long shadows on the walls, his skin shimmering ominously under the harsh, unforgiving glare of the fluorescent lights. Abigail enters with a near ethereal grace, her movements fluid and precise, her eyes piercing and calculating, as if she is a warrior readying herself for battle.

I lean against the edge of the large table, its polished surface cool beneath my fingers, which tap out a relentless urgent rhythm mirroring the tension that grips us all. "We don't have much time," I declare, my voice taut with urgency and tension, each word carefully measured and weighted with the gravity of our situation. "The police's temporary distraction with Alisha's case grants us a brief window of opportunity, and we must act swiftly."

Gudmundur nods, his deep voice rumbling through the room like distant thunder, a sound that seems to reverberate off the walls. "The disappearances and murders are escalating at a terrifying rate. If we don't contain this threat immediately, the risk of exposure explodes exponentially," he warns, his expression grave, filled with the knowledge of the looming danger.

"And with exposure comes chaos," Abigail interjects, her tone laced with grim determination, her words slicing through the air like a finely honed blade. "The fragile balance we've fought so hard to preserve could shatter in an instant, unraveling everything we've worked for."

My mind races frantically, stitching together fragments of information, trying to make sense of the chaos: the potential presence of wendigos on the loose, the chilling trail of gruesome murders, the disappearances that seem to defy logic, the whispers of something ancient and malevolent stirring, lurking in the shadows, ready to unleash havoc upon an unsuspecting world.

"We need to find the source," I say, my voice steady, my eyes hardening with determination as I meet the gaze of each team member. "This isn't just a rogue wendigo. There's something else at play here, something bigger, more insidious, that threatens to consume everything if we don't act decisively and with precision."

Gudmundur leans forward intently, his brow deeply furrowed with concern. "I suspect there is a darker force lurking behind these recent attacks. An entity with enough power and malevolence to control and direct the wendigo's relentless and insatiable hunger," he speculates, his voice tinged with unease.

A shiver runs down my spine at the very thought of such a formidable enemy. The idea of an adversary capable of manipulating such a terrifying creature as a weapon poses an enormous threat to us all.

CHAPTER 15

"Then our investigation must begin there," I declare with determination, my voice ringing with firm authority and resolve. "We must carefully trace the wendigo's movements, looking for any discernible patterns or clues that might lead us to whoever or whatever is orchestrating these attacks from the shadows."

Abigail's eyes gleam with a predatory light, filled with both excitement and determination. "I have contacts within the city's shadowy underworld," she reveals. "They might have overheard whispers in the dark or sensed a shift in the delicate balance of power."

I nodded slowly in acknowledgment, a meticulously detailed plan starting to take shape in my mind as every detail of the situation mapped itself out with precision. "Gudmundur," I began in a calm yet commanding tone, "I need you to reach out to your contacts within the Dragon Council immediately and ascertain whether they've pieced together any fresh intelligence, any nuanced insights that might prove useful down the line. And Abigail, please mobilise your network of contacts, but do so with the utmost discretion—we simply cannot afford to reveal our hand too soon."

I paused, ensuring everyone fully grasped the gravity of our task, before continuing with quiet determination. "As you both follow up on these leads, I'm going to head back to the most recent crime scene to search for any previously overlooked clues—is it still your wish to inspect the scene with me?" Their silent nods of agreement confirmed that we were all on the same page.

Turning my attention to another crucial detail, I pressed on, "Mini, I need you to proceed with extreme caution alongside Alisha. Should you uncover any promising leads—no matter how faint—they must be relayed to me immediately, too much is riding on this investigation." With that, the air was thick with resolve as each one of us rose and set off to pursue our respective leads with determined urgency.

After orchestrating these initial movements, I instructed Gudmundur and Abigail to wait in the conference room. Stepping outside, I sought a moment of privacy to speak with Mini about Alisha. Once we were well clear of potential prying ears, I inquired softly yet firmly, "What have you managed to glean from our new guests? Anything of substance?"

Mini's eyes flickered with a mixture of curiosity and caution. "They're controlling their emotions very well," she reported, "but there have been a few subtle slips. From what I can tell, at times they seem to find you amusing, and they're clearly intrigued by the way you react. I don't sense any intention to cause you harm—in fact, it almost feels as though they have some sort of intention to protect you."

Her words echoed in my mind, prompting a cascade of perplexed thoughts: "What? Why would they want to protect me?" I recalled my earlier assumptions—surely the dragon breed would have been all too eager to see my downfall, and the vampires' behaviour left me baffled. Yet, such mysteries could only be unraveled in their time. "Mini," I continued, my voice now edged with a note of urgency, "I need you to work very closely with Alisha. Dig deep for any details, especially any clues pointing to why someone might target her family or shed any light on the nature of the attack."

Concluding our private exchange, Mini returned to Alisha, and the two settled into a serious discussion, their heads together over the details. Once more, I made my way back to the conference room to assemble my two new allies. The moment I entered, a heavy and eerie silence descended,

CHAPTER 15

as if the room itself were holding its breath. Locking eyes with them, I declared, "I know that you two are up to something. I'm not entirely sure what it is, and frankly, I'm not overly concerned with the details—as long as you promise not to hinder this investigation. If you can share your assistance in making sure no more lives are needlessly lost, then we are on the same side." In response, they exchanged a fleeting yet significant glance. After a moment of charged silence, Abigail finally spoke up, "We will assist you—but on one condition: once this case is resolved, you must sit down with us. There is so much we need to discuss with you."

Inside, I exhaled a long sigh and mused silently, "Great, another headache I didn't need right now." Yet, resolution steeled my tone as I replied, "Alright, deal—case first, then you both can have your say. For now, I'm heading back to the Silvers' home; I'm convinced there's something there we're missing."

CHAPTER 16

Return to the Silver Residence

Pulling up to the Silvers' house and seeing the bright yellow police tape fluttering in the breeze, along with the stationary patrol car parked prominently in the driveway, twisted my stomach into knots. A sense of dread settled over me as I stepped out of my vehicle. I approached the officer standing guard at the perimeter to present my credentials, preparing to explain my presence. However, before I could even reach into my pocket, the officer nodded, indicating he had already been informed of my arrival. I turned to gesture for Gudmundur and Abigail, to join me as I prepared to enter the scene.

With a deep breath, I ducked under the cordoned-off area and opened the door to the house. The moment I stepped inside, I was hit by an overpowering, nauseating stench—a stale smell of dried blood intermingled with the acrid scent of fear. It was as though the air itself was thick with terror, wrapping around me like an invisible shroud, and sending an involuntary shiver down my spine. The atmosphere within the living area was oppressive, almost as if the emotions of fear and panic had solidified into a palpable force that assaulted each of my senses relentlessly.

Behind me, Gudmundur and Abigail began their meticulous survey of the home. They moved cautiously, taking great care not to disturb any potential evidence, yet their eyes were sharp, absorbing every detail with practiced precision. Their presence was reassuring, their expertise evident in every step they took. "Call out anything you see as you see it," I instructed them, my voice cutting through the thick silence of the room. "I'm assuming you have both done this sort of thing before." I received a couple of affirmative grunts in response, confirming their familiarity with such grim scenes.

Before we divided to cover more ground and continued our investigation, Abigail paused, a thoughtful expression crossing her face that suggested she was deep in contemplation. "Where was Alisha found?" she inquired, her question hanging in the air like a mystery waiting to be solved. It struck me as peculiar because I was quite certain I had previously informed them of Alisha's exact location. She had been discovered in the wine cellar, cowering in fear and brandishing a knife in a desperate attempt to protect herself from whatever threat she perceived. The image of her, trembling and terrified, was still vivid in my mind. "She was in the wine cellar," I replied, my curiosity piqued by her unexpected inquiry. "Why do you ask?"

Abigail's gaze turned more intent as she explained, "I'm picking up her scent. From what I'm smelling, she ran to the cellar when she heard the sirens from the police approaching the scene." Her observation was intriguing and added a new layer to the unfolding mystery.

"What do you mean?" I asked in confusion, trying to piece together her revelation. "I got here after the police, but the kid was in there, and she was scared out of her mind." My mind raced with questions and possibilities as I tried to make sense of the timeline.

"What I'm saying," Abigail continued, her voice carrying a weight of conviction, "is that there is more going on here

CHAPTER 16

than we think." I couldn't disagree with her. Things weren't exactly adding up, and the pieces of the puzzle seemed scattered in every direction.

"Okay, keep looking," I instructed, attempting to formulate a comprehensive plan. "I'm thinking Mr. Silver must have witnessed something significant during his work that prompted his superior to take such drastic actions. He has an office downstairs, so I'm going to head there and search for any files or papers that might provide a connection to his work activities. Additionally, see if you can locate any computers or laptops so we can scour them for further clues."

With our strategy firmly established, we embarked on a thorough search, leaving no stone unturned as we meticulously combed through every inch of the house, garden, and garage. It was an exhaustive search that spanned several hours, but our tenacity eventually paid off. We stumbled upon some documents that appeared to hold promise, particularly those detailing some containers slated for delivery to a warehouse. From what I could discern, the documents we unearthed were filled with falsified reports and papers, indicating the existence of an elaborate cover-up. The deeper we delved into the pile of evidence, the more intricately woven the web of deceit became, suggesting something that was only just beginning to reveal itself.

As I pored over the documents, I noticed another container was scheduled for delivery, which seemed to be exactly what we were looking for. I turned to Gudmundur and Abigail, who had been reading the documents over my shoulder. "Well, do you think it's worth investigating the warehouse location to see if this is connected to the case, or should we hand this information over to the officer stationed out front?" I asked, weighing our options as we stood on the brink of unraveling a potentially significant lead in the unfolding investigation.

Abigail flashed me a wide, toothy grin that seemed to light up her entire face. "Well," she began, her voice dripping with enthusiasm, "we all know the police force is seriously overworked, so why don't we take matters into our own hands and handle this little stakeout ourselves? I have just two questions before we head out. My first question is for you, Gudmundur: do you happen to sell blood at that bar of yours?"

I was taken aback, almost gasping in horror at the suggestion. Surely she didn't believe that the place where we had met him would serve something as morbid as blood. Gudmundur, however, replied with ease and good humour, as if this were the most natural thing in the world. "I've only had the establishment for a brief period, as you are well aware, my dearest Abigail," he said with a chuckle, "but I have made sure to stock a few bottles of blood types A, B, AB, and O. One of the witches I employ is diligently working on a process to add flavours to the blood, so that's something you can look forward to if you decide to become one of my regular customers."

I felt a powerful surge of indignation swelling within me, my cheeks flushing with the heat of my anger. "What on earth are you saying?" I exclaimed, my voice laced with disbelief and incredulity. "Please don't tell me you actually go out and bleed people just so you can bottle their blood and sell it for a profit!" My temper flared up like a wildfire, and the air around us seemed to grow thick with tension, charged as if with electricity, crackling with the raw intensity of my emotions. Realising I needed to rein in my temper, I began taking deep, calming breaths to steady myself.

CHAPTER 16

As I was trying to calm down, I heard Gudmundur begin to explain in a measured, soothing tone, "We do not condone anyone using humans in such a manner, but vampires do need human blood to survive. However, we have found that humans are willing to donate blood freely if they receive financial compensation in return. So, in simple terms, we pay humans to donate blood. We never take too much, and we ensure they have a meal before they leave our supervision. I believe the vampire council enforces something similar, and those who choose to kill humans for blood are considered renegades, hunted down, and dealt with accordingly."

Hearing this explanation managed to quell the storm of emotions within me. I looked at both of them and was just about to apologise for my overreaction when the little bloodsucker burst out in uncontrollable laughter. "Wow, you really are amazing! Everything I've heard about you is true. You punch first and ask questions later, but you really need to control that temper, especially if you don't fully understand the supernatural world."

I grumbled under my breath, feeling a bit sheepish. "Yeah, I guess I just kind of freaked out a little when you said you sold blood. I apologise.»

"Alright, now that we've got that sorted out," Abigail continued smoothly, as if the earlier conversation hadn't even occurred, "do you have all the surveillance equipment you think we'll need at the agency?"

"Yeah, I'm pretty sure we've got all the latest technology and a fully stocked armoury," the response came with assurance. "I can drop you both off at the Dragon's Keep, then head back to the agency to gather whatever we might need and meet you once you're finished!"

Gudmundur interjected with an air of authority, "No, you will accompany us to the Dragon's Keep. You'll eat there, and don't concern yourself with any supplies. Just inform me of anything specific you require, and I will ensure it is provided." He stated this as if it were the most natural thing in the world, leading me to reassess my initial impressions. These two individuals might be more significant figures than I had initially perceived. They exude a level of confidence and poise that I've only ever seen in Alexander and lyn. I suspect I may have a few probing questions for them as we prepare for our little stake out.

***

I parked the car near the entrance of the Dragon Keep, observing that it was just as bustling with activity as it had been earlier in the day when we first visited.. Upon entering, we were greeted by the familiar sight of the waitress who had attended to us in the morning. With a warm smile, she led us to the exact same table we had occupied earlier. Gudmundur, with a certain air of sophistication, requested her to bring over two bottles of the prestigious 2009 Chateau Petrus, along with a warm bottle of the exclusive top-shelf special, and three glasses to accompany them. She nodded and hurried off to fulfil his request.

As we settled into our seats, Abigail playfully pointed a finger at Gudmundur, remarking with a knowing smile, "You're really pulling out all the stops with that wine, aren't you? That stuff doesn't come cheap, and even with your usual clientele, I doubt their pockets are that deep." Gudmundur responded with a slight chuckle, "Actually, this wine is from my personal collection. I've heard that Lady Jessica enjoys a glass of red wine, and this particular vintage happens to be a favourite of mine. Moreover, I've been informed that it pairs exceptionally well when mixed with Type O, and I was hoping you might join us while we dine and strategise for our upcoming reconnaissance mission."

CHAPTER 16

Before we delved into ordering food, Gudmundur leaned forward, his expression shifting to one of seriousness. "Now, before we make any decisions about our meal," he began, his voice carrying a weight of importance, "I would like to hear your thoughts on any equipment you think we might require for our stakeout. It's crucial that we're fully prepared and have everything we need."

This was my cue to jump in. I had been racking my brain, trying to think of everything we might need while also ensuring we wouldn't be burdened with too much equipment, allowing us to remain agile and manoeuvrable. However, before I could present Gudmundur with the list of equipment I had in mind, I realised I needed to gather some information on the capabilities of my two companions. Turning to Gudmundur, I said, "I have an idea of what we need, but I need to know more about your capabilities first. So you're up, Gudmundur. What are your experiences, and what do you bring to this operation?"

Gudmundur nodded, acknowledging the wisdom in my question. "You are wise to ask," he replied, his tone reflective. "Very well, I have participated in numerous wars and battles throughout my long years, both in my dragon form and in my human guise. But given our current situation, I'll focus on my experience in human conflicts. Over the past century, I've been involved in many of the significant wars that have unfolded—World War I, World War II, the Korean War, the Vietnam War, and the Gulf War. In most of these conflicts, I have been utilised for covert operations. I am proficient with most modern weapons, surveillance equipment, and communication systems. As for my attributes, as you might imagine, I am stronger and faster than any human and even more so than most vampires, except perhaps the oldest among them. I am an ice dragon, so I wield some influence over ice and frost. Additionally, I have a modest ability when it comes to compulsion, although I have a sneaking suspicion that Abigail might be even more skilled in that particular area, isn't that right, Abigail?" Gudmundur remarked, giving Abigail a sly and knowing wink as he spoke.

"Well, he's got me there," Abigail responded with a playful smirk. "I am indeed much better at tinkering with people's minds than the big guy is." Wow, note to self: don't get on either of there bad side," i thought, contemplating silently. "Alright, Abigail. What other unique skills can you bring to the party?" i inquired, eager to learn more about her abilities.

"Well," Abigail began, "all of my senses are heightened to a remarkable degree, so I can usually tell when someone is lying to me just by hearing the subtle variations in their heartbeats or by detecting the minute fluctuations in their body temperature. This makes me an expert tracker, able to follow even the faintest of trails," she continued, her voice filled with confidence. "I can use most firearms available, but I have a distinct preference for blades. In addition to that, I have the ability to elongate my fingernails into claws that are sharper and more durable than most other blades you might encounter. And then, of course, there's my enhanced strength, speed, and stamina, which are all above average. Unfortunately, I can't use magic or anything along those lines," she admitted, with a hint of regret.

"Wow, these two are like a walking arsenal," I mused, marvelling at the formidable team they embodied. It dawned on me that I would need to eliminate most of the items from my shopping list, but this adjustment would ultimately make us lighter and more stealth-like, a potential advantage in our mission.

CHAPTER 16

"Okay, in that case, we should consider acquiring tactical fatigues for each member of the group, along with light sidearms. An L9A1 Browning would be a solid choice if you have access to them, although an SA80 might prove to be an even better option. Additionally, we would require night and thermal vision systems to enhance our capabilities in low-light conditions, and standard communication devices to ensure we stay connected, especially in the event that we get separated. Oh, and if there are any tactical blades available I have my own but its always good to have back ups." I say as I gently caress my swords. "Do you believe you can procure everything we need?"

Before anyone could utter a response, our waitress materialised beside us as if by magic. She placed three glasses carefully in front of us and positioned several bottles in the centre of our table. With a professional demeanour, she straightened up and extracted a digital tablet from her apron pocket, then inquired if we would like to place an order for food. Before I could form a reply, my stomach betrayed my hunger with a loud growl, making it clear to everyone at the table that I was incredibly famished. "I would like to order the biggest steak available on the menu," I declared, "accompanied by a baked potato, seasonal vegetables, and a generous helping of peppercorn sauce."

Gudmundur, seemingly unbothered by my rather enthusiastic appetite, merely offered a casual shrug, as if my extensive order was the most typical thing in the world. Without missing a beat, he mentioned that he would stick to his usual choice. Turning to the waitress, he politely requested that she send out his assistant, Max, to join us at the table.

Shortly thereafter, a young man who appeared to be no more than 18 years old and had a slender frame approached our table. He gave a slight bow and respectfully inquired, "My lord, how may I be of service to you?"

"Max," Gudmundur began, gesturing towards us, "I would like to introduce you to Lady Jessica and my esteemed friend Abigail. I have a task for you; I need you to prepare a vehicle equipped with the following items." As Gudmundur began listing the necessary supplies, I couldn't help but notice that Max was casting a disdainful look in my direction, his expression as if I were something utterly repulsive stuck to the sole of his shoe.

This unfriendly demeanour was something I had been warned to anticipate from those of the dragon breed. Gudmundur, picking up on Max's insolent attitude, abruptly questioned, "Max, is there something you wish to express?"

Max's attention snapped back to Gudmundur, and upon meeting Gudmundur's unwavering gaze, spoke "My lord, I mean no disrespect, but it is the abomination. It should not be allowed to live, and you should not be compelled to endure its presence."

Before anyone could even blink, and so silently that none of the other patrons in the bustling pub took notice, Max found himself bent forward at a precarious angle. It seemed as though he and Gudmundur were merely exchanging a few hushed words. However, from my vantage point, I could clearly see the terror etched onto Max's face. Gudmundur had a firm grip on Max's collar, pulling him uncomfortably close, as his right arm underwent a startling transformation. It was suddenly covered in interlocking scales, his hand morphing into menacing claws. He brandished these newly formed claws right in front of Max's eyes and, with a growl so deep it seemed to resonate from within his very core, he issued a grave warning, "If you dare disrespect Lady Jessica

CHAPTER 16

again, and I hear about it, I will not hesitate to kill you. Do I make myself clear?"

Max, visibly trembling with fear and with eyes widened to the size of dish plates, nodded his understanding slowly, almost mechanically. "Very well," Gudmundur continued, his tone as icy as his glare, "you have a task to complete, so remove yourself from my presence at once. And do it promptly!" I could easily imagine that Max might have lost control of his bladder right then, so profound was his terror. "That wasn't necessary," i said through gritted teeth" , recalling the forewarnings I'd received about the kind of behaviour to expect from those of the dragon breed. Admittedly, it irked me, yet as long as they refrained from causing me physical harm, I knew I could endure. What I didn't voice aloud was the deep emotional sting their derogatory comments and disdainful looks inflicted on me. After all, it wasn't my fault that some lunatic had experimented on me against my will. I hadn't asked for this burden, nor did I need a bunch of self-important twats to heap scorn upon me for it.

"Lady Jessica, I must express that you do not deserve to be treated in such a manner. You have been dealt an exceptionally harsh hand in life, and yet the way you have carried yourself throughout these challenges is nothing short of exemplary and commendable. Your conduct is above reproach, and for that, I offer my sincerest apologies for the way the dragon breed has treated you. However, let me assure you that the behaviour and sentiments of individuals like Max do not, in any way, reflect the thoughts and feelings of the majority among us," he concluded with a sincere tone. As his words hung in the air, our meals arrived, and a tantalising aroma wafted up, causing my mouth to water in anticipation. The dishes set before us looked absolutely exquisite, and I could feel my anticipation playing out in my expression. Noticing this, Abigail chimed in with a playful remark, "Are you going to savour that wonderful meal or simply gaze at it longingly with your eyes?" Her teasing comment brought a rush of warmth to my cheeks, and feeling embarrassed, I blushed deeply. Without further delay, I eagerly dug into my meal, savouring each bite and complementing the flavours with the rich, smooth wine that accompanied it. We quickly polished off our scrumptious meal, savouring every bite, and I knew without a doubt that I would need to return to this cozy spot again in the future. Having thoroughly discussed our plan of action for the evening, we were just about ready to depart when my phone began to ring. Glancing at the caller ID, I saw it was Mini. I answered the call as the others began gathering their belongings, and I followed them towards the back of the pub. "Yeah, Mini, what's up?" I asked, curious about what she had to share.

Mini's voice came through, slightly muffled but filled with urgency. "Hey, I just finished talking with Alisha, she's explained as best as she can what transpired when her family were killed" she began, her tone dropping to a more serious note. "What those bastards did... it's absolutely disgusting. They barged in while the family was having dinner, just relaxing for the evening, and all Alisha could say was that a monster came through the door. As soon as she saw it, as soon as they all laid eyes on it, they were frozen in terror. She tried to call out, but she couldn't find her voice. Then she heard the monster say that they would make her mother watch. A man followed the monster inside, placing a hand on its shoulder, and the beast calmed instantly, like a dog responding to its master's silent command. He reprimanded the beast as if it were a child and announced that the mother

CHAPTER 16

would be first, followed by the brother. Then, he said he would interrogate the father, but the girl was deemed too valuable. They had already administered some of the compound to her, and since there was no adverse reaction, they intended to take her with them to join their growing army."

Mini paused for a moment, letting the gravity of the situation sink in before continuing. "Once he finished his chilling speech, he unleashed the beast on the mother and brother. All Alisha could do was watch in horror and sob helplessly. When they came to her father, they took their time, ensuring his suffering was prolonged as they questioned him and cruelly tore him apart. Alisha couldn't remember what they had asked him—I think she was in shock by then. The next thing she knew, the man approached her, attempting to drag her from the house. But something snapped inside her, and she fought back, managing to escape.

That's why she lashed out with that knife. When the door opened and she faced a man, I completely understand why she reacted as she did. I would have done the same in her position."

As I stood there, absorbing every detail of Mini's distressing account, my heart throbbed with empathy for Alisha and the unimaginable ordeal she had been subjected to. The gravity of the situation pressed down on me like a leaden weight, clinging persistently to my shoulders as I trailed my companions into the dimly lit back room of the bar. Words faltered on my lips; even the brief version of events Mini shared was enough to churn my stomach, leaving me on the brink of losing my dinner. Yet, I sensed that Mini's narrative wasn't complete, and indeed, she continued, her voice quivering with a mix of fear and urgency. "Jess, it's worse than you think. When she mentioned the compound,

I asked the lab to analyse a blood sample and conduct a comprehensive spectrum test to detect any anomalies. I have the report right here, and it mirrors yours. It reveals similar anomalies, though they aren't quite as potent," she explained, her voice trembling slightly with unease. "Jess, what are you planning to do?" she inquired, her worry palpable.

"Sorry, Mini," I replied, feeling a surge of anger rising within me like a wildfire. "I need to go kick a dragon in the balls," I declared, my voice laced with determination. Before she could offer a response, I had abruptly ended the call. The mention of confronting a dragon in such a manner caught the attention of Abigail and Gudmundur, who both turned to see what I was referring to. Abigail, quick to react, leaped out of harm's way just as my fist made a swift and forceful connection with Gudmundur's jaw. "You son of a bitch," I spat, fury evident in every word. "Was she the reason you wanted in on the case?" The room seemed to shrink around us, the tension palpable, as Gudmundur reeled from the impact, the question hanging heavily in the charged air.

As he began to rise from my initial strike, I quickly aimed a solid kick at his head, hoping to land a successful hit that might jog his memory. However, he was incredibly swift, and I couldn't even decipher how he managed to block my attack. Suddenly, with a lightning-fast move, he swept my other leg out from under me, sending me crashing down into an ungraceful heap on the floor. I landed squarely on my backside, and before I could even catch my breath, he had me pinned down with an iron grip. In the background, I could just barely make out the sound of Abigail giggling, her laughter cutting through the air like a knife. I promised myself that once I managed to get back on my feet and finish giving this dragon a proper beating, I would definitely have

CHAPTER 16

a word with her about finding humour in my predicament. "What do you think you're doing, Jessica?" he inquired, his voice dripping with condescension. I shot back, my voice laced with defiance, "You have some nerve asking me that. Just how many people have you and your band of idiots given blood to? How many of them didn't make it and died in sheer agony, all so you could have your little army of freaks at your beck and call?"

"I don't know what you're talking about, but if you take a moment to calm down, I'll do my best to assist you," he said, trying to soothe the rising tension.

"I've just hung up the phone with the agency. They informed me that Alisha has the same type of anomalies in her blood as I do. So, please explain how you could possibly claim ignorance about this situation. How many dragons are out there injecting kids with cocktails of paranormal and dragon blood?" I demanded, my voice sharp with accusation.

The expression on his face turned icy, enough to chill the very marrow in my bones. "I have already informed you that we do not engage in such activities. The last time something like this occurred, it resulted in too many lives being lost. Are you absolutely certain about these results?" he asked, his tone laden with gravity.

"I'm as certain as I can possibly be under the circumstances. Why do you ask?" I replied, my suspicion unwavering.

"Would you be opposed to having someone from the council meet with the child and examine her blood results? We need to understand precisely what is happening," he suggested, a hint of urgency in his voice.

I paused for a moment to weigh the implications of his proposal. "Alright, go ahead and make the necessary arrangements. But let me be clear—if anything happens to her,

I will hold you personally responsible," I warned, my voice firm and resolute, leaving no room for misunderstanding.

He nodded in agreement, a silent acknowledgment that conveyed mutual understanding. As he moved away from me, he lifted his phone to his ear, his expression darkening with each passing second. The tension in his body language was unmistakable; he was visibly pissed. His voice rose and fell in a heated conversation that seemed to stretch on for an eternity. Finally, with a sharp motion, he hung up on the person on the other end of the line and turned back to face me.

"One of the medics from the council will be heading out to assess her condition. It'll be someone I know and trust, and I promise they will treat her well," he assured me, his voice firm yet tinged with lingering frustration.

"Fine," I responded, my tone clipped but accepting. "Let's get going; we are already running behind schedule." With urgency in my movements. I swiftly gathered my gear from the waiting assortment, making sure everything was in place, and headed towards the waiting car, ready to embark on the next part of our journey.

CHAPTER 17

Warehouse Surveillance

The warehouse stood ominously before us, its massive form a dark and foreboding silhouette against the pitch-black, moonless sky. We were huddled together, crouched low behind a rusted, decrepit dumpster that offered little comfort or protection, while my heart thrummed violently against my ribcage, each beat a resounding echo in the tense silence. To my right, Gudmundur was a study of focused intensity; his nostrils flared slightly as he scanned the imposing structure, his eyes narrowed to slits, scrutinising every shadow and corner for signs of danger. Abigail, to my left, was like a wraith, a silent and motionless presence that seemed almost unreal in her stillness, yet I felt the strength of her resolve and readiness.

My mind was a whirlwind of thoughts and worries, each one tumbling over the other in a frantic race. What horrors lay hidden within those looming walls? What monstrous surprises awaited us in the darkness beyond? I felt a cold dread clawing its way up my throat, threatening to choke me, but I ruthlessly pushed it down. There was no room for fear now—I had a mission, a critical task that could not be abandoned. Lives hung in the balance, and failure was not an option.

"I don't sense any active magical wards," Gudmundur rumbled, his voice a deep, resonant whisper that barely disturbed the tense quiet of the night. "But there's a... wrongness in the air. Something unnatural." His words hung heavy, like a foreboding cloud.

I nodded with a grim determination, acknowledging the weight of his observation.

"Abigail, what do you see?" I inquired, my voice subdued, as I sought her insight, hoping it would shed some light on the murky situation we found ourselves in. The atmosphere hung thick with tension, pressing down on us like a tangible weight.

The vampire, her eyes unblinking and fixed on some distant point, seemed momentarily lost in thought. "Two guards," she finally murmured, her voice a cool, detached whisper that carried to where I stood. "They're patrolling both the east and west sides. They're armed, but they're human. I don't see any visible cameras." Her face, carved with the precision of a sculptor's hand, remained an impassive mask, yet I couldn't miss the flicker of disgust that flared briefly in her eyes. "They reek of cruelty," she added, her tone laced with contempt.

My jaw tightened involuntarily as I digested her words. "Right," I said, determination steeling my voice. "We stick to the plan." I paused for a moment, making sure I had their full attention. "Abigail, you take the west guard. Gudmundur, handle the east. Do it silently. I'll locate our entry point." My gaze met each of theirs in turn, seeking and finding the same resolve mirrored back at me. "We go in, gather the evidence, and get out. No unnecessary risks. Is that clear?"

In unison, they nodded, already slipping into their designated positions with the fluid grace of seasoned operatives, leaving me with the task of finding our way in.

I observed them as they disappeared into the shadows with a fluidity that seemed almost otherworldly. Abigail

CHAPTER 17

became a blur of motion, moving with a speed that defied comprehension, while Gudmundur, despite his considerable size, displayed an unexpectedly nimble agility that belied his formidable presence.

Taking a deep, calming breath to steady myself, I began to creep cautiously along the perimeter of the area, all my senses heightened and alert for any potential signs of danger or alarm. The cold, rusted metal of the warehouse wall was a reassuring presence against my fingertips, grounding me as I moved.

There it was. I spotted a small side door, cleverly concealed behind a disordered stack of rotting pallets, its presence almost imperceptible at first glance. As I examined the lock, my lips twisted into a humourless smile, recognising the simplicity of the challenge before me. This was mere child's play to someone with my training.

With a practiced flick of my wrist, I slipped a set of lock-picks from the hidden compartment within my sleeve and deftly manipulated the mechanism. The lock yielded quickly to my expertise, and I caught the door just in time, preventing it from creaking open and betraying our presence. Beyond the threshold, only the inky darkness awaited, shrouding whatever lay inside in mystery.

"Point of entry secure," I whispered into my earpiece, my voice barely more than a breath. "Regroup at my position."

Within moments, Abigail and Gudmundur appeared at my side, materialising from the shadows as soundlessly as spectres. I met their gazes, noting the same grim determination etched into every feature of their faces, a shared resolve that needed no words to convey.

With an unspoken agreement, we moved as one cohesive unit, seamlessly slipping into the waiting shadows of the warehouse. We were ready to face whatever challenges awaited us in the oppressive darkness that seemed to swallow everything whole.

The corridor stretched before us like an endless gaping maw of darkness, broken only by the feeble glow of emergency lights that flickered sporadically. I took point with my SA80 rifle held firmly in position, my footsteps barely more than a whisper against the cold, unforgiving concrete floor. Behind me, Gudmundur and Abigail moved with a predatory grace, their enhanced senses finely attuned, probing the thick gloom for any hint of danger that might be lurking within.

With each step we took, the air seemed to grow increasingly thick and oppressive, the sterile bite of antiseptic mingling with an undercurrent of something darker, more insidious. It clung stubbornly to the back of my throat, a cloying sweetness that set my teeth on edge and made my skin crawl.

"Something's not right here," Gudmundur rumbled in a low voice, his words barely more than an audible growl. "The scent... it's off. Unnatural."

I nodded, the hairs on the back of my neck prickling with unease. "Stay sharp. We don't know what we're walking into," I cautioned, my voice barely above a whisper yet filled with a steely resolve.

We pressed onward, the corridor twisting and turning like the guts of some great, malevolent beast. Doors lined the walls at irregular intervals, each one sealed tight, their small windows opaque with layers of grime that had accumulated over time.

Abigail paused for a moment, her head cocked to one side as if listening intently. "Do you hear that? Sounds like... medical machinery?" she whispered, her voice barely disturbing the silence.

CHAPTER 17

A low, rhythmic thrumming drifted from somewhere ahead, the pulse of it vibrating through the floor beneath our feet. My heart quickened, adrenaline surging through my veins, heightening my senses and sharpening my focus as we moved cautiously forward, deeper into the unknown.

"I don't like this one bit," I muttered under my breath, reaching for the comforting, familiar weight of my gun, feeling the cold metal steady my nerves. "Stay close to me, don't wander off."

As we moved cautiously forward, the narrow corridor suddenly opened up into a vast, cavernous chamber, the sudden expanse of space seeming to swallow us whole. I came to an abrupt halt, my breath catching painfully in my throat as I tried to take in the unsettling scene before us.

Stretching out in neat, endless rows were hospital beds, each occupied by a small, unmoving form. Children, there were dozens upon dozens of them, their faces ghostly pale in the dim, oppressive gloom. From their fragile bodies snaked a tangled web of tubes and wires, connecting them to softly beeping machines that punctuated the heavy silence with their rhythmic sounds.

"My God," Abigail breathed, her voice trembling with horror, each syllable heavy with dread. "What is this place? How could something like this exist?"

Gudmundur's eyes glinted with an intense, fiery light, reminiscent of glowing embers in a dying fire. "An abomination," he snarled, his voice laced with fury as his talons flexed menacingly. "We cannot allow this to continue. We must put an end to this nightmare."

I swallowed hard, feeling the bile rise in my throat like a tidal wave threatening to overflow. With immense effort, I pushed it back down, steeling myself for the task at hand. I forced my eyes to remain open, taking in every heart-wrenching detail that lay before us. This was the reason we had come, the mission that drove us forward. This was the atrocity we were determined to halt in its tracks.

"Spread out," i commanded, my voice as unyielding as flint, resonating with the authority of someone who had seen too much and could bear no more. "Document everything you see. We'll ensure this place is reduced to ashes, but first, we must guarantee the paranormal world understands the magnitude of what occurred here. And we will hunt down and catch the bastards responsible for this horror."

With heavy hearts laden with grief and a simmering, righteous fury, we moved through the rows of beds. Each step felt like a journey through a nightmare. The children appeared so small, so heartbreakingly fragile, their tiny chests rising and falling in an eerie, synchronised rhythm. What unspeakable horrors had they been subjected to? What kind of monsters could inflict such cruelty upon innocent lives, lives that had barely begun?

My hands trembled uncontrollably as i lifted my camera, capturing image after damning image, each one a testament to the darkness we had uncovered. Beside me, Abigail moved with a gentleness that belied the storm of emotions within her. She softly brushed a lock of hair from the forehead of a young girl, whose innocence had been shattered, her eyes glistening with tears she refused to shed.

"We'll save you," Abigail whispered, her voice a tender promise, as much a vow to herself as it was to the unconscious child before her. "I swear it," she murmured, her words a quiet beacon of hope in a world that felt overwhelmingly dark.

Gudmundur worked in grim silence, his movements precise and controlled. But the fury in his eyes spoke volumes, the ancient wrath of a dragon stirred to life.

CHAPTER 17

we worked quickly, efficiently, a well-oiled machine even in the face of such horror. But with each passing moment, the weight of what we'd discovered settled heavier on our shoulders.

This was only the beginning. A single battle in a war we never even knew we were fighting. But now that we have seen the truth, there could be no turning back.

we would have justice. And God help anyone who stood in our way.

As we ascended to the next floor, we were met with a scene worse than the one below, leaving us breathless and horrified. In the dim, sterile light, row upon row of pregnant women lay shackled to cold, clinical medical tables. Their bellies, rounded with the promise of new life, seemed grotesquely vulnerable as they writhed in agony and terror. Their faces were masks of suffering, eyes wide with unspoken pleas for mercy, for salvation from this living nightmare.

Nearby, young men, mere boys, were subjected to grotesque and invasive procedures, their youthful bodies violated in the name of some perverse and twisted form of science. The sight of them, stripped of dignity and humanity, made my blood run cold.

"Dear God," Abigail whispered, her voice quivering with horror and disbelief, each word barely escaping her lips. "What are they doing to them?"

I swallowed hard, struggling to suppress the rising tide of nausea and bile that threatened to choke me. "Experimenting," I managed to say, my voice heavy with the weight of unspeakable knowledge. "Harvesting. They're using them like lab rats." The scene before me triggered a flood of memories, recalling the torment Jeremiah had inflicted upon me, but now it was magnified, multiplied to monstrous proportions.

Determined to document the atrocity, I raised my camera. Each click of the shutter was an act of defiance, a solemn vow to expose the horror and bring the perpetrators to justice. The mechanical sound resonated like a promise, a commitment to shine a light on the darkness.

Gudmundur approached one of the women, his touch tender and careful as he checked her vital signs. "They're alive," he said softly, a note of urgency in his voice, "but barely. We need to get them out of here." His words echoed with the urgency of the situation, a call to action that could not be ignored.

I nodded, my mind racing. We had to document everything, gather irrefutable evidence. But we couldn't take all these people with us we were only equipped for recon.

"We'll have to come back for them," I said, a heavy weight settling in my chest, self-loathing creeping in as the words slipped from my lips. It was a decision I despised, yet I knew it was the only rational course of action. "We need to gather more intel and regroup at the agency, then figure out an actual plan that won't get us all killed in the process."

Abigail and Gudmundur exchanged a glance, a silent understanding passing between them like a shared secret. Neither of them liked the idea of leaving without completing the mission, but they also understood that, given the circumstances, there was no other viable option. They nodded, acknowledging the necessity of our retreat.

We continued our meticulous search of the cavernous warehouse, carefully avoiding the roving patrols that seemed to appear out of nowhere. As we moved stealthily through the shadows, we documented as much as we could, making our way toward one of the isolated labs. Inside, we discovered an array of computer terminals and filing cabinets, each potentially holding crucial information.

CHAPTER 17

Gudmundur's fingers danced across the keyboard with remarkable speed, his brow furrowed in intense concentration as he navigated through the multiple layers of security protocols. The computer terminal hummed softly, its rhythmic sound the only thing breaking the oppressive silence of the dimly lit room. as he began doing a data transfer to a thumb drive. Time was slipping through our fingers like sand, and Gudmundur was acutely aware of it. Every passing second amplified the risk of detection, threatened to unravel our carefully orchestrated operation right before our eyes.

"Come on," he muttered under his breath, his dragon-enhanced senses on high alert for any sign of impending trouble. "Just a little more..."

The progress bar on the screen inched forward at an agonisingly slow pace, a visual representation of the tension that filled the room. Gudmundur gritted his teeth, his muscles coiled like springs, ready to react at a moment's notice. We needed this data, the valuable secrets hidden within the facility's encrypted files. It was the key to unraveling the tangled web of the conspiracy, to bringing the perpetrators to justice and restoring order.

Abigail, stationed vigilantly by the door, suddenly stiffened, her body tensing like a coiled wire. "Movement," she whispered, her voice barely more than a breath, yet tinged with urgency. "Adjacent room."

Gudmundur and I froze in place, paralysed by the fear of being discovered at such a crucial moment. The consequences of getting caught now were too dire to contemplate. With deliberate caution, I inched closer to the small, rectangular window embedded in the wall. My breath caught as I peered into the dimly lit neighbouring chamber, trying to make sense of the scene that unfolded before my eyes.

What I saw sent an icy chill coursing down my spine, leaving a trail of goosebumps in its wake. There, in the sterile, clinical environment, were children—innocent young souls—dressed in sterile white gowns that seemed to swallow their tiny frames. They were being herded like cattle through a series of decontamination chambers, robbed of any semblance of individuality. The harsh, unforgiving lighting created stark shadows that danced ominously across their pale, expressionless faces. Their eyes, devoid of any spark or semblance of life, stared blankly ahead, as if their spirits had been extinguished.

"It's worse than we thought," I murmured, my voice taut with a barely contained rage that threatened to boil over. "They're not simply experimenting on them. They're systematically breaking them down, stripping away their humanity piece by piece." The realisation filled me with a sense of helpless fury, as I stood there, a silent witness to the atrocities being committed.

Gudmundur's jaw tightened like a vice, his fingers clenching the keyboard with a firm, unyielding grip. "Almost there," he murmured, his voice a quiet, unwavering beacon of determination. "Just a few more seconds." The anticipation hung thick in the air, almost palpable as they waited for the moment that could change everything.

The progress bar inched its way to completion, finally reaching its terminus. The portable drive blinked in acknowledgment, a small yet significant signal that the download was complete. Gudmundur handled it with the utmost care, gently removing it and sliding it into a secure pocket as if it were the most precious treasure ever to exist. We had obtained what we had come for—the evidence that could potentially dismantle this entire operation and bring its dark deeds to light.

CHAPTER 17

With the files successfully downloaded and the crucial photo evidence securely in hand, I signalled to Gudmundur and Abigail. It was our cue to initiate our escape, moving with precision and stealth through the dimly lit corridors of the sprawling warehouse. Each step was carefully measured, our footsteps barely audible, muffled by the thick soles of our boots and the deafening beat of our own hearts, which echoed like a drum in the silence.

My mind raced relentlessly as we navigated the maze of paths, the magnitude of our discovery weighing heavily on my shoulders like an oppressive burden. The haunting images of unconscious children, pregnant women, and young men subjected to unspeakable horrors were seared into my memory, fuelling an unwavering resolve to expose the truth and seek justice for those who had suffered.

Gudmundur's voice sliced through the chaos of my racing thoughts with a low, urgent tone that commanded immediate attention. "We're almost there. The exit should be just around the corner," he said, his words becoming a lifeline that pulled me back to the immediate task at hand. We pressed forward with renewed determination, driven by the gravity of our mission and the flickering hope that soon, the world would be privy to the truth of what had transpired in the shadows.

Relief washed over me as we rounded the final bend in the dimly lit corridor, the faint glow of moonlight filtering through the exit door a beacon of hope amidst the darkness. With a final, desperate burst of speed, we reached the threshold, pushing through the door and emerging into the cool embrace of the night air.

Outside, our chests heaved with the exertion and adrenaline that coursed through our veins. I glanced at Abigail and Gudmundur, their faces etched with a mixture of relief and grim determination that mirrored my own.

"We did it," Abigail breathed, her voice trembling slightly with a blend of exhaustion and triumph. "We got the evidence we needed."

I nodded, feeling the weight of the situation pressing upon me. "This is just the beginning," I replied. "We have to get this information back to the agency, expose the truth of what's happening here ."

Gudmundur's eyes flashed with fiery anger, a reflection of the injustice we had uncovered. "Those bastards won't get away with this," he declared, his voice filled with steely resolve. "We'll make sure of it."

As we made our way quietly back to our vehicle, the enormity of the mission settled upon us like a heavy cloak. Despite the fatigue that tugged at my limbs, I felt a surge of resolve. We had uncovered a nightmare, a twisted conspiracy that threatened the lives of the innocent. But we would not rest until justice was served, until the perpetrators were brought into the harsh light of day.

"Let's go," I said, my voice steady and determined despite the whirlwind of emotions swirling within me. "We have work to do, and we won't stop until the truth is out there for all to see."

CHAPTER 18

Strategic Briefing

Back at the agency, Gudmundur and Abigail lent a hand in compiling comprehensive briefings for the entire team. It was the usual mundane office work, but it kept us preoccupied while we awaited the arrival of everyone else. As I meticulously added the finishing touches to each team member's files, Gudmundur entered the room, balancing a tray brimming with steaming cups of coffee for us all. The rich, dark aroma of the coffee wafted through the air, and it suddenly dawned on me just how long it had been since I last had a decent night's sleep. A wave of bone-deep exhaustion washed over me, but there was no time for rest—no rest for the wicked, as they say. "Thanks, dragon boy," I said with a grateful nod, "I needed this. Just make sure you keep it coming."

Not long after I drained my cup of coffee, everyone began to trickle in. Abigail, Gudmundur, and I maintained a relatively quiet demeanour as the team members took their seats. By the expressions and the sidelong glances people exchanged, I could only surmise that everyone had gathered information that they were eager to share with me, and I had a sinking feeling that not all of it would be pleasant to hear. "Alright, everyone," I announced, gathering my thoughts.

"I'm going to outline what we have gathered so far," I began, projecting my voice over the quiet hum of the room. "Afterward, I invite you all to ask any questions you might have or contribute any additional information you've managed to ascertain thus far." Once I finished the quick outline, I turned to Kieth and Mini, seeking any updates on Alisha's blood-work. As I looked at them, both seemed a bit apprehensive, exchanging glances before Mini finally spoke up. "Sweetie, we need you to sit down and try not to react while we call in Gudmundur's associate. You're not going to like what he has to say, but we need you to remain calm. Can you do that for us?"

Their demeanour alone suggested the news was dire, but I nodded, signalling my agreement to stay composed. I took a deep, calming breath, feeling the cool air fill my lungs, and gripped the metal armrests of my chair with determination. I focused all the tension coursing through my body into maintaining an unyielding hold on the armrests, ensuring I wouldn't lose control and lash out.

Mini then ushered a very thin man into the conference room. At first glance, he appeared to be the quintessential bookworm, his glasses perched askew on his nose, hair a tousled mess, shirt half-untucked from his jeans, and an overall look of someone who had been immersed in research for days on end, oblivious to the passage of time or the day of the week. However, as soon as his penetrating gaze landed on you, it felt as though he was peeling back layers, dissecting your very essence with a keen, analytical eye.

This man was undeniably an apex predator masquerading as a scholar, and with just a single look into his eyes, one could perceive a latent violence simmering just beneath the surface, ready at any moment to be unleashed upon his adversaries. His presence was both commanding and unsettling, as if he carried the weight of untold power within him.

CHAPTER 18

"Greetings, everyone. I am Ogma," he announced, his voice resonating with a cold, somewhat analytical tone that cut through the room's tension. "As you are all aware, I am here at the request of Gudmundur to conduct an assessment on the young Miss Alisha. The purpose of this examination is to determine whether she has been infused with dragon blood," he continued, his words deliberate and methodical, each one meticulously chosen.

"I can confirm," he declared with a deliberate pause, letting the gravity of his words seep into the room, "that the child is indeed like you. She has been infused with dragon blood and other abnormal genetic materials. However," he continued, his voice taking on a tone of bewilderment, "it has not been done in a manner I would have expected." As his revelation unfolded, the atmosphere in the room seemed to grow colder, each word he uttered lingering in the air with an ominous weight. Those present were left to ponder the profound implications of his findings, the silence thick with unspoken questions and apprehension.

We all stared at him, our expressions blank, as though he were speaking an unfamiliar language. "As Lady Jessica has experienced personally," he elaborated, "infusing someone with paranormal genetic cells is a painful process, and most of the time, it proves fatal. The reason for this is that we paranormal entities are overflowing with magical energy and power. Humans, for the most part, possess very little magical ability. Although there are exceptions, those who are capable of holding power are never born with any magical abilities. Introducing all this power into a human vessel often overwhelms and ultimately destroys it.

However, when a paranormal creature dies, the magic in its blood and tissue degrades over time, and the remains do not decompose as rapidly as most other living things. It can take centuries for the remains and the magic within them to deteriorate to the point where they become worthless. I believe what has been done to Alisha, as well as the others you have discovered, is that they have been injected with dead tissue and blood. The results of Alisha's blood tests show a degree of necrosis in the foreign cells and a much lower concentration of magical power than I would have expected."

His explanation plunged us all into a profound state of stunned silence, as we struggled to grapple with the chilling reality of what had been done to Alisha and potently others. The room was thick with unspoken fears, hanging heavily in the air, along with the daunting questions that lay before us, as we endeavoured to comprehend the full extent of this dark and twisted experimentation that had been inflicted upon them.

"So, what does this mean exactly? Is she going to remain like me, or will this work its way out of her system eventually? Is there any possibility of reversing it for others?" I asked, my voice tinged with a mixture of hope and despair.

"From what I can discern, her system has already adapted to the blood, and the changes that have occurred are irreversible," Ogma replied, his tone calm yet grave. "She likely experienced cold or flu-like symptoms during the transition, so she avoided the weeks and months of torturous pain that you endured. The changes she is undergoing are only slight at this point, but I believe that, in the fullness of time, she will experience more dramatic manifestations of her newfound power. What I propose is that I take Alisha into my care so that I can guide her, ensuring she is not a threat to herself or others. I understand that until this investigation is concluded, you will need to keep her here to ensure her protection, and I am more than willing to stay with her to

CHAPTER 18

assist in her protection. Additionally, I can help explain what might begin to happen to her in the future with her powers. I can also try to introduce her to the supernatural world so that she isn't so overwhelmed. My offer will remain open once your investigation is completed, and I extend the same offer to anyone else who is being affected by this situation."

I paused for a moment, absorbing the gravity of what he was proposing, and I scanned the faces around the table to see if anyone was poised to object. But it seemed that everyone was taken aback by what Ogma was suggesting, leaving me with only one question that came to mind. "And what do you gain from extending such kindness to these people?" I inquired, my tone skeptical and laced with suspicion. "In my experience, dragons very rarely act out of the goodness of their hearts. Even Gudmundur and Abigail are only assisting me in this matter because they want to discuss something with me once it's over ." As I concluded my statement, I fixed a glare upon him, my eyes burning with an intensity that would cause grown men to cower in its wake.

"I see you hold a deep-seated distrust for the dragon breed, and I cannot blame you for it. We have done much to earn your mistrust, having not treated you with the kindness or respect you rightfully deserve. I am aware that even in the presence of my master, you have endured disrespect and outright hostility from us. However, I want you to know, with all sincerity, that I bear you no ill will. I am prepared to lay down my very life to defend these victims against any threat that may come their way, even if those threats come from my own kind. On this matter, I give you my solemn word," he declared with utmost gravity. At the conclusion of his statement, I distinctly felt the magic infused in his words. It was not merely an attempt to persuade me of his sincerity; it was an oath, a binding promise made in front of witnesses.

My jaw dropped in sheer astonishment, and then, in unison, everyone gathered around the table rose to their feet and chanted, "On your word, we bear witness." The atmosphere in the room shifted dramatically, filled with a solemnity that made it clear things had just become very real, very quickly. "Alright, Ogma, I believe you genuinely mean no harm to the victims, and I will accept your offer to protect them.

"Mini, if there is nothing pressing that you need to report at this moment, would you be so kind as to accompany Ogma to Alisha? It would be immensely helpful if you could assist in explaining to her that he will be staying with her for a while. Please do your utmost to ensure that they develop a harmonious relationship and get along well with one another."

A wave of guilt washed over me as I burden Mini with this particular task, but there was no denying that she was the most capable person for ensuring everything unfolded smoothly. Her expertise would prevent any issues or temper tantrums, whether they originated from the dragon or the young girl. Mini, with her characteristic grace, led the dragon out of the conference room. As she passed by, she gave me a pointed look that clearly conveyed her displeasure, a silent message that I would eventually pay for assigning her to this unexpected babysitting duty.

As I watched them leave the room, I turned my attention to Kieth. I inquired if he had any insights from a forensic standpoint that might aid our investigation. In response, he launched into a detailed explanation, confirming that he could substantiate all the conclusions we had already reached. He assured me that he would have his team thoroughly analyse the recovered information from the warehouse.

CHAPTER 18

Keith made a solemn promise to keep me informed if they uncovered any intelligence regarding who might be orchestrating events from behind the scenes. The rest of our meeting continued in a similar manner, with Keith expressing his deep suspicion that the sifters were aware of something significant unfolding in the background. Yet, they remained stubbornly silent, adamantly refusing to engage or share any insights they might possess. In stark contrast, the mages had shown an entirely different attitude, extending their full cooperation and demonstrating a remarkable willingness to assist in any way they could. They had already provided Keith with vital information, detailing a strategic approach on how we might successfully subdue a wendigo, a creature of formidable power and ferocity. Recognising the importance of this opportunity, I took the chance to ask Keith to follow up on that specific project, ensuring that all the necessary equipment and weapons were gathered and prepared to confront the beast effectively. With a newfound sense of purpose, Keith bolted out of the office, his eyes gleaming with excitement and determination, invigorated by the prospect of the challenging battle that lay ahead.

Left alone in the expansive conference room, the atmosphere heavy with tension, I found myself flanked by my two new shadows the imposing figure of Aldrich walked in and took a seat. The silence was deafening as I faced him, his deep, penetrating eyes meeting mine. They were like an endless abyss, dark and unfathomable, drawing me in with an almost magnetic force. It was as if I was teetering on the precipice of being lost in their enigmatic beauty forever. I had to mentally shake myself free from their hold, forcing my thoughts back to the grim realities at hand.

"Sir," I began, my voice carrying a weight of urgency and frustration, " should I assume your presence menace you want an update on the case?" I asked nervously

With out a word he just gave a slight nod for me to proceed.

"this case is becoming more disastrous with every twist and turn. We are at a loss, unable to pinpoint the mastermind orchestrating this chaos. We're entangled in a web of gruesome murders, People infused with the blood and tissue of deceased paranormals. There's also a warehouse brimming with cutting-edge medical experiments and potently the involvement of a wendigo.»

Pausing, I took a deep breath, feeling the crushing weight of the decisions before me. "I'm at a crossroads, uncertain of my next move. Should I take the risk and storm the building to rescue the victims trapped inside, or should I bide my time, hoping to gather more intelligence on the elusive mastermind, aiming to dismantle the operation from its very foundations? Who in their right mind could possibly have the resources to orchestrate something of this magnitude, and what could their motivations possibly be? What piece of this puzzle am I missing, and what should my next step be?" I asked, my voice tinged with despair, fully aware that I probably sounded as if I were whining, yet desperately seeking guidance amidst the chaos.

"Jessica," Aldrich began, his voice gentle yet firm, "you are standing at a crossroads with questions swirling around you and countless paths stretching out in every direction, more than even I can foresee. My opinions on what you should do don't really matter here. This is your case to handle, your responsibility to shoulder, and the decision about which direction to take lies solely with you. Rest assured, I will support whatever choice you make.

CHAPTER 18

Nevertheless, I must emphasise the importance of rest at this juncture. I understand it's probably not what you want to hear, but trust me when I say that rest brings clarity. Whatever path you decide to pursue will require you to be operating at full capacity, with your mind sharp and focused. Therefore, I urge you to return to the dorms and get some sleep. It's essential that you recharge. I will inform the rest of the team to follow suit. Consider yourselves off duty until tomorrow morning. At that time, I expect you to come to my office with a well-thought-out plan of action for your next steps in this case."

Having delivered his advice and instructions, Aldrich rose from his leather chair, straightened his tie, and left the room without further comment or even a backward glance. I slumped back in my chair, feeling the weight of frustration settle over me like a heavy blanket. I guessed I needed to recharge, but it drove me absolutely crazy knowing that innocent people were out there, possibly being experimented on, while I was being advised to sleep and do nothing about it. I signalled for Abigail and Gudmundur to follow me out of the conference room. When we reached the long, dimly lit hallway, I turned to them, dismissing them with a wave of my hand. "We can meet here tomorrow at eight in the morning," I said, attempting to mask my irritation. "That should give us some time to plan before I have to report back to Aldrich.»

With that, I walked away, my mind already drifting to the comforting thought of a glass of wine and a hot shower in the dorm rooms. It was a small respite from the chaos swirling around us. As I made my way down the corridor, I noticed Abigail trailing behind me, her steps echoing softly. I raised an eyebrow at her in question, and she gave a slight shrug, as if to say she had no intention of leaving me alone.

"I'm not letting you out of my sight," she explained with a faint smile. "Gudmundur is going to see if he can extract any additional information from Ogma than what's already apparent. He plans to brief the Dragon Council about what we've uncovered. He'll be at the agency bright and early, and hopefully, he'll have information that may significantly influence the course of action you wish to take moving forward."

"So, what, are you going to be my bodyguard for the evening?" I asked, my voice dripping with sarcasm, though secretly I was a little relieved to have her company. Abigail chuckled softly, her eyes glinting with determination, and we continued down the hallway together, the weight of uncertainty still pressing down on us.

She merely laughed in response, her eyes twinkling with amusement, and said, "I think I'm the one who should have a bodyguard to protect me from you, but how about we just watch each other's backs while we relax in your dorm?" Her suggestion hung in the air, lighthearted yet reassuring. I couldn't help but let out a resigned sigh, filled with mock exasperation, and replied, "Alright, alright, let's get moving." With that, we made our way to my room. We finally reached the elevator, its doors sliding open with a soft ding, and stepped inside. As the elevator ascended, we exchanged knowing glances, the quiet hum of the machinery our only companion. Soon, we arrived at my dorm, ready to unwind and enjoy each other's company.

CHAPTER 19

Cozy Confines of Desire

Back in the cozy confines of my dorm room, I swung the door open and invited Abigail inside with a welcoming gesture, encouraging her to make herself at home. I mentioned, quite casually, that if she preferred a bit more privacy, I could certainly make arrangements for her to have her own dorm room. Her response was a warm smile, accompanied by a gentle assurance, "No, I think I will be quite comfortable in here with you." Her decision was clear and confident, and I acknowledged it with a nod, accepting her choice without hesitation.

"Fine, suit yourself," I remarked, waving a hand nonchalantly in the air as if to dismiss any formality between us. "But at least make yourself useful and check if they have any food in the kitchenette area. Also, a glass of wine wouldn't go amiss either," I added, my tone half-joking, hoping to break the ice and dispel the subtle tension that seemed to linger in the atmosphere.

With that settled, I excused myself and retreated to the en-suite shower, seeking a moment of solitude. Once inside, I securely locked the door behind me, ensuring a brief sanctuary of privacy. I pressed my forehead against the cool, solid surface of the door, closing my eyes as I inhaled deeply, drawing in a calming breath. As I exhaled slowly, I endeavoured to steady myself. My mind was a chaotic whirlwind of thoughts, spinning with such intensity that I felt disoriented, unable to discern whether I was coming or going. The day's events and the looming decisions of the near future weighed heavily on my mind, like an oppressive burden pressing down relentlessly, and I desperately craved this momentary pause to gather my scattered thoughts and regain some semblance of clarity.

I turned on the shower, hoping that the soothing sensation of hot water cascading over my weary muscles would somehow help unravel the tangled web of choices and guide me towards determining my next course of action. The warmth enveloped me, providing a fleeting respite from the turmoil within. After what felt like only a brief moment of solace under the comforting stream, I reluctantly stepped out, wrapping myself snugly in a towel, and made my way to the kitchenette.

To my surprise, there stood my little vampire shadow, Abigail, with a mischievous grin lighting up her face. She held a bottle of wine and two glasses, her efficient handiwork evident. "Well, damn," I remarked, raising an eyebrow at her quick and thorough work,

"You certainly don't waste any time, do you? Did you happen to conjure up any food while you were at it, or is your grand plan just to get me thoroughly drunk and see what unfolds from there?" I said, my words laced with a playful tone. I was teasing her, of course, marvelling at her resourcefulness and the unexpected twist she had added to our otherwise ordinary evening.

With a sly smile, she responded, "I ordered a pizza for you. It should be here shortly, but I thought I would join you for a glass of wine while we wait. Maybe we can use this time to get to know each other a little better."

I paused, weighing my options. It was a moment of decision, and I thought to myself, to hell with it. If she was

CHAPTER 19

going to stick around, I might as well try to glean some information from her. "Well," I started, "if you intend to hang around, do you wish to enlighten me about what your interests are in me while we have this little impromptu slumber party?"

Abigail's gaze locked onto mine, her eyes burning with an intensity and depth that suggested whatever she was about to disclose could potentially alter the very essence of my existence. Her demeanour was contemplative, as if she was weighing the significance of her words before letting them spill into the open air. Finally, she broke the silenceher voice, which was soft yet carried an undeniable weight and purpose. "Perhaps," she began, "I simply take pleasure in being around you. You truly are an amusing person to spend time with. I can't remember the last time I enjoyed myself this much."

"Really?" I responded, my tone laced with a touch of skepticism. "Is that how you're going to play your hand? Fine, keep your secrets if you must. But once all this is said and done, I expect some answers from you—and from that giant lizard of yours as well." I concluded with a grin, feeling my curiosity rise, and a sense of anticipation building for the revelations that lay ahead.

With that exchange hanging in the air, I made my way to the lounge area, Abigail trailing behind me like a shadow. Upon entering, I sank into the embrace of a plush cuddle chair, getting comfortable as Abigail settled herself on the sofa directly across from me. The room was warm and inviting, the perfect setting for an intimate conversation. I took a slow sip of my wine, savouring the rich flavour, before speaking again.

"Well," I began, gently breaking the comfortable silence that had settled between us, "if you're not quite ready to share the reasons behind your keen interest in me, perhaps you could at least indulge me with your thoughts on the case we've been diligently working on together."

After a brief pause, Abigail replied, "I believe you're definitely on the right track. The information we discovered at the warehouse is going to provide us with a fantastic opportunity to gather the crucial leads we need on everyone who's involved in this situation. However, the shifter's reluctance to get involved is really concerning me. In supernatural communities, word spreads like wildfire, and the fact that the agency has dispatched people to all factions, combined with Gudmundur and I immersing ourselves so heavily in this matter, should have been more than enough to encourage the shifters to join our cause.

My thoughts are that whoever is orchestrating all of this has either resorted to blackmailing the shifters or is offering them payment to act as mercenaries. It's not unusual for the packs to take on mercenary jobs, but I wouldn't have thought they would voluntarily choose to engage in something like this. It's troubling, to say the least.

I think it might be wise for you to ask any of the agency shifters to look into the local packs and try to uncover what they know about the situation. There's a chance they might have some valuable insights or hidden knowledge that could help us untangle this web of mystery."

Before I could formulate a response, an unexpected knock resonated at the door. Perfect timing, as it signalled the arrival of the food delivery, and it couldn't have come at a better moment. I craved something substantial to occupy my thoughts while I mulled over the implications of what Abigail had just mentioned. Did she genuinely believe that the shifters might be entangled in this situation?

CHAPTER 19

As I swung open the door, it revealed a delivery guy standing there, balancing the food with a practiced ease. The tantalising aroma of garlic, cheese, and spicy sausage from the pizza, accompanied by the savoury scent of wings and garlic bread, was enough to make my mouth water instantaneously. I expressed my gratitude to the delivery guy for his timely arrival and handed him a generous tip of £20. I always ensure to tip the delivery personnel well, as it encourages them to remember my address and prioritise my orders for swift delivery.

With the food in hand, I made my way into the lounge and carefully set the boxes down on the table before me. The anticipation was mounting as I prepared to dive into the feast. I reached for my wineglass, only to discover that Abigail, had already refilled it for me. Perhaps keeping the little bloodsucker around had its perks if she continued to ensure my glass was never empty.

"So, do you genuinely believe we have shifter involvement in this case?" I posed the question, pondering aloud. "I concur that their unwillingness to assist is troubling, yet they, too, have individuals who are missing. Perhaps they are conducting their own discreet investigation, or maybe the cases are entirely unrelated, and they simply have their hands full at the moment."

I wasn't necessarily expecting a detailed response from the cheerful little vampire, but my statement seemed to spark a contemplative expression on her face, as if she were considering the intricacies of the situation. Meanwhile, seizing the opportunity,

I carefully selected the largest, most enticing slice of pizza from the box, savoring the cheesy aroma that wafted up as I lifted it. As I began to chew, my mind was not only processing the delicious food but also the myriad of thoughts swirling around in my head. We sat like this for a considerable amount of time in comparative silence, with only the occasional rustle of cardboard as i reached into the box to grab another piece of food. This quiet period allowed our thoughts to deepen and settle, and by the time every last morsel was gone, both of us wore troubled expressions on our faces. Abigail, who usually spoke with an upbeat tone, broke the silence first, her voice stripped of its former cheerfulness. "I need to make some calls to verify some of my suspicions," she announced with determination. "I'm also going to get a monitoring unit out to the warehouse as soon as possible. You need to get some rest. I'll wake you in a few hours and brief you on anything I find."

Her brisk dismissal made me realise just how exhausted I truly was. I resigned myself to the undeniable fact that sleep was necessary. Once I reached my bed, the moment my head hit the soft pillow, the weight of the day's events caught up with me, and I fell into a deep, immediate slumber.

***

The sharp and distinct sound of raised voices cut through the thick veil of my slumber, abruptly jolting me into wakefulness. It took a few disoriented moments for me to gather my wits and recognise that the voices belonged to Abigail and Gudmundur, who were engaged in a heated discussion with a third person—a voice I did not immediately recognise. As I lay there, straining my ears to catch bits and pieces of their conversation, it became clear that their disagreement, though intense, was not likely to escalate into any form of violence or physical confrontation, at least not imminently. Feeling a wave of relief wash over me, I decided to rise from my bed and head toward the en-suite bathroom, discarding my sleepwear along the way in a trail behind me.

CHAPTER 19

Once in the bathroom, I stepped into the shower, allowing the hot water to cascade over my body. The warmth of the water seeped into my skin, and I hoped that it would jolt me into full consciousness, preparing me mentally and physically for the patience I would undoubtedly need to navigate the chaotic whirlwind that was sure to descend upon my doorstep today. The case promises to bring a level of upheaval and complexity that demanded both my attention and composure.

I lingered under the soothing spray for as long as I dared, using the time to mentally brace myself for the impending turmoil and the challenges that this particular case was certain to introduce into my life. After feeling sufficiently prepared, I dressed in my usual attire, which to the casual observer might appear as nothing more than comfortable, loose-fitting clothing. However, to those who knew me well, my choice of attire was a calculated decision rooted in practicality. I donned steel-toe boots, lightweight combat pants, an Under Armour shirt, and a loose-fit hoodie. Beneath this seemingly relaxed exterior, I was armed to the teeth, prepared to face down a small army if the situation required it.

Feeling somewhat under-caffeinated but nevertheless fully equipped and alert, I exited the bedroom with my senses sharpened and ready for whatever awaited me. As I made my way to the kitchen, I encountered the three individuals whose voices had roused me from my slumber. They were gathered around the table, each one sipping coffee from their respective mugs. The atmosphere in the room seemed deceptively calm at first glance, yet there was an undeniable undercurrent of tension that lingered in the air, almost palpable. Each of them appeared deeply absorbed in their own thoughts, the remnants of an earlier argument now lying dormant but still simmering just beneath the surface, waiting for the opportune moment to flare up once more.

"So, can someone please enlighten me as to why there's a complete stranger in my dorm room, raising his voice at an ungodly hour of the morning and sipping coffee like he owns the place, or should I consider starting my day by cutting off some balls?" At my decidedly unfriendly and rather direct morning greeting, both the stranger and Gudmundur swivelled their heads in my direction, their mouths hanging open, clearly at a loss for words. Whatever they saw on my face must have been quite intimidating, as the colour visibly drained from their cheeks. True to her usual form, Abigail merely leaned casually against the counter and purred, "I'll get you a coffee, and Dragon Boy over here will take it upon himself to introduce your guest. Please, try not to injure them."

I have an intense dislike for people who are cheerful in the morning. "Alright, I'll take my coffee black with two brown sugars! Now, while she's busy with that, would one of you care to fill me in on what's happening here?" I demanded, casting a stern glare at both men. Gudmundur, looking rather apologetic, finally spoke up: "I must apologise; it was never my intention to cause you any distress. However, this gentleman is an envoy from the United Packs of London. They wish to solicit your assistance because they believe that a prominent child from one of the packs has been abducted, and they suspect it might be connected to your ongoing investigation."

"They had the audacity, the sheer nerve, to turn us away when we reached out for assistance. This was after we laid bare the tragic fact that a child had been forced to endure the nightmare of witnessing the brutal murder of her entire family. They shrugged off our plea for help, dismissing it as if it were a mere inconvenience. And now, in a twist of irony that

CHAPTER 19

borders on absurdity, they believe they can just stroll into the heart of my investigation and assert their right to be involved. Why? Because the missing child in question belongs to some high-profile figure with influence and connections? Are you seriously suggesting to me that the disappearance of shifter children isn't a common occurrence, and yet they expect us to roll out the red carpet for them in this particular case?"

The stranger, clearly trying to diffuse the escalating tension and restore some semblance of calm, interjected in a measured tone. "Please, allow me to introduce myself. My name is Milo, and I sincerely apologise for this unannounced intrusion into your affairs. However, I must express that I have a genuine belief that the child we are concerned about has unfortunately fallen into the grasp of the very individuals you are currently investigating. We have received an ominous message, one that speaks of dire consequences. It warns us that should we choose to cooperate with your agency, the boy will vanish from our sight forever, and our people will continue to disappear without a trace. My presence here is as an envoy of the United Packs, and it is imperative that this role remains strictly confidential. As the situation stands, I find myself akin to your colleagues who are shifters. I have no ties to any particular pack, you see I am a loner. This ensures that my involvement cannot be leveraged against them. To maintain this delicate cover, I am presently working under the guise of being aligned with Gudmundur."

"That all seems to make sense," I snapped, my irritation cutting through the air like a knife slicing through silence. My frustration was palpable, a tangible force that seemed to ripple outwards. "So, what do you have for us? Is it just that the packs are being bullied into steering clear of this investigation? Are they being strong-armed into submission, or is there more beneath the surface that we haven't seen?"

"I've compiled a comprehensive list of every shifter we suspect has been snatched by these predators," he replied, urgency and a note of desperation lacing his voice. "Reports coming in from various sources indicate that they're kidnapping people right off the streets, in plain sight, without a care for the chaos they leave behind. From the intel I've gathered and the facts I've managed to painstakingly verify, they're taking anyone they can get their hands on—not just paranormals, but regular humans too. The warehouse you infiltrated is just the tip of the iceberg, a mere drop in the vast ocean of their operations. I know of at least four other sites. Two appear to be research facilities, not housing many abductees, while the other two are sinister testing grounds. The site you breached seems to be where they bring them after whatever twisted experiments they conduct at the testing grounds. I've tried to track down the ownership of these buildings, but they've been bought through labyrinthine of shell and dummy corporations. Every lead I've chased has hit a brick wall, a dead end at every turn. That's why I'm here. I'm hoping that by joining forces, we can put a stop to this madness, dismantle their operations, and bring those responsible to justice."

I locked eyes with him, searching for any flicker of deceit or hidden motives, but all I sensed was sincerity, burning brightly like a beacon in the darkness. His determination was evident, and his resolve seemed unshakeable.

"Alright," I said with a slight nod, acknowledging the gravity of the situation, "I genuinely appreciate the assistance you're offering us. Has Gudmundur filled you in on the current circumstances, especially concerning Alisha? She's the young girl who is under the dual protection of our agency and, quite remarkably, a dragon. Her safety is of

CHAPTER 19

utmost importance, and we must ensure that her security remains intact as we confront this escalating threat."

He confirms with a nod, indicating he has been thoroughly briefed at this juncture. Just then, Abigail arrives with my coffee, its rich aroma wafting through the air, promising a momentary comfort. I motion for everyone to find a seat. "So, Milo," I begin, turning my focus to him, "what are your thoughts on how the silvers might be involved in all of this? Our intel so far indicates that Alisha has been infused somehow, but the details of when or how it happened remain elusive. Our lab technicians are diligently examining all the evidence, but I fear we won't be receiving any breakthroughs from their end in the near future," I say as everyone around the table nods in agreement. "Also during your independent investigations, have you come across any indications that they might be using a wendigo?"

Milo nods solemnly. "Indeed, I have reason to believe they subjected at least one of the test subjects to extreme torture, feeding it a diet of raw human flesh. It seems these were the unfortunate individuals who did not survive the experiments. From what I've gathered, their intention is to form their very own army of monstrous entities!"

I sat there, utterly stunned, my mouth agape at the horrifying revelation Milo just shared. This was far worse than anything I had imagined possible. However, it was now crystal clear what needed to be done. These people had to be stopped, and the first step involved shutting down these facilities and uncovering the identities of those orchestrating this madness. It had to be someone with immense power, wealth, and significant influence. I knew I had to make my way to Aldrich's office and rally the troops immediately, and my instincts told me it would undoubtedly culminate in a bloody confrontation.

CHAPTER 20

Under Pressure

My palms were slick with nervous sweat as I stood before Aldrich, briefing him meticulously on our latest findings. The room felt both cavernous and suffocating, filled with an air of expectation that pressed down on me. Every word that left my mouth felt like a substantial weight, each one carrying the potential to either impress him with our diligence and strategic foresight or disappoint him with a flaw he might find in my reasoning. I carefully outlined what we had discovered through extensive investigations, detailing the intricate web of connections and evidence we had painstakingly gathered. Then, I presented my comprehensive plan for synchronised raids on all the confirmed locations, to ensure maximum impact and efficiency. He took a long, contemplative moment to consider my proposal, his fingers steepled beneath his chin, his eyes a piercing gaze that studied me carefully. He was searching for any trace of hesitation or doubt in my expression, any crack in my confidence that might suggest a lack of preparedness or conviction in our operation.

The silence was palpable, stretching endlessly and amplifying every beat of my heart until it echoed like a drum in my ears. I stood resolute, my gaze fixed and unwavering, waiting for him to deliver his verdict. At last, he spoke, his voice resonating with authority and a quiet strength that left no room for doubt. "I agree with your assessment," he articulated slowly, each word deliberate and measured. "And I am convinced that a synchronised assault is our optimal strategy. Based on the extensive information you have gathered, I can assert with confidence that there is someone with significant connections orchestrating this from the shadows. We must act swiftly and decisively, targeting these sites today, before they have any opportunity to destroy crucial evidence or any suspects escape." His words sent a shiver cascading down my spine.

"Before you proceed to initiate your preparations," he continued with a thoughtful pause, "I would like you to remain here while I verify something of importance." I nodded in agreement, a wave of relief washing over me as I realised he was taking my plan with the seriousness it warranted.

As he stepped out of the room, leaving me enveloped in solitude, my mind became a tumultuous sea of emotions, a whirlwind of anticipation and anxiety swirling uncontrollably. I was grappling with the magnitude of what lay before us, the enormity of the tasks that awaited. This was no ordinary moment; it was a critical juncture in our ongoing investigation. Everything we had tirelessly worked for, the painstakingly crafted plans and operations, hinged upon this crucial meeting with the boss. It was a pivotal moment where the lines between success and failure blurred, and the stakes had never been higher.

Despite the pressing urgency of the situation, a sense of helplessness washed over me as I found myself alone in his expansive office. The minutes stretched into what felt like an eternity, each second dragging by with agonising slowness. The rhythmic ticking of the clock on the wall seemed to mock me, its relentless cadence a reminder of the precious

CHAPTER 20

time slipping through my fingers. My impatience grew with every passing moment, a gnawing frustration that I couldn't shake. I yearned to be engaged in something productive, whether it was refining our strategies, planning our next move, or even charging through doors with determined intent. Anything, absolutely anything, would have been preferable to sitting here, feeling like a chastised schoolchild awaiting a reprimand. Unable to endure the oppressive stillness any longer, I began to pace back and forth across the room, my footsteps echoing softly as I tried to channel my nervous energy into movement, seeking some semblance of relief.

Just as my restlessness threatened to consume me, the door swung open, and Aldrich returned, accompanied by a striking figure. A tall, dark stranger materialised at his side, capturing my attention entirely. My jaw dropped in sheer awe as I took in the sight of this imposing man, who towered at least seven feet tall. His skin was a rich shade of smooth milk chocolate, radiating an air of quiet confidence. His eyes, gleaming like molten silver, seemed to penetrate my very soul, drawing me in with their intense, piercing gaze. Long, ebony dreadlocks cascaded down his back, adding to the already captivating aura that surrounded him.

He wore a sleek silver-grey suit, tailored to perfection, hugging every contour of his muscular frame with precision. It was abundantly clear that this man didn't rely on the gym for his extraordinary physique; his every movement exuded an aura of strength and control, reminiscent of a seasoned martial artist or a battle-hardened soldier. His body spoke of years spent honing it for survival, a testament to his discipline and dedication.

As he stood there, dominating the room with an undeniable presence, it was abundantly clear that he was not just a figure of impressive physical strength but a formidable force whose very being commanded attention and respect. His stature was imposing, and the aura he exuded seemed to fill every corner of the space, making it impossible to ignore him. Our eyes met for a fleeting moment, and in that brief exchange, he offered me a knowing smirk, a silent communication that spoke volumes of his self-assured nature. With a casual, almost leisurely stride, he sauntered over to the Aldriches plush leather sofa, settling into it with the ease and familiarity of someone who seemed to own not just the furniture, but the entire room. Confidence emanated from him in waves, creating an impression that he moved through life without a single worry or care, as if the world itself was merely a stage for his performance.

The sudden, stern voice of Aldrich practically screamed, shattering the silence and jolting me out of my pleasant daydreams about the strikingly beautiful man standing before me. "Jesica," he said sharply, his tone leaving no room for misunderstanding, "I would like to introduce you to Enlil, a distinguished representative of the watcher's council. They have expressed serious concerns about your recent findings, and Lord Enlil has graciously offered to serve as our point of contact with the council moving forward."

My mind was spinning, trying to catch up with the rapid shift from my daydream to the reality of the situation. As I attempted to compose myself and focus on the conversation at hand, I couldn't help but feel a wave of intimidation wash over me, emanating from the formidable figure of Lord Enlil. His piercing gaze seemed to cut right through me, as if he could see into my very soul, and his entire presence exuded a palpable aura of power and authority that was impossible to ignore. The air seemed to thicken with the weight of his importance, making it difficult to breathe as I stood there,

CHAPTER 20

wrestling with the urge to both meet his gaze and avert my eyes.

"Do not burden yourself with concerns about my presence, young one," Enlil spoke, his voice resonating with a soothing and authoritative timbre, as if his words were masterfully carved from the very air that enveloped us. "I shall only intervene as a measure of last resort. My visit here is prompted by a multitude of reasons, and although your particular case may have contributed in a minor way to my arrival, it does not occupy the forefront of my attention. Rest assured, my presence is not meant to overshadow your efforts."

Despite the comforting nature of his assurances, an unsettling sense lingered within me, like an invisible shadow casting doubt over the room. A nagging suspicion gnawed at my thoughts, suggesting that he was scrutinising our every action with an intensity that belied his calm demeanour. It was as if his eyes pierced through the veil of our intentions, seeing far beyond what was openly displayed. However, I had little opportunity to dwell on these unsettling thoughts, for Aldrich was in the midst of detailing the intricacies of our current predicament to Lord Enlil. His explanations, filled with both urgency and clarity, demanded my attention.

With a concise yet meaningful nod, the lord addressed us once more. His words were carefully chosen, each syllable imbued with a depth of meaning that resonated long after they were spoken. "I possess great confidence in your ability to navigate this challenge with success, and I eagerly anticipate receiving further updates as events unfold. Your perseverance and ingenuity shall surely illuminate the path ahead." His statement, though wrapped in genuine encouragement, carried an underlying caution—a subtle reminder of the stakes involved—leaving me to ponder the true nature of his visit and what additional purposes might lie hidden behind his composed exterior. His presence, while seemingly benign, hinted at complexities that were yet to be unraveled.

As I grappled with the bewildering shock of Enlil's abrupt arrival, I tried to focus my thoughts and redirect my attention to Aldrich. The unexpectedness of Enlil's presence had thrown me off balance, but I knew I had to push past my initial surprise. My voice quivered with a blend of determination and trepidation as I addressed Aldrich, "Aldrich," I began, trying to steady myself, "if there's nothing more urgent that demands our immediate attention, I'd like to gather the team without delay. We need to initiate our strategic plan to shut down these facilities and uncover the underlying truth of what's truly happening here."

A shiver of unease rippled through me as I locked eyes with Aldrich, whose gaze was as unyielding as steel. His exterior seemed calm and composed, yet the slight tension in his jawline subtly betrayed the tumult of emotions simmering beneath his calculated surface. "That is an acceptable plan," Aldrich replied, his voice carrying an authoritative weight that underscored his position. "Nonetheless, I expect to be kept informed at every juncture. In fact, I will be establishing a backup command centre within these walls, ensuring that all communications are monitored meticulously."

My heart thudded against my ribcage as the full magnitude of the situation dawned on me. Enlil's unexpected presence signalled that our mission was fraught with more peril than I had initially realised. Time was of the essence, and we needed to act with both swiftness and precision to resolve this case before it could inflict further damage. My mind raced, filled with a whirlwind of potential scenarios and possible outcomes as I prepared myself to brief the team

CHAPTER 20

on this critical operation. Each passing minute now held immense significance, and the weight of responsibility bore down on me heavily as we set forth on this perilous mission.

With my heart pounding fiercely in my chest, I hurriedly navigated my way out of the Aldrich's office, the immense weight of our critical mission pressing heavily on my shoulders.

CHAPTER 21

Unease in the Conference Room

As I navigated the corridors leading to the conference room, an unsettling sensation took root in the pit of my stomach. The unexpected arrival of Enlil, coupled with the mysterious and looming interest of the watcher's council, had left my nerves frayed and on edge. It crossed my mind that perhaps I should have reached out to Alex for some much-needed guidance or advice, but circumstances no longer allowed for such a luxury. Time was of the essence, and my concentration had to be wholly dedicated to ensuring the successful completion of this mission. Only after this pivotal point could I begin to unravel the enigma and shed light on the peculiar events that had been unfolding. Upon stepping into the conference room, I was greeted by a larger gathering of individuals than I had initially anticipated. The air was thick with a palpable mixture of tension and anticipation, as we all prepared to embark on our perilous journey. It was my hope that by the end of the day, we would be armed with more crucial information to aid our cause and edge us closer to our ultimate goal.

As I entered the room, I could feel every head pivoting in my direction, their eyes filled with a complex blend of curiosity, tension, and perhaps a hint of expectation. Dominating the back wall was a large monitor, broadcasting a live video feed from the very office I had departed moments ago. Enlil, maintaining his impeccable posture and exuding an intense, unwavering gaze, sat confidently in front of the camera, while Aldrich, visibly restless and fidgeting in his chair, seemed unable or unwilling to meet Enlil's penetrating eyes. My arrival seemed to introduce an additional layer of unease, as if a heavy, invisible weight had descended upon the room, suffocating the space with a density akin to thick molasses. After a polite clearing of my throat to gain composure, I made my way to the head of the long table and settled into my designated seat, acutely aware of the multitude of eyes still fixed intently on me.

The atmosphere in the room crackled with an electric intensity, charged with a silent tension and a shared anticipation that lingered in the air like a storm teetering on the edge of unleashing its fury. My presence was familiar to some, yet remained a mystery to others. As the leader of this critical mission, it was my responsibility to inform everyone about the purpose of our assembly. I began, addressing my team as we gathered around the large table, where maps and schematics were meticulously spread out before us. "I have been tasked with organising five strategic raids on facilities that are culpable for committing atrocious crimes, including kidnapping, murder, and inhumane experimentation on innocent people," I explained, ensuring that the gravity of our mission was clear to each team member.

Before moving forward, it was essential to ensure everyone was acquainted with one another. "As for introductions, Keith, I believe you have a good grasp of who everyone is here. Could you kindly introduce each member for the benefit of those who may not yet know?" I asked, turning to him.

Keith responded with a voice that exuded a sense of unwavering confidence and authority, effortlessly addressing

CHAPTER 21

the team with a natural ease that seemed to put everyone at ease. "Certainly, it would be my pleasure," he replied warmly, a welcoming smile gradually spreading across his face like a sunrise. "Allow me to introduce everyone present," he offered, gesturing with open hands as if to embrace the group. "First up is Mini," Keith continued, his tone subtly shifting to a more personal and engaging touch as he introduced each member of the team with careful consideration. "She is not only an empathetic healer but also a remarkably skilled water mage," he indicated, turning his attention to Mini. Her bright blue eyes shone like sapphires, and a gentle aura surrounded her, radiating an undeniable sense of calm and tranquility. As she nodded graciously in greeting to the rest of the group, it was clear that her presence alone had a soothing effect on those around her.

"As for Gudmundur and Abigail," Keith continued, gesturing with a wide sweep of his arm towards two imposing figures who stood at attention with an air of authority. "They serve as enforcers for the esteemed dragon and vampire councils, respectively. Furthermore, they also take on the role of representatives for their respective councils in important matters such as these." The very air around them seemed to shimmer and crackle with an invisible power as they acknowledged their crucial roles in this assembly.

"Milo," Keith went on, his gaze moving thoughtfully over the assembled group, "is a shifter who is closely affiliated with Gudmundur." He paused for a moment before continuing. "And then there's Osaki," he said, inclining his head respectfully towards a striking figure whose six magnificent tails fanned out gracefully behind her. "She is a six-tailed kitsune and serves as the formidable leader of one of our elite strike teams based out of the London office."

Standing beside her was Danielle, another formidable presence and a respected leader from the same London office.

"And last but certainly not least," Keith concluded with a broad grin, turning the attention towards himself with a hint of pride. "I am a mage by profession. While my expertise primarily lies in the realm of defensive magic, I do have a selection of offensive spells in my repertoire that I can employ when the situation demands."

The team nodded in understanding, each member exuding their own unique aura of strength and unwavering determination, ready to face whatever challenges lay ahead in the mission. Their confidence was palpable, and it filled the room with an infectious energy. "Thank you, Kieth," I said gratefully, giving him a small nod of acknowledgment. "I truly appreciate the introductions you provided; however, there are two important details that were missed during your briefing. First and foremost, it is crucial for everyone to know that I am the girl who was subjected to experiments by Jeremiah. We hold a strong belief that the facilities we will be raiding are conducting similar unethical experiments. Therefore, if anyone among you has any reservations about participating in this mission, please speak up now so we can arrange for suitable replacements without any delay."

As I scanned the room, my gaze met each member of my team. Their eyes, filled with a mixture of amusement and challenge, met mine, clearly indicating their readiness to proceed. It seemed like no one had any objections or hesitations, which came as a great relief to me. "Good," I said, feeling reassured.

"It seems we're all on board with this operation," I continued after a brief pause, allowing the silence to stretch out and emphasize our shared commitment to the task at

CHAPTER 21

hand. "Now, onto the second matter at hand—Danielle." I shifted my attention deliberately towards Keith, directing my focus specifically and intently on him. "You failed to mention what type of 'other' she is. Is she a vampire? A shifter? A mage? Or perhaps something else entirely different? I mean no offence by asking, but it's crucial information that we absolutely need in order to determine which facility your team will be assigned to, ensuring that we are fully prepared for any and every situation that may arise."

Her piercing gaze swept over me with a calculated precision, akin to that of a hungry predator meticulously stalking its unsuspecting prey. Her breaths were shallow and controlled, each intake and exhale revealing an unwavering sense of self-control. The stillness in the room was fleeting, an ephemeral quiet broken only by the sound of her voice. "I am a descendant of Melusine, the mythical serpentine lady of French folklore," she declared, her words dripping with supreme confidence. As I gave her a blank look, trying to comprehend, she elaborated further, "Think of me as a shape-shifter, blessed with the extraordinary ability to transform into a reptilian form."

My mind raced furiously at this unexpected revelation—the very idea of someone, apart from dragons, possessing such incredible abilities to shift into a reptile form had never crossed my mind before. But she wasn't done yet. "And to make things even more interesting," she continued without missing a beat, "I have a few additional abilities, much like our kitsune friend Osaki."

My thoughts were a whirlwind of disbelief, spinning chaotically as I endeavoured to fully comprehend the magnitude of her extraordinary powers and remarkable abilities. This revelation certainly introduced an unexpected and intriguing twist to our already eventful meeting, which had been filled with surprises. "Okay, thank you. That information will undoubtedly prove to be incredibly helpful," I said, while carefully contemplating which site would be best suited for her and her team's unique skills and talents.

As I surveyed the room, my mind was occupied with the task of meticulously assigning teams to their respective designated raid locations, ensuring that each group was perfectly matched to their mission. "Osaki," I said, addressing the exceptionally skilled kitsune, "your unparalleled expertise in the art of illusions and misdirection will be invaluable for this particular mission. I would like you and your team to focus your efforts on targeting the Millennium Mills. This is a derelict, turn-of-the-20th-century flour mill that stands in West Silvertown, on the south side of the Royal Victoria Dock. It is strategically positioned between the formidable Thames Barrier and the expansive ExCel London exhibition centre."

My gaze flicked down to the meticulously detailed information that Milo had painstakingly gathered over independent investigation. This data clearly indicated that the location in question was primarily utilised for specialised research purposes. As such, it was deemed highly unlikely to host a large number of live test subjects, reducing the complexity of our mission significantly. Instead, the facility was more likely to be sparsely occupied, with only a few dedicated medical researchers conducting their experiments and a handful of security personnel keeping watch. "Your unique skills will undoubtedly be of immense value here," I remarked with emphasis, "as we absolutely cannot afford to set off alarms or draw any attention to ourselves during this operation."

"That should be a simple task," she replied, her words spoken with an ease that belied the gravity of our mission.

CHAPTER 21

Her voice was infused with the natural mischief and illusions that seemed to come effortlessly to her kind. The glint in her eye caught my attention; it was a playful spark that hinted at a mischievous nature lurking just beneath her calm and composed exterior. Despite the seriousness of our mission and the potential dangers we faced, I found myself captivated by her unique energy and was increasingly curious about the mysterious qualities of her kind. As we continued with the intricate planning of our operation,

I made a mental note to dedicate more time and effort to truly getting to know her once our mission was successfully completed. I was eager to unravel the enigma she presented and understand the depths of her intriguing personality. However, for the time being, we had to remain intensely focused on avoiding any unwanted attention from the public eye and utilising our unusual abilities to take our enemies by surprise with precision and stealth.

"The next target," I continued, "is nestled beneath the towering structure of the Battersea Power Station. Beneath this iconic landmark lies a covert research facility. Our intelligence suggests that this facility is primarily occupied by medical researchers, which makes this infiltration operation all the more intricate and challenging. The once purely industrial building has now been transformed into a bustling hub of luxury retail and high-end housing, teeming with unsuspecting bystanders who are completely unaware of the hidden activities below. Our knowledge of the facility remains limited, and we only have information regarding the location of the main entrance.

"Do I have any volunteers willing to bravely take on the challenging task of infiltrating this heavily guarded site and gathering the crucial intelligence we need?" The room was filled with a tense silence until Danielle's confident voice sliced through it like a knife. "I will take on this site," she declared with unwavering assurance. Her confident tone and determined stance conveyed that she had a well-thought-out plan in mind. Her eyes sparkled with a hint of excitement, revealing her anticipation for the mission ahead. With her unique set of skills and abilities, I was certain that Danielle could gain access to the site without using the main entrance and skillfully avoid detection. Once inside, she assured us, "I will be able to take care of the security measures in place and shut down all communications to prevent any alarms from being triggered when my team breaches the main entrance and we secure the site."

I found it hard to believe she was so eager and willing to take on such a daunting task. In my surprise, all I could ask was. "Do you feel confident that your team will be able to handle it, or do you think you might need any additional support?" I asked, genuinely concerned. Danielle paused for a moment, carefully considering her answer before responding with confidence, "No, I think we have everything under control." Her determination was evident in the firm set of her jaw and the spark of resolve in her eyes, which gave me a renewed sense of confidence in her abilities and the mission's potential success.

The next site on our agenda is a testing ground located at the historic Abbey Mills Pumping Station. The imposing structure of the abandoned building stood forebodingly against the skyline. Its once-pristine walls were now a canvas for layers upon layers of graffiti, each layer telling a story from a different era that had passed through this place. The windows, now cracked and shattered, permitted only fleeting glimpses of the murky and mysterious interior. Yet, as the old saying goes, appearances can be deceiving. According to the intelligence reports we had gathered, the

CHAPTER 21

interior of this structure had been meticulously retrofitted with cells and medical examination rooms, all outfitted with cutting-edge equipment, making it fit for conducting experiments. This mission was not going to be a simple one; we were all acutely aware of that fact.

"Milo," I addressed him with a serious tone, ensuring he understood the gravity of the situation, "this one's yours." Although Milo wasn't officially a member of the agency, meaning he didn't have a dedicated team to support him, I had absolute confidence in his abilities. I believed he was more than capable of taking on the challenge of leading a new group without any issues. "We'll pull members from other units to support you," I continued, my mind already racing with thoughts about who would be the most suitable candidates to assemble into an efficient and effective strike team designed to tackle this particularly dangerous undertaking. It was imperative that we put together a group that was not only skilled but also adaptable to the myriad challenges that lay ahead.

"Keith," I began, addressing him with a steady voice. "I need you to take the helm at the Springfields asylum location. This task is critical, and I trust you to manage it effectively. In addition, Keith, I require you to collaborate closely with Milo. Together, you'll be responsible for assembling a strong and capable team tailored to his needs, while simultaneously establishing your own infiltration squad. Can you both rise to this challenge and accomplish these pivotal tasks for me?" My eyes, sharp and unwavering, swept across them, ensuring they were fully cognisant of the gravity of their responsibilities. The mission's weight loomed heavily in the air, but Keith and Milo possessed a steely determination to succeed. They exchanged resolute nods, turning back to face me, prepared to embrace the daunting task that lay ahead.

"Alright, so that leaves me with the responsibility of the abandoned Surveils psych hospital," I said hesitantly, shifting my attention to Mini. "I realize this will be difficult for you, and I had initially promised that you would stay with Alisha. However, circumstances have changed, and I believe your presence is crucial here as backup. The victims will need someone on site who can connect with them swiftly, and you are undoubtedly the best we have for that role." A pang of guilt touched my heart for placing her in such a challenging position.

"Not a problem at all," Mini replied with unwavering confidence. "I was actually hoping you would assign me to this one. I have a feeling that I might discover something there that could significantly aid the victims." Her voice was infused with determination, her resolve shining brightly.

"Gudmundur, Abigail," I said, turning my focus to the two remaining members of our group. "Should I assume that you will be remaining with me, or do you wish to lend your considerable strength to one of the other teams?"

"Abigail and I will stay with you," Gudmundur answered promptly, without a second's hesitation, his voice steady and resolute. "And if it meets with your approval, I would like Alisha to remain with Ogma during these operations for added support and oversight." He paused for a brief moment, allowing the weight of his proposal to settle in the room, before addressing the image of Aldrich displayed on the large screen in front of us. "In addition, I have taken the initiative to organise a specialised team, comprised of both dragon breed and elves, to establish a dedicated facility just outside London. This facility is specifically designed for these victims, where they will receive all the necessary treatment and care they require to ensure their well-being."

CHAPTER 21

Aldrich's eyebrows furrowed in confusion, his image leaning slightly towards us from the wall monitor as Gudmundur's words hung in the air like a dense fog. The tense silence in the room was almost tangible, everyone on edge, holding their breath as they awaited an answer. Aldrich turned his discerning gaze towards me, as if seeking silent confirmation, and then redirected his attention back to Gudmundur, his expression stern and unyielding.

"And who exactly gave the order for this arrangement?" he asked sharply, his voice cutting through the silence like a knife.

Gudmundur stood his ground, unwavering and unflinching under Aldrich's intense scrutiny. "I made a brief report to my Queen last night," he explained with calm assurance, "and this morning I received word that preparations have already begun in earnest. However, I can stop them if you prefer to make other arrangements or if there are any adjustments you wish to suggest."

Aldrich's jaw visibly tightened as he methodically processed the influx of information, his thoughts clearly churning and shifting behind his eyes. After what seemed like an eternity, he let out a long, heavy sigh that seemed to release some of the pent-up tension in the room, allowing a brief moment of reprieve. "No, that won't be necessary," he finally replied, his voice softening slightly, as though adopting a more conciliatory tone. "Please, I ask that you pass along my most sincere thanks to your esteemed Queen for her cooperation and her prompt action in this matter." As Aldrich spoke, the tension in the room seemed to ease, albeit only slightly, yet it was still abundantly clear that there were underlying concerns about these sudden preparations and the implications they might carry for the future.

A slight tremor of fear slipped into Aldrich's usually confident and commanding voice, sending an involuntary shiver down my spine. His expression, however, was in stark contrast to the broad, Cheshire-cat grins adorning the faces of Enlil and Abigail. What crucial detail had I missed? I made a mental note to myself, vowing to uncover that mystery later.

I checked my watch, the hands pointed to 10 am. The clock was ticking, and time was slipping away with each precious minute that passed. We needed to act swiftly and decisively if we were going to pull this off successfully. "Okay, listen up, everyone," I commanded with authority. "We launch at dusk. That gives us roughly ten hours to get everything ready and in order. Will everyone have their teams assembled, recon done on the designated sites, and be fully prepared for combat by then?"

Each member of the team responded with a resounding "yes," accompanied by a determined nod that spoke volumes of their commitment. They scattered quickly, each one intensely focused on their specific tasks at hand, preparing diligently for what was to come at dusk. The air was charged with an electric mixture of anticipation and nerves as we all worked together towards our common goal.

As the heavy door clicked shut behind them, my heart began to race with an increasing tempo. The pressure of Gudmundur's intense gaze, combined with the formidable presence of Abigail and Mini, made me feel small and vulnerable, as though I were shrinking in their presence. Even the monitor displaying Aldrich's office had shut down, adding to the overwhelming sense of isolation. I slumped back into my chair, feeling the weight of everything pressing down on me, and began to rub my temples in an attempt to ease the tension building up inside me.

CHAPTER 21

"Jess, hun, I can feel your emotions...they're all over the place," Mini said gently, her voice overflowing with genuine concern and empathy that was palpable in the air. "What's going on? Please, talk to us. We're here to listen and help in any way we can."

I took a deep, steadying breath, struggling to find the right words to articulate the unease that had been gnawing at me ever since this situation began. "Something feels off. I can't quite put my finger on it, but there's something about this whole situation that just doesn't sit right with me," I admitted, hoping they could understand my vague intuition.

Mini nodded understandingly, her expression filled with warmth and reassurance, while Gudmundur and Abigail exchanged worried glances that spoke volumes about their own concerns. Then, as if a light bulb had turned on in my mind, an idea struck me.

"Gudmundur, Abigail...do you think we could use your people for our infiltration team? I don't know any of the London teams, and I would feel much more comfortable if at least someone on our team was familiar with the people watching our backs," I proposed, hoping they would see the wisdom in my request.

There was a moment of tense silence as they processed my request, the weight of the decision hanging heavily in the air. Finally, Gudmundur nodded in agreement, his face resolute, and promised to arrange for some of his best operatives to meet us at the dragon's keep. A surge of relief washed over me like a wave crashing onto the shore - at least now I knew we had some trustworthy allies on our side, ready to support us in whatever lay ahead.

***

My heart began to race uncontrollably, each thunderous beat pounding against my chest as I fixed my wide eyes on the unfolding scene. Slowly emerging from the oppressive darkness were not one but five distinct teams, their figures materialising like spectral warriors stepping forth from the shadows. Every individual in these teams was intricately armed, their bodies bedecked with an assortment of lethal weapons strapped tightly onto their skin, evoking the image of a modern, deadly suit of armour. They advanced with an almost poetic precision and fluid grace, each step perfectly coordinated with the next, much like the parts of a grand, well-oiled machine working in unison. While my initial impression was tinged with incredulity, as I thought for a fleeting moment that they bore a resemblance to Rambo wannabes flaunting muscle and bravado, I could not help but acknowledge the unmistakable aura of professionalism and intense danger that radiated off of every single one of them.

And then, my eyes were taken captive by an even more extraordinary sight—a singular, unforgettable detail in each team: one member per squad was in a warrior state so formidable it defied simple description. These individuals were a majestic fusion of dragon and human, their shining forms covered in a kaleidoscope of shimmering, iridescent scales. With these fierce, almost mythical creatures now among their ranks, the entire group exuded an even greater sense of danger and prowess, transforming them into a force that seemed nearly unstoppable. As they pressed ever closer, my muscles grew taut with anticipation, and an electric charge of readiness permeated the air.

A commanding figure soon took centre stage—a tall man with a prominent scar running dramatically down one side of his face—clearly the leader of this elite assembly. With a deliberate and confident stance, his unwavering gaze pierced the distance as he turned his attention to

CHAPTER 21

address Gudmundur. In a voice filled with authority and unmistakable respect, he declared, "Sir, as requested, I have organised the troops." His words, resonating with both unwavering confidence and steely determination, showcased the formidable strength of this well-prepared team.

Then, Gudmundur's own voice, rough-hewn and imbued with authority, resonated as he spoke directly to me. He detailed the readiness of his five highly trained units, each meticulously prepared to infiltrate and dismantle the fortified psych hospital facility. Every team had already been assigned a specific side of the building to target, with one additional unit held in reserve, ready to jump into action should unforeseen emergencies arise. Additionally, a medical team was positioned and prepared on standby, waiting to provide vital assistance to Mini immediately after we secured the area. In that moment, I found myself swept away by a cocktail of nervousness and reassurance, fully aware that the presence of such a skilled and strategically arranged team left no doubt that this mission would be fraught with difficulties and high stakes.

A short exclamation escaped me—a subdued "Wow"—a clear acknowledgment of my deep admiration and surprise at how quickly and efficiently the operation had come together, far swifter than I had ever imagined possible. Then, with the tone of absolute authority, Gudmundur made his intent crystal clear: "I want it understood that this is Jessicas operation, and if any of you have any misgivings or issues with who she is, then I expect them not to tag along. The stakes are unbelievably high, and it is imperative that we are all united in purpose. Do I make myself clear?" His words hung heavily in the air, demanding unwavering loyalty and absolute commitment from everyone in his presence.

After a thoughtful pause that stretched into a few brief moments of silence, he continued with the gravity of his command, "We have too much riding on us executing our assignment flawlessly. We know that the location we are about to face will be guarded by overwhelming defences. Our mission objectives are clearly defined: first, subdue all hostile forces with the utmost care to avoid unnecessary collateral damage; second, rescue every captive and ensure that they receive any and all necessary medical treatment; and third, safeguard all digital systems and hard copies of vital files from being wiped out, so that we can uncover not only what they are up to but also the underlying motives behind their actions and the puppeteers orchestrating it all."

Every soldier standing there snapped to attention, their posture rigid and their expressions fixed with determined focus as they responded in perfect unison, "SIR, YES, SIR." With that reaffirming response, Gudmundur's command resonated throughout the room, reinforcing the seriousness of our task ahead.

"Excellent," he pronounced, before adding that each one of them had been assigned a particular role critical to the mission's success. "But before we embark on our task, I must forewarn you that a wendigo—an entity of unpredictable power—might be among the enemy. Therefore, remain alert, vigilant, and prepared at every moment."

With those final words resonating in the air, Gudmundur, accompanied by Abigail Mini and myself, took deliberate steps away from the secluded back room of the dragon's keep. Our carefully coordinated and meticulously assembled group then began to navigate its way toward the expansive dining hall, each step fraught with heavy expectation and the underlying knowledge that the journey ahead would challenge every skill and resource we possessed. As we

CHAPTER 21

walked, I couldn't shake the growing sense of anticipation building within me. This was the pivotal moment we had been tirelessly working toward, the culmination of countless hours of preparation and planning.

In the dining hall, a vibrant and colourful array of food awaited us, with a large, steaming pot of freshly brewed coffee sitting proudly at the centre of our table. The enticing smell of the coffee permeated the air, mingling with the mouthwatering aroma of sizzling bacon and perfectly cooked eggs. Mini surveyed the enticing spread, her eyes widening in eager anticipation as she poured herself a generous cup of coffee and turned her penetrating gaze toward me.

"What's bothering you?" she asked in that straightforward, no-nonsense tone of hers. "I can sense it in your emotions, and it's ruining my coffee experience." Mini had always been an empath, uniquely attuned to picking up on other people's feelings and moods, which made her an invaluable and essential member of our team. However, there were times when her abilities could be a bit of a nuisance, like this moment when I found myself unable to hide anything from her discerning perception. I could attempt to fabricate a lie and blame my erratic emotions on the stress of the mission, but deep down, I knew she wouldn't buy it. She knew me far too well for that.

I turned to face the three of them, my expression both serious and urgent, my mind churning with questions that demanded answers. "Something doesn't add up here," I began, my voice carrying the weight of the situation. "The Watcher's Council is suddenly taking an active interest in our affairs, which, correct me if I'm wrong, is something that rarely ever happens. And with all the major players involved in this situation, it's baffling that I am still allowed to lead this operation. Then there's Aldrich's peculiar reaction when you mentioned your Queen and the elves setting up a recovery site. I need answers, and I need them now. Can any of you shed some light on what's really going on behind the scenes?" My heart was pounding in my chest as I awaited their response, my mind racing with a myriad of possibilities and suspicions. The air in the room was thick with tension and uncertainty, like the ominous calm before a brewing storm. Every word spoken felt weighty and laden with hidden meanings, as if each syllable carried an unspoken truth. It was clear that there was much more at play than any of us realised, and I couldn't shake off the unsettling feeling of being ensnared in a tangled web of secrets and deceit.

Gudmundur was the first to respond, his voice carrying a note of surprise and intrigue that piqued my curiosity. "The Watchers involving themselves isn't as unheard of as you might initially think," he said thoughtfully, his gaze shifting towards the others in the room, searching for any sign of agreement or dissent. "But I do agree, it is indeed rare," he continued, nodding in my direction to acknowledge my point. "With as many influential people taking an active interest in this case, I would have thought Aldrich would have inserted himself more prominently." Gudmundur's brows furrowed deeply in thought as he continued, as if delving into a memory long buried.

"As for his reaction to my Queen and the elves...well, let's just say that Aldrich was embroiled in a very public scandal a few centuries ago," Gudmundur began, his voice carrying a hint of amusement intertwined with the seriousness of the story. His tone suggested there was a deeper, more intricate narrative lurking behind these words, a tale perhaps too complex or dangerous to share in its entirety. "My Queen was the one who uncovered and brought it to light. Needless to say, Aldrich ended up very humiliated, his reputation in

CHAPTER 21

tatters." A faint smirk tugged at the corners of Gudmundur's lips, a subtle indication of the satisfaction he derived from recounting this piece of history. "It has taken him several centuries to live down his shame and regain some semblance of dignity."

"Okay, that somewhat clarifies why he reacted that way. But it couldn't have been too severe if he's now in charge of one of the agency branches," I remarked, my brows furrowed in confusion as I tried to reconcile the pieces of this puzzle.

"It wasn't necessarily a terrible offence, nor was it explicitly illegal. However, it went against the deeply entrenched societal norms and ultimately caused significant damage to his career. If he hadn't been caught, he could have ascended to Alexander's position on the elves council and within the agency; the loss of that influence has haunted him ever since.

Even the mere mention of the Queen is enough to ignite his anger and stir up old grievances," Gudmundur explained with a resigned tone, his gaze distant as he reflected on this past indiscretion and the enduring consequences it had wrought. His eyes seemed to glaze over, as if replaying the scenes of some long-forgotten drama that still held its grip on his heart, each memory a ghostly echo of what once was.

Impatiently, I leaned forward in my chair, the rich aroma of freshly brewed coffee beckoning me irresistibly from across the table. The steam curled upwards in delicate tendrils, weaving intricate patterns in the air, teasing my senses as I inhaled deeply. I couldn't resist any longer. "Are you ever going to tell me who this elusive queen is, or is that another one of your dragon secrets?" I asked, my voice tinged with a palpable sense of frustration at the constant veil of secrecy that seemed to shroud everything in this enigmatic world that I had only just begun to unravel.

The dragon across from me smirked, as if deriving a certain enjoyment from my growing frustration. His eyes twinkled with a mischievous glint, as if he relished the mystery that surrounded him. "If my sources are correct, she will be at the recovery site when we arrive after the mission. You will have the pleasure of meeting her there," he said, his voice smooth and assured, as if orchestrating an encounter of great importance.

I rolled my eyes, already dreading the encounter with yet another important figure in this society. It seemed like everyone I encountered was someone I needed to impress or please in some way, each interaction a delicate dance of diplomacy and intrigue. But I knew I couldn't back down now - too much was at stake. The weight of my responsibilities pressed heavily upon my shoulders, and I steeled myself for the challenges that lay ahead, determined to see this journey through to its uncertain conclusion.

As the concerns about Aldrich were temporarily pushed to the back of my mind, another nagging worry began to surface, demanding my attention. My thoughts shifted to the upcoming series of raids, and try as I might, I couldn't shake the unsettling feeling that these operations would require more support than initially anticipated. The weight of responsibility pressed heavily on my shoulders as I contemplated the potential consequences of any oversight. With urgency in my voice, I asked, "Can you or Abigail arrange for non-agency affiliated backup teams to be present at the other raid sites?" I paused, emphasising the gravity of the situation. "But we must be exceedingly discreet.i don't want them to reveal themselves unless absolutely necessary. And no one can know that we've arranged this additional aid. If a mole were to discover our plans, it could spell disastrous repercussions for all of us involved." The tension

CHAPTER 21

in the room was almost tangible as we navigated the delicate balance between preparedness and secrecy.

Abigail, with a determined expression etched on her face, rose from her seat. "I will take charge of arranging the backup teams," she stated with conviction. "The dragons have already committed a significant amount of manpower to this operation, so it's time for me to put my resources to use. As you rightly pointed out, maintaining discretion about our backup is crucial, so I propose that I handle all planning and coordination for this aspect of the operation. This way, if the backup teams aren't needed, their presence will remain unnoticed. And until the entire operation is complete, I suggest that I am the only one kept in the loop about our plans." Her voice was firm and confident, a reflection of her years of experience and leadership within the vampires' organisation.

I readily agreed to her request, but I made sure to emphasise the critical importance of her role in my team for the upcoming assault. After meticulously reviewing every last detail, both the formidable dragon and the formidable vampire departed, leaving me alone with my swirling thoughts and my ever-faithful companion, Mini, by my side. The room fell silent, save for the rhythmic ticking of the clock, each second a reminder of the challenges that lay ahead.

I spoke in a hushed tone, my voice barely audible over the sound of our hearts beating like thunder in our chests. "Do you truly believe this plan will succeed, Mini?" I asked, my words laced with a mixture of hope and uncertainty. She didn't respond with words; instead, she chose a different way to communicate her confidence. She wrapped her arms tightly around me, pulling me close, pressing her cheek against mine in a gesture that spoke volumes. We sat there together, enveloped in a comforting silence that stretched on for what felt like hours, drawing strength and resolve from each other's presence. Finally, after what seemed like an eternity, we gently pulled apart, ready to set our carefully crafted plans into motion.

CHAPTER 22

Infiltration Alert

As our team cautiously approached the sprawling facility, we immediately noticed an unexpected surge of activity that caught us off guard. The once quiet and unassuming location, which had been so tranquil and easygoing during our previous visits, was now bustling with frenetic movement and palpable energy. It was as if the entire area had come alive with purpose and urgency. The number of security personnel had clearly increased since our last reconnaissance mission; their tense postures and vigilant gazes were unmistakable signs of their readiness to defend their operation at all costs, no matter what challenges they might face. We instantly realised that our initial plan would not work under these changed circumstances - we needed to devise a new strategy on the spot, one that could adapt to these unforeseen developments. As we observed files and equipment being hastily loaded into unmarked vans, the air was thick with frantic chatter from radios. Our team was in constant communication with other raid teams stationed at different sites, each of us trying to coordinate our efforts. However, despite our attempts to maintain contact, their communications seemed to have gone dead, leaving us in a state of anxious uncertainty. All I could do was hope fervently that our comrades were safe and sound, even as we continued to press forward towards our objective with unwavering determination. The tension in the air was palpable as we moved ahead, unsure of what obstacles might lie in wait for us but resolutely determined to complete our mission regardless of the challenges. With beads of sweat forming on our brows and trickling down our faces,

We made a split-second decision, an impulsive, adrenaline-fueled choice to charge headlong towards the building, our hearts pounding fiercely, like war drums echoing in our chests. There was absolutely no time for meticulous planning or careful deliberation. Instead, we sprinted with every ounce of strength we possessed, an unstoppable force hurtling towards the compound, driven by an unwavering, singular focus: to thwart their insidious operation before it could spread its malignant roots to another unsuspecting site.

As we closed in on the entrance, we instinctively divided into teams, each of us knowing our roles in this high-stakes gambit. One group swiftly established a blockade, strategically positioning themselves to prevent any vehicles from escaping, while others stealthily moved to the sides and back of the building, poised to capture anyone who dared to flee. It was a perilous manoeuvre, fraught with risk, but it was the only option left. It was now or never if we wanted to dismantle this dangerous operation once and for all.

With a firm tap on Gudmundur's shoulder, I motioned towards the looming truck convoy ahead. "We need to create a massive diversion," I whispered urgently, "something that will pull their attention away while Abigail and I sneak inside." Gudmundur's eyes sparkled with a mix of excitement and determination as he nodded, already focusing intently on the targets that lay ahead.

"Make it big and showy," I added, flashing a defiant grin, "we want every eye locked onto you."

CHAPTER 22

Abigail joined in with an unwavering voice that cut through the pandemonium like a beacon of steadiness. "And don't forget," she commanded with authority, "we must secure any incriminating evidence from those vehicles. But above all else, remember that saving innocent lives is our foremost and sacred duty. We cannot afford to lose a single soul in the relentless pursuit of evidence." Her words echoed with profound gravity, a stark reminder of the high stakes and the perilous nature of our mission.

As we stealthily advanced towards the looming building, Abigail and I swiftly devised a strategy, ensuring our communication channels remained open and clear. "If you need backup, don't hesitate to request it," I urged the team, my voice firm and resolute. "We absolutely cannot afford to lose anyone to reckless heroics."

Gudmundur's smirk widened into a sinister grin, transforming his countenance into a terrifying mask of sheer determination. His muscles rippled with raw power, expanding as if fuelled by some primal force, before he charged towards the trucks with unstoppable momentum, like a war god on a mission of divine wrath. The cacophony of metal screeching and glass shattering erupted around us as he plowed through the barriers, drawing the frantic attention of guards who scrambled in a desperate attempt to contain the escalating chaos.

My stomach twisted with a mix of dread and adrenaline as I cast a nervous glance at Abigail, who stood beside me with a mischievous glint in her eyes, betraying a hint of excitement amidst the tension. The air hung heavy and oppressive, nearly suffocating us with its palpable intensity. The only sounds punctuating the oppressive silence were our laboured breaths and the soft crunch of gravel underfoot as we anxiously awaited Gudmundur's audacious plan to come to fruition.

Suddenly A thunderous explosion violently tore through the distance, its deafening roar echoing across the landscape as the shockwave reverberated through the very ground beneath us. It was as though the earth itself shuddered in response, and my heart was seized by a relentless, pounding frenzy, akin to a caged animal desperate to escape. The sheer, overwhelming force of the blast served as a visceral reminder of the chaos we had recklessly unleashed, and the electrifying urgency of the moment surged through our bodies like a jagged lightning bolt, crackling with life.

"I'm not sure if this is a good idea!" I stammered, my voice barely audible, swallowed by the tumultuous roar of the explosion. The air was thick with tension, yet Abigail just smirked, her eyes dancing with mischief and laughter barely contained. Her expression was a stark contrast to the chaos, as if she thrived in the madness.

"Well, you did tell him to get their attention," she quipped, her voice tinged with a mischievous lilt, barely able to contain her bubbling laughter. Indeed, Gudmundur had not only achieved that goal but had surpassed it magnificently. The night sky erupted into an awe-inspiring display of flickering orange and red flames that surged upwards, each explosive burst more ferocious and captivating than the last. It was as if the heavens themselves had become a canvas for this vivid, chaotic masterpiece.

The ground beneath us trembled as a thunderous explosion shattered the stillness of the night, reverberating through the air with a force that sent shivers down our spines. Our hearts pounded furiously in our chests, adrenaline coursing like wildfire through our veins, as we stood there, triumphantly witnessing the fruition of our audacious plan. Yet, beneath the surface of our exultation, a lingering doubt gnawed at me—was this truly a wise decision?

CHAPTER 22

With hearts racing and breaths held tight, we meticulously counted down the excruciatingly long 30 seconds before springing into action. We launched ourselves like shadows into the heart of the heavily guarded facility. Abigail moved with an almost superhuman swiftness and precision, dispatching the remaining guards with a lethal grace, as if they were nothing more than inconsequential hurdles in her determined path.

Our blood pulsed with an electrifying intensity, coursing through our veins and propelling us forward with unstoppable momentum as we finally breached the heavily fortified doors. We dove for cover with a sense of exhilaration, the thrill of the moment consuming us entirely and leaving us ready for any resistance that might come our way. Yet, to our utter surprise, the scene inside was one of chaos and frenzy, with guards scrambling in every direction as if their carefully laid plans had been completely foiled. With cautious precision, we scanned the area, ensuring it was clear of immediate threats before we hesitantly agreed to split up and search for our elusive objective. The air was thick with tension, and a palpable sense of danger loomed over us as we worked in unison to reach our goal.

As I cautiously traversed the labyrinthine corridors of the building, I meticulously took note of every detail that could prove significant.

Every room I cautiously stepped into seemed to have been caught in the throes of a tempestuous storm, each one more chaotic than the last, as if a ferocious whirlwind had rampaged through, leaving nothing untouched. The hospital cots, which where once full of patients, now stood starkly empty and unwelcoming, their surfaces barren except for the faint, ghostly imprints of past struggles and the chaos that had ensued. The air itself crackled with an almost tangible feeling of urgency and an underlying unease, pushing us forward with a blend of steely determination and careful caution. We understood all too well that each footfall carried us ever closer to revealing the hidden truths cloaked within these ominous walls.

As I navigated the disordered spaces, my eyes fell upon furniture lying in disarray, some pieces overturned, while others bore the marks of violence, and dark, ominous stains that marred the floors and walls—the unmistakable remnants of blood. My senses were heightened to the point of near-overload as I traversed the chilling, silent corridors, my body wound tight with a palpable fear. A battle waged within me, torn between the compulsion to forge ahead and the instinctive urge to retreat, as the haunting memories of my past captivity at the hands of Jeremiah loomed large, threatening to engulf my consciousness. Allowing myself to become attuned to the unsettling environment, I could almost taste the residue of fear and desperation that lingered in the air, mingling with the metallic, coppery scent of long-dried blood. Yet, beneath this, there was an additional, fresher aroma that stirred a deep-seated unease within me. It was a potent concoction of primal instincts—an unsettling blend of hunger, raw desire, acute pain, and twisted pleasure.

This place was far more than just a deserted asylum; it was a vast repository of secrets, a vault containing unspeakable horrors that seemed to beckon me back with an irresistible pull to those shadowed and forgotten days of the past. I found myself ensnared in a tangled web of conflicting emotions—on one hand, there was an unyielding drive within me to unearth the hidden truths buried deep within its walls, but on the other, there was a paralysing dread that gripped my heart at the mere thought of the terrifying revelations that might lay in wait for me.

CHAPTER 22

As I moved through the desolate halls, a heavy, oppressive feeling settled like a weight in my chest, making it difficult to breathe. The energy surrounding me was not just dark; it was twisted and malevolent, as if some sinister force was calling out to me from the shadows. Despite the deep unease this sensation caused, I couldn't help but feel irresistibly drawn towards it, much like a moth helplessly attracted to a blazing flame.

I let myself be guided by the pull of this ominous wrongness, carefully navigating through the dimly lit and eerily silent corridors. My footsteps echoed softly off the peeling walls until I arrived at a rusted, foreboding door that led down into the very depths of the facility. Every instinct screamed at me that it was a terrible idea, that I should turn back immediately, but something deep inside, an unquenchable curiosity perhaps, urged me onward, compelling me to face whatever lay ahead.

Determined to uncover the source of this dark and disturbing energy that seemed to permeate every corner of the abandoned facility, I reached for my comms unit with a sense of urgency, clicking it on in a desperate effort to get Abigail's attention. Her voice, familiar and reassuring, would be a welcome comfort amidst the creeping fears and the oppressive darkness of this enigmatic place that seemed to close in on me with every passing moment.

"Abby, do you copy?" I spoke into the device, my voice trembling with uncertainty and a hint of desperation. The silence that followed was almost unbearable, each second stretching into an eternity until finally, crackling through the static, came Abby's concerned response.

"What's going on, Jess? Are you okay, do you need backup?" her voice was tinged with worry, and even through the distorted connection, I could sense her anxiety for my safety. Her words wrapped around me like a lifeline, momentarily steadying my racing heart.

"Not yet," I replied, striving to project a confidence I didn't truly possess. "But I'm heading down to a lower level. The energy here feels utterly wrong, unlike anything I've ever encountered before. It's as if the very air is charged with something dark and sinister. If you don't hear from me in the next ten minutes, I need you to come looking for me. Bring backup if possible. I have no idea what I'll find down there, but I can't shake this unnerving feeling that I'm not alone."

My words came out in a rushed torrent, fuelled by the adrenaline pumping fiercely through my veins. I was trying to prepare myself, both mentally and physically, for the potential dangers that lay ahead. I took a deep breath, attempting to calm the turbulent storm of emotions swirling within me, and steeled myself for the descent into the unknown darkness below, where the source of this disturbing energy seemed to be lurking.

I paused, my breath held in anticipation, waiting for Abby's response. But there was only silence. "Abby," I repeated, my voice tinged with urgency, "what's wrong? Do you need backup?" I pressed on, concern lacing my words. "Is there a problem at your end?"

Her reply came after a moment of hesitation, her voice strained and slightly distorted through the static of our radio communication. "No, Jess, it's fine," she finally answered, though her tone was anything but reassuring. There was a tremor in her words that suggested otherwise. "But I might encounter some logistical issues if you need backup," she continued, her voice tinged with concern and wrapped in the fuzzy interference of the airwaves. "I've stumbled upon a group of survivors, and they're not in great shape. I'll do my best to get them to safety and then return to assist you.

CHAPTER 22

Just please, please be careful out there." Her plea resonated deeply, every repetition of "please" emphasising the urgency and care she felt for my wellbeing.

Her words hung in the air with a tangible weight, adding to the already tense atmosphere that surrounded me. I nodded instinctively, even though she couldn't see me through the invisible thread of our communication. Taking another steadying breath, I felt the gravity of the situation pressing down on me. The path ahead was shrouded in uncertainty, its twists and turns unknown, but one thing was clear: I had to face it head-on. With Abby's cautious words echoing in my mind like a mantra, I braced myself for whatever awaited in the depths below.

Her concern for my safety was palpable, even through the crackling of the radio. It was almost as if her worry was a physical presence, seeping through the airwaves and wrapping around me like a protective cloak. I could feel the urgency of her emotions, as they mingled with my own apprehensions. Carefully, I began to plan my next move, the eerie silence around me broken only by the faint, ghostly sounds of distant screams and sporadic gunshots that seemed to echo from another world. My heart raced, thudding like a relentless drumbeat in my chest as I prepared myself for the dangers that lay ahead, determined to make it out alive no matter what.

"Okay, get them out safely and maintain radio contact," I replied, my voice steadying as I tried to convey a calm I didn't entirely feel.

Taking a deep, steadying breath to fortify my resolve, I began my descent down the spiral staircase. With each step, a sense of foreboding washed over me, like an invisible force was pulling me further into this mysterious place. The stairs creaked and groaned beneath my weight, their protestations adding to the eerie atmosphere that enveloped the scene. The sound echoed in the hollow space, amplifying the tension that coiled within me.

After what felt like an eternity of cautious descent, I finally reached the bottom of the seemingly endless staircase. Before me stood a formidable door, crafted from what appeared to be solid iron or another equally unyielding material. Taking a deep, steadying breath, I pressed my palms against the cold surface and pushed with all my might. Slowly, with a groan that echoed ominously through the still air, the door began to creak open, revealing a vast, open area beyond. This expansive chamber, in its former life as an asylum, must have served as a storage room, a place of mundane utility. Yet now, the remnants of its original purpose clung to the air like a ghostly memory, overshadowed by an aura of encroaching darkness and malevolence. The once ordinary space had morphed into something decidedly sinister, its walls appearing to close in with a palpable, oppressive energy that weighed heavily on my soul. Shadows flitted along the edges of my vision, whispering secrets from a bygone era and hinting at unseen dangers that lurked in the silent, foreboding corners. As I stood there, absorbing the somber and unsettling scene before my eyes, my heart raced uncontrollably, pounding in my chest like a drum of impending doom.

Chained to the walls were several grotesque creatures, hideous abominations that seemed to be a twisted amalgamation of half-human, half-beast—wendigos. Their eyes gleamed with a terrifying hunger and malevolence, reflecting a deep-seated malice that chilled me to the bone. Their distorted forms writhed in a grotesque dance of agony or perhaps grotesque pleasure, provoked by my unwelcome presence. Tears welled up in my eyes, blurring my vision as

CHAPTER 22

they trailed down my cheeks, each droplet a testament to the overwhelming horror I struggled to comprehend. How could such monstrous beings exist in our world, a world that was supposed to be grounded in logic and order? And what unfathomable forces had brought them here, to this place of darkness and despair? Questions swirled relentlessly in my mind, a chaotic storm that threatened to sweep me away, as fear gripped me with icy fingers, tightening its hold with every heartbeat, threatening to consume me whole.

I had been warned in advance about them, cautioned with a gravity that weighed heavily on my conscience. Despite the serious warnings, no amount of mental fortification or emotional readiness could have adequately prepared me for the grotesque spectacle that unfolded before my eyes in chilling detail. Their eyes, glowing ominously like sinister lanterns in the enveloping gloom, were fixed intently upon me, with a gaze so unwavering and penetrating that it seemed to pierce through my very soul. The owners of these eyes were grotesque creatures, hunched over in a manner reminiscent of ghoulish sentinels, as they ravenously devoured the scattered bodies that lay in chaotic disarray around them.

Each of these monstrous beings was a horrific amalgamation, a terrifying fusion of sharp, yellow claws that gleamed malevolently in the dim light, dripping, razor-like fangs ready to tear apart anything in their path, and flesh so desiccated and drawn that it seemed to cling to their skeletal frames like parchment stretched tightly over brittle twigs. Their grotesquely distended bellies were bloated and misshapen, evidence of the sickening feast they had indulged in, a macabre testament to their insatiable hunger.

The air was thick and oppressive, laden with the nauseating stench of blood and saliva that mingled seamlessly with the metallic tang of death, creating an atmosphere so suffocating that it choked the breath from my lungs and seemed to wrap around me like an inescapable shroud. It was a tableau torn straight from the darkest recesses of my nightmares, a scene of horror so vivid and viscerally detailed that no imagination, no matter how twisted or depraved, could have conjured such a vision. Strewn across the ground in this terrifying tableau were bodies, some unmistakably lifeless, while others writhed in sheer agony, making desperate and futile attempts to escape the horrifying fate that had befallen them. Limbs were grotesquely absent, cruelly severed from their owners, while others bore grave and gruesome injuries, and some lay deathly still, their faces frozen in a ghastly mask of terror, a silent testament to the unspeakable horror they had endured in their final moments.

Every fibre of my being, every instinct I possessed, screamed at me with an urgency that was almost palpable, urging me to flee, to escape this waking nightmare that threatened to consume me whole. Yet, I stood paralyzed, caught in the unyielding grip of an indescribable fear, unable to tear my eyes away from the hellish scene that unfolded before me, a haunting vision that would be forever seared into my memory.

In that chilling moment, I realised that nothing in my life could have possibly prepared me for this harrowing encounter. The atmosphere was thick with tension as I clutched my comms set, desperately hoping for a lifeline. "Abigail? Gudmundur? Can either of you hear me?" I called out, my voice trembling with urgency and fear. The only reply was the deafening silence, which seemed to wrap around me like a suffocating shroud. I tried once more, my voice now shaky with both fear and a growing sense

CHAPTER 22

of desperation. "Abigail? Gudmundur?" I pleaded again, but the only response was the eerie static that filled my ears, a haunting reminder of my isolation. It was at that moment, with a heavy weight in my gut, that I understood with unsettling clarity that I was utterly alone in this dire situation.

Confronted by the terrifying presence of the Wendigo's—those monstrous figures with their sinister shadows cast upon the cold, dimly lit walls—and surrounded by the utterly helpless survivors, whose very lives now teetered on the precipice of my impending decisions, I swiftly began to assess my precarious situation, my mind racing with an urgency I had never before experienced. Time was of the utmost essence, slipping through my fingers like sand, and the weight of the mounting pressure was nearly suffocating in its intensity. Could I possibly muster the courage and the sheer strength necessary to confront and subdue these fearsome creatures that stood menacingly before me, and then proceed to seek aid for those in dire need? Or should I entertain the gut-wrenching option of abandoning the innocent victims, fleeing for my own life in a desperate bid for self-preservation, knowing the moral implications that such a choice would carry? Alternatively, perhaps the only course of action was to remain steadfast, to stand my ground and hold off the monstrous being until reinforcements arrived, a decision fraught with uncertainty as to how long such assistance might take to reach us.

As if responding directly to the whirlwind of thoughts swirling inside my mind, a door on the opposite wall slid open with an eerie soundlessness. Suddenly, a flood of dozens more survivors poured in, each of them wide-eyed and terrified, clad in their hospital gowns and barefoot, huddling together in small, trembling groups. These new arrivals brought with them an atmosphere charged with fear and uncertainty. Then, from behind this influx of people, there came an unsettling symphony of sounds—a peculiar, eerie laughter mingled with the clatter of heavy footsteps. This noise was starkly different from the soft patter of bare feet on the solid floor, and it echoed hauntingly through the cavernous storage hall, reverberating off the walls and heightening the tension in the air. This unsettling orchestration provided a chilling backdrop to my internal debate, making the decision I was grappling with feel all the more urgent. In that very moment, it seemed as though the universe itself had taken the reins of my decision-making, guiding me inexorably toward one clear and undeniable path—I would have to protect these survivors with every ounce of strength and determination I possessed, no matter the cost to myself. My mind suddenly made up and my resolve crystallised within me.

With resolve hardening my voice, I summoned it to its loudest, most commanding timbre, aiming to rally the courage of everyone around me and prepare us all for the impending clash with the creatures that threatened our very existence. I steeled myself for the battle that lay ahead, feeling a surge of determination course through me. My voice echoed through the expansive hall, loud and authoritative, as I shouted to the scattered group: "All survivors, gather around me! We must band together to defend ourselves!"

I could see the surprise and fear etched on the faces of some of the survivors, yet they quickly summoned their own resolve. Despite the pain from their injuries and the disorientation from the bewildering situation they found themselves in, they began limping and crawling towards me. The struggle was visible in their every movement as they fought to move away from the encroaching threat.

CHAPTER 22

Upon closer inspection, I noticed something peculiar—the chains securing the wendigo seemed to be pulling them towards the walls, dragging them further away from their intended prey. The entire scene was one of chaotic frenzy, filled with cries of pain and terror that pierced the air, creating a cacophony of distress. From the shadows on the other side of the hall, the eerie sound of laughter transformed into a low, menacing voice that sent shivers cascading down my spine.

"So you made it all the way down here, little girl," the voice hissed with a sinister certainty that seemed to wrap around me like a suffocating shroud. I couldn't quite place the voice, yet its eerie familiarity only deepened my sense of unease, leaving me on edge as the tension in the room continued to escalate, the atmosphere thick with impending danger and palpable dread. The voice, dripping with a hint of malevolence, continued its taunting. It slithered through the air like a serpent, each word laced with a twisted glee that sent shivers down my spine. The owner of that voice was clearly reveling in my predicament, delighting in the power they held over me.

"Can you believe it?" it cackled, the sound of its laughter echoing eerily as it drew closer and closer, its presence almost tangible in the dimly lit room. "Jeremiah captured and the great Alexander taking you in like a lost little kitten." Its mocking tone seemed to bounce off the walls, filling the space with a sinister energy that threatened to overwhelm me. I searched frantically for the source of the voice, my heart pounding wildly in my chest as if trying to escape the confines of my ribcage. As it drew nearer, I could feel its presence looming over me like a dark cloud casting a shadow over my very soul.

"All this work to prepare and set up these experiments," it sneered with disdain, each word dripping with contempt and a chilling sense of purpose. "But any progress we may lose will be worth it when we have you under our control." A chill ran down my spine as I realised just how devoted this individual was to their cause. They saw me as nothing more than a means to an end, a tool to achieve their twisted goals, and their determination was as intimidating as it was terrifying. "You are my golden ticket," they whispered, their voice filled with a madness that sent a wave of nausea through me. "My key to success. The organisation will reward me generously, and I will be set for life."

A sickening feeling settled like a lead weight in my stomach as I listened to their delusions of grandeur, their voice growing louder and more fervent with each passing word. "And when we finally make our move," they hissed, their voice surging with an almost palpable fervour, "no one will be able to stand in our way. No longer will we hide in the shadows, for we shall rule over the humans as is our right. And the paranormal community will kneel before us and treat us like gods." My mind reeled at the thought of such power-hungry individuals gaining control over innocent lives, the very idea sending a wave of horror crashing over me.

It was clear that this person was truly committed to their twisted beliefs and would stop at nothing to achieve their goals, their determination as unyielding as it was terrifying. And as I cowered in fear, the shadows of the room pressing in on me from all sides, I knew that I was just a pawn in their deadly game of power and control, a helpless participant in their nightmarish vision of the future.

The voice that reverberated through the dimly lit room was laced with a toxic blend of venom and arrogance, almost palpable as it sliced through the tense silence. The speaker, this unfortunate soul whose audacity was only matched

CHAPTER 22

by their apparent lack of sanity, seemed to be missing a few crucial parts in the machinery of their mind. "Look," I sneered with a derisive curl of my lip, "I couldn't care less about your so-called master plan, whatever grandiose scheme you've concocted in your deluded mind. But let me make one thing abundantly clear: if you believe that your life will miraculously transform simply because you acquire some title or position, you are sorely mistaken. Power and status, true power and status, aren't commodities that can be handed to you on a silver platter; they are prizes that must be diligently earned through grit and tenacity. And individuals like you, who lack even a semblance of a backbone, will never achieve such distinction. You're destined to remain a mere errand boy, a dispensable pawn in someone else's elaborate game. You will always be at the beck and call of others, perpetually following orders, because you neither possess the intelligence nor the courage required to think and act independently. Now, reveal yourself." The air, already heavy with tension and disdain, hung oppressively as my challenge lingered, a daring invitation for the unknown figure to step into the light and confront the harsh truth of their existence.

"You stupid bitch, I will show you that you're nothing," he hissed, his words dripping with venomous disdain, each syllable steeped in deep-seated hatred and malice. His voice was a vile sound, each word like a dagger, and it hit me with the force of a physical blow. I recoiled instinctively, my stomach churning with a profound sense of revulsion. "I'll show you just how worthless you are, a mere failed experiment," he sneered, his voice laced with cruel intent. Fear wrapped around me like an iron chain, and I tried desperately to back away, but I was trapped. The saviours, those who we had been here to save were huddled around me, their bodies seeking refuge behind mine, while others frantically attempted to drag the severely injured away from the wendigo to safety.

The wendigo, those nightmarish creatures, were now securely fastened to the walls, their chains fully retracted into the cold stone. Yet, these predatory beasts remained poised, ready to pounce on any unsuspecting prey the moment they were set free. Their eyes glinted with a feral hunger that sent shivers down my spine.

Suddenly, the dim light in the room brightened, casting away the shadows that clung to every corner. As the illumination spread, it revealed a figure standing amidst armed guards and the last remnants of the survivors. My heart sank as recognition dawned upon me, and disbelief crashed over me like a tidal wave. It was someone I had trusted implicitly, someone I thought to be an ally. The shock of betrayal was overwhelming, a bitter taste in my mouth. "No, it can't be... you were supposed to be on our side," I whispered, my voice trembling with disbelief and profound disappointment.

The realisation that everything we had fought for might have been in vain crushed me, and my entire world seemed to crumble into dust around me. The weight of betrayal was suffocating, and I felt as though I were standing on the edge of an abyss, the ground beneath me crumbling away. The trust I had placed in this person, in our shared mission, was shattered, and I was left grappling with the harsh reality that I had been a fool to believe in them. Everything I had believed in, everything we had worked for, now seemed like a cruel joke, and the sense of hopelessness was overwhelming.

CHAPTER 23

Malicious Intent

Aldrich emerged from the shadows with the stealth and sinuous grace of a serpent, his facial features twisting into a menacing grin that promised nothing but malevolence and ill intent. The dim light cast eerie shadows on his face, amplifying the sinister effect. With a gun held steadily in his grip, its muzzle trained unwaveringly on me, he advanced with the assuredness of a predator closing in on its trapped prey. "Alexander and that dragon queen bitch never saw this coming," he sneered, his voice dripping with venom and laced with an arrogant disdain that was impossible to ignore. The barrel of the gun glinted ominously against the faint illumination, reflecting the malevolent wickedness of his twisted smile. My heart pounded like a war drum in my chest, each beat resonating with the terror of the imminent danger that loomed over me.

"But I left you at the office with Enlil," I stammered, my voice quivering with a tumultuous mix of disbelief and dread. The shock of his presence was almost too much to process, defying all logic and reason that I clung to. How could he possibly be standing here, right before me, as if mocking the very laws of reality? I felt my heart race, pounding in my chest like a relentless drumbeat as I struggled to comprehend the surreal scene unfolding before my eyes. "How did you get here?" I asked, my mind spiraling into a chaotic storm, desperately trying to untangle the threads of the nightmare that had insidiously woven itself into the fabric of my reality. Each thread seemed to tighten around my consciousness, pulling me deeper into a whirlpool of confusion and fear.

"I had my extraction team take down that blowhard after you and your friends left," he replied nonchalantly, as if discussing the weather on a pleasant afternoon. His tone was disturbingly calm, a stark contrast to the turmoil consuming me. "He didn't stand a chance. By the time he wakes up, all this will be over and you'll be back in one of our labs." His eyes gleamed with a sinister glint, a cold and calculating light that sent shivers cascading down my spine. "We're curious about what makes you so different from the rest, and we won't let you escape again." His words hung heavily in the air, their weight pressing down on me like a suffocating fog.

A heavy silence settled between us as his words sank in, causing a chill to run down my spine. The distant sounds of battle echoed through the air above, a constant reminder of the danger surrounding us. Explosions and gunfire punctuated the silence, each sound a testament to the chaos that lay just beyond our immediate surroundings. In this moment, the possibility of being saved seemed like a distant hope, an elusive dream slipping further from my grasp with each passing second. Unless some unforeseen change occurred, the shadows of despair threatened to swallow me whole.

I could sense Aldrich's flawless plan looming ominously over us, casting a foreboding aura of tension and imminent peril that seemed to seep into every corner of the dimly lit room. It felt as though one wrong move, one misstep, could trigger a deadly outcome for us both. The weight of the

CHAPTER 23

situation pressed heavily on my shoulders, and a chill ran down my spine as I realised just how precarious our position truly was.

Aldrich's hand trembled with barely contained anticipation as he expertly pulled the trigger, his fingers moving with a precision that spoke of countless rehearsals and a steely resolve. The deafening silence that followed the muted click was only broken by a sudden, sharp sting on my neck. Instinctively, I reached up and pulled away the small tranquilliser dart, my fingers fumbling with urgency. It was clear that Aldrich was leaving nothing to chance in his desperate attempt to maintain control over the situation, ensuring that every detail was meticulously accounted for. His presence alone seemed to weigh heavily upon the air, a tangible force that pressed down on me, making it difficult to breathe. I could feel his power emanating from him, an invisible aura of authority that seemed to amplify his already imposing stature. He towered over me, his gun still unwaveringly pointed in my direction, a silent threat that underscored the gravity of the moment.

The tension in the atmosphere was palpable, a living entity that seemed to wrap itself around us, coiling tighter with each passing second. I could sense the danger lurking behind Aldrich's cold, calculating eyes, a ruthless determination that sent a shiver through my soul. Desperately, I tried to fight against the encroaching haze that clouded my mind.

"Son of a bitch, what did you just shoot me with?" I managed to utter with a voice that was a trembling concoction of anger and disbelief. My mind was racing, trying to comprehend the situation, but even as the words left my lips, I felt a strange sensation overtaking me. My eyesight began to blur, the world around me dissolving into a haze of colors and shapes. A numbing sensation spread through my body like wildfire, blazing a trail that left me feeling disconnected from my own limbs. I stumbled forward, my legs turning to jelly beneath me, as the tranquilliser dart took effect with brutal efficiency, determinedly dragging me toward an abyss of darkness that threatened to swallow me whole.

My once steady grip on my firearm slipped away, the familiar weight of it now foreign and useless against Aldrich's approaching men, who advanced with calculated precision. In a desperate attempt to regain some semblance of control, I reached out with trembling fingers, fumbling for the sword that hung at my waist. It was a weapon that had waited patiently, eager to taste the metallic tang of blood. As I withdrew the blade with shaky hands, its steel glinted ominously in the dim light, a beacon of defiance in the encroaching shadows. I knew all too well that Aldrich was too much of a coward to soil his own hands with the dirty work, but I was damned if I would let his hired goons take me down without a fight.

As they closed in, the air thick with tension, I could feel the adrenaline surging through my veins, igniting a fire within me that fought against the numbing effects of the drug. It gave me the strength to face them head-on, a resolve burning brighter than ever. Today, they would have to earn their paycheque with every drop of blood I shed, for I was determined to go down fighting, defiant and unyielding, with every last breath in me.

The impending battle loomed over me like a storm, one that promised to be neither simple nor swift. Yet, I was resolute in my determination to make this day unforgettable, to engrave it into the annals of their memory as the day they had to struggle fiercely against a warrior who refused to bow down or concede defeat. The sound of the guard's

CHAPTER 23

heavy, metal-studded boots resonated ominously against the cold, unyielding concrete floor, each step echoing like a death knell as they charged towards me with eyes narrowed in unwavering determination. My head felt like it was being crushed in a vise, throbbing painfully, and my vision wavered as I fought to maintain my stance. The bitter, acrid aftertaste of the drug they had injected into my veins lingered on my tongue, a constant reminder of its numbing effect on my senses, slowing my reflexes to a frustrating crawl. Despite this, I was adamant in my refusal to let it sap my strength or resolve. With a swift sidestep, executed with precision and a deft slash of my blade, I managed to evade his grasp and draw first blood, a thin crimson line appearing on his forearm. The rush of adrenaline that surged through my veins was like a brief, flickering candle in the dark, sharpening my focus momentarily before the oppressive effects of the drug once again clouded my mind. Taking precious seconds to catch my breath, I cast my gaze around the dimly lit chamber and observed more guards filing in, their expressions twisted with malice as they fixed their eyes on me.

Each one of them was driven by Aldrich's ruthless and unyielding orders to capture me alive, ensuring that I would be taken prisoner once more. Meanwhile, the unfortunate souls who had already been dragged into this nightmare were left behind to confront the merciless hunger of the ravenous Wendigo, which lurked ominously in the shadows, waiting to feast upon them. As I surveyed the dire situation, panic rose sharply within me. I realised with grim clarity that I was both outnumbered and outmatched by my Aldrich's men. My mind raced wildly, frantically searching for any possible avenue of escape, fully aware that every precious second counted before additional reinforcements would inevitably arrive to seal my fate.

Then, without warning, a heavy iron door that I had used to enter the room suddenly slammed shut with a resounding clang, effectively trapping all of us inside together. The air immediately grew thick with tension, as we all prepared for the inevitable battle that lay ahead.

The mere thought of losing consciousness, drifting into that abyss only to awaken once more bound and trapped, ignited a powerful surge of fear and rage that coursed violently through my veins. It was as if my blood had transformed into molten lava, boiling and pulsating with an uncontrollable, frenzied energy that threatened to engulf me entirely. In that heightened, almost surreal state, my skin seemed to vibrate with an invisible current, humming with electricity as though I were a conductor for some formidable and unseen force. Arcs of crackling energy began to snake across my body, like serpents of light, shooting out sparks that danced chaotically between different parts of my form. I could feel an almost primal transformation taking place; my nails lengthened and sharpened into lethal talons, while a peculiar tingling sensation overtook my teeth, morphing them into razor-sharp fangs capable of tearing through flesh with ease. All of this was unfolding simultaneously, even as I remained ensnared in a state of sheer panic and terror, a state which paradoxically served to fuel the raw, untamed power swirling violently around me, building to an unstoppable crescendo that seemed to defy the very laws of nature itself.

The guards, who only moments before had received orders to capture and subdue me, now stood frozen, their eyes wide with a mixture of awe and fear. The terror etched on their faces was almost palpable, with some appearing to be on the brink of losing control of their bladders, such was the depth of their fright. The intensity of this sensation is beyond words, indescribable in its magnitude. It's akin to

CHAPTER 23

staring straight into the heart of an oncoming tornado, its swirling winds and ominous clouds threatening to devour everything in their path. And yet, amidst the chaos, there exists a rush of exhilaration and pure, unadulterated joy, reminiscent of the moment you first kiss your true love and finally grasp the essence of what it means to be truly complete. The adrenaline surging through my veins merges seamlessly with a profound sense of contentment and fulfilment, creating a tempestuous whirlwind of emotions that leaves me both breathless and fiercely alive, teetering on the precipice of something extraordinary and unknown.

Without any prior warning, a guard suddenly swung the barrel of an MP5 submachine gun in my direction and let loose a rapid burst of bullets. The deafening sound of gunfire reverberated violently throughout the room, creating an overwhelming cacophony as I stumbled backwards, struggling to maintain my balance. Each bullet seemed to slam into my body with relentless force, and I could feel the shock of every impact. My legs, unable to bear the brunt of the assault, gave way beneath me, and I crumpled to the floor, desperately gasping for air, my lungs burning with the effort.

Amidst the chaotic noise and confusion, Aldrich's voice sliced through like a blade. "What do you think you're doing?" he roared, his voice filled with anger and urgency. "We need her alive!" His words sent a wave of panic crashing over me as the full weight of the situation settled upon my shoulders. It became painfully clear that this shadowy organisation would go to any lengths necessary to keep me under their control, and they were not about to let anything stand in their way.

Aldrich's orders came sharp and unyielding, his tone icy and commanding. "Go over there," he directed, pointing with authority to a prone figure on the ground—me. "Check her vitals and restrain her, even if she appears deceased. We cannot risk losing her." As the guard approached with mechanical precision, I couldn't help but think, what an arrogant jerk. He doesn't even have the decency to check if I'm still alive himself. But then again, why am I still breathing after such an onslaught? There was no time to ponder the miraculous fact that I had somehow survived a barrage of MP5 ammunition. My mind raced with more pressing concerns: the necessity of stopping Aldrich, ensuring the victims' safety, and protecting the welfare of my team members at all costs.

As one of Aldrich's guards leaned over me, his breath warm and moist against my skin, a primal awareness surged through me, and I could feel the beat of his pulse racing like the rhythm of a war drum. Without a moment's hesitation, I slid the sharp edge of my blade across his throat, watching with a detached fascination as a crimson gush of blood spilled out onto the ground, painting the earth with his lifeblood. As his body fell to the side in a graceless collapse, I sprang to my feet with a fluid grace that belied the chaos around me, ready to face whatever formidable challenges awaited me next.

My eyes, sharp and calculating, scanned the rest of the guards surrounding me, their weapons raised high and their faces twisted with a grotesque mix of anger and fear. Yet, in the midst of this volatile scene, I felt no fear. Only an intense, burning determination surged through my veins, propelling me forward with a singular purpose—to put an end to this madness before any more innocent lives were lost to the brutality of the conflict.

I could feel the simmering anger within me, fuelling my actions and pushing me forward with an unbreakable focus

CHAPTER 23

that was as steady as my heartbeat. The combat training sessions with Hiyori and Hargreaves came rushing back to me in vivid clarity, flooding my mind with their teachings and guiding my muscles and joints in a perfect, synchronised rhythm.

I moved with the precision and fluidity of a well-oiled machine, a testament to the countless hours of gruelling practice and dedication I had invested in my craft. Each movement was deliberate and calculated, allowing me to swiftly and efficiently strike down each guard that dared to approach. Their attempts to subdue me proved utterly futile against the unyielding force of my relentless resolve. I expertly turned my opponents' momentum against them, using their own strength to my advantage, swiftly disarming and incapacitating them with a deftness that left them bewildered. A few unlucky one ended up dead on the ground, my swords having sealed their fate, never to provide any answers about Aldrich's insidious plans. In that intense moment, my thoughts were not consumed by notions of justice or the quest for answers. My singular focus was on stopping Aldrich from unleashing further destruction and chaos upon the world.

The once formidable guards, now reduced to either lifeless forms sprawled on the ground or writhing in agony, were utterly unable to come to Aldrich's aid. A look of fear crept into his eyes, and I could almost taste its bitterness on my tongue, a flavour that mingled with the adrenaline coursing through my veins. A small, involuntary smile tugged at the corners of my lips as I relished the sight of him so vulnerable, stripped of his power and rendered helpless in the face of my determined pursuit.

"So, Aldrich, you want me to meet with this organisation?" I inquired, my voice as cold and detached as the barren winds of winter. My words sliced through the air like a finely sharpened knife, sending an involuntary shiver down Aldrich's spine, as though I had struck a nerve within him. "Perhaps you can start by enlightening me on where exactly I might find them. That way, we can all gather around for a nice little chat, don't you think?"

I paused deliberately, allowing the weight of my words to hang in the air as I studied his fearful expression, which betrayed a mixture of dread and uncertainty. After a moment, I added with a sly smirk, "And who knows, perhaps you might even earn yourself a reduced sentence, assuming your information proves to be valuable enough." My tone dripped with mocking sarcasm, as I toyed with the tantalising prospect of manipulating Aldrich's fear to my advantage.

In response, the venom in his voice oozed like toxic acid, unleashing a torrent of ferocious hatred and defiance that seemed to scorch the very air between us. "You ignorant bitch," he began, his words dripping with disdain and arrogance, "do you honestly believe that I will accompany you willingly?" He spat each syllable with such contempt that it felt like a physical blow. "You are nothing but a powerless pawn in this intricate game we play, and even if by some miraculous twist of fate you managed to overpower me, I have far too many connections, too many allies, to ever find myself rotting away in some hellhole like Tuataras." His defiance was as fierce and primal as that of a cornered animal, yet beneath the surface, there was a flicker of desperation that could not be entirely hidden, a hint of fear that belied his bravado.

A cruel, serpentine smirk twisted his lips, a vile expression that seemed to distort his very visage, as he continued his taunting speech with relish, savouring each

CHAPTER 23

excruciating moment of tension he created. "No," he began, his voice dripping with mockery and disdain, "I think I will indulge in some entertainment at your expense." His eyes, alight with malevolent amusement, gleamed in the dim light, reflecting his dark intentions. "Let's see how you compare to my pets," he sneered, his tone laced with a chilling arrogance. "These wendigo were once innocent test subjects, mere pawns in our grand scheme, but now they serve me faithfully as my loyal clean-up crew, my glorified garbage disposals for when our experiments have outlived their usefulness. We simply drop them down here and listen to the symphony of screams from their unfortunate victims, a haunting chorus of terror that echoes long into the night, a melody that never fails to delight."

The atmosphere around us seemed to grow colder, more oppressive, as Aldrich took enjoyment in the fear he instilled in his captive audience. His sinister pleasure was palpable, a dark energy that permeated the chilling atmosphere enveloping both himself and the unfortunate souls caught in his web. With a dramatic wave of his arm, Aldrich commanded the chains holding six monstrous creatures to the wall to release. The rusted metal links fell away, sending the creatures crashing to the floor with a resounding clatter that echoed through the room.

As the monstrous wendigo shook off their restraints, their hulking forms loomed large, their eyes blazing with an inner fire that spoke of untamed fury. Their primal growls, resonating deep within their massive chests, filled the air with a terrifying symphony of impending doom. My instinct screamed at me to follow Aldrich as he made a swift break for the door, his footsteps echoing in the cavernous space, but a stronger sense of duty anchored me to the spot. I knew I was bound to protect the innocent victims trapped in this room with me, to stand as a shield against the encroaching darkness.

The beasts, with their bared teeth and rippling brawn, closed in on me, their intent clear and menacing. I could feel the heat of their breath and the weight of their gaze as they advanced, and I braced myself for the impending battle, my resolve hardening into unyielding determination.

In a voice that reverberated with commanding authority, I bellowed out a series of urgent commands to the victims who were huddled together in fear behind me. "Listen carefully!" I shouted, my voice cutting through the tension-filled air like a knife. "If any of these creatures manage to slip past me, I need each and every one of you to step up and defend those around you with everything you have. Reinforcements are on their way, but until they arrive, we must hold our ground."

Despite the lingering effects of the tranquilliser that was still coursing through my veins, threatening to sap my strength and dull my senses, I concentrated all my remaining energy on the massive, terrifying beasts that were charging towards me with unrelenting ferocity. There was no time to develop elaborate defensive strategies or to hesitate in the face of danger. I cast aside all pretences of caution and launched myself headlong into an aggressive attack, driven by sheer survival instinct. My target was clear: the vulnerable knee joints and ankle tendons of these colossal creatures. I knew that if I could manage to immobilise them, my chances of survival, as well as those of the people depending on me, would greatly increase.

With a fierce determination, I landed several powerful strikes, my blows precise and fueled by desperation. One of the beasts let out a piercing howl of pain, a sound that echoed through the chaos as it crumpled heavily to the

CHAPTER 23

ground, momentarily incapacitated. Adrenaline surged through my body like a raging river, propelling me forward as I continued to battle against seemingly insurmountable odds. I was driven by an unwavering resolve to protect those who stood behind me, their lives resting in my hands. The acrid smell of sweat and fear pervaded the air, mingling with the sounds of battle as I fought with every ounce of strength I had, determined to ensure our survival against these creatures.

The other wendigo, having learned from their previous mistake, were now lurking just beyond my immediate reach, their eyes filled with a cunning intelligence. They expertly dodged my every attack, moving with a swift, almost serpentine grace that forced me to restrain my boiling rage and mounting frustration. The presence of the wendigo was overwhelming, their insatiable hunger was suffocating in its intensity, like a heavy fog that clouded the air around us. The fear radiating from their helpless victims was tangible, a thick wave of terror that seemed to only add fuel to the fire of the wendigo's relentless pursuit.

Nevertheless, I had been meticulously trained for situations just like this one. Hargreaves had drilled into me the crucial importance of being on a protection detail, emphasising the necessity of always knowing where the next potential victim might be. But this time, the situation seemed overwhelming. There were simply too many lives to protect, too many terrified faces looking to me for salvation. So, instead of spreading myself too thin, I concentrated on maintaining my own barrage of attacks, determined to hold the line.

"Someone check if the door behind us is open and start evacuating the others!" I shouted over the chaos, my voice rising above the cacophony of panic and desperation, hoping fervently that someone would hear and heed my instructions, moving swiftly to ensure the safety of those we had sworn to protect.

Yet, just as I was about to fully articulate my command with clarity and precision, two of the wendigo, taking advantage of my momentary lapse of attention, launched a meticulously coordinated assault in my direction. In a flash, a sudden surge of energy coursed through my veins, and with a purposeful focus, I summoned and Channeled power into my blades, amplifying the force of my counterattack to an extraordinary degree. The first attacker met its demise in a gruesome display, as its head was severed from its body with a shocking finality that momentarily jolted me out of my concentrated state. The result was so startling that it lingered in my mind for a brief moment, a testament to the lethal precision of my strike. However, The second wendigo, its eyes alight with an unquenchable, savage fury, wasted no time in exploiting the brief window of my distraction. In a single, terrifying motion, it lunged forward with wicked precision, its massive, gnarled limb slamming into my abdomen with such brutal force that instant pain exploded throughout my body like a series of relentless, overlapping shockwaves. Each pain-stricken pulse felt sharper and more merciless than the previous one, sending burning searing shocks across every nerve as if trying to incapacitate me in the very instant.

Desperation surged within me, and with a mix of frantic energy and honed instinct, I scrambled to realign my focus. I managed to raise my arm just in time to intercept and block the creature's other snapping limb—a desperate, last-second act that stood in the way of a potentially fatal blow aimed straight at my neck. Every muscle in my body tensed as I called upon every shred of strategy and skill that I had

CHAPTER 23

ever cultivated through countless training battles. Using the creature's own momentum as an unintentional ally, I sharply pivoted on my right foot, twisting its arm behind its back with a precision borne of grit and determination. In that agonizing moment, as I felt the sickening discharge of force that dislocated its shoulder—a horrifying pop that seemed to echo in the space between us—the beast let out a primal howl of agony. For an ephemeral moment, a profound sadness washed over me. I briefly mourned the tragic realisation that these creatures, now twisted in their monstrous forms, were once innocent beings torn from their humanity by forces utterly beyond their control.

There was no time to linger on sorrow, however. I pressed onward in my assault. With every ounce of strength and bitter resolve coursing through me, I drove the beast relentlessly to its knees. Then, summoning what felt like the last reservoir of fortitude within me, I thrust my blade deep with unyielding resolve into the very base of its skull, ending its misery in one final, decisive act of mercy amidst the chaos of our battlefield. The sound of its last ragged breaths filled the air, each note a somber reminder of the grim necessity behind my actions, the heavy toll exacted to protect not only myself but any others who might suffer from such hellish fury.

As I slowly withdrew my bloodied blade from the lifeless, limp body of the wendigo, a reeking miasma of decay and death overwhelmed my senses, the stench an acrid reminder of the carnage that had just unfolded. Around me, the scene was one of utter disarray and macabre horror— two lifeless forms sprawled in gruesome pools of blood, one writhing in pain with a groan that split the silence, and three remaining foes snarling and drooling with raw, untamed, primal ferocity. The beat of my heart thundered in my ears as time itself seemed to slow, each moment stretching into an eternity as I struggled with the harrowing realisation that, without swift and decisive action, those predator eyes could soon fix themselves solely on me.

Before I had a chance to form a plan, a small, tremulous voice echoed from behind me—a voice laden with fear and desperation as it admitted, "The door won't budge and it looks too heavy to break." With that whispered confession, the oppressive weight of our entrapment in this confined, nightmarish space pressed down on me like a physical force. The soft, heart-wrenching sob of a woman behind the voice only amplified the gravity and uncertainty of our peril. There was no longer time for hesitation; it was a race against the rising tide of imminent destruction as I scoured the disordered surroundings for any viable means to survive the savage onslaught of these relentless, ferocious wendigo.

With my heart pounding erratically in my chest, I quickly surveyed the area, my vision darting from one menacing figure to the next. A low, bitter curse slipped past my lips—"Shit," I muttered under my breath—while my inner monologue wrestled with the grim reality: I would have to endure this relentless barrage until, hopefully, help found us in the nick of time. Even as my voice resonated with a strength I hardly felt,

I summoned even more inner power, drawing from the swirling cocktail of rage, anger, and raw fear that electrified the air around me. It was as if the very atmosphere pulsed with a frenetic energy, a vibrant and chaotic dance of emotions that both fuelled and consumed me. I recalled a crucial lesson from my time training with Alex, a lesson that whispered to me in the recesses of my mind: harnessing the dragon aspect of my powers could unlock limitless potential from the energy constantly surging around us. This was not

CHAPTER 23

just a skill but an art, a delicate balance of control and release that promised untold strength if mastered.

With a deep, determined inhale that seemed to fill my very soul, I shifted my focus to channel that latent, formidable power. Almost immediately, my body began to hum with electricity, the sensation akin to thousands of tiny sparks igniting beneath my skin. The crackling energy erupted around me like a tumultuous river breaking free from its banks, cascading in wild torrents that fuelled every cell in my body with a wild, unpredictable vigour. I felt as if I was standing at the precipice of a great and dangerous power, preparing myself for the next inevitable wave of attack.

Focusing my mind with an intensity that bordered on desperation, I commanded the energy to form a protective shield around those behind me. It took shape slowly, its form conjured from sheer will and determination, imperfect yet solid enough to withstand an initial attack. The barrier shimmered with an ethereal glow, a testament to the sheer force of will required to maintain it. With this vital defence in place, I could finally concentrate on the three enemies before me without the gnawing worry for those I protected gnawing at my resolve.

But I was acutely aware that this shield wouldn't hold forever. It was just a temporary defence, a fragile bulwark against our relentless attackers, one that required all of my concentration and strength to maintain. Yet, despite the mounting pressure and the weight of the task upon my shoulders, I clung tightly to the hope that we would be rescued soon, that we would somehow survive this dangerous ordeal. With the shield firmly in place, I shifted my focus back to the wendigo, my eyes blazing with a fiery determination.

Feeling like a caged animal pushed into a corner, I reached deep inside myself, unlocking the pandora's box of my emotions. With each passing moment, the restraints and shackles that had bound my spirit began to fall away, as I released the torrent of pain and sorrow that had weighed so heavily on my heart. I allowed the anger, sadness, and grief from losing my mother to surge through me, the guilt over my father's untimely death, and the haunting memories of what had been done to me in those dark, suffocating caves. I channeled it all, transforming the raw, searing emotions into a concentrated wave of power that radiated from me like a living storm.

I could feel an incredible surge of strength coursing through me, invigorating my senses and awakening dormant muscles that yearned to be used with a newfound vitality. Despite the overwhelming intensity of my emotions, I felt as light as a feather and utterly invincible, as if nothing could touch me. The wendigo continued their relentless assault, pouncing and lunging at me with ferocious intensity, their eyes burning with a primal hunger. Yet, with an effortless ease and the grace of a seasoned ballerina, I dodged their vicious attacks, revealing in the exhilarating thrill of battle that surged through my veins. As I fought with an unrestrained ferocity, a realisation struck me like a bolt of lightning—this was why paranormals often carried an air of arrogance. With such immense power at their disposal, it felt as though no one could ever stand in their way. A sense of cockiness washed over me, as I basked in this formidable power that coursed through every fibre of my being. However, my momentary lapse in focus caused by my newfound arrogance allowed the wendigo to cunningly herd me toward the far end of the room, away from those who depended on my protection. Now cornered, I found myself

CHAPTER 23

in a precarious situation, and I had to devise a way to escape before it was too late, before the chance to protect those who relied on me slipped through my fingers like sand.

My blade sliced through the air with a deadly elegance, glinting like a serpent of polished steel with an insatiable hunger. With each swing, I landed blows that should have been devastating, yet no matter how much damage I seemed to inflict on these monstrous creatures, the relentless wendigo just kept advancing. In the heated frenzy of battle, all that truly mattered was the raw fury boiling within me and the primal instinct driving my survival. My vision narrowed, focusing solely on their contorted, enraged faces; my senses heightened, feeling nothing but the adrenaline coursing through my veins and the ferocity that powered my every attack. The pungent stench of fresh blood mingled with the acrid scent of sweat, overpowering any other aromas that might have lingered in the air.

The wendigo were relentless, their grotesquely twisted forms moving with a predatory grace that was both mesmerising and terrifying. They encircled me, a living ring of malevolent intent, their eyes glinting with an otherworldly hunger. As if responding to some unspoken, sinister command, the fourth wendigo, the very one I had injured earlier in our brutal clash, rejoined the fray with a vengeance. Together, they moved with chilling coordination, a seamless unit of destruction, their movements as precise and fluid as if choreographed by some dark force. We danced a deadly waltz across the chaotic battleground, each step a testament to the life-and-death struggle unfolding in the shadows.

Despite my best efforts and unwavering determination, the overwhelming numbers and strategic manoeuvres of my adversaries began to exact a heavy toll on me, each brutal strike testing the very limits of my endurance and my will to survive. Hemmed in on all sides, their relentless blows landed with sickening force, leaving me drenched in my own blood and struggling to remain upright. My once powerful arms, which had served me well , now felt numb and useless, hanging limply at my sides, unable to rise in defence against the onslaught. Yet, with every ounce of strength I could muster, I fought on, driven by a fierce resolve to defy the insurmountable odds and overcome this merciless onslaught of creatures that seemed to have been pulled from the darkest depths of nightmare.

My body had become a canvas of slashes and stab wounds, each mark telling a vivid story of the brutal attack I had endured. The jagged, crimson lines stood out in stark contrast against my pale, sweat-drenched skin, serving as a cruel reminder of my impending defeat. In the eyes of my attackers, I could see the triumphant glint of victory, a chilling indication that they knew they had won, and I was powerless to stop the inevitable. My legs, once sturdy and unyielding, finally gave out from under me, and I collapsed to my knees, the crushing weight of my injuries at last catching up to me. With each laboured breath, the searing pain screamed through every fibre of my being, but despite my desperate desire to fight back, I found myself unable to summon the strength to continue the battle any longer.

It was over, or so it seemed. As I started to fade into unconsciousness, a deafening BOOM reverberated through the atmosphere, shaking the very ground beneath us. A sudden burst of blinding light and searing heat erupted, enveloping us in its fiery embrace, signaling some kind of catastrophic explosion. In that fleeting moment, a glimmer of hope flickered; perhaps, just perhaps, there was a slim chance that the captives might survive this terrifying ordeal.

CHAPTER 23

Yet, the formidable Wendigo's , relentless and unaffected by the chaos, remained singularly focused on delivering the final, lethal blow. And as the encroaching darkness began to close in around the periphery of my vision, I found myself welcoming it with open arms, yearning for release and ready to escape the relentless horrors and nightmares of this world.

CHAPTER 24

Awakening in Unfamiliarity

As I gradually emerged from the depths of unconsciousness, my mind was a swirl of confusion and disorientation. It took a moment for me to gather my scattered thoughts, but the first thing I became acutely aware of was the unfamiliar bed beneath me. The sheets were crisp and cool, a stark contrast to the warmth of my skin, and the sensation was both comforting and unsettling. My senses were slowly coming back to life, and I felt something sharp and foreign lodged in my arm—a needle, perhaps—and the unmistakable chemical scent of a hospital invaded my nostrils.

My ears were bombarded by the incessant beeping of machinery, a rhythmic yet jarring sound that seemed to echo through the room. In the distance, I could discern the faint sound of a heated discussion, voices rising and falling with urgency, though the words were indistinguishable. With great effort, I managed to open my eyes, squinting against the harsh brightness of the sterile room. The white walls and glaring lights momentarily blinded me, causing me to blink rapidly as my eyes adjusted to the overwhelming brightness.

As my vision cleared, I noticed tubes and wires snaking across my body, connecting me to an array of medical equipment. An IV drip was inserted into my arm, and various monitoring devices were taped all over me, their purpose unknown but their presence undeniably important.

An oxygen mask covered my face, its tight fit making it difficult to speak or even breathe properly.

I could feel a deep warmth spreading across my cheeks, a flush of heat that signalled a mingling of embarrassment and worry as I came to the daunting realisation that my condition might be far more severe than I had initially assumed. My mind raced, trying fervently to piece together the sequence of events that had led me to this unfamiliar place, but the hazy fog of confusion made it difficult to recall anything clearly. My current reality was dominated by the uncomfortable sensation of being tethered to an array of medical machines, each one a stark reminder of my fragile state. I yearned desperately for a return to the comforting embrace of normalcy, a time when my body was not constrained by wires and tubes.

Feeling defeated and utterly exhausted, I found myself unable to endure the thought of remaining bedridden without understanding the circumstances that had brought me here. Summoning what little strength had, I took a deep, steadying breath and carefully pushed back the heavy blanket that enveloped my battered body. To my surprise, I discovered that I had been dressed in a fresh, matching set of bra and panties, a small mercy that offered a fleeting sense of dignity amidst the chaos. A tiny, hopeful part of me wished it hadn't been Abigail who had taken on the task of dressing me, as I could already envision her playful teasing at my expense in the future.

a sharp wince escaped my lips at the sight that greeted me as I looked at my reflection . My reflection revealed a tapestry of bruises, a vivid, almost artistic array of yellow, green, and purple hues that painted a staggering 70% of my body. Each bruise was more than just a mark on my skin; it was a testament to the ordeal I had endured, a silent witness

CHAPTER 24

to the trials that had tested my spirit. It was painfully clear that the road to recovery would be long and arduous, a winding path filled with both physical and emotional challenges. Yet, despite the daunting prospect of healing, there was a flicker of determination within me, a stubborn resolve to reclaim the life and the identity that had been momentarily overshadowed by this harrowing experience. It was an experience that had left scars, both visible and unseen, but I knew it wouldn't kill me. As I examined myself further in the mirror, I noticed deep lacerations crisscrossing my thighs, chest, and stomach. The thought of counting them, of acknowledging each line carved into my flesh, made my stomach churn with unease. Steeling myself for the challenge ahead, I swung my legs over the edge of the bed, feeling the cool air brush against my skin, and forced myself to stand. It was time to see if I was strong enough to face the outside world, even with my wounds still raw and exposed, to test if my spirit was as resilient as I hoped.

With trepidation, I gingerly placed my feet onto the cool ground, mindful of any sudden movements that could send me toppling over like a fragile tower of cards. After a few tense seconds that felt like an eternity, I straightened my posture, relieved to find that my body could support itself without collapsing under its own weight. Taking a deep, calming breath, I peeled off the monitoring tabs that had been perpetually tracking my heart rate and blood pressure—those incessant, beeping reminders that seemed to dictate my life within the sterile confines of this hospital room. But just as I thought I was in the clear, just as I began to feel a small sense of victory over my situation, chaos erupted around me. Alarms blared with piercing intensity, and doors flew open with a force that seemed to shake the very walls, as a horde of medical staff rushed into the room

They were undoubtedly drawn in by the sudden explosion of activity on their screens, the unexpected deviation from the calm and routine they had been anticipating. The abrupt commotion jolted me, leaving me both startled and disoriented. In a reflexive move, I stepped back, only to find my legs, still unreliable and unsteady, betraying me as they buckled beneath me. This sent me tumbling back into the chaotic mess of wires and cables that surrounded me.

As I lay there, gazing up at the sea of doctors and nurses who hovered anxiously above me, their faces painted with worry and illuminated by the harsh, flashing red lights, I felt a wave of vulnerability wash over me. In that moment, I couldn't help but feel like a helpless child, overwhelmed by the situation. Intermingled with the concerned voices of the medical staff were the familiar tones of my closest friends—Lyn, Alexander, Gudmundur, and Abigail—who had evidently been drawn to the scene by the uproar just as the medical team had been.

Once they had determined that I was not in immediate danger and assured themselves that everything was indeed under control, the medical team began to gradually disperse. Their departure left us enveloped in an awkward and uneasy silence that permeated the room. This space, which had just moments before been filled with frantic activity, bustling with urgent voices and the clatter of medical equipment, now seemed eerily still and quiet. My friends and I exchanged glances, each of us silently grappling with our own tumultuous feelings of relief mingled with lingering anxiety that clung to us like a shadow.

Lyn, with her grace as fluid and natural as a swan gliding effortlessly across a tranquil lake, knelt down beside me. She gently lifted me up from the cold, hard floor

CHAPTER 24

where I had been lying, cradling me in her arms with the tenderness of someone holding a precious, delicate flower that might wilt at the slightest touch. Her touch was warm and reassuring, and for a few moments, we remained in that embrace, surrounded by a silence that was both comforting and profound. Her warmth and love enveloped me like an unyielding shield, offering protection from the turmoil that had just unfolded.

After what seemed like an eternity Lyn carefully placed me back onto the soft, welcoming mattress. She tenderly pulled the warm blanket up to my chin, shielding me from the chill that lingered in the air, a reminder of the cold reality we had just faced. Her voice, typically gentle and soothing, now held a firmness that surprised me and sent shivers cascading down my spine. It was a tone that betrayed a mix of anger and concern.

"My little dragon," she said with a sternness that was uncharacteristic yet undeniable, "would you care to explain how you ended up in this bed?" From the corner of my eye, I could see Abigail and Gudmundur shifting uncomfortably, clearly feeling the weight of guilt for whatever part they played in the circumstances that led to my injuries.

With a heavy heart and a sense of resignation, knowing that recounting this nightmare would be an excruciating ordeal. The horrors of the sub-level replayed in my mind with relentless clarity, like a never-ending horror film that refused to let me rest. As I began to recount the details to Gudmundur, Abbey, Alex, and Lyn, their faces mirrored my own, each twisted in shock and disbelief at the unimaginable atrocities we had witnessed together.

Gudmundur and Abbey meticulously filled in the gaps of my fragmented recollection, painting a vivid and terrifying picture of the events that I had missed while I was desperately clinging to life against our relentless foes. Gudmundur recounted, with a voice tinged with both awe and horror, the harrowing experience of wielding weapons that were imbued with potent magic. He described the deafening roar and fiery chaos of setting off explosives, each detonation a desperate attempt to repel the unending waves of attackers who seemed to emerge from every shadow and crevice. His tales of these fierce battles chilled my blood, a stark reminder of the merciless nature of our adversaries.

Meanwhile, Abbey shared her own nerve-wracking exploits, detailing her courageous attempts to reach the upper levels where prisoners were held captive. Her story was one of daring and audacity, as she manoeuvred through corridors fraught with danger to liberate those trapped souls. Yet, even as she fought valiantly for their freedom, the enemy, much like vultures waiting to scavenge, began to close in on her and Gudmundur, tightening their grip with lethal precision. They soon found themselves ensnared in a treacherous game of cat and mouse, their communication lines severed and every conceivable escape route cut off, with each passing moment bringing them closer to an ominous fate.

Just as the last flicker of hope began to dim, and despair threatened to consume us all, salvation arrived in the form of three formidable figures – Alexander, Lyn, and Enlil. Their appearance was nothing short of miraculous, akin to avenging angels descending from the heavens. With unmatched prowess and terrifying ease, they tore through our enemies, obliterating them within moments. It was due solely to their swift and decisive intervention that any of us survived that perilous encounter.

Once the dust had settled, and the battleground lay silent, they began their search for me. Guided by the residual

CHAPTER 24

energy wave I had emitted in a desperate bid to shield the remaining survivors during my battle with the wendigo, they honed in on my location. Lyn, according to those who witnessed the rescue, was the first to reach the sub level where I lay. With her extraordinary strength, she demolished the door with little effort. From this point, my memory fades into darkness, for I was unconscious, sprawled on the cold floor, with the wendigo's looming menacingly over me.

I was informed that when Lyn became aware of the perilous situation I was ensnared in, an intense and fiery rage overtook her. In that moment, she unleashed her entire formidable power against the grotesque creatures, becoming a tempest of nature in her own right. Her fury was so overwhelming that the creatures, monstrous and terrifying as they were, were ultimately reduced to nothing more than lifeless forms sprawled at her feet. The specifics of what transpired remain shrouded in mystery, as no one was forthcoming with further details about the savage intensity of her wrath or the chaotic battle that followed. Nevertheless, I was reassured that every single wendigo had been transformed into mere corpses, devoid of life.

As these reports reverberated in my mind, I found myself overwhelmed by a profound wave of shock and disbelief. It had never occurred to me just how deeply Lyn cared for my well-being, nor had I realised the true danger I was in, teetering precariously on the brink of death. My thoughts raced uncontrollably, filled with concern and anxiety. "What happened with the other strike teams?" I wondered aloud, desperation creeping into my voice. "Did the backup arrive in time to assist them? Were there any casualties suffered on our side?" My heart pounded in my chest as I contemplated the grim possibility that others might have lost their lives as a result of Aldrich's treacherous betrayal.

Suddenly, I felt a familiar touch as Alexander's reassuring hand gently landed on my leg, pulling me back from the spiral of my racing thoughts to the present moment. His voice was calm and steady, like an anchor in a stormy sea. "Relax," he said with a soothing tone, "the other sites were warned ahead of time and were more prepared than we initially anticipated. Your quick thinking, especially in sending in those backup teams, was crucial. It saved us from facing any fatalities. Though, I must admit, some team members did sustain injuries, but they are expected to recover in due time."

He paused for a moment, allowing the weight of his words to sink in before continuing, "From what we've gathered, it appears that once Aldrich realised his plan was unraveling, he shifted his focus entirely. Instead of trying to conceal his involvement further, he turned his efforts towards capturing you. He must have thought that having you would give him some sort of leverage or perhaps he planned to offer you up to his superior as a bargaining chip. That's the conclusion we've drawn from the evidence we've managed to recover so far."

As he elaborated on the intricate situation, a chilling and unsettling sense of dread began to slowly wash over me like a cold, creeping tide. The mere thought of being used as a pawn in such a dangerous and convoluted game left me feeling utterly cold and vulnerable. It was terrifying to consider how perilously close I had come to becoming a mere tool in the hands of someone as manipulative and calculating as Aldrich, a master of deception and intrigue. I nodded slowly, taking in every detail of his explanation with a deeply furrowed brow, my mind grappling with the implications. "From what he was saying before he left me to die," I began, my voice barely above a whisper, low and

CHAPTER 24

grave with the weight of the situation, "the organisation that he is a part of was also linked to Jeremiah. And although he didn't come out and say it conclusively, he made it sound as though he, along with others, had been to the caves where Lyn and I were held captive. He claimed to have seen me there and even insinuated that he had taken part in some of the brutal tests we were subjected to. But I can hardly recall anyone other than Jeremiah being present during those torturous moments." I paused, my mind racing with a tumult of doubt and confusion, trying to piece together the fragments of information. "Do you think he was telling me the truth? Or was he purposely trying to rattle me, throwing me off course, and sowing seeds of doubt in my mind?" My fingers clenched into tight fists as I spoke, my suspicions and unease growing stronger and more insistent by the second, like a storm gathering on the horizon.

Alex and Lyn exchanged a knowing glance, their eyes filled with a mixture of worry and a hint of fear that seemed to linger like a shadow in the room. "Based on what we've uncovered today, it appears that there is something far more sinister at play than any of us had originally anticipated," Lyn began, her voice trembling slightly, betraying the unease she tried to conceal. "We will need to delve deeper into this matter at another time, but for now, I'm asking for your patience and understanding," she concluded, her tone pleading yet firm.

Alex, picking up where Lyn left off, added in a voice that was both firm and reassuring, though the underlying tension was palpable. "The gravity of the situation weighs heavily upon us all as we speak. We need you all to stay healthy and strong because I foresee a difficult and trying path that lies ahead for each of us," he declared, his words hanging in the air like a foreboding cloud. The room fell into a profound silence as the weight of their predicament began to sink in for everyone present. This was no longer just a simple mystery to unravel; it was something far larger and more perilous than they could have ever imagined.

My voice broke the silence, emerging as a nervous, jumbled rush of words. "Well, about that," I started hesitantly, feeling the tremor in my voice as I spoke. "I made a promise to Gudmundur and Abigail to assist them with an urgent matter once this case was resolved. But with the way things stand now, it doesn't seem feasible. And by agreeing to help them, I may have unwittingly placed myself under the authority of a Dagon queen whom I have yet to meet." As my words faded, an oppressive silence descended once more, heavy and tense, as if the room itself was waiting for a verdict to be rendered. In that moment, all I could think was, "Shit, I'm in trouble," as the full scope of my predicament became all too clear.

Suddenly, the room was filled with the joyful and infectious sound of laughter, shattering the heavy tension that had hung over the group like a dark cloud for days. It was a welcome and much-needed relief, lifting their spirits and bringing a sense of lightheartedness and camaraderie into the space. Lyn settled down next to me, her smile so infectious that it seemed to illuminate the entire room as she assured me, with utmost confidence, that everything had been handled and there was absolutely nothing left for me to worry about. But despite her soothing reassurance, I couldn't quite shake off the nagging feeling of unease that clung to me, especially knowing that even Aldrich harboured fear of the formidable dragon queen.

As I voiced my concerns, hoping to find some understanding, they all erupted into another round of laughter, their mirth echoing off the walls. Abigail

CHAPTER 24

laughed so hard that tears streamed down her face, her joy contagious. Yet, in the midst of this merriment and shared laughter, I couldn't help but wonder if there was more to the situation than they were letting on. The uncertainty only added fuel to the fire of my nerves, leaving me feeling even more unsettled.

Standing my ground with a resolute and stubborn look etched on my face, it must have been clear to Lyn that I was not backing down easily. She took a deep, calming breath, trying to ease the tension that lingered between us. "My little dragon," she said softly, her voice full of warmth and understanding, "you don't need to fear the dragon queen. She loves you dearly. I can assure you of that." Despite her gentle reassurances, I still didn't fully understand. So, in a burst of frustration, I blurted out, "Most dragons hate me. Why would she love me? Can someone please explain? My head is starting to ache from all this thinking." With a defeated sigh, I gave Lyn the saddest puppy dog eyes I could muster, hoping for some clarity.

In response to my unspoken plea, she enveloped me in a warm and comforting embrace, her arms wrapping around me with an abundance of love and tenderness that felt as though it could shield me from all the uncertainties of the world. "I know she loves you because I am the dragon queen," she revealed with a gentle, knowing smile that seemed to hold the wisdom of ages, "and I see you as though you're my own daughter." Her words were like a soothing balm to my troubled mind, offering a profound sense of belonging and acceptance that I had longed for, even amidst the laughter and uncertainty that often surrounded us. It was as if her declaration had the power to mend the invisible fractures within me, stitching together the fragments of doubt with threads of reassurance.

As much as I wanted to delve deeper, to ask the myriad of questions swirling in my mind, Lyn's voice took on a firm yet caring tone as she declared, "Now no more questions. You need your rest." Her words, though gentle, held a finality that brooked no argument. With that, she gently guided me to lay down, her hands softly urging me to close my weary eyes. As if on cue, the exhaustion I had been holding at bay finally caught up with me, wrapping me in its embrace. I drifted off into a dreamless sleep, comforted by the steady, rhythmic beating of Lyn's heart beneath my ear, a constant, reassuring presence that promised safety and peace in the midst of everything unknown.

***

In the tumultuous aftermath of Aldrich's shocking betrayal, the paranormal world was plunged into utter chaos and disarray. The council representatives, a diverse and influential group from various factions, erupted into a frenzy of outrage and concern, vociferously calling for thorough investigations into the treachery and demanding swift and severe justice for the numerous victims who had suffered as a result. The air was thick with tension and conflicting opinions as discussions turned heated and impassioned.

Within the council, some factions vehemently advocated for the immediate and uncompromising disposal of those affected by Aldrich's actions, viewing them as potential threats that needed to be eradicated to restore order. On the other hand, other more cautious parties proposed a different approach, suggesting that the victims should be studied meticulously in hopes of unraveling the mysteries surrounding the events that had transpired and perhaps gaining insights into preventing such betrayals in the future.

After extensive and fervent debate that spanned several tense sessions, a resolution was finally reached. It was

CHAPTER 24

ultimately decided, in a rare moment of consensus, that the victims of Aldrich's betrayal should not be held accountable for the actions that had been unjustly imposed upon them. Recognising the complexity of the situation, the council agreed that the agency would bear the responsibility of providing comprehensive training and rehabilitation for these individuals, aiming to integrate them back into society while ensuring their well-being and safety.

This new chapter, marked by a reality fraught with its own unique set of challenges and uncertainties, demanded resilience and adaptability from all involved. However, amidst the turmoil and unpredictability of the situation, I found a sense of solace and reassurance in knowing that Ogma, a wise and trusted figure, would also have a significant role in this crucial rehabilitation process. His steady presence filled me with a sense of calm and confidence, providing a beacon of hope and stability amidst the turbulent seas of change and uncertainty.

***

Finally, after what felt like an eternity spent under the watchful gaze of the onsite nurse, I was at last granted the elusive green light to leave the confining embrace of the hospital. As the doors swung open, I stepped out into the cool, invigorating air, my lungs gratefully filling with the fresh scent of freedom and possibility. Each step I took towards the hospital's exit felt like a small victory, a tangible return to the world beyond sterile walls and beeping machines.

However, my peaceful thoughts were abruptly interrupted by the low, resonant thrum of a powerful engine that pulled up beside me with a commanding presence. My eyes widened in astonishment as they took in the sight of an electric pink Shelby Mustang GT 500, a vehicle whose sleek, aerodynamic curves and audaciously bold colour demanded attention and admiration from all who beheld it. As the tinted window smoothly rolled down, it revealed a bright-faced vampire with an impish glint sparkling in her eyes, her expression one of playful amusement.

"Hello Jess," she chirped with a voice as cheerful as a songbird's, her words carrying a melody of mischief. "What are you doing here?"

I made a conscious effort to maintain a veneer of neutrality in both my voice and body language, suppressing any hint of surprise or curiosity that might betray me. "Just getting some fresh air," I replied, my tone carefully measured.

Curiosity thoroughly piqued, I leaned forward eagerly, craning my neck to get a better view inside the car. To my utter astonishment, my gaze landed upon the unmistakable figure of Gudmundur, who was seated in the back seat with a distinctively grumpy expression etched across his features. His presence was unexpected, yet familiar, and with a slight nod, I offered him a small, respectful greeting. Acknowledging his presence, I then redirected my attention back to the vampire driver, a whirlwind of anticipation and curiosity swirling within me as I awaited her response.

"Oh well, we were just out and about when we heard that you were being discharged today," she continued, her tone casual yet infused with a hint of excitement, as if the day's unfolding events were part of a larger, unwritten adventure waiting to be explored. Her words seemed to carry the promise of unexpected journeys and new beginnings. "We thought it would be a good idea to come and pick you up, to take you back to the dorms," she explained, a sly smile playing on her lips, suggesting there was more to her plan than she was letting on.

CHAPTER 24

"That sounds good. I need to gather my things and arrange transport back home," I replied, feeling a wave of relief at the unexpected yet timely offer of help. It was comforting to know that I wouldn't have to navigate the complexities of travel arrangements alone.

"What do you mean 'transport home'?" Abigail asked, her eyebrow arching in curiosity, clearly intrigued by my mention of returning home.

"I mean going back to HQ. I have some more training to complete and then I'll receive orders for my next assignment," I clarified, elaborating on my plans with a sense of duty and purpose. The path ahead was clear, and I was ready to follow it.

"You mean you won't be staying at the London office for an extended period?" Gudmundur's voice came from the back seat, tinged with genuine surprise and perhaps a subtle hint of disappointment. It was clear he had anticipated my stay to be more prolonged, and now he was grappling with this sudden twist that was at odds with his initial expectations.

"Well, as far as I'm aware, that's not the plan," I replied, as I settled into the plush confines of the car. "Unless, of course, you two have some insider information that I'm not privy to," I added, casting a glance in the rearview mirror to catch a glimpse of Gudmundur's expression.

Abigail, seated right beside me, let out a melodious and lighthearted laugh, her voice resonating with a sense of camaraderie and shared amusement. "Oh, we're far too insignificant to have access to such top-secret plans," she replied, her eyes twinkling as she added a playful wink. "We're merely here to offer a ride to a friend in need," she continued, as if the very idea of being involved in something more significant was utterly preposterous.

The interior of the car was nothing short of opulent, an exquisite blend of luxury and comfort that seemed to cocoon its passengers in a realm of elegance. The seats, crafted from the finest leather, enveloped you in a comforting embrace, while the doors were adorned with glossy mahogany panels that caught the subtle glow of the streetlights, reflecting it in a warm, inviting manner. A faint yet captivating aroma of vanilla and sandalwood lingered in the air, weaving an intricate tapestry of both luxury and mystery around my unexpected chauffeurs. This car, with its understated sophistication, seemed to elevate the simple act of being driven to a whole new level of experience, transforming it into a journey of refinement and class.

I merely shrugged at Abigail, not letting myself be drawn into the familiar game of intrigue and secrecy. I was well aware that both she and her partner held high-ranking positions within their respective councils and were known as powerful enforcers in their own right. However, if they chose not to disclose their secrets to me, I had no intention of pressing the issue. As we continued our smooth drive through the city, I allowed myself to relax, closing my eyes and surrendering to a light slumber.

The sound of their voices gradually transformed into a distant murmur as I began to drift off into a light slumber, only barely registering snippets of their ongoing conversation as it floated aimlessly in the background. Time seemed to slip away like sand through an hourglass as I rested, my awareness fading with each passing moment. Before I knew it, the journey had come to an end, and we had arrived at the agency's expansive London office. Slowly, I opened my eyes, blinking against the sudden brightness that filled the interior of the car. I stretched my arms as best as I could within the confines of the luxurious vehicle, preparing both body and

CHAPTER 24

mind to disembark and face whatever awaited me at our impending destination.

My two ever-present shadows, who had accompanied me throughout the entire journey, unbuckled their seat belts with a synchronised click. They followed my lead, stepping out of the vehicle and joining me on the bustling sidewalk. The city hummed with life around us, the noise of traffic and chatter forming a symphony of urban existence.

"What are you up to?" I accused, my voice tinged with suspicion as I narrowed my eyes at Gudmundur. My gaze lingered on him, searching for any signs of deceit. "And don't try to play innocent with me," I warned, my tone carrying an edge of distrust.

"Well, as you pointed out, we do have official titles," Gudmundur retorted, his voice carrying a tinge of grumpiness as he met my gaze. "We're just here for a progress update on the state of various investigations. We have no nefarious intentions, I swear!" His words were laced with sincerity, yet I found it difficult to completely trust him.

"I find that hard to believe, dragon boy," I shot back, my voice dripping with skepticism. But if they were determined to accompany me, so be it. With a resigned huff, I turned and strode purposefully towards the building, the imposing figures of a dragon and vampire following close behind me, their presence felt like a constant shadow.

The sun beat down on us mercilessly, casting long, distorted shadows across the pavement as we approached the grand entrance of the building. The glass doors gleamed brilliantly in the sunlight, reflecting the towering structures that surrounded us. My heart raced with a mix of anticipation and dread as we stepped inside, the cool air of the lobby washing over us. I was unsure of what awaited us within those walls, but I steeled myself for whatever challenges lay ahead, determined to face them head-on with my unlikely companions by my side.

As I made my way towards the front desk, I was immediately enveloped in a tight bear hug from Mini and Keith, who had obviously been planning this ambush for quite some time. Their excitement was palpable, and it was clear that they had been eagerly waiting for my arrival the moment I stepped inside the building. Keith's booming voice filled the air, resonating off the walls with a warmth that was both welcoming and invigorating. "Well, if it isn't our fearless saviour," he exclaimed with an infectious enthusiasm. "Come on, Alex is waiting for all of us."

With a broad smile that seemed to light up his entire face, Keith took the lead and guided us down the familiar hallway to what used to be Aldrich's office. However, as we approached, it was evident that the space had undergone a complete and rather impressive transformation. The once formal and somewhat sterile room had been reimagined into a wonderfully inviting environment. It now featured an array of cozy sofas and armchairs, thoughtfully arranged around a large coffee table. This table was generously adorned with an assortment of snacks, ranging from savory to sweet, and flanked by a variety of laptops poised for work or leisure.

The atmosphere of the room had shifted entirely from its previous incarnation; it was now a comfortable gathering place for the team, one that exuded a sense of camaraderie and collaboration. The changes made it abundantly clear that this was no longer just an office. Instead, it had become a vibrant hub of activity where ideas could be shared, friendships fostered, and creativity unleashed in a setting that felt as comforting as a living room.

As I made my way into the office, I was greeted by the sight of Lyn and Alex standing before me, their faces lighting

CHAPTER 24

up with genuine joy that radiated warmth and welcome. They greeted me with open arms and enveloped me in a warm, affectionate hug that spoke volumes of their sincerity and affection. "We sincerely apologise for not coming to see you sooner," Lyn said softly, her voice carrying a soothing tone that was filled with genuine concern. "With everything that has happened recently, we've been trying to manage a lot of chaos, but please know that you have never been far from our thoughts and hearts." As she gently guided me to a comfortable sofa, my heart swelled with a complex mixture of gratitude and a tinge of fear. The warmth of their gestures and the sincerity of their concern showed how deeply they cared for me, yet I couldn't shake the feeling of apprehension about what they were about to reveal.

Alexander's commanding presence seemed to fill every corner of the room, his deep, resonant voice cutting through the thick, anticipatory air like a knife. The tension and sense of anticipation were almost palpable as he addressed the gathered group, his words laden with significance and urgency. Every pair of eyes in the room was fixed intently upon him, hanging on every word that he uttered. "Thank you all for being here today," he began, his gaze sweeping thoughtfully over each individual present. His eyes held a complex mixture of gratitude and seriousness, conveying the gravity and importance of the situation at hand. Lyn reached over and gave my hand a reassuring squeeze, her calming touch providing a sense of solace amidst the chaos of emotions swirling around us. As Alexander continued to speak, I couldn't help but feel a profound sense of gratitude for Lyn's comforting presence by my side.

"Everyone assembled in this room is intensely aware of the ongoing investigation that has recently cast a shadow over the entire paranormal community, stirring unease and apprehension among us all. With considerable effort and strategic communication, we have managed to keep widespread panic to a minimum, maintaining a semblance of calm amidst the chaos. However, the undeniable truth remains: someone has orchestrated a complex and treacherous situation, wherein the head of the London facility has committed an unforgivable betrayal against his own people. This individual has engaged in forbidden and reckless experiments, targeting both the human and paranormal communities. As a result, the delicate balance that keeps the secret existence of the paranormal communities hidden from the world at large is now at risk of unraveling. This situation is fraught with immense complexity and potential danger, demanding our immediate and undivided attention. If we fail to get to the bottom of this dire situation, we truly run the risk of destroying the world as we know it, jeopardising everything we have worked so hard to protect.

As of this moment, I am assuming full control of the London branch to ensure a focused and effective response to these developments. Jessica, Mini, I am transferring both of you to London as well. Please understand that this is not a punitive measure, but rather a strategic decision on my part. Given the tumultuous events that have transpired, I feel more secure and confident having you both by my side as we endeavour to unravel the true scope and depth of these events. Additionally, it is my pleasure to introduce you to two of the three new hires we have brought into this branch as part of our expanded efforts. Allow me to present agents Abigail and Gudmundur. They have recently resigned from their esteemed positions on the paranormal councils and will now be working with us as both liaisons and active field agents. Alongside our third new member, they will form a

CHAPTER 24

dedicated team tasked solely with uncovering the layers of this mystery and identifying the individual or individuals responsible for setting it all in motion. Jessica, Mini, and Keith, you will also be assigned to this team."

Before any objections could be raised, Alex decisively pressed the intercom button, summoning Ogma to join them. His fingers danced over the controls as he leaned in to speak clearly into the speaker system. "Please come in; we are ready for you now," he announced with a sense of urgency that seemed to fill the room. A few minutes slipped by, marked by the ticking of a nearby clock, before the door swung open, revealing the entrance of two men who walked in with a purposeful stride. As they took their seats, I exchanged a puzzled glance with Lyn, my brows furrowed in confusion. "Why is a police officer here for this discussion?" I inquired, my voice tinged with curiosity and a hint of apprehension. Lyn merely offered a mysterious smile, her eyes twinkling with a secret knowledge. "Be patient," she advised calmly, "everything will be explained in due time."

I let out an exasperated sigh, the sound echoing slightly in the room, and settled into my seat, my mind a whirl of questions as I eagerly anticipated the unfolding of events. Rising from his chair to formally greet the new arrivals, Alex extended a welcoming hand towards DCI Lancaster. "Welcome, Mr. Lancaster," he began with a cordial nod. "Please come in and make yourself comfortable. I trust your tour with Ogma has been quite enlightening thus far?"

Lancaster, a man of composure and poise, nodded in response, though his expression betrayed a mixture of intrigue and disbelief. "It has certainly been... interesting," he confessed, his voice carrying the weight of the revelations he had encountered. "But I must admit, all of this information is overwhelming. And from what Ogma has told me, it seems that ordinary individuals like myself don't typically gain access to such knowledge. So, why have you brought me here?" His gaze flickered between us, keenly seeking an explanation that would satisfy his growing curiosity.

Lancaster's sharp and perceptive observation skills did not go unnoticed by Alex, who leaned forward with a glint of interest in his eyes, as if recognising a kindred spirit. "You possess a rare talent for this line of work," Alex remarked in a low, confident tone that resonated with authority. "I would like to extend an offer to you – join our agency and become a crucial member of Jessica's team. Together, we will meticulously comb through every clue and track down those responsible for the missing persons you have tirelessly searched for." He paused, allowing the gravity of his proposal to settle in the room, his gaze fixed intently on Lancaster, carefully studying his reaction. "Do you have what it takes to see this through to the very end, or will you simply walk away?" The weight of Alex's words hung heavy in the air, a challenge that tested Lancaster's dedication and determination to solve the case. The atmosphere was charged with a sense of impending responsibility, and I could almost feel the immense burden that came with accepting such a proposition. It was no surprise when Lancaster, after a moment of contemplation, nodded in acceptance, officially joining my newly formed team, ready to embark on this daunting journey with us.